BY HANNAH BONAM-YOUNG

Out of the Woods

Out on a Limb

Next to You

Next of Kin

Set the Record Straight

Out of the Woods

Out of the Woods

A Novel

Hannah Bonam-Young

DELL BOOKS
NEW YORK

Published in the United States by Dell, an imprint of Random House,
a division of Penguin Random House LLC, New York.

Dell and the D colophon are registered trademarks of
Penguin Random House LLC.

Library of Congress Cataloging-in-Publication Data
Names: Bonam-Young, Hannah, author.
Title: Out of the woods: a novel / Hannah Bonam-Young.
Description: New York: Dell Book, 2025.
Identifiers: LCCN 2024042972 (print) |
LCCN 2024042973 (ebook) | ISBN 9780593871867 (trade paperback) |
ISBN 9780593871874 (ebook)
Subjects: LCGFT: Romance fiction. | Novels.
Classification: LCC PR9199.4.B6555 O978 2024 (print) |
LCC PR9199.4.B6555
(ebook) | DDC 813/.6—dc23/eng/20231010
LC record available at https://lccn.loc.gov/2024042972
LC ebook record available at https://lccn.loc.gov/2024042973

Printed in the United States of America on acid-free paper

randomhousebooks.com

2 4 6 8 9 7 5 3 1

Book design by Jo Anne Metsch

For Abi, for not letting it break you.

And, for all my fellow Amy March girls out there.
You don't have to be great or nothing.
You can just be.

AUTHOR'S NOTE

WELCOME BACK, FRIENDS.

Out of the Woods is an interconnected stand-alone set after book one, *Out on a Limb*. Sarah and Caleb are the "happily" married best friends to Win and Bo, book one's protagonists. I'd suggest reading *Out on a Limb* first, but you absolutely don't have to, to enjoy *Out of the Woods*.

Win and Bo, from *Out on a Limb,* will always be incredibly special to me. They launched my career in a big way, and I poured so much of myself into their love story—my disability, my experience of motherhood, and many pieces of my own love story. I had told myself that I'd write one deeply vulnerable book, hope for the best, and leave it at that. I had believed that I'd be better off closing my bleeding heart before I poured it out on page again . . . but then along came Sarah and Caleb.

My husband, Ben, and I began dating in high school and got married when I was eighteen. Which, in hindsight, is a batshit thing to do. Thankfully, we're still happily together. Not without effort. Not without painful lessons. Not without struggle. But ultimately, I'm lucky to say that I'm married to my best friend. There's no one else whom I'd rather spend time with. No other person can make me laugh harder or make me feel safer. We were just among the lucky (and not-so-lucky) few who met their person a little too young—which is the inspiration for this novel.

Out of the Woods is my love letter to all of us who met their soulmate before they had the chance to fully meet themselves. I wanted to write a story that reflected the delicate dance of being madly, deeply in love with your significant other but desperately seeking independence, evolution, and change.

It's also for all of us who, following a traumatic event, felt frozen in time.

Sarah and Caleb have been together for more than half of their lives by the time we meet them in *Out of the Woods*. Their love story is one filled with hopefulness, familiarity, inside jokes, shared history, grief, friendship, and intimacy. I hope you love them as much as I do.

—HANNAH BONAM-YOUNG

Content Warnings:

- Death of a parent from amyotrophic lateral sclerosis (ALS)
- Medical treatments, illness, hospitalization, terminal diagnosis
- Questioning religious practices/spirituality, Catholicism
- References to alcohol and marijuana consumption
- Descriptive sex scenes
- Accident resulting in hospitalization

"You find the path by walking it."

—MAYA ANGELOU

Out of the Woods

"SARAH!" WIN'S VOICE COMES AROUND THE CORNER OF the school's hallway before the rest of her follows. She's running faster than I've ever seen her move—outside of a swimming pool that is. "Would you *please* get out of the way?" she shrieks at a pair of seniors who seem about ready to dry hump each other, parting them as Moses did the Red Sea as she continues running like a puppet freed from its strings.

"What on earth . . ." I say, just as she, panting, stops and bends over to catch her breath in front of me. "Are you okay?"

"We really need to stop faking our periods to get out of gym class." She straightens, placing a hand on her heaving chest. "Coach Smith is right; cardio is important. I will not make it past tryouts if—"

I hold my right hand out to silence her, reach into my locker for my inhaler, and present it to her with an open palm.

"I'm good." She shakes her head, slowing her breaths as she moves to lean against the row of lockers next to mine. "Plus, we both know that thing expired in middle school."

"Mom says that expiration dates are a tool from the government to take more of our money and limit resources." I toss my inhaler into the abyss behind the neat row of library books that sit front and center. What lies beyond those books is no longer my concern. At this rate the inhaler's fall is probably cushioned by hundreds of discarded gum wrappers and abandoned scrunchies.

Win nods slowly, making no effort to hide her disgust. "Let's hope Marcie doesn't have the same attitude about the food in our fridge."

I wince but shake it off. "Wait . . . why were you running? And yelling? And—"

"There's a new boy," Win interrupts. "A *cute* one. A tall, well-dressed, *glasses*-wearing boy . . ." She waits for my reaction eagerly while *I* await a valid reason for her behavior.

"Okay? And?"

Win grins like the devil herself. "He was reading a book . . . like a *real* book. A hardcover with a broken-in spine. Something old."

I gasp and slam my locker shut. "Where is he?"

"By now?" Win looks around the hallway which is only growing more crowded as the clock ticks closer to first period. "He could be anywhere."

I chew my lip, my grin growing lopsided. "Let's go find him."

ONE

MY MOTHER WAS RELIGIOUS IN THE SAME WAY THAT leggings are pants. By that I mean whenever times were desperate or for comfort. Never one to shy away from a passive-aggressive "Bless her heart" or an exasperated "Lord give me strength," my mom mostly expressed her beliefs in empty platitudes that I often flat-out dismissed.

But she did teach me to pray. Not before bed every night, as her parents so rigidly instructed her, or at a Sunday mass, or to apologize for a laundry list of transgressions that one didn't need to feel all that sorry for. Instead, my mother, the no-nonsense woman that she was, taught me to treat my one-way calls to the big man in the sky as more of a crisis hotline and less as a suggestion box. "God's got enough problems," she'd said. "Don't waste his time with things you can handle yourself." Or, at the very least, have the saints handle.

And so, over the course of many years, I discovered what qualified as worthy of God's attention. Like the time my mom's shitty Ford Mondeo broke down on the highway during a snowstorm, an hour from home without a pay phone in sight. Or, when my aunt June's—who's not actually my blood-relative but rather my mom's best friend who we shared an apartment with—boyfriend started throwing shit in the adjoining room. Or when my best friend and daughter of Aunt June, Win, didn't come home right away after swim practice one time and we'd watched a little too much *Dateline* that week for comfort. Then, of course, when Mom's doctors said there was nothing left to be done but to make the most of the time she had left. After that, we started to pray a lot.

Desperate prayer is the only kind I've ever known.

After Mom passed, I relied on my own instincts to tell me when it was appropriate to pull on that heavenly pair of tin cans tied together with angel's-harp string. I'd shut my eyes tight and ask something *bigger* than myself to intervene. A force of some kind. Some deity. Some all-powerful, all-knowledgeable, all-capable *thing*. Something my mother called God. Something I haven't been bold enough to name for myself just yet.

And even though I've never seen an answered prayer, I still find myself giving it a go. Rarely and only when there's nothing left to be done, just as Mom taught me. Like right now, for example. Because this event, the gala that I'd decided to host in honor of my late, brilliant mother, is about to fail spectacularly. And there's nothing I can do to fix it.

"Sarah? Are you back here?" Win, my lifelong best friend, turns the corner of the darkened hallway where I've hidden myself away. Her black hair is tied into a low bun, curtain bangs framing either side of her face. The squiggly horizontal lines she gets between her brows when her nose bunches up with worry are visible from here. The moment she sees me leaned against the wall, her shoulders slump and she picks up the bottom of her floor length, purple silk gown to hurry over to me at the far end of the corridor.

"You caught me," I whine pathetically, wishing there was somewhere left inside of myself to hide.

"I did." She looks me over, head to toe, with increasing anxiety behind her eyes. "Caleb sent me to find you. The auction is almost over." After growing up in the same home as Win for our entire childhoods, we know each other at a level deeper than most friends would. Closer to sisters, I'd like to think. Twins maybe, given that we're the same age. And so, because of that, I know that Win's tone, the slight hesitancy in her voice when she said the word *auction,* means that I was right to be back here praying for a miracle. We're still nowhere near to our fundraising goal—no nearer than we were when I snuck away.

In quick succession I clear my throat, shake my head, and look up to the ceiling—all attempts at avoiding the onslaught of tears threatening to spill over. But they still come, slow and burning as they gather along my bottom eyelids. "Fuck . . ." I whisper, dabbing under my eyes with the sides of my thumbs. The last thing I need is mascara running down my cheeks when I eventually make my way back out there.

"It was a beautiful evening," Win offers gently, her mouth tilting up on one side. She reaches into her handbag, pulls out a tissue, and offers it to me.

I take it, holding it up to my water line to dab tears away. "Beautiful doesn't exactly fund research though, does it?" I reply, snarkier than I intended before I sniff back more tears. "Sorry," I whisper. I'm not mad at Win, I'm angry with myself. *So* fucking angry.

"No . . . I guess not." I watch as Win hikes up her dress past her knees, and then lowers herself to sit on the floor, letting the silk material pool between her crossed legs.

I ungracefully drop to sit next to her, my knee-length forest green dress is too tight to do anything but keep my legs extended out in front of me. "I don't want to go out there," I say through a heavy sigh as my ass hits the ground.

Win nods slowly, looking back toward the door at the end of the hallway. "Do you want me to tell Caleb to handle it? I'm sure he could—"

"No," I say forcefully. "No, definitely not." The last thing I want is for my husband to come to my rescue *again*. I've already wasted so much of our money on this event. *His* money, if I'm being completely honest with myself. I can't ask him to also step in to give the saddest goodbye address to a crowd mostly consisting of his business associates and their far-more-accomplished-than-his-own spouses. This isn't Caleb's failure; he shouldn't have to own it. It's all mine.

Isn't that what you wanted? some malevolent part of my psyche whispers. *Something that's only yours?*

"Then I don't really see any other option here, babe." Win pats my thigh and lowers her head onto my shoulder. "You still pulled off an incredible event and it was your very first one. I know you wanted to do it all yourself, but maybe that's too big a task for anyone to take on. It was also a *really* big fundraising goal. Maybe next time—"

I tense, straightening my posture, which forces Win to sit up, removing her head from my shoulder. The last thing I want right now is the gentlest possible version of *I told you so* from the person who's consistently cheered me on since we were in diapers.

"How much have we raised?" I ask abruptly. "When you left to find me, what was the total?"

Win clears her throat, looking at the hem of my dress, just above my knobby, freckle-covered knees. "Just under one-hundred-and-eighty thousand."

Shitting-fuckity-fuck.

The goal for tonight is three hundred thousand. Between the

hall rental, catering for a crowd of almost four hundred people, entertainment, auction items, décor, and advertising, the event cost just over a hundred and twenty thousand.

I automatically do the math. "Sixty grand," I murmur, barely audible.

"That's a *lot* of money, Sar." I don't even think Win heard me; she can just see my obvious disappointment.

I struggle to stand in my tight dress by clawing for a grip at the wall. I begin pacing back and forth as Win's eyes track me like I'm the ball at Wimbledon.

"Caleb and I could have saved everyone a Saturday night and donated double that amount without all of this . . ." Fanfare. Effort. Time and energy. Ego. Performance. "Bullshit," is what I land on.

"But you raised awareness, too. Doctor Torres's speech moved people to tears, Sar. This doesn't just end tonight. The impact—"

"Dammit," I whimper, grinding my high heel into the ground as I move my hands to my hips and grip tightly. "Am I some fucking cliché? Some bored, rich housewife who has to have a cause?" I throw my hands up, then wrap them around my shoulders as I gently sway side to side. "What the fuck am I doing, Win?" I ask in soft desperation, clinging on to her eye contact like a lifeline. "I could have stayed at home and toasted to Mom with a glass of her favorite Pinot Grigio and made *more* of an impact by writing a check for what this stupid event cost. What a waste of fucking time. What a waste of money. What a *waste*."

"Sarah, you're not being fair to yourself. You didn't know it was going to—" She stops herself, but I hear the last, unspoken word regardless.

"Fail?" I ask, my chest falling on a wounded breath.

Win's lips tighten, as she holds eye contact, firm yet pleading. As if to say, *Don't make me say it.*

"Fail," I repeat, raising my palms to press against my neck, cradling my jaw in both hands.

"Marcie would be so proud of you," Win says gently. "I don't want you doubting that for a second."

I shake my head stubbornly as I turn away from her. Mom may have been a mother figure to Win from the moment she and Aunt June brought Win home from the hospital, but she was *my* mom. I'm the one with her DNA flooding my veins. Her auburn hair, her tea-stain eyes, her slightly crooked left incisor, her long legs and disproportionately short torso, her ugly feet with bent-in toes she'd joke were our family's curse. A stranger's nose, I once pointed out. A parting gift from my poor excuse for a father, she'd less-than-affectionately replied.

All that to say, I know my mom better than anyone. I am the closest thing to her left living. And I don't think she'd be proud of me. Not tonight. Maybe not for a long, long while. Because at thirty-one years old, I've accomplished next to nothing.

My mom was seventeen when she got pregnant and eighteen when she had me. She scraped every penny together with my *also* knocked up Aunt June, got a half-decent apartment, and did the best she could with so little.

Marcie Green could throw together a Michelin-star-worthy meal with a couple of cans, whatever else we had in the pantry, and a few bags of frozen vegetables if you gave her an afternoon and a Shania Twain CD to blast on repeat. She'd transform a dilapidated, thrift-store dollhouse into Barbie's Malibu dream home with a little bit of paint, time, glue, glitter, and effort. She wasted *nothing*. Not a dollar and certainly not a moment of her life.

While I can proudly claim I have all the physical attributes of my mom, it often feels as if Win inherited the majority of Mom's personality. After quite literally being dealt the short hand in life—that joke will never get old—Win has overcome so much to be the woman she is today. Her limb difference never once held her back. Hell, I think it somehow even propelled her forward. Stubbornness, maybe. Pride, partially. Tenacity, mostly. All of Mom's best qualities. Eventually, she found herself in the arms of her dream man and accidental baby daddy, Bo. Ever since those two collided they've been unstoppable in making Win's dreams come true. Dreams they now share.

In just under two months Win and Bo will officially open Camp Cando. A summer camp she has designed for kids with varying disabilities, and their families, to explore nature and have community with one another. And she'll do it all with my adorable not-quite-two-year-old niece, August, strapped to her back. So, believe me, if Mom's somewhere looking down on the two of us with pride, it's sure as shit not me she's watching.

"Win? Sar?" Bo, Win's husband, rounds the corner from the opposite end of the hall.

Bo is six foot five, conventionally handsome in a nerd-next-door kind of way, has swoopy blond hair with a middle part, and a beard that could probably use a trim. But I know for a fact that Win likes him to keep it more unkempt. I like to think that Bo was cosmically forced to knock up Win's stubbornly independent self because the universe knew we needed him and she had sworn off dating.

Since their infamous Halloween romp—at *my* party—he's become an irreplaceable member of our family. He reaches all the shit off the high shelves and changes out lightbulbs, for example. But mostly it's his big heart that we were missing. The affection he gives so easily to all of us but to his daughter and my best friend the most.

I usually refuse to call him by the same name more than once per time spent together, just to keep things interesting. It started as new-kid hazing but Bo, like he does with most things, took it in stride and now it's just for fun. Variations of his name include Bo, Robert, Roberto, Rob, Robbie, Rob the Builder, Bo-Nus, Bo-bonic plague, Robo-Nerd, Bo the hoe, Daddy Bo, Father Roberts, and—his personal favorite—Bil*bo* Baggins.

"This place is a fucking labyrinth," Bo says, looking over his shoulder toward the dimly lit hallway behind him. "Did you two get lost?" He slows, assessing me with just as much care as his wife had only a few minutes ago.

With an audible sigh he steps around me, offering a hand to his wife who holds out her arms in the air expectantly. He pulls her up, and then they both turn toward me, matching worry across their features. I swear they're starting to meld into one mutant, overly astute, annoyingly cute being.

"You doing okay?" he asks, wincing playfully in a way that tells me he already knows the answer.

I sniff, feeling my sadness metamorphize into bitter resolve. "You're in finance, Robert . . . so, tell it to me straight. The event cost one hundred and twenty thousand and we've made . . . ?"

He swallows heavily, making his throat bob. "About one-ninety when I came to find you both."

"Right." I nod, my eyes falling closed. "So . . . Good investment?" I ask.

I look up at Win's gentle giant as he nervously paws at the edge of his beard. "You made a profit," he says, avoiding eye contact.

"Hmm," I mumble indifferently.

"And the night isn't over yet," he adds, lowering his hand to his trousers' pocket.

"You're both too nice." I check my watch to find that we have about ten minutes before my scheduled farewell address. It was my mom's watch, actually. Chain-link, gold-plated. It probably cost her less than thirty dollars at a big-box store. I don't usually wear it, but I thought it might have been a good luck charm tonight. I fiddle with it, fighting the urge to take it off. "I should probably get out there," I say, brushing my finger across the clock face.

"Caleb told me he can handle it if you want him to. He—"

"No," Win says, interrupting Bo with a gentle pat to his chest. "She wants to do this herself."

Bo turns to face me and nods once, wearing a sweet smile. His hand finds his wife's arm, still draped across his chest, and squeezes her wrist.

Without a single word being spoken, the three of us nod, share a wistful sigh, and then begin walking down the hall. We pass by the storage rooms containing extra tables and chairs, the bustling kitchen as the caterers tidy up for the night, and the side corridor where staff are running back trays of emptied champagne flutes and water glasses, until we reach a set of double doors.

The venue on the other side of the doorway is a classic ballroom containing glistening crystal chandeliers, white draped linens, thin carpeting with intricate swirls of a similar gray color. At the far end there's a stage, brought in specially for tonight. On top of it sits a clear plastic podium, a large sky-blue backdrop featuring the clinic's emblem, and, off to the side, a photograph of my mother set upon a white easel.

The photo, from my and Caleb's wedding, is the only one from Mom's last year of life that I can stand to look at. She doesn't look sick at first glance. In it, Mom's wheelchair is parked next to the first row of pews with Aunt June and Win out of focus behind her in the frame. She's smiling subtly toward the front of the tiny sanctuary, wearing a feathered, wide-brimmed blue hat. Pride shines across all her features as she watches her blissfully naïve nineteen-year-old daughter promise forever to a man who would have been better described as a boy.

"Ready?" Bo asks, hand on the door in front of us, ready to push.

I force a smile, and feel it does not reach my eyes.

"You've got this," Win says, rubbing my shoulder as Bo opens and holds the door ajar for us to pass through.

Immediately, my ears perk up in confusion. The room we enter is not at all what I was expecting. The vibe is . . . joyous. It's celebratory. The guests are applauding . . . Smiling . . . Cheering.

Win squeals at my side just as Bo turns on his heels, his face lit with excitement as he stares down at me. I look past them toward the stage where my husband stands tall, presenting an obnoxiously large check written out to the ALS Research Institute of Southern Ontario for three-hundred-thousand dollars to Dr. Torres.

Something in my gut twists as they turn to pose for a photo, laughing like old friends, and the photographer's flash flares.

This is *not* an answered prayer.

This is Caleb's doing.

"DON'T MOVE; JUST ONE MORE PIN . . ." MY MOTHER IS on her knees in front of me, her back to the large standing mirror in her bedroom. She's got her pincushion tied around her wrist like a bracelet as she tugs at the hem of the dress she's making me for the school dance. I watch in the mirror as she folds over one last piece of the green, silky underlay with a steady concentration.

"Marcie, have you seen my—" Aunt June appears in the doorway, and I spin around to face her, unable to contain my prideful smirk. "Holy shit, Sarah Abilene! Look at you!"

"I said don't move," Mom cries out, laughing anxiously. "You're lucky I didn't poke you!"

Aunt June nods, a grin lifting her rose-tinted cheeks. "You look hot as hell, girlie."

"I know, right?" I giggle, twirling the fabric around my knees. "Mom thinks it's too short."

Aunt June smiles knowingly toward my mother. "Your mom forgets that you're fifteen now."

"If you keep moving around like that your dress will end up crooked," my mom mutters, but I can hear the humor in her tone as she slips in a final pin and pats my bum, so I make room for her to stand.

"That Caleb kid better keep a tight grip on you at the dance or he'll lose you to another boy," Aunt June says, wandering further into my mother's bedroom. She begins rifling through Mom's drawers without any sort of permission. "Once Win sees that she's going to ask you to make her a dress as well, Mars."

I turn to face the mirror again, catching the tail end of my mother rolling her eyes. "Win has a swim meet the night of the dance, remember? You're picking her up early from school Friday and driving her to Toronto Prep for—"

Aunt June slams a drawer shut. "Course. I remember." She slips a set of bangles onto her wrist and moves to stand behind me to admire her reflection, fussing with her bleached-blond hair tied up into a high pony. She's a petite woman, shorter than me, and voluptuous. She's not the least bit shy about showing off her curves. "I'll be back late tonight, don't wait up!"

"Ooh-la-la," I sing out as Aunt June spins on her six-inch heels and sways out of the bedroom.

"Do not encourage her," Mom says, shaking her head. "And, speaking of *dates,* when am I going to meet this Caleb of yours?" She holds gentle eye contact in the mirror, with one slightly quirked brow. "You're not embarrassed of your old mom, are you?"

I roll my eyes as she wraps her arms around my shoulders, leaning over me. "Of course not . . . and you're *not* old." I giggle, pressing the side of my forehead into her chin as I stare at our reflection.

"So?" she asks, smiling.

"Soon . . . I promise."

Soon arrives three days later when Caleb comes to pick me up for the dance. He knocks twice before I open the apartment door. His fist is still raised for what would have been a third rap, but I intercepted it—not bothering to hide that I'd been anxiously awaiting his arrival. "Don't break up with me until *after* the dance, okay?"

"Uh, hi?" Caleb says, before his stunned gaze dips down. "Whoa, you look—"

"I know it's not a nice building."

"What? No, Sar, it's—"

"It smells like cigarettes and the paint is chipping off the walls but that's just in the hallways! It's nicer in here," I interrupt, speaking so fast I think I might strain my tongue. "Not as nice as your parents' house obviously and—"

"Sarah—"

"And my mother is going to ask you a lot of questions. She'll probably insinuate that she knows a guy who can make people disappear but—" Caleb circles his arm around my waist, tugs me to him, and kisses my lips before they've had the chance to stop moving. I relax into his hold.

"My turn now." He places his hand on my neck, which always makes my knees weaken, then kisses me softly again. "You look amazing," he says, leaning back to admire my dress once more before a final, light kiss. "I don't think I've seen you nervous before, Green . . . I think I like it."

I glare at him playfully. "It's just . . . I know it's not . . . It's different than what you're used to."

He smiles mischievously and it lights up his entire face. "You may have mentioned that once or twice."

It's then that I notice he's matched his tie to the color of my dress, as I'd requested, and that he's clearly tried to style his hair in the way I told him I liked best—pushed to one side with one dangling, perfect curl resting against his forehead. "You look very handsome. Thank you."

"You don't have to thank me, weirdo." His nose scrunches up over the top of a grin as he leans down to kiss me again. Just before his lips meet mine, we're interrupted by the sound of a purposefully cleared throat.

"Is this the famous Caleb, at last?" my mother says, leaning her hip against the kitchen island. "How about you leave my daughter's lips alone for a moment and come say hello?"

Caleb rallies quickly, to my surprise. "Hi, Miss Green," he says, confidently waltzing toward my mother, his hand extended at the ready. "It's great to meet you."

Mom's teasing smile grows lopsided as she tentatively puts out her hand to shake his, her eyes softening enough for me to notice from across the room. "Well, hello . . . How *polite*."

TWO

"THERE SHE IS," CALEB SAYS EXCITEDLY AS HE STEPS up to the podium, pointing me out to the crowd with his hand extended before initiating another round of applause. I smile politely toward the stage, my head bowed as I weave my way through tables of wealthy acquaintances and well-to-do philanthropists—all the while trying to conceive any other possible explanation for this sudden financial uptick and failing.

Caleb looks handsome standing up there in his black suit jacket . . . but I *do* wish he'd have paired it with something other than his favorite dark denim jeans. Though, in his defense, a lot of the men here tonight are wearing a similar ensemble. The tech-guy wardrobe, as Win affectionately calls it. *Her* husband is in a custom-fit suit, however.

Caleb's curly, maple-brown hair is trimmed short and pushed to one side, as it has been since I told him I liked it that way forever ago. He's not switched up his style of glasses either, wearing the same thinly framed, rounded gray metal over his espresso-colored eyes. The prescription has strengthened with the years, but other than that, nothing about Caleb has changed all that much since we were fourteen.

He's still exactly six feet tall, though his license says 180 centimeters, which would place him at about five foot eleven. I told him to have it fixed, but he was far too polite to correct the sweet older woman behind the counter at the licensing office. He still has a perfect megawatt smile from braces provided by his parents' superior dental coverage. The same purplish arrowhead birthmark on his collarbone that I love to press my lips to. The same scar on his right hand from a run-in with a Bunsen burner in the eleventh grade that he teasingly blames me for, and that same casual ease about him that at best can calm you down and at worst make you feel jaded. And while my body has filled out after the second puberty of my mid-twenties, Caleb has kept his lean, rectangular frame. He is my steadfast, easy, contented man. Something solid in a world that constantly seems to shift on its axis.

Caleb has always been *safe*.

As my whole world began falling apart, when losing my mother became inevitable, there was this kind, if a *tad* dorky, high school sweetheart who promised to never leave me. Who loved *me*. The girl from a single-parent home who developed an affinity for drinking a little too much and sneaking the occasional cigarette out of her aunt's packs. The girl with a shocking amount of overdue library books, an unquenchable desire to be liked, and the vocabulary of a sailor who came with a variety of baggage no teenager ought to have.

I've known Caleb for over seventeen years now and loved him for nearly as many. Which is why I know in my gut that this wasn't some surprise last-minute donation, or high stakes bidding on the final auction item that brought my fundraising goal to completion. This check has *Caleb* written all over it, even if it doesn't literally say his name.

It's the cursed roles we've been stuck in since the eleventh grade. The gallant knight riding in on his white horse is here to save me once again. And *shit,* if being the damsel in distress isn't getting old.

I eventually find my way to the bottom of the stage and a polite stranger from the closest table extends his arm to help me up the stairs while my husband remains unmoving, wearing his classic, carefree grin. Dr. Torres stands to the left of center stage holding the check loosely in front of his lower half, his eyes held on me with warmth and appreciation.

Just as I finish greeting the doctor, Caleb embraces me once again with a subdued smile, pulling me tight against him.

"How?" I whisper into his ear.

"Later," he answers, using a hand on my lower back to help me toward the podium center stage.

I clear my throat, looking over the round tables filled by guests evenly spaced around the ballroom. I shake myself and perform a smile, however bewildered it may appear. "Whoa," I say softly into the microphone, which is followed by a faint high-pitched ringing from the speakers. I swallow thickly, adjusting the microphone stand to my height. "I was only gone ten minutes. . . ." I laugh timidly. The guests laugh too, a polite rumble throughout the room, and I feel better for it.

Though I refused her help in all other preparations for tonight, Win did assist me in writing my speech. Mostly, I had planned to talk about my mother. I *was* going to say how I'd do anything to have had more years with her. How this research, helped with tonight's funds, will buy more time for families just like mine. And isn't that all we ever want? More memories with the people we love?

But now, it feels wrong. I don't deserve the speech that I suspect was bought for me. I didn't earn it.

My tongue feels swollen, and my palms begin to sweat as I white-knuckle grip either side of the podium. Suddenly, in my mind's eye, the podium is a bathroom sink at a high school party and I'm looking at myself in the medicine cabinet's mirror above it. I can see her reflection—seventeen-year-old me. Her lip-gloss is smudged, her hair is askew, and her face is pale. Shame washes over me like a familiar thick fog at the memory. Have I really changed? Have I truly grown from that scared, messy girl?

It took only one hit to my pride for me to give up. To throw away all of my potential. How *pathetic* is that . . .

Caleb clears his throat behind me, and the room comes back into focus. I force a deep breath, straightening my shoulders.

"Thank you all for coming this evening to help support Doctor Torres and his team at the ALS research institute of Southern Ontario," I start, my voice steadier than I'd expected it to be. "My mother, Marcie Green, died from complications of ALS eleven years ago. Since then, Dr. Torres's team has made massive strides in . . ." I trail off momentarily as I look toward the photo of my mother on stage. "In their research. The money we raised to-night, and the donations I hope we all continue to make in the future, will only help their efforts." *Mom's smile. Her proud, happy smile.* "God, I miss her. . . ." I whisper before laughing somberly. "And . . ." I duck my head as I swallow back another wave of heartache. I struggle to catch my breath, as if I haven't had over a decade's worth of practice.

When I lift my chin, I can see the general unease across the faces of the attendees. Tilted heads, tilted smiles, tilted cham-pagne flutes. Some well-meaning guest initiates applause and the crowd claps halfheartedly, nodding in sweet, if a bit condescend-ing, encouragement.

I interrupt it. "Truthfully—I could stand up here and say so many things but the heart of it is this . . . I wish that my mom had more time. . . ." I instinctively bring a hand to my chin as I feel it begin to tremble.

Caleb crowds me from behind, his hand slipping onto my hip, his thumb swiping up and down on my lower back. "D'you want me to?" He whispers into my hair.

I turn over my shoulder to shake my head and allow myself a brief moment to study his face. He's so familiar to me now that I feel myself having to concentrate to *truly* see him. As if he was a mural passed every morning on the way out the door or the lyrics to a favorite song I've sung along to a million times. Beautiful. Special, even. But known.

What would have happened if my mom had more time? I wonder, noticing the crow's feet at the corners of his eyes that, I suppose, haven't always been there. *Would we have gotten married so young? Did I jump from one safety net to the next?*

My heart desperately misses the answers that I thought I had at nineteen. The confidence to promise forever to a safe-house boy with a kind heart and the naïveté to believe that would be enough.

As Caleb retreats backward, I take yet another deep breath, fastening on the mask I've gotten used to wearing as a well-seasoned hostess. The false face you're granted when you begin taking advisory meetings at the bank and learn to throw around questions like *Where are you summering?* It's clean and polished and shiny, has no discernible emotion, and does not leave a lasting impression—at least with the way I wear it. The moment I feel the mask slip into place, I find the missing parts of my speech within the backlogs of my memory.

"Your generosity tonight will help fund research that can give people living with ALS just *that;* more time to live. More time to discover who they are. To dance in darkened clubs and fall in love with strangers. To make mistakes and find forgiveness. To drive with music blasting and windows down on a long dirt road. To lie under a tree from dawn to dusk with a good book. To work jobs they hate until they find what they're meant to do. To spend more hours with their loved ones, doing nothing whatsoever at all, and yet everything, at once. The chance for them to feel as if they got to live a full, consequential life."

Win nods enthusiastically from the back corner, wrapping her arm around her husband's waist as he bends down to wipe a tear from her cheek.

"If my mother taught me anything, it was to waste nothing. Not time, opportunities, or resources. So, I encourage you all to continue asking yourselves after tonight: What would Marcie Green do? Because the answer is, probably, drink a glass of white wine, give when you're able, help when you can, and not waste a moment."

Caleb steps closer and I turn to find him holding two champagne flutes. I can't help but smile up at him, taking one. "May I?" he mouths, and I nod in response. "To Marcie," Caleb says, bending toward the microphone as he toasts the crowd.

"To Marcie," the room responds in unison, followed by a collective sip.

I let the sparkling bubbles fade off my tongue before I speak again. "Thank you again to Doctor Torres and the team at the research institute and to all of you for being with us tonight. Please get home safely."

Once I finish, and a gentle applause fades out, the speakers begin playing soft jazz as they had the rest of the evening. I look over the crowd as most guests return to their previous conversations while a few stand to collect their belongings for a quick exit.

"You were amazing, baby," Caleb says, in a cavalier tone that instantly reminds me of who paid my speech's acceptance fee.

I spin on him, fast enough that my hair swings over my shoulder. "What did you do?" I enunciate each word in a menacing, slow whisper.

Caleb instantly recoils, his brows twisting together. "What? I—"

"Your mother would be so proud." Dr. Torres's voice booms as he makes his way across the stage, his hand reaching out to grasp my arm, which he squeezes tightly. "Nice save," he says, winking at Caleb. "You've got a good man here." He switches hands to hold the check as he drops my arm and clasps Caleb's shoulder instead.

Caleb turns his attention toward me, his lips pulled into an uncomfortable smile.

"I do," I reply, as genuinely as I'm able, though I feel my eyes glaze over with the sheer amount of effort it takes.

"Have a good night, you two," Dr. Torres says. "You deserve it!" he adds, sauntering off the stage, the obscenely large check in hand.

"Are you *seriously* mad?" Caleb asks in a near whisper, his eyes scanning over my head to the tables and guests below.

"Well, that depends." I glare at the underside of his jaw until he tilts his chin back down to face me.

"On?" One of his brows ticks upward in challenge. *I accept.*

"*On* how we managed to raise an extra hundred thousand dollars within the ten minutes it took for Bo to find me."

His thumb scratches the side of his nose, then just slightly above his lip as he looks down, a crooked smirk pulling at his lips. "Would you believe me if I said it was a very last-minute, anonymous donor?"

"No," I answer with a short sigh. "I would not." He reaches for my free hand, but I step back, placing it on my hip instead. Then, I bring my champagne flute to my lips as I stare at him unflinchingly over the top of the glass, swallowing every last drop. His fingers toy with the golden wedding band on his left hand, twisting it around his ring finger as he waits for me to finish. Once I do, I wipe my thumb across my bottom lip, and tilt my head expectantly, purposefully keeping a blank expression.

Caleb bends toward me, speaking in a hushed tone. "You worked so hard for tonight, Sar . . . What was I supposed to do?"

I scoff. He just doesn't get it. "*Nothing,* Caleb. You were supposed to do nothing," I say, a little too loudly. I only register that because Caleb's eyes move sharply to the crowd beyond the stage with a hint of panic.

His jaw flexes, the tendon in the side of his neck visible as he begins to speak in a low, ragged tone. "I don't even really know why we're arguing at all right now but . . ." He pauses, crossing his arms. "Can we discuss this later? Without an audience?"

I don't answer. Instead, I turn on my heels and storm off the stage; knowing that he'll follow. I make my way across the ballroom toward the kitchens and the familiar darkened hallway where I'd gathered my courage earlier, nearing the double doors where Bo and Win are still standing.

"We're gonna get going. Our babysitter can't stay late and . . ." Win doesn't finish her thought, gently shoving her purse into Bo's arms as she bends to take off her heels. I pass them without a second glance, too angry to stop. I hear Bo whistle long and low, signaling that I must look as pissed off as I feel.

When the familiar footfalls behind me stop abruptly, I look back to see Caleb saying a thoughtful goodbye to them both. Rage boils up closer to the surface at the sight of him taking the time to chat with our friends when he *should* be following me.

Now, on top of everything else, Caleb wins the *better friend award* too.

Pushing past the double doors, I move into a storage room lined with spare tables and place my emptied champagne flute onto a storage shelf. I forcefully remove my heels and drop them onto an emptied dolly before I begin pacing in frantic circles, rubbing at my chin so forcefully that I'm sure a layer of makeup has come off onto my palm.

"Sarah?" Caleb calls out apprehensively from the hallway. I hear the double doors shut behind him, the sounds of the crowd and music muffling as they do. "Are you back here?"

"In here," I respond, crossing my arms. In doing so the clasp of my watch—my mother's watch—gets stuck on the tulle overlay of my dress. Groaning, I begin tugging at it.

"Where?" Caleb replies, sounding no closer.

"The storage room!" I snap, struggling to pull the watch free. Growing hot behind the eyes, I wrench my wrist a little too hard. Helplessly, I watch as the watch's clasp breaks before it falls onto the linoleum floor. When I bend down to pick it up, I notice that the tulle of my dress now has a small tear in it as well. "Of course," I mutter to myself, slipping the broken watch into my cleavage for safekeeping.

This dress doesn't have pockets. The dresses my mom made me *always* had pockets.

"Sarah?" Caleb calls out again, *apparently* attempting to start up a friendly game of Marco Polo.

"Oh my god!" I yell, stepping out into the hall with my arms extended above my head as if to wave down a plane. "There's one open fucking door in this hallway with a woman inside of it losing her mind 'The Yellow Wallpaper' style. Did you even attempt to move from that exact spot? Get in here!"

Caleb's nostrils flare as his chest inflates with a deep breath. "Sarah, I know tonight is emotional for you but—" He begins walking toward me as my sharp laugh cuts him off.

"Right, of course, *emotional*. I'm emotional! I couldn't possibly be justified in being angry with you."

"Maybe if you could explain *why* you're angry with me?" Caleb asks, moving closer until I'm backed into the room. He shuts the door behind him after a quick, nervous glance into the hallway.

"This was *my* fundraiser, Caleb. Mine. Not yours. Not anyone else's. I did all of this by myself, and I intended to fail *or* succeed by myself."

"By yourself, huh?" he asks, voice verging on mocking.

"Yes," I spit back.

Caleb huffs exasperatedly, glancing up to the ceiling as he undoes the top button on his white dress shirt, exposing his Adam's apple and a whisper of chest hair. "All right, sure . . ." he says, sarcasm rolling off his tongue. "The guest list, then. How *exactly* did that come about?"

I grind my molars together, dead-eyeing him.

He nods as if he can hear my snarky thoughts under my vacant expression, his lips pouting in a shitty type of smug expression that I'd like to rub off his face with a dig of my own. "Because I *distinctly* remember sitting at our kitchen counter as we pulled that list together from *my* contacts."

"Yeah, thanks for those. Turned out great. Ree-aally generous friends you've got there. And so nice of your parents to show!" They'd not even bothered to RSVP, never mind attend, but Caleb saved them seats at our table regardless.

That knocks the smug look off his face. No one in the history of ever has held two such lousy people in such high regard as Caleb does his parents. "I told you to start smaller, Sar." He did. I *hate* that he did. Win did too, in less direct wording. "I told you to—"

"You understand that you've made this night meaningless, right?" I ask, tears threatening to pour. I force them away, choking them down until the sadness rests heavy in my throat. I know the moment Caleb sees me cry, he'll stop fighting. To him, tears are a white flag in battle—an immediate call for ceasefire. Perhaps it's reckless of me but tonight I'd rather us both be wounded than experience another silent car ride home with unspoken frustrations continuing to pile between us.

I'm done pretending that everything is fine. I'm done pretending that *I* am fine. Honestly, I think part of me wants Caleb to be mad at me. I can't *always* be harder on myself than everyone else is, surely.

"Before you stepped in, I could have at least said I turned a profit. Now between the cost of the event and our own donation, we haven't."

"That's crap and you know it. It was a loss either way," he says, one of his shoulders lifting as he points toward the ballroom. "You told me *weeks* ago that you wanted to raise at least *double* what it cost us. That's what *you* said. You were nowhere close to that."

Out of all the moments to be on the exact same page, I wish it wasn't this one. "I'm really loving the times you're choosing to use *us* and then *you*," I say, trying to force my voice even.

"Pardon?" Caleb crosses his arms and hunches forward.

"You said what it cost *us* and that *I* was nowhere near close."

"Well, you made yourself clear. It's your event, not mine."

"But it's *our* money I spent, not mine?" I retort.

Caleb purses his lips. "What's mine is yours," he replies pointedly.

Allowing that shitty turn of phrase to breathe for a moment, I stare at the tactfully closed door. It reminds me of Caleb's urgency to get off the stage when I spun on him. And, sure, I care what the people out there think of me too, so it shouldn't bother me that Caleb does the same and acts accordingly. But it brings up an old wound that time never seems to fully heal.

No matter how many times he'll tell me otherwise, I feel like I embarrass him. That I'm the unerasable red-wine stain on the otherwise perfectly clean tablecloth that is the Linwood family.

His mother's indifference toward me over the years, in stark contrast to her unbridled pride in her son, is only ever expressed in fleeting, passive-aggressive comments that hint at my lack of career or ambition. Questions like: How have you been keeping busy? Or comments such as: You must be lonely in that big house all day. And these are immediately followed by news of Caleb's sister, Cora's, career achievements or phone-tree gossip about their friends' daughters—who would have been much better wives, no doubt—and their bright, shining, somehow-still-single lives. As if to remind Caleb that other women still exist in the world. Successful women. Women ready to give him children if he so desires because *of course* it's solely my decision for us to not have kids.

Caleb's dad, Cyrus, is universally indifferent to anything that doesn't fill his pockets. He met Caleb's mother, Michelle, during her first year of college when he, thirteen years her senior, taught a guest lecture on networking in business. I wasn't there but I'd wager to guess that the keynotes were: Be born rich and use daddy's contacts to get ahead. After that first encounter, Michelle quickly became "Chellie" to him and, soon after, everyone else. The Linwoods have a long, eerie tradition of all family members having first names that begin with the letter *C*. He didn't call her Chellie out of affection or familiarity—he did it so she'd fit the mold.

Sometimes I wonder if Cyrus would like me more if my name was Claire or Charlotte or Cecelia. *No . . . not that last one.*

"I'm sorry tonight failed," I say, turning to face him—my eyes wide and smile insincere. "I'll be sure to pay you back."

Caleb's shoulders sink as he drags a hand down from forehead to chin. "Fuck's sake, Sarah. You know I don't think about it like that. That's not fucking fair!" His voice rises, startling us both— Caleb rarely yells. Never at me. The moment freezes, as do I.

"Fuck . . . Sorry." He blows out a long breath, bringing his wrists to his temples. "I—I didn't mean to upset you. I didn't think that it would upset you." His shoulders fall on another sigh. "I really was just trying to help."

"Yeah," I say, then mumble, "always so helpful."

"Do you expect me to apologize for that?" he asks, letting his arms fall heavy to his sides. "You were off pouting somewhere, the auction was done, I sent Bo and Win to try and find you, but time was running out and I had to make a decision. I'm sorry that I thought you'd rather save face, but clearly, I underestimated your pridefulness."

"Well, times are tough!" I laugh bitterly. "I have to reserve the resources when my supply of pride runs so goddamn low."

Caleb rolls his eyes. "Don't be dramatic. You have plenty to be proud of."

"Really?" I smile near hysterically, shaking my head as the tip of my nose burns with the threat of tears once again. "What, exactly? Name *one* thing that I should be proud of, Cay. Something that's *only* mine. Something that I've done entirely on my own."

I watch as the man who's known me for seventeen years, the very same man who's been hailed as a genius and received endless awards for his innovative, brilliant brain, struggles to come up with a single answer.

And there's no fighting it anymore, his silence cracks me wide open. Tears spring loose on a broken sob.

Caleb's eyes close softly as he lessens the distance between us and wraps me in his arms.

That's enough, I think.

White flag.

Take me home.

THREE

"THAT'S STILL GOING ON, HUH?" WIN SAYS, HER EYES held on the door to the garage as it shuts behind Caleb, who leaves without so much as a goodbye. Every other Friday night Caleb goes to Win's place to play Dungeons and Dragons with Bo and their friends, and she comes here for a telenovela marathon with me. "The silent treatment?"

"Yep . . ." I pour this evening's second helping of merlot. "Since the fundraiser." I take a large sip, let the wine rest in the back of my throat, then gulp. Setting my glass down, I look to see my best friend, biting at her thumbnail as her eyes slide nervously between me and the door to the garage. "It'll be fine," I say, attempting to set her at ease. "We'll be fine," I reiterate.

Honestly, I'm beginning to wonder if that's true. Caleb's never been *this* upset with me before. For the entirety of our marriage, our longest fight prior to this one lasted only two days. And it was *me* moving around our place like some sort of petulant poltergeist—with the slamming of doors, cupboards left ajar, and laundry piles the only evidence of my presence—not Caleb. He's always been the calm one. There's no experience to help predict how long this could go on for. Or, if it will ever end.

Maybe this is it. Maybe he's finally had enough of my bullshit. I wouldn't blame him.

"It's been almost a month," Win says, delicately picking up her glass with her smaller right hand to carry a bowl of popcorn in her left toward the living room and my cozy, white L-shaped couch that awaits us. "This is you and Caleb we're talking about; you guys don't fight. Not like this."

"I don't know . . ." I follow Win, balancing a tray carrying several bowls filled with candy and my multiple beverages. One for hydration, one for fun, and one for comfort—water, diet Coke, and wine—just as Aunt June taught me. I set the tray on my marble coffee table and throw myself back onto the couch, shuffling into the corner seat. "I think maybe that's the issue. We've been letting shit pile up for years, ignoring it like the bills on our moms' kitchen table. But now they're all past due and we're too tired to deal with it all."

"If I didn't know better," Win says, placing a pillow in her lap and hugging it, "it would seem like you're giving up."

"Would that be so bad?" I ask, throwing a handful of popcorn into my mouth. "I mean . . ." I say, voice muffled by half-chewed-up kernels before I swallow. "How many people do you know who got married as teenagers stay married into their thirties? Statistically couples who get married before twenty are fifty percent more likely to get divorced and divorce rates are *already* high to begin with."

Win inhales sharply, causing me to turn my gaze toward her, my hand filled with popcorn freezing in midair. The expression on her face is one of offense mixed with blatant confusion. As if my blasé attitude uninvitedly slapped her ass at the bar before asking for a donation to the Girl Scouts.

"You googled it?" she asks, her voice slow. "You *googled* divorce rates?"

"Yeah . . . I—" I can't bring myself to look at her. I nearly apologize, feeling the discomfort seeping out of her. "Yeah."

"You and Caleb are *not* a statistic, Sarah," she says, in a way that feels like I'm required to agree with her. "You two were fine just a few months ago, right? More than fine, I thought. Help me understand . . ."

I drop my fistful of popcorn back into the bowl between us and brush my hands free of crumbs. "I don't know, Win. Just, lately, I've been questioning everything." I look up to find her eyes on me, gentle but visibly concerned. I want her to relax, to not worry about me, but I also need to get this off my chest.

"I've been thinking a lot about Mom lately and I've been questioning over and over and over again: What do I have to show for the last decade of my life? Who *am* I? And so much of that answer is wrapped up in Caleb. I mean, we started dating when I was fourteen." I suck in a breath, having failed to breathe for quite some time. "I've been Caleb's other half for more than *half* of my life. I honestly am starting to wonder if I'm some sort of . . . NPC or something."

Win blinks, her eyelashes fluttering rapidly. She opens her mouth to speak, shuts it, then shakes her head. "Wait—what's an NPC?"

"A non-player character," I answer. She's still confused, open mouth staring at me. "Like from a video game? The characters who exist the moment the main player needs them to and then, presumably, disappear when offscreen—existing in some empty void. Caleb explained this to me years ago, but I suppose you're still relatively new to the whole married-to-a-nerd gig."

"You think you're a background character?" Win asks, her tone far more concerned than I'd like it to be.

I hide my face from her, plucking lint off the couch cushion next to me. "On the night of the fundraiser I asked Caleb to name *one* thing I should be proud of. Something that's just my own. Do you know what he said?" I keep my face pointed away but sheepishly look toward her.

Win's frown deepens but her eyes narrow and harden with determination. "Your generosity? Your thoughtfulness? Your humor? Your banging bod? Your—"

"Winnifred," I interrupt, shaking my head softly. Her chest raises on a deep breath, sensing what comes next, I presume. "He said nothing." I shrug one shoulder, tugging my lips between my teeth as I watch her look away, visibly disappointed. "Caleb couldn't think of a *single* thing."

"He's never been good under pressure," Win says. "You know that."

"Would we call that pressure?" I ask, swallowing back my hurt.

The corner of her lip twitches further downward. "I guess not but—"

"How would you feel if Bo couldn't name a single accomplishment of yours? If he couldn't point to one thing and say *You did that, look how amazing you are,* after over a decade of marriage? Hell, after the two-ish years you two have been together."

"Awful," she answers, resigned. Deep down I know I shouldn't feel accomplished having gotten her to see how dire the situation truly is, but I do. "I'd feel awful," she repeats, quieter.

"Right," I say, leaning back into the couch cushions, straightening my posture. "Now take the men out of the picture—imagine *you* couldn't find a single thing to be proud of yourself for, either."

"Sarah . . ."

"I need a change, Win. Something *has* to give. And, maybe, that thing is Caleb. Maybe I need to survive on my own. And, maybe, he'd be better off." I sigh. "Maybe he's finally seeing what his parents have thought all along. I'm a loser."

"Sarah Abilene Linwood, you are *not* a loser," Win says decisively.

"I'm not a winner," I reply, reaching for both my diet Coke and wine and taking back-to-back sips.

"You're in a funk. This is a funk. An early-thirties crisis. We can find something that's just yours." She reaches for my knee and pats it forcefully. "You could go back to school, you could take up pottery, you could become an astronaut for all I care . . . But you'll find something." She hesitates, then squeezes my leg. "You know, Mom always thought you'd eventually write some books of your own. We all did."

Yep, I know. Tried that and failed, thank you *so much* for the reminder. "It's fucked up, right?" I attempt to divert the conversation. "That I have all this time, good health, and resources at my disposal, and I do *nothing* with it, but Mom—"

"What you've got to do first is *stop* comparing yourself to Marcie." Win drops her hand as she raises an eyebrow at me. "Because that won't help you figure your shit out and it sure as hell won't help save your marriage."

The words *save your marriage* send a cool shiver down my spine. "Damn, Winnie . . . You switched up your tone fast."

"I took a moment, gathered intel, and figured out what you needed. I decided it's tough love. You've got to talk to Caleb, Sar. Tonight. You cannot throw your whole life away because one event didn't go as planned. You cannot just call yourself a loser and will it into existence by giving up. You deserve far better than that. *You* are better than that."

Really? Am I? Doubt it.

"What if it all unravels?" I ask.

"Unravels?" Win repeats, her brows pinching.

I place both of my drinks onto the coffee table then stare at the cuff of my cardigan. "What if Caleb and I are like a nice, cozy sweater. A favorite sweater. The one you cannot wait to pull out as soon as the weather turns. The one that you've worn through your highest highs and your lowest lows. Comfortable. Dependable. But one day, you notice a broken stitch and tug on the thread a little too hard. Then, you keep tugging and tugging trying to find the end of the loose thread. But instead, the whole thing falls apart and you're left wearing nothing—your tits out to the wind—with a pile of yarn at your feet."

"Then, I guess, you'd pick up the yarn and knit another sweater."

"But it'll never be the same," I say, looking at her, allowing her to see the fear behind my eyes that I've tried so hard to hide from her for so long.

"Well . . . *is that such a bad thing?*" She throws the phrase back at me with a coy smile. "You want a change, right?" She pushes on my knee with a teasing force. "You and Caleb have made a beautiful sweater together, babe. But it's been over a decade and clothes wear out over time. Maybe it wasn't made well enough to begin with, considering all that you were going through when it was first put together and how young you both were. But now, you have the chance to make something new. Something that will last. And the yarn *is* good."

"This analogy is getting tired," I mumble, picking lint off my sleeve.

Win presses her foot into my leg, until I look back at her. "Pull on your thread and unravel your sweater, then wind up a new ball of yarn and begin again."

I look at her with exaggerated disgust. "I may choose to strangle myself with the yarn if you keep going."

"Well then, perhaps you should make yourself a nice scarf instead." Win reaches toward the coffee table to throw a gummy bear in her mouth. "Hmm," she mumbles, chewing as her eyes dart side to side. "You remember my old lifeguarding manager? Helen? From Westcliff Point?"

I look at her suspiciously. "I guess. Why?"

"Helen, married to Yvonne? I worked with her for four summers. . . ."

I glance up to the ceiling with my palms presented as if to say, *help me please.* "How did our conversation get here from my marriage-crisis sweater? Do Helen and Yvonne knit? Did Helen strangle Yvonne with a scarf? What is the context? Take me along on your thought process here."

Win rolls her eyes, smirking. "It's annoying you can't read my mind by now." She finishes chewing her candy, then swallows hard. "Helen and Yvonne run this camping trip every year for couples. They invited Bo and me, but we can't make it, given that it's only a few weeks before Cando's opening and, *you know,* our Velcro-kid. . . . It's seven nights away at the end of June."

"End of June . . . as in just over a week from now?"

"According to the Gregorian calendar, yes."

"Okay? And?"

"It's called *Reignite.*"

"Reignite," I repeat incredulously.

"Yes," Win replies in a snarky tone, tossing a lace of licorice at me. I pick it up off my chest and bite into it, tugging it away from my mouth until it breaks. "Yvonne is a counselor and Helen is an outdoor and recreation therapist. She said that the couples they help come back closer and better off than ever before."

"But it's outdoors?" I can't help but show my distaste.

"If I had to put money on it? I'd think the hiking and camping excursion is outdoors; yes."

"Caleb and I are not outdoorsy people, Win. You know that."

"Didn't you just say you needed a change?"

"Well, yeah but—"

"To try something new?"

"Yes, however—"

"I think this could be good for you. Seven days, no distractions, a little bit of couples counseling in the great outdoors. Might give you some time to think. To talk. To dream about what you want out of life. What's the worst that could happen?"

"I squat to take a shit in the woods and my vagina grazes poison ivy."

She blinks at me, stunned. "Wow, your mind didn't even hesitate to come up with that scenario."

"We both know how sensitive she is," I say, looking down at my lap. "I'll be nursing her back to health for the rest of my days. Now *that* wouldn't be good for my marriage."

"We'll get you a collapsible bucket to shit into," Win says, reaching for her drink. She uses her tongue to fetch her straw, takes a long, drawn-out sip and then sets it back down. "Ooh, and one of those lady urinal things."

"So according to you," I hold up both hands to perform air-quotes, "to *save my marriage,*" I drop my hands into my lap, "I have to shit in the woods? Or piss into a funnel?"

"People have done a lot more work for a lot less reward."

"I'd have to convince Caleb to take the time off work."

"Something tells me that won't be so difficult."

I scoff. "He's not Bo."

Win turns her body to face me, her bent knee touching mine. Her glacial-blue eyes drift off to the left as my uncomfortable remark fills the space between us. I don't typically compare our husbands, out loud or otherwise. It's just, they *are* different. One man is possessed with a type of love that seems to command his every thought and action and the *other* man . . . less so. But maybe Caleb was like that in the beginning too. I can barely remember it now.

"Listen, Sar. I love you more than anybody on this planet. You're my top three with my husband and my little girl. But . . . I've also had seventeen years to love and learn Caleb's ways. That man *loves* you—whether he's always great at showing it or not. I think if you tell him you want to try and go fix this weirdness between you, he'll be on board. I think if you explain to him how you've been feeling, he'll want to do this for you both."

I nod slowly, thinking it over. *I can at least approach him with the idea, right?* "Do they have a website?"

Win pulls out her phone, types into her browser, then scoots closer on the couch to show me. The first photograph on the website is a group picture. Ten or so hikers, covered in varying amounts of dirt and grime, all smiling brightly. Below the photograph reads, "*Spend some much-needed time with yourself, nature, and your partner during our one-week wilderness retreat. We've all been guilty of getting caught up in the daily routines of life. We're here to help you and your partner reflect, reconnect, and reignite your spark.*"

"So . . ." she says after a few minutes of scrolling. "What do you think?"

"I do like it . . ." I let the *but* die on my tongue. Win's right, Caleb and I need something different. Something to help us out of our rut and comfort zones. Something to remind us of who we were before so many years together buried us under.

"So?"

"It's Caleb," I say, in a cautious way that translates to: "I should just ask him, right?"

"It's Caleb," Win repeats, in an assured way that translates to: "Absolutely."

"I SHOULD GET YOU HOME, IT'S ALMOST CURFEW," CALEB says, peppering my shoulder with kisses as he squeezes me tighter from behind my back. "But I *really,* really don't want to," he whispers.

"Five more minutes." I sigh blissfully, feeling the cold winter air fighting its way in through the frost covered windows and nipping at my cheeks. Caleb was prepared for the weather and brought a few heavy wool blankets. We're currently on top of one and under another. The other was lost somewhere on the floor below sometime after my bra came off and the windows began fogging up. "When do you need to be home by?" I ask, rolling within his grip to curl myself into him. Thank goodness for this generously wide backseat.

"My dad's away for work and my mom is probably asleep by now. So, whenever I want."

I wonder if Caleb knows his demeanor changes whenever he talks about his parents. How unconvincing his usual carefree tone becomes. "It's your birthday, you don't think your mom stayed up to say goodnight?"

"No, I doubt it. She gave me my gifts this morning before school."

I cringe internally. That is *not* the sole purpose of seeing your child on their sixteenth birthday. Or *any* birthday, for that matter. But I don't have the heart to break that to him. "No one can top Opa's gift, anyways," I say, changing the subject somewhat as I admire the moonroof above our heads. Opa is, without a doubt, my favorite of Caleb's family members. He cannot stand his son-in-law, for one, and he sees his grandson the way I do—kind, gentle, smart, thoughtful. Not weak or easily distracted, as his father does. I think Opa decided to gift Caleb his old car because he knew Caleb needed to be out of his house as much as possible.

"I think I like your gift the most," Caleb coos against my neck, spreading goosebumps across my exposed skin as he sucks on my pulse point.

I hum playfully in response. "I hope you're not implying that my virginity was *given* to you . . ."

A laugh rumbles from the back of Caleb's throat. "*No,* never. I meant the hat your mom made."

"Hey!" I say with a breathy laugh as I turn to face him. "I made that hat!" *It was actually Win who made it. I wrote her essay on* The Crucible *in exchange*.

"That *is* what you said, yes." He tilts down to smile at me, and I'm struck by just how beautiful he is. How *good* this feels.

I never allowed myself to imagine that having sex for the first time would feel so safe or warm or comforting. Hell, the way my mom described losing her virginity was almost enough to put me off the idea of sex forever. But Caleb is not my father—whoever that guy is. Caleb is something else entirely.

Caleb's contented sigh vaporizes into a fog in the cool winter air between us. "I love you," he says, bringing his lips to my forehead. "I love you a truly stupid amount."

And I understand what he means by *stupid* because I've come to the same realization . . . We are *far* too young to be feeling this way. Far, far too young to give ourselves over to someone else *this* much. That this will most likely end, as most first loves do. Meaning, we're both running headfirst toward heartbreak. And what else could you call that other than stupid?

But, even still, in this moment I cannot bring myself to care about that possibility at all.

I choose to hope that maybe, just maybe, fate will have something kinder in store for us. That I'll never need to know a day without Caleb, his ease, puns, or comfort, ever again.

That, just maybe, I got lucky earlier than most.

I tuck my smile against his throat. "I love you too."

FOUR

CALEB IS TAKING A LONG ENOUGH SHOWER THAT I know he's either masturbating, avoiding me, or had turned the water on before realizing he needed to take a shit. Behold: the intimate knowledge held within marriage.

Because we've not had sex for almost two months, it's reasonable to presume that he's masturbating *and* avoiding me. He's probably got his forehead pressed against the tile while he strokes himself, billows of steam surrounding him as hot water cascades between his shoulder blades and down his back, ass, and thighs—just as I've gotten to see countless times.

I love walking in on Caleb showering, propping myself up on the bathroom counter between our his-and-her sinks, and watching him get himself off. There's something uniquely hot about the way the tendons in his forearms flex, his small grunts of pleasure as he releases, his sigh of relief once he comes, and the slow turn he does afterward toward the showerhead to rinse off that allows me the perfect view of his ass.

He's told me that he doesn't mind if I watch but doesn't particularly understand why I want to. I am quick to point out the hypocrisy of such statements—because he *loves* to watch me play with myself, with my fingers or with toys. He's begged to record it on his phone more than a dozen times, at least. And I mean *truly* begged. Like, fully pleading and whimpering while on his knees—usually as he's positioned between mine for an up-close-and-personal private show.

The *act* of sex has never been our issue. Although our first few times were comically awkward in hindsight, as is the rite of passage. We were both virgins, after all. For a while Win and I referred to Caleb as "Oliver-Oil" because he was *extra virgin*. Meaning, I had also been his very first kiss. Turned out I'd be his first and *only*.

The thought has occurred to me that I could be terrible at kissing and Caleb would have no idea as he's got nothing to compare me to. But I don't think I am. I'd kissed a *lot* of boys—and a few girls—before Caleb and I shared our first kiss at fourteen and hadn't received any complaints.

I had my first kiss at eleven, which I suppose is fairly young, but I was an early bloomer, according to my mom and Aunt June. Puberty hit me like a truck the summer before seventh grade. I went from not needing a bra to wearing a training bra to a full B-cup in the span of two months. My new boobs acted like a bat-signal to the boys in my class, some of whom came back that September different (i.e., taller) themselves. Regardless, I had their attention, and I loved it.

It was always just kissing until I was thirteen and one unremarkable boy asked if he could put his hand up my shirt after soccer practice behind the sport's equipment shed. He gingerly placed his hand on the outside of my bra as Win kept watch around the corner for teachers and other students. I lied afterward and told her that it was *awesome,* but I purposefully never spoke to that boy again.

Then, I met Caleb. He'd made the bold decision to defy his parents' wishes and transfer from private to public school because of our high school's computer science lab donated by some well-to-do alumni.

We dated for over a year before we *finally* started doing more than kissing. He wanted to take things slow, and I respected that—though I did my fair share of crying to Win about whether he was into me or not. Fourteen-year-old-me mistook his chastity for indifference. After all, boys are supposed to be the ones doing the pressuring, right? At least, that's what I believed at the time—confirmed by the afterschool specials my mother made us watch about the dangers of teenage boys and their hormones or teenage boys and their drugs or teenage boys and their alcohol or, well, just teenage boys in general.

The lesson was: Boys will pressure you, and you should just say no!

Except Caleb never once pressured me and I *definitely* would have just said yes!

Eventually, Caleb got his learner's permit and his Opa's 1995 LeSabre as a sixteenth birthday present and we celebrated the occasion by ripping each other's clothes off twenty minutes from my house in the dimly lit parking lot of an abandoned Zellers. That car really did get some mileage after that.

Caleb would never dare to have sex under his parents' roof and my mom was *very* strict about having my bedroom door always open given how young she was when I came to be. The car's backseat was all we had until Caleb moved out for his first year of university. To this day I still can't drive past a Buick dealership without blushing.

For a while, our relationship was simple. Our biggest argument had been about Caleb opting to travel around Europe with his family during our summer breaks instead of staying home with me to . . . go to some local fair or, I don't know, the used bookstore that hadn't gotten any new stock since the late nineties. I was a teenage, lovesick idiot who'd not yet experienced Italian gelato so, truthfully, I didn't know what I was asking him to give up.

Then, in the eleventh grade, Mom got her diagnosis. It had been a long, difficult process up until that point. She had undergone countless tests, seen dozens of specialists, coming up empty time and time again and I could see her exhaustion, even though she worked hard to disguise it. It would have been a relief to finally have an answer if that answer hadn't been ALS.

When Mom and Aunt June sat Win and me down to tell us the news on what had otherwise been an average Friday evening, they didn't ask Caleb to leave. Instead, they asked all three of us to sit together on our thrift-store couch as they sat across from us and delivered what felt like a death sentence to our lives as we'd known them. When all five of us hugged afterward, sniffling and teary-eyed, I realized that, at some indiscernible point in time, Caleb had become a part of our family.

From that day on, Caleb drove out of his way every morning to pick Win and me up for school and every afternoon to drop us off.

Sometimes the other girls at school would comment about how *cute* it was that Caleb drove us every day. And they weren't wrong, it was. But that was the simplistic perspective of the young and carefree. In reality, those extra thirty minutes that I'd have otherwise wasted on the bus allowed me the time before school to make sure my mom was up, fed, and comfortable. I didn't know how to tell them that Caleb and I weren't just your average high school sweethearts desperate for every extra minute we could have together. How serious and grown-up it all felt to have a routine that served my family. How to convey the gratitude I felt to have someone take on a burden of their own to relieve one of mine.

Caleb wasn't like their silly, fair-weather boyfriends. He was a provider. He was a caretaker. I convinced myself that we were *practically* adults. On the days that I just smiled and said, "Yeah, he's the best," in response to a girl's sweet sentiments—I'd give Caleb head in his car during lunch period. I figured it was the least I could do to say thank you.

Regardless of the reason, those car rides each day that the three of us shared hold some of my most favorite memories.

Our mothers' apartment was on the second floor and our rusted balcony sat just above the building's main entrance. Every afternoon, Aunt June would be out there—smoking the *one* cigarette she'd allow herself per day after "quitting"—and taunt Caleb lovingly from her high perch. She'd often be in her scrubs, after just getting home from her shift at the retirement home, and her hair would be in a comical state of disarray.

Caleb took it all in his stride. After a few days of drop-offs, he started eagerly rolling down his window before we made the turn into the semicircle driveway. I loved that about him. That despite the echo chamber of polite society he'd grown up in, he accepted our household as it was. Chaotic, brash, messy, and teasing in our love.

He'd chat with Aunt June about her guy of the week as she forced him to help her fold laundry, or my mom about her appointments while she taught him to cook, because he'd never learned to do those things at home. And, after some time, it was hard to remember what life was like before Caleb *or* Mom's diagnosis. They'd both always been there, it seemed.

God, I miss that shitty apartment. I miss crawling into my

mother's bed with her. I miss feeling like there was so much that was still to come, and not already passed. I miss the gratitude I felt to Caleb for taking care of me when I had someone to take care of too. When he was lightening my burden and I wasn't the burden.

Blinking back to focus, I realize that our shower is still running. It has to have been at least thirty minutes since Caleb got in there. That amount of water usage alone would be enough to warrant a scathing David Attenborough documentary. Maybe Caleb slipped and fell? Do people in their thirties die from slipping in the shower?

Fuck . . . if Caleb is found dead in our shower there will certainly be people who point an accusatory finger at me after our little public spat at the fundraiser. *Wealthy young entrepreneur found dead*—the tabloids will read—*his dumbass wife waited twenty minutes longer than a normal fucking person would before discovering him and calling for an ambulance.*

I cannot afford to go to jail, I have a gluten sensitivity. Prison food would turn my gut into a tear-gas factory.

I throw my blankets off my bottom half, tiptoe over to our ensuite bathroom, and begin attempting to telepathically communicate with my husband as I slowly open the door.

I'm not peeking at your private time, okay? I know things are still weird between us. I'm just making sure that you're okay. All right, maybe just a tiny peek too . . .

"Cay?" I call out softly, poking just my head in.

Caleb's back straightens, lifting his head off the shower wall. He keeps his back to me as he drops his hands to his sides and clears his throat. "Uh hey," he responds. His voice is raspy and echoes in the tiled room. "I'll be out in a minute. . . ."

I know what you were do-ing, I long to sing teasingly. *Dirty, dirty boy!* "Okay," I say, instead.

"I don't really want you to—"

"I was worried you fell," I interrupt for the sake of my dignity. Or his. Or both?

"Oh, uh, no. All good."

"Okay. Well, um . . . Enjoy." As soon as the last word escapes my mouth, I feel the energy shift. Caleb's shoulders tense and he wipes both hands through his hair, standing under the steady stream of water. I acknowledged what he was doing in there and that was enough to quell his arousal. That's a new low.

With his head hung, Caleb shuts off the shower and forcefully slides open the glass door. I'm momentarily treated to the sight of his entirely naked, dripping wet body right before he wraps a towel around his hips and makes his way over to the bathroom sink in a way that can only be described as sulking.

I stand awkwardly in the doorway, unmoving. If I walk away from him now, when he's visibly upset, I'd be sending a very clear-cut message. One that reads: I don't give a shit. But alternatively, standing here gawking at him doesn't exactly help matters.

God . . . I've popped zits in the mirror as this man takes a piss next to me too many times to count. Why is just being near him while he brushes his teeth suddenly so unsettling? I *hate* it.

"I was hoping we could talk," I mumble as I aimlessly tug at the tied knot of my robe.

He looks over his shoulder, toothbrush buzzing in his mouth with a film of toothpaste coating his lips. "Yeah?"

"Yeah," I answer. "When you're ready."

Caleb spits into the sink then pulls the hand towel from the holder on the wall. The washcloth that had been folded neatly above it falls to the floor. I fight the urge to police which towels he should use for what and where they should go—not on the floor!—even though I desperately want to. Caleb drops the now toothpaste-covered towel onto the counter and turns, placing his hip against the basin's frame as he stares at me expression-less.

My mind goes blank as to how to best bring up Win's wilderness retreat idea. So, stupidly, I think of the other available topic for discussion in an effort to not bring up proper towel etiquette.

"Sorry I interrupted," I offer, glancing toward the shower stall. "You looked . . . good."

His bottom lip pouts as his eyebrows raise. But he *still* doesn't speak.

"I—I know it's been awhile. Since we—"

"Is that what you wanted to talk about? Our . . . hiatus?" he asks.

"Well, no. Partially, I guess. Our *other* hiatus, maybe."

"Ah."

"From . . . talking?"

"Right." Caleb crosses his arms in front of his chest, then brings one hand up to his face where his thumb begins scratching the side of his nose. "I know, I'm sorry."

"We haven't had a real conversation since the night of the fundraiser. I feel all this . . . distance between us."

He nods as he closes the distance between us with exaggerated, slow steps. "Better?" he asks, offering me a shy smile. I sigh softly, lowering my eyes from his face to the tile floor between us. "Not better," he whispers, in lieu of an answer from me.

A few beats pass in lingering silence. I look at my slippered feet, trying to find the strength to admit to all that I'm feeling. Struggling to figure out how to express this unnerving sense of being lost within myself and needing to go searching elsewhere. Every part of my psyche is flooded with worry that he won't want to take that journey with me. That this—I—will be the end of us. *What would that even look like? A life without him . . .*

Caleb clears his throat again, capturing my attention. I watch him rub his lips together before he opens his mouth to speak. "I've been wrestling with my feelings since the fundraiser, and I've not really landed on how to talk about them just yet. I thought that approaching you before I sorted myself out would just cause another fight and, honestly, I've just got a lot on my plate at work right now. When I get home, I want to relax. The last thing I want to do is fight and end up sleeping on the couch."

I scoff. I shouldn't, but I do.

I don't have time to regret it before Caleb jumps back in, his tone defensive. "I know that's perhaps not what you'd like to hear, Sarah, but that's the truth."

"Sleeping on the couch?" I ask, my eyebrows rising as I tilt up to face him. "When we have *multiple* guest bedrooms?"

"It was a figure of speech."

"So, you're saying that you've been avoiding me for the sake of your peace—which . . . yeah, you're right, sucks to hear. But did it ever occur to you that maybe this wouldn't end up with us in a fight? That *maybe* we could discuss our hurt feelings like grown-ass adults?" It's not lost on me that the attitude I leveled onto that last question doesn't help my argument.

Caleb straightens before rocking back onto his heels, slowly narrowing his eyes on the center of my forehead as if he's attempting to search my mind. "No, not really. A fight seemed unavoidable since I wasn't ready to back down yet."

"What is *that* supposed to mean?"

He smirks, eyes glancing up to the ceiling. "Just that our arguments typically end one of two ways." He lifts a finger, his expression more playful than I'd like. I want him to take me seriously. To take *this* seriously. "One . . . I back down, apologize, and ask for forgiveness or two," he lifts a second finger, "Win tells you that you were in the wrong, you stomp around for a few extra days, and then eventually you admit defeat and extend a peace offering."

I scoff again, crossing my arms. "Okay. *Sure.* . . ."

His eyebrows rise in a taunt, a dry laugh making his throat flex. "Am I wrong?"

"I apologize when I need to, Caleb."

"In your own way; I guess."

I stare at him expectantly. If he's going to make accusations, he better be ready to present examples.

He crosses his arms and rubs his biceps with his left hand. "Okay, then. For starters, you'll text me at work about what movie you want to watch when I'm home that I know for a fact you do not want to watch. I can recall *Back to the Future, Ferris Bueller's Day Off,* and *Monty Python and the Holy Grail,* off the top of my head."

Oh. "Who said I didn't want to watch those?"

"You, on several occasions. Then there are times I'll come home to find that you'd ordered Poncetti's for dinner because it's my favorite even though you think their pizza tastes like feet. Or when you've stopped by the office midday to drop off baked goods for me and my team. Or, my personal favorite, when you climb onto my lap in nothing but your robe the second my ass hits the couch." His eyes glance down my body, a little too lewdly for the conversation we're *supposed* to be having.

I notice myself unconsciously pull my robe tighter across my chest. As he steps closer, I can feel the heat from his shower wafting off his body along with the intoxicating scent of his mandarin and bergamot body wash. His smell attempts to overwhelm my other senses and, apparently, my better judgment.

We could talk *after* sex, right? Maybe that's all this is . . . distance caused by our lack of intimacy recently. Maybe it's all in my head. Maybe with a few orgasms everything would just sort itself out . . .

"And, given that Win was over tonight"—he tilts his head

arrogantly—"and you're in my favorite of your robes"—his hand finds my hip, forcing me to arch my back to see his face—"and you so *boldly* walked in on me in the shower . . ." He begins lowering his face toward mine.

"I want to go hiking," I blurt out, his lips mere seconds from making contact. "Sorry, I, uh, that's what I wanted to talk about. Hiking."

"Hiking," Caleb repeats slowly, his eyes narrowing on my parted lips as he pulls back slightly. "You and me . . . the two of *us* . . . in nature?"

I nod, swallowing. "It was Win's suggestion."

"Well, I could've told you that; but why?"

"I was talking to Win about us and I, uh, she . . ." I look up to the ceiling, trying to find the right words. "Her boss from West-cliff, Helen, and her wife, Yvonne, run this camping excursion thing. For couples. To help them reconnect."

"Reconnect?"

"Yeah," I reply dryly. "Yvonne is a relationship therapist."

Caleb steps back, his hand moving from my hip to rub his chest as if he's been struck. I watch silently as he kneads the center of his chest with the heel of his palm—moving back and forth over the same spot. "Th-therapy, huh?" he says, voice breaking before he swallows air.

"Mm-hmm," I mumble, raising my chin slowly until our eyes meet. Caleb's eyes have lost the darkened, lust-filled appearance that they had only moments ago. Now, they're watching me keenly as if I'm an uncaged bird.

Caleb nods, three times too many for it to be played off as anything but unsure. "We can do that . . . if—but do we have to camp?"

I look over my shoulder to our bedroom beyond the half-opened bathroom door. "Could we maybe go sit?" I don't know if the steam from his shower, the topic of conversation, my husband's naked proximity, or *all* of it combined is making me dizzy—but I need to sit down.

"Do you—do we . . ." Caleb stammers, running a hand through his wet hair. "I'm sorry I shut you out, baby, but—"

"C'mon," I say gently. "I'll show you." I open the bathroom door without turning my back to him and tilt my head, gesturing for him to follow. I grab my laptop from my nightstand, open it, and place it in the middle of our bed. Caleb emerges from the bathroom in his robe, fastening the tie around his waist as he drops down next to me on the mattress.

"This is it?" he asks, a little breathless. I nod. Caleb swallows tightly, his Adam's apple jutting out as his eyes scan the screen and he moves to control the trackpad and read further. "So it's a week-long thing?"

I wince. "Yeah, it is."

"Seven days of hiking and sleeping in tents . . ."

"Seems that way."

"No real showers or toilets," he says, scrolling, "or beds," he adds, his eyes darting over to his phone on the nightstand as it begins vibrating with a slew of notifications. The familiar doorbell-like sound for incoming emails that he *refuses* to turn off at any time of night or day chime repeatedly back-to-back.

"Or phones," I add pointedly. "Or work," I mumble as his phone begins to ring. Caleb's shoulders tense as he looks over and reads the caller ID. "It's late," I say. What I *mean* is, don't pick it up. Not now. *Please.*

Caleb hesitates, looking between me and his nightstand.

"Please," I whisper, disheartened.

He sighs, just as it goes to voicemail. Leaning toward the laptop, Caleb explores Reignite's website further. "Is this . . . is this really what you want? I mean, if you want us to get counseling, we could start nearby." He winces. "Maybe an office where we could sit on a couch instead?" he adds, half serious. "Do you—do *we*— really need something so drastic?" He turns to me.

The desperate, anxious look on his face reminds me *so* much of that sweet teenage boy I once knew that it nearly stops me in my tracks. It's the same expression I remember catching glimpses of when his dad didn't make our high school graduation—despite Caleb being valedictorian—as he'd gone on yet another last-minute business trip. Or when, years later, we found out his mother's father, Caleb's sweet Opa, passed away two days shy of our long-awaited visit that Caleb had postponed three times because of his own busy work schedule. It's the face that matched mine as we cried in the parking lot of the funeral home before my mother's service.

Grief, helplessness, and heartache all rolled into one and aging him in reverse.

Immediately, *everything* inside me wants to set him at ease. To push that singular piece of damp hair away from his forehead and kiss the spot it had occupied. I want to say: *No, you're right, let's try something else first.* Something easier. Something *safe*.

We could start tomorrow by finding a therapist who comes highly recommended. And sure, they'll have a full roster of patients, so we won't be able to start seeing them for another month or two. . . . *But* they'll have a cushy office downtown with a welcoming receptionist who will bring us artfully crafted lattes before each session. Then, we'll talk to them for about an hour each time.

Well, maybe more like forty minutes given the amount of time it'll take for either of us to settle in enough to properly address anything remotely important. But we'll get there eventually. Then, when we leave, we'll endure an unpleasantly silent car ride home, having left with unresolved arguments, unfinished conversations, and unanswered questions that we won't have the guts to discuss until our next appointment.

But it could work, right? We *could* make it work. . . .

No, a voice in my head whispers, softly letting me down.

I can't fully explain why this all feels so suddenly urgent, though I wish I could. I don't know why these feelings I've sat with have come to the surface, demanding immediate attention when they've been dormant for so long. But that is the truth of it.

It doesn't feel like enough to be here, day in and day out, living the same daily routines and monotony with some therapy-lite sprinkled in. I need bold, decisive action. I need Caleb and me out of this house and routine and into something that I hope shakes us out of the familiar and the pleasant and the comfortable. I feel the urge to get *out* vibrating under my skin, a sensation impossible to ignore that refuses to remain silent any longer.

I turn my attention toward my husband, and coil that damp, stray piece of hair around my finger before releasing it to rest my palm on his cheek. "I think we do," I tell him, so quietly it may as well have been telepathic. "I really think we *have* to do this."

Caleb's frown deepens as his eyes scan the computer. He leans his cheek into my hold, as if his head is too heavy for him to hold up on his own. "Okay," he says, voice determined yet faint, as his lips caress the edge of my wrist, his breath warming my pulse point. "Then . . . we'll go."

"IS CALEB STILL COMING OVER?" WIN ASKS BETWEEN herculean spoonfuls of cereal. "I asked to use his laptop for my assignment," she says, her mouth full as milk streams off her chin.

"You're disgusting," I reply, shutting the fridge door. "But yeah. He'll be here soon."

"When are *you* going to get a rich boyfriend with a computer?" Aunt June teases her daughter, tossing a piece of her crust at her from across the table as I pour myself orange juice.

"Maybe when her tits finally come in," I add on, smiling cruelly as Win glares my way.

"Girls!" my mother yells, clearly agitated, from down the hall. All three of us freeze, sheepishly looking toward her as she appears from around the corner. "Have you seen my wallet?" I shake my head. "Shit . . . June? My wallet?" she asks frantically, turning toward the dining table.

"My pickpocketing days are behind me," my aunt mindlessly replies into her mug of steaming coffee.

"Fuck! I've searched everywhere twice." Mom drops her bag

onto the counter with a loud thud. "I *cannot* afford to replace all of my stuff right now. I don't have time for this!"

My mother *rarely* curses and when she does, it takes the oxygen out of the room. Win and I exchange giddy, anticipatory glances at her use of colorful language.

"All right, well . . ." Mom says, her voice firm as she scans our faces and pinches the bridge of her nose. "We'll pray to St. Anthony." None of us move, staring at her blankly. "Now, please!"

"Not you," Aunt June says, waving a flippant hand toward Win. "You're Protestant."

"I am?" Win asks, before shoving more cereal into her mouth. "Since when?"

"This is an all-hands-on-deck situation! C'mon!" Mom falls to her knees and crosses herself.

When Caleb walks in five minutes later after a polite knock signaling his arrival, we're all on our knees with our hands clasped in front of our chests. Without hesitation, he calmly shuts the door, removes his shoes, drops his backpack, and slowly lowers himself to the ground next to me. "What's happened?" he whispers, wearing a hesitant, curious pout.

"Nothing bad . . . just a lost wallet," I reply, trying to signal for him to lower his voice.

"Hush!" my mother snaps, then does the sign of the cross, as if she has to start all over again.

"We're praying to St. Anthony," I somewhat explain, quieter this time. Caleb nods, then assumes the position, though he certainly isn't familiar with the patron saint of lost things. Or any of the others for that matter. Minutes go by before I catch him peeking at me with a mischievous grin and I have to glare back at him.

Half a second later, Aunt June breaks the prayer-filled silence by asking, "Mars, did you check the car?"

Mom opens her mouth to argue, then closes it just as quickly. Then later, she's slipping out the front door. When she comes back wearing an apologetic grin with her wallet in hand, we all burst into laughter.

"False alarm, Anthony. . . ." I mutter under my breath as Caleb helps me stand with an outstretched hand. He locks his fingers with mine, then runs his thumb up the side of my wrist.

"Missed you," he says softly, pushing up his glasses with his free hand.

"It's been like *one* day," Win mocks as she digs through Caleb's backpack for his laptop.

"I missed you too. Sorry for . . ." I hold his soft eye contact. "All of them."

"I like it. My family is hardly ever all in the same room," he tells me.

"Well, we don't have many other rooms," I jest.

"Still." He shrugs.

Win pats his shoulder before taking his laptop over to the dining table. "Thanks, loverboy!"

"You're going to need my password," he tells Win, squeezing my hand just once before he drops it and follows after her.

I hadn't noticed my mom standing by the door, hovering before she slips out for the day. We smile at each other, more like friends than parent and kid, and she winks at me. I can practically hear her thoughts: *He's a good one.*

I agree, I reply silently.

FIVE

WHEN OUR TIRES HIT GRAVEL, I LOOK UP FROM MY BOOK to see a group of seven people, and what is either a very short adult or a child, huddled under a red and blue motel sign, seemingly unaware that rain is beating down onto them and all their luggage. Sorry, not luggage. Onto them and their oversized backpacks.

They're similar to the ones Caleb came home with a few days ago. He enthusiastically informed me that they were sixty-five-liter rucksacks recommended to him by some guy from Focal's marketing department named Kent who has successfully hiked Mount Kilimanjaro. My first reaction to this was wondering why any business would measure the capacity of their product with how much water it could hold when it's built to hold clothes and other nonliquid items. Then my thoughts turned to the grotesque amounts of ball-chafing Kent must have experienced on his nineteen-thousand-foot journey in the Tanzanian heat. What I said out loud to Caleb was: *Thank you.*

Once Caleb warmed up to the idea and got Kent's two cents, I think his distaste for the outdoors was overtaken by the excitement about what sort of gadgets he could buy. The heavy-duty backpacks, the sleeping bags that fold impossibly small, the cooking and eating supplies, the tent that he pitched in our living room, disassembled and built again in repetition until he got his assembly time down to "just under eight minutes." He even bought a multiknife tool with a built-in compass—as if the guy hasn't relied on an app to direct him from our home to his office daily for the past six years.

Unfortunately, Caleb deciding to take a full week off—like *off the grid,* off—meant that he's been working pretty much nonstop in the past week. So other than expressing his enthusiasm over his gizmos-and-gadgets-a-plenty, we've not had much time to talk about what comes next. Regardless, I've chosen to take his enthusiasm as a good sign.

Win was right, convincing him to do this wasn't hard. That counts for something. At the very least, it means that we *both* want to work on this. That we recognize we can do better by and for each other.

As Helen recommended in her email after registration, I've bought us both journals. She didn't say what to write in it, other than to bring it along, but I have already filled the first few pages with issues that I think Caleb and I should work through together during our sessions. The sessions I *assume* we will have, that is. Because, other than being told to meet at this dodgy-ass motel on the side of the highway at noon today, I have no clue what else awaits us.

I hope we haven't accidentally joined some sort of children-of-the-forest, cultlike situation. I do think, admittedly, I'd easily fall victim to becoming a cult member. Win has dragged me away from many a street preacher and pamphlet-giver over the years, just before I was about to hand over my email address or signature. There's something about a charismatic person speaking with confidence that acts like a golden, flickering light to my mothlike brain.

Why yes, kind stranger . . . I *do* want to know that I'm loved unconditionally, thank you so much! And yes, please *do* tell me about the afterlife—what is it like? And, *sure,* please tell me what to do and how to do it and when and where so I finally feel like I'm doing something right *and* understand whose judgment to measure that by. Perhaps my mother was onto something with her vague relationship with religion. If this doesn't work, maybe I'll give that a go.

Is divorce shameful if you choose to give up your life and join a nunnery? No one could judge Caleb for being left for another man if that man was Christ, right?

As Caleb begins reversing into a parking spot, I pull out my phone to text Win.

> SARAH: You're sure this isn't a cult, right? It's got cult vibes.

> WIN: Has Yvonne already started a sound bath? That was fast, even for her.

> SARAH: What have you gotten us into?

> WIN: You can thank me later.

Win's next text is a photo of Gus, my niece, sitting on the toilet without an ounce of context.

> SARAH: Since when does she do that?!

WIN: Bo put her on there because she'd been yelling "shit!" for the past hour.

SARAH: And?

WIN: She pooped. I'm weirdly proud?

I quickly glance to my left, noticing that Caleb's concentrated on his phone as well. Though, I suspect, it's more last-minute vitally important work emails and less potty-training related text messages.

SARAH: As you should be!! How many almost two-year-olds potty-train themselves by using potty words? She's a genius.

WIN: At least she used the word in the right context, I guess, but her daycare won't be thrilled. Also, I'm assuming this is goodbye? I'm going to miss you!!

SARAH: Just seven days and then I'll be blowing up your phone once more.

WIN: Until you sign the million-year soul contract and join their fray.

SARAH: Well, then I guess this is goodbye. See you in a cool mil.

WIN: Be careful out there, okay? I know I'm the one who suggested it but imagining you and Caleb in nature has been keeping us up at night.

SARAH: Surrre . . . THAT is what is keeping you two horndogs up at night. I appreciate the concern, but we'll be fine.

WIN: Did you pack the baby wipes? U got to keep downstairs clean for when you two make up and make out.

SARAH: Never fucked in a tent . . . any tips?

WIN: Not shocking considering you've never slept in a tent?? But seriously, did you remember the wipes? Nobody wants hiking-crotch.

SARAH: I have the wipes! Stop being so obsessed with my sex life, weirdo!

WIN: Pot. Kettle. Black.

SARAH: KK! Losing signal! In the woods! Byeeeee!

WIN: BE SAFE! And, as for tips, don't fuck on the air mattress if you can avoid it. There's nothing sadder than popping an air mattress and having to sleep on the hard ground.

SARAH: We have mats, not a mattress.

WIN: Then put those mats to good use, babe.

"What's got you smiling like that?" Caleb asks warmly, reaching over my lap to place his phone in the glove compartment.

"Win and Gus."

"You've got a group chat already? Man, Gus is growing up so fast."

I roll my eyes, smiling. I turn off my phone but toss it back and forth between my hands, hesitating to lock it away with Caleb's just yet. "We won't be able to take any photos," I say, holding up the phone between us.

Caleb's eyebrows raise alongside his crooked smirk.

"And, what if there's an emergency? How would we call for help?" I ask.

"I'm sure that Helen and Yvonne have a plan for that."

"What if someone mentions a movie or television show but no one can remember the name of the lead actor? Or song lyrics but not the title? What will we do? Sit in the frustration of not knowing for *seven* days?"

"I suppose we'll just have to find the nearest cliff and put ourselves out of our misery." Caleb leans over the center console and rubs his thumb along my chin as he cups my face. It feels oddly intimate. Emphasis on *odd*. Something about the juxtaposition of such a tender touch with the very reason we're in this motel parking lot makes me uneasy. "Is this okay?" Caleb says, his smile faltering as his eyes focus on my face.

"Yeah, I think I'm just in my head a little bit."

He nods, his hand stiffening the smallest amount, but not withdrawing. He takes a long breath that flares his nostrils, as his eyes hold on mine tenderly.

"Hi," I whisper, the corner of my mouth resting against his palm.

Caleb smiles softly. "Hi, baby. I want to say, before we start, that I love you . . . and, I'm glad we're here."

I blink wordlessly at him. It's strange that after many years of predicting his next move and hearing those three words time and time again, that I'm caught off guard. But I realize, upsettingly, that it's been at least a few months since either of us have said *I love you* intentionally. We say it every day in routine. When we hang up a call, in the morning as Caleb leaves for work, and before we fall asleep—or, more accurately, before we roll onto our sides in bed to scroll on our phones. And it's even stranger that hearing those three words said with intention and focus and purpose makes us being here feel redundant.

Let's go home, I think. Intentional love is enough. We can go home, and I can find a job and hope that it gives me purpose, or at least leads me in some sort of productive direction, and then I'll have something to point at and say *that is just mine*. We'll go to therapy once a month and fuck like bunny rabbits again. We don't need all of this. This was a stupid idea anyways. Caleb is practically allergic to the outdoors, and I didn't properly break in my new hiking shoes that will most definitely give me blisters.

I open my mouth to laugh, to say *What on earth are we doing?* To say *Let's get out of here.* To say *I love you too and I think that can be enough.*

But Caleb has the next word. "If this is what we need to do to get you out of your rut, then I'm happy to do it. Team Linwood, right?" He leans back and presents me his fist to bump with my own.

Annnnnd, there it is. Reality crashes in once again.

Caleb looks down at his fist, then to my face, and then slowly drops his hand to his lap. "No?" he asks, followed by an unsure, shaky laugh.

I stare longingly at him, holding eye contact for a lingering, quiet moment as his eyes narrow in confusion. Then, I delicately move to unbuckle my seatbelt, turning my body toward the front of the car. "This isn't *just* for me, Cay." I wait, listening diligently for his next words. Instead, the only sound between us is the rain that continues to fall against the windshield and roof of the car. "This is supposed to be for both of us," I remind him. "To learn to communicate better. To look inward. To . . . reconnect," I add.

"Right, of course, yeah." Caleb's eyes search the space between us as if he's looking for a clue or memory *or* escape as he begins fiddling with his wedding ring. "I know."

"But what you said kind of made it all about me. . . . Like I'm the broken cog in this otherwise functioning machine." I smile disingenuously, attempting to hide my hurt. I don't know why I do it, but it comes naturally.

"I didn't mean it like that," he says defensively, lifting his chin to face me. "You know that."

Caleb will often say *You know that* when defending himself. Nothing gets under my skin quite like that phrase from his lips. To me, *You know that* is the equivalent of saying: *You're being irra-*

tional. Because if I *did* truly know what Caleb intended prior to every time he says *You know that*—I'd be creating a problem where there was none. I'd be choosing to believe that his intention *is* to hurt my feelings, which I never once have. I know Caleb is kind. I know he's not the type of person who actively tries to harm someone. But just because he's never *trying* to hurt me doesn't mean he can't and I'm tired of him throwing out that phrase like it's some sort of get-out-of-jail-free card.

"I'm telling you how it felt to hear you say we were here to get out of *my rut.*" I put my phone in the glove compartment with his and shut it. *Goodbye world.* "I don't know what you meant by it, but I do know how it made me feel."

"Okay," he says, taking off his own seatbelt with a *hefty* attitudinal flare. "Well, sorry, then. I only meant that it was your idea to come, and I am happy to do it. I was only trying to have a nice moment before we got going."

"Right," I reply, in a matching, short tone. "But—" I stop myself, letting my eyes fall shut on a frustrated sigh, needing a moment to choose my next words wisely. Doesn't he understand that *this* is part of why we're here? I thought I'd made myself clear after the fundraiser—the roles of rescuer and rescued need to be put to rest. Do they not suffocate him in the same way?

After collecting myself, I hesitantly reach toward him, cupping his face like he'd done to me earlier. I rub my thumb along his stubble, thinking of the beard that will soon take its place after he goes seven days without shaving. Caleb's mother passed along her *very* Greek genes to her son. He can grow a five-o'clock shadow by noon a few hours after a morning shave. He's only grown it out once, and not on purpose. It was the week leading up to when Mom died, when we rotated between sleeping in brief shifts at home and sitting by her hospital bed. That memory fills my heart with a nostalgic sort of melancholy, and I fight to refocus my attention as I continue brushing his cheek.

"I'm grateful that you agreed to come, and that you want me to feel better . . . but I also need to know you're receptive to this experience and what it can give *you* too."

"I am," he says, timidly placing his fingers onto the back of my hand before he looks down shyly. "I know I've got work to do. I didn't mean to imply otherwise."

There it is, I think, *we're talking again.* "See . . ." I smile up at him. "We're communicating better already, and we haven't even left the parking lot." I dip down to catch his sight line. "And I love you too"—I say it with every bit of purpose that Caleb had, enunciating each word— "so much."

His shoulders relax on a sigh, a small smile overtaking his lips. Looking at his mouth, I wonder if I should lean forward for a kiss. But as we breathe in and out together in tandem, letting the tense moment wash away, it doesn't feel right to. It feels *more* intimate this way. Looking into each other's eyes as we overcome the first of what will probably be several difficult conversations to come in the next week. Too often we're guilty of sealing things with a kiss, to move past a moment. In the same way we've been saying I love you; a little peck here and there has become routine. I don't remember the last time we kissed to *only* kiss. Not for a greeting or to say goodbye or as a precursor to sex. We can work on that too.

"I'll get the bags," Caleb says, pressing his forehead against mine. I nod as he leans away from me. Wearing a soft frown, he puts his jacket's hood up, presses the tailgate button next to the steering wheel, and exits the car into the rain.

I lower the sun visor to check my reflection in the small rectangular mirror. *It's going to be okay,* I silently inform the nervous woman with my mother's eyes. I wonder if there will ever be a day where I look in the mirror without a tinge of bittersweet sadness—the sense of missing her but having her close.

"You coming, baby?" Caleb asks from the trunk, projecting his voice over the sound of rainfall as he slings his bag over his shoulder.

"Yep, sorry!" I answer, putting up my hood and stepping out of the car *directly* into a puddle.

Here we go.

"SARAH GREEN!" THE SLIGHTLY GOOFY-LOOKING GUID-ance counselor calls from down the hall.

"What does *he* want?" Win asks me, glaring toward him. I don't blame her natural distrust of men, given her mom's never-ending conveyer belt of loser boyfriends, but I roll my eyes at her immediate skepticism just the same.

"I'll let you know . . ." I nod politely toward Mr. Nadeau as I approach his office door. "Hi, sir."

"I'm glad I caught you. I was just chatting with Ms. Vaccaro about you." *Oh, god.* Is this because I called out the blatant sexual tension between Frankenstein and his creature? I didn't mean to make people laugh . . . The *first* time. "She was *very* impressed by your recent short-story assignment. We wanted your permission to submit it to a province-wide competition. The winner will re-ceive two thousand dollars and a one-on-one mentoring session with author Cecelia Floodgate."

"Cecelia Floodgate?" I gawk. "Like *the* Cecelia Floodgate? The author of The Champion series?"

"Yes." Mr. Nadeau chuckles at my obvious excitement. "Did you know she was from Ontario?"

Yes. I also know her mother's maiden name, the precise location of her father's hardware store two towns over, and the names and ages of all three of her cats . . . But that's probably not information worth sharing. "I *did,* actually."

"Well, if you're interested then—"

"I am!" I interrupt, then nervously bite at my lip. "But maybe, could—could I have a week to edit it some more? I didn't think . . . Well . . ."

"You didn't think Cecelia Floodgate would be reading a random assignment not even worth two percent of your grade that you probably wrote on the bus ride in?"

I smile up at him. "Exactly."

"You can have until the end of next week, then we'll get you signed up."

"Okay." I nod far too eagerly. "Thank you, sir!"

"See you next week," he says, turning back toward his office. I spin on my heels, finding Win, who's been joined by Caleb, both looking at me expectantly.

"I'm going to be rich!" I shriek, running and jumping into Caleb's arms.

Nearly four hours later I'm bursting through our apartment's front door, in search of my mother. "I'm home!" I call out, dropping my backpack by the shoe rack. I lock the door behind me, mindlessly flip through the mail on the counter, and then wander toward the back hallway lined with the doors to each of the three bedrooms, realizing I've yet to hear a response from Mom, who I'm almost certain is home. "Mom? You here?"

"In here," she responds softly, the sound of her voice coming from behind her half-shut bedroom door.

My top lip catches between my teeth when I realize that she's in bed in the middle of the afternoon again. Mom has been really tired lately. Aunt June and I finally convinced her to go to the doctor at the beginning of the summer, when she started having sensations of tingling and numbness alongside her exhaustion, but it's been months and they've still not figured out what's wrong. Aunt June has picked up extra shifts at the nursing home so my mom could cut back her hours but that doesn't seem to be helping much anymore. She hasn't started asking any of us to pray about it yet, so, there's probably no reason to worry.

"Hey, baby," she coos warmly, her eyes fighting to open. "Sorry, I must have dozed off. Is it already past three?" I nod. "Ah, I'm sorry . . ."

"You don't have to be sorry," I say, lifting the edge of her duvet and crawling in next to her. "How was your day?"

"Fine, yeah. Did a whole lot of nothing." She swallows, loud enough for me to hear. "You?"

"Something cool happened during lunch period today." I place my head on her shoulder, and she starts playing with my hair. I know that most teenage girls probably don't lie in their mother's bed and fight the urge to suck their thumb when cocooned in their hold, but it can be our little secret. "Ms. Vaccaro wants to submit my assignment to a writing competition."

"That's amazing, baby," Mom says excitedly. "My grandma always said we'd have a writer in the family. It's certainly too late for me, so I'm glad it's you." Mom doesn't talk about her dreams of being a journalist, though Aunt June has mentioned it once or twice. I think, like most things my mom chooses to leave out of her history, it's because my *unplanned* entrance into the world put an end to it. Just like her relationship with her parents, her dreams of college, and her good-girl reputation. I plan to make it up to her. I just don't know how yet. "Is this your short story I read last week?"

I nod, resting my face against her chest. "Cecelia Floodgate reads the winner's piece."

"The Cecelia that you love so much? The fantasy writer?" I nod again, smiling to myself.

"You'll win," she states boldly, but I scoff. Mom reaches down, curls her finger under my chin and lifts it so I can look at her. "You, my darling, are brilliant."

I'll try to be. For her. "Thanks, Mom. . . ."

SIX

WE APPROACH THE GROUP OF OUR FELLOW HIKERS standing under the motel sign with weary smiles as Caleb takes his glasses off and tries to wipe them free of water. He does this even though it is *still* pouring rain. I wonder if it would be rude to point out the awning less than ten feet away that could probably offer shelter to our group. Surely they've noticed it and they're choosing the rain, right? And if so, *why*?

"Welcome!" Helen says cheerily as we approach. I recognize her from the times I visited Win while she was working as a life-guard over the summer a few years ago. Helen is white, though her skin is tanned in a way that suggests she spends a lot of time outside and probably drinks kombucha—an inner-peace and good-health sort of glow. Her hair, or the part of her hair that I can see from under her clear plastic poncho, seems to be chopped short with strands of silver and gray among the black. She's got wrinkles around her eyes and the tips of her smile, and a quiet confidence about her that reminds me of Win. Under her poncho she's wearing a teal pullover sweater with white quilted patches and black nylon pants with several large pockets down the side of each leg. "Hello, hello! You must be Caleb and Sierra."

"Close! It's Sarah," I say, projecting my voice over the sound of cars speeding past on the highway and the slosh of water under their tires. I smile softly, readjusting my coat's hood for more coverage as lightning strikes nearby. Caleb places his glasses back on, no less wet than before, then nods politely toward the rest of the group. I watch his resolve give way as the rain floods his vision and he loses contact with the outside world.

"Right, Sarah, of course, sorry," Helen replies. "Caleb and *Sarah,*" she says, overly enunciating my name, "I'm Helen." She puts her palm on her chest, pausing as she bows her head slightly and smiles. "Honored to meet you both."

Extending her hand out to her left, Helen begins introducing us to the three other couples. "We're a smaller group this year, but a good one. These are your fellow hikers, Maggie and Phil, Jai and Nina, and Henry and Kieran. And this," she says, throwing her arm over the shoulders of the child next to her, "is Libby." Libby is so bundled up under a black, puffy raincoat that I can only see her mouth, nose, and eyes. She's pale with freckles like my own, and her eyebrows are so fair they're nearly nonexistent. She does *not* look pleased to be here. "My granddaughter," Helen explains. "My wife is wandering around nearby, pleading with Mother Nature to stop the rain."

Caleb and I both chuckle, but no one else does. *Noted . . .*

"Well, now that we're all here we should probably get going. I'll go fetch Yvonne," Helen says, looking at her watch. "Come with me, Lib," she adds as she walks away, gesturing for Libby to follow behind her. The young girl sighs, her shoulders falling as she stomps after Helen.

"First time?" Phil, if I'm remembering his name correctly, asks, looking between Caleb and me. Phil's eyes hold on Caleb as he removes his glasses again, and Phil grins as he scratches his white goatee. If I had to guess, Phil, in his younger years, was probably a football player. He comically towers over the rest of us. His broad shoulders and deep, deep voice only add to his friendly larger-than-life aura.

"Is it that obvious?" I ask, wincing as I realize that they're *all* similarly dressed—specifically noting the waterproof nylon pants they're all wearing—in contrast to my leggings that are already drenched, and Caleb's . . . that *fucker!* He's got the fancy-pants too.

The woman next to him, Maggie, waves me off. "We've been coming for years, and we haven't met you two yet, that's all." Maggie's skin is a dark, rich brown, the same as her husband's, but she also has patches of depigmented skin on her cheek and forehead that are a paler cream color. If I remember correctly from a *Vogue* article a few months back, it's called vitiligo. She's strikingly beautiful, and, if I had to guess, probably in her early fifties.

"Right."

Caleb quietly moves to wrap his arm around my hips, pulling me closer to him. It's unexpected, but not totally surprising. He's far less extroverted than I am, and often seeks out touch for comfort. I like that I can offer him that, even still.

"It's good to meet you both," I say, leaning into Caleb's hold, threading my thumb through the belt loop on his pants. "All of you," I add, smiling subtly at each stranger around the circle.

Next to Maggie and Phil is a couple closer to our age, or perhaps a bit younger, who appear to be silently arguing with each other with exchanged dagger-sharp side glances, crossed arms, and clenched jaws. I decide it's probably best to not approach them at the moment.

"Sorry, I missed your names," Caleb says directly to the surly couple. "Was it Jai and . . . ?"

Let it be known that Caleb, bless his sweet soul, has never once read a room.

"Nina," the woman answers, forcing her agitated expression away for a second to offer Caleb and me a polite, tight-lipped smile. Nina is a brunette with the kind of bone structure people spend thousands of dollars to mimic and few actually achieve— striking cheekbones and a perfect, straight nose. Her eyebrows are bushy in that fashionable way and her skin is buttery and tanned and blemish-free. She's tall and slender, probably just under six feet, standing at the same height as her partner.

"Have you also done this before?" Caleb asks, gesturing between them. Nina turns to Jai, wearing an expression that tells me Caleb has just stepped on a land mine.

Jai smiles arrogantly, staring straight ahead and successfully avoiding eye contact with his . . . girlfriend? Fiancée? I don't see a ring on either of them. Jai is classically beautiful—tall, dark, and handsome. He has warm, reddish-brown skin, black hair, and his appearance is expertly manicured. His stubble perfectly trimmed, his eyebrows tidy, his teeth shining brighter than Heaven's gates.

"I have, yeah," Jai answers in an unexpectedly *thick* British accent. God, where did Helen and Yvonne find these two? A hot-people-r-us catalog? They must come straight here from a magazine shoot with their gorgeous faces and perfect bodies and then you throw in a Peaky-Blinders-esque accent? My jealousy continues to increase as my husband continues to stick his foot *directly* into his mouth.

"So, you've come here before but . . ." Caleb twists his head, looking at me in confusion. I blink up at him in a way that I hope communicates: *Stop digging yourself a deeper hole and do not try to hand me a shovel.*

Nina laughs dryly. It's a sarcastic sound that is punctuated by an exclamation mark and serves as a warning. "I found out about an hour ago that Jai brought his fiancée on this trip last year. Oh, *and* that he had been engaged too—which he never bothered to tell me before now." Nina answers, smiling sweetly in a way that makes *me* fearful. "But no, I haven't been here before."

"Oh, nice," Caleb says, then immediately shakes his head, chastising himself. "Well, not nice but—"

"For what it's worth, Nina, none of us thought they'd last," Kieran interrupts, throwing something from his pocket into his mouth and cracking it between his teeth. Kieran is shorter than the rest of us and is probably in his late thirties or early forties. He's got lip and eyebrow piercings, both neon blue, black short hair, and a cheeky grin that seems to be his resting expression.

"Yeah, they were *not* a good fit," adds Kieran's husband, Henry, taking a sip from a canteen with steam pouring out the top. He attempts to pass the thermos to Kieran, but he snubs it. Henry is just a few inches taller than his husband, and his auburn hair is tied neatly into two braids that fall to his collarbone. "We all said so," Henry says, looking toward Maggie with a lopsided, expectant grin. "Didn't we?"

Nina bends forward, looking around Jai to see Phil and Maggie, who are busy looking at their shoes and then the muddy puddle in the center of our circle, and then the sky, and then just about *anywhere* and *everywhere* else.

"Help me out, big man," Jai says to Phil, nudging him with his elbow.

"It is *none* of our business," Maggie replies, patting her husband's chest just as he opens his mouth to speak. "Right?" She looks at me for some reason, so I nod, shrugging my shoulders.

When the others look away from Maggie, and Nina and Jai start bickering with each other *just* above a whisper, she shakes her head at me, smiling in a way that makes me feel like one of the gang. Which is nice, considering all these people, other than Nina, have already met.

Caleb presses his chin to the space behind my ear and whispers, "I don't want to jinx it . . . but I think we have a shot at winning this."

I huff a laugh, glancing up at him. "It's not a competition," I whisper, biting my lip to stop my smile from growing. Our eyes meet playfully and the creases on either side of his eyes deepen with a smile of his own.

"It's not?"

"No!"

"But if it was?" he asks, his tongue darting out between his lips, his eyes fixed on my mouth.

"Then . . . I would say we have a fair shot. Phil and Maggie will be tough to take down, though . . ." I say, looking toward them as they make lovey-eyes at each other, giggling about something. "They seem solid."

The sun appears from behind a dark storm cloud, making all of us look up to the sky. Then, the rain abruptly stops. "Huh . . . would you look at that. Go, Yvonne," Caleb says, nodding approvingly.

"I have a feeling it's going to be a very strange week," I reply, looking up to the sky, then around the circle at each of our new acquaintances.

"It'll be good," Caleb says, lowering my hood and tucking a wet strand of hair behind my ear.

"Yeah?" I ask, my voice smaller than I'd expected.

"Yeah," he says, stepping back to unzip his jacket. "It'll take me a minute to warm up to everyone, but the way they all tease each other reminds me of home." I snort a breathy laugh as Caleb removes his outer layer. His athletic shirt underneath is dry, but skin-tight. I unconsciously bite my lip, admiring him. It really has been awhile since I raked my teeth across his stomach and kissed my way further down. . . . Thank god for Win's baby wipes suggestion.

"Remind me to put our tent up far away from you two," Kieran says loudly, interrupting my trail of dirty thoughts.

"Now, now, don't go forgetting Reignite's *evil* golden rule," Henry singsongs, wagging a finger at us. I have zero idea as to what he's talking about.

"Fuck," Jai grumbles, itching above his eyebrow. "Forgot about that."

"Something else you didn't share?" Nina says, tilting her head toward Jai.

"They'll go over all the rules later, and there aren't many," Phil says, looking between Nina and Caleb and me. "But I believe what Kieran is referring to is the abstinence agreement."

"Abstinence? I haven't heard that word since prom night," I say, as Caleb lowers to unzip his backpack resting on the ground in front of him. Surely, they cannot be serious.

"What sort of agreement?" Caleb asks, folding his jacket to fit inside its small, waterproof carrier bag.

"No sex," Kieran says. "It apparently helps us focus on *other* kinds of intimacy."

Caleb freezes, mid-fold.

"Personally, I find that other kinds of intimacy are overrated," Jai says, crossing his arms across his chest. "I do my best talking with my lips and hips."

Nina squints at him, her expression dumbfounded. "Everyone talks with their lips, you buffoon."

"Careful, darling. You know I like it when you're mean," Jai sends air-kisses toward her and she turns away, glaring even still.

Caleb stands, leans toward me and mouths, "Did you know about that?"

I shake my head. "But it wouldn't be the first time we broke a rule," I whisper with a wink.

"Here they are. Finally," Maggie says.

Approaching us is a willowy-framed, gray-haired woman with Libby and Helen trailing behind her. She's wearing a white shirt, loose-fitting blue-linen pants, and enough bracelets to start her own foundry. She floats toward us, her eyes scanning all of us with a watchful regard that leaves me uneasy. "Thank you for waiting," she says, her voice lower than I'd expected, and each word is drawn out as if she's never once been in a hurry. Just like Jai, she's British, but her accent is smoother than his, with a posher lilt to it. "Best to wait for better weather though, wouldn't you agree?" she adds, turning toward Nina. "You must be Nina." Yvonne's lips purse together as she admires her. "Hello."

Caleb and I exchange a subtle what-the-fuck look as she bows at the waist.

"Hi," Nina says, extending the same tight-lipped smile she'd given Caleb and me.

"And you must be Sarah and Caleb," Yvonne says, slowly turning to face us. It's then that I realize Yvonne is not wearing any shoes. I blindly reach for Caleb, and grip tightly onto his arm as I suppress a shudder, imagining her toes squelching into the muddy earth around us.

"Hiya," I say, attempting to sound casual. "Yes, that's right," I add. I've never once said *hiya* in my entire life.

"Good to meet you," Caleb says, his voice audibly strained.

Yvonne smiles knowingly, her eyes held where our bodies are joined. "Well, welcome," she says, then purses her lips as she continues observing us.

I don't like the way her large, eerily blue eyes take us in. It's as if she's seeing the past, present, and future. Maybe this woman *is* a witch. The rain did stop, after all. I drop Caleb's hand, moving both arms over my stomach. Which, of course, she notices, her eyes narrowing.

"All right . . . Well," Helen says, her eyes darting between Yvonne and me. "Welcome to Reignite!" Helen claps her hands together and Libby sidesteps further away from her grandmother as Yvonne falls in step next to her. "We are so thrilled you all decided to join us this year whether it's your tenth time with us or your very first. Yvonne and I began Reignite to help couples spend intentional time together, away from life's distractions. We believe that there is no better place to reconnect with ourselves and our partner than in the glory of nature. We accept everyone here, wherever they're at in their healing journey. We extend grace and consideration for you all and we ask that you do the same for one another and us as well."

"This will be our eleventh year leading this retreat," Yvonne says, "but this year will look a tiny bit different. As some of you may know from our blog, my daughter . . ." Yvonne's voice falls away for just a second as she seems to gather herself. "My daughter passed earlier this year. Helen and I now have the honor of raising our granddaughter, Libby. As you have probably guessed by now, she will be joining us this week."

I look at Libby, who cannot be much older than nine or ten, and feel my heart twist tightly. I was double her age when my mom passed, and it's almost completely derailed my life. I can't help but wonder how it will affect hers.

Caleb squeezes my hand twice in quick succession. When I turn to look up at him, he searches my face. "You okay?" he mouths.

I nod weakly, but even still, he brings the back of my hand to his mouth and kisses across my knuckles.

"Welcome Libby!" Phil says brightly. "I'm glad there will finally be someone here with the same maturity level as me," he teases. Libby doesn't so much as look in his direction.

"Because of that, we will be taking it a bit easier and stopping for rests whenever necessary. As always, we travel as a group. If one of us needs a break, we will all stop. And just like the rest of our practices—there will be a zero-tolerance policy for shaming or judgmental remarks. Libby and I will be having adventures of our own, ahead of the group, when possible," Helen adds, smiling softly at the scowling little girl. "So, there's no need to censor your conversations."

"Well thank fuck for that," Jai says, smirking. I watch as Libby's armor falls away for half a second, a small grin visible, fighting to grow from the corner of her mouth.

Helen takes a centering breath, smiling blankly toward Jai, and then the ground. "Well, that's it for now. We will discuss more tonight over dinner once we make camp."

"How long is the first hike?" Henry asks, lowering into a lunge.

"About fifteen kilometers."

"Holy mother of god," Caleb's voice trembles, barely above a whisper.

My eyes flash at him in panic. "That's like what? An hour?" I ask loudly, looking around for assistance. "Right?" I squeak.

"Closer to three, maybe more," Helen answers matter-of-factly.

"We're going to die," Caleb says for my ears only.

I turn to him, whispering hoarsely. "We haven't prepared for this at all. I don't even know where my gym membership card is . . . Do I even have a card? Is it digital now? Has it expired?"

"I take back what I said, we're absolutely *not* going to win." He turns his body to face mine, our boots nearly touching when he bends to catch my eyes. "Are you *absolutely* sure you want to do this?"

"We're not even allowed our phones," I say, distantly. "Who can exercise that long without listening to music?"

"Sociopaths," Caleb says, looking suspiciously over my shoulder at the group.

"I suppose it's not too late for us to leave," I say, only half joking. "But . . ."

Caleb takes a deep breath in, surveying the landscape around us. Then he shakes his head, wearing an expression of stubborn pride. "No. Fuck that. We're Linwoods," he says, raising his chin with performative confidence. He then pushes his glasses up his nose, which, truthfully, lessens the effect somewhat. But still, the sentiment is sweet.

"Yeah," I agree halfheartedly, as if our last name *truly* carries any weight, and then present my fist to bump with his. Instead, he grabs my wrist and tugs me toward him so our chests collide.

"We've got this," he whispers, lowering his lips to mine. He kisses me fiercely, which is very much unlike Caleb while in the company of near-perfect strangers. His lips engulf mine as his thumb strokes the side of my face, his fingertips pressing against my jaw with delicious pressure that's removed too soon. "Right?" he asks, pulling back.

"Yeah . . ." *We're definitely going to die.*

"Oi-oi," Jai says, before I have the chance to turn back toward the group. "The newbies are getting hot and heavy," he adds, grinning as he bends into a stretch with his body arching toward us.

"We should probably do that too," Caleb says matter-of-factly, shucking off his backpack.

"Shit, probably," I say, attempting to drop into a forward bend, copying Nina's positioning and posture without her natural poise.

I laugh so hard that I snort as my legs start to burn and quake, nearly giving out. Caleb laughs too, purposefully exaggerating his grunts and moans as he stretches for my benefit. And damn it feels good to laugh with him like this. Even if we are *truly* fucked.

SEVEN

I'VE APPLIED ENOUGH MOSQUITO REPELLENT TO CATCH
on fire if someone lights a cigarette four towns over, but the fuck-
ers are still after me. The terrain is muddy, dense, and wet. So,
while we suffer—the bugs are thriving. We're halfway, according
to Phil's enthusiastic updates, and I'm happy to report Yvonne
put appropriate footwear on prior to our departure and is no longer raw-dogging the mud.

The hike isn't so bad when we're all making light conversation,
but thus far, the group has mostly moved in silence—concentrated
on not slipping or getting stuck in the mud.

"What do you do for fun?" I ask Maggie, or whoever else is
listening, as the path narrows between overgrown trees. It's not
my best conversational cue, sure, but my body is currently pump-
ing all my blood and oxygen into my legs, depriving my brain.

"Oh, uh . . ." She's caught off guard, but her pleasant tone tells
me she doesn't mind making small talk. "I like to paint," Maggie
responds softly, as if it's something she doesn't discuss often.

I hold tightly onto my pack, hopping over a puddle. "Really?"

I ask, out of breath. "That's great. What sort of things do you paint?"

"Oh, just this and that . . . Scenery, mostly."

"I bet she's incredible," I say, looking over my shoulder to Phil, egging him on.

"She won't let me see any of it," he answers, his happy expression unwavering. "I've yet to snoop, but . . ." Phil groans, walking up a steep patch of rocks. "If I do, I'll report back."

"Secret hobby," I say mischievously, smirking at Caleb as he holds out a hand to help me over a fallen branch. "You'd know something about that."

"Oooooh," Kieran says from up ahead. "What did *he* do?"

Caleb shakes his head, grinning. "Sarah likes to tease me for playing Dungeons and Dragons."

"He told me he was going to the gym but I caught him playing at my best friend's house with her partner and a gaggle of dorks."

Caleb sighs, looking forlorn at the path ahead. "I wish I had been going to the gym . . ."

"What is Dungeons and Dragons?" Jai stops, waiting for us to catch up to him. "Is that some sort of kink thing?" he says lowly, tilting his chin down to conceal his voice.

"Even I know what Dungeons and Dragons is," Libby says loudly from up front. I hear my mother's voice in my head say, "Oh! She speaks!" in that teasingly affectionate cadence that she'd use when I'd been moping around our house or giving her the silent treatment. I resist repeating it out loud.

Caleb perks up. "Do you play?" he asks her enthusiastically.

Libby stops, slowly turns over her shoulder, and looks him up and down with nothing less than disgust. "No . . . obviously."

I push my lips together, fighting a laugh as she twists back around and continues walking on.

"That was humbling," Caleb says, forcing my laugh to spill free. He looks at me with humored annoyance then up to the sky, his tongue pushing against the inside of his mouth as he smirks. "Guess I shouldn't tell her about Glinera, then?"

I gasp. "You wouldn't dare!" Glinera is the name of the two-headed witch Win and I created to join Bo and Caleb's campaign last year. We were only three sessions deep before Caleb, Bo, and all their friends voted unanimously to kick us out for inappropriate behavior. Allegedly, we made the group uncomfortable with our sexual innuendos and double entendres. I maintain that they just felt intimidated by our superior role-playing abilities and unmatched creativity.

"Well, that depends. . . . Do you have *more* anecdotes to tell the class?" he asks, his eyes piercing mine. "Or will you behave?"

I readjust my backpack, stretching my neck. "I'll behave," I grumble, throwing a suggestive side-glance his way.

WE CONTINUED MAKING polite conversation for the following hour with our hike-mates, swapping small pieces of information with one another. I learned that Phil and Maggie both work at the same high school, that Phil is nearing retirement, and Maggie isn't too far behind him. They were both previously married but have been together for almost twenty years. He teaches gym and coaches the basketball team—which just won some sort of provincial championship—and she's the school's librarian.

I didn't get much of a chance to chat with Jai, as he seemed to be catching up with Yvonne ahead of us all, but I did get to briefly talk with Nina. She's an aspiring stage actress and just moved back home to Toronto after studying at the Royal Academy of Dramatic Arts in London. She's only twenty-three but is used to being mistaken for older due to her unwavering confidence, height, and beauty. She didn't *actually* say that last part, it's purely speculative.

She and Jai met through a mutual friend, and bonded over their love for the UK, theater, and appreciation of Canada's recreational marijuana laws, evidently. Her exact words were, "We shared a joint and a cab and the rest is history."

Kieran and Henry kept to themselves, mostly. They smuggled in a set of wireless headphones with a solar-panel charger and they're using an old iPod to listen to music together. We should have thought of that. This steep climb would be a lot better if I had music drowning out the embarrassingly loud sound of my breathing.

As we near the end of today's hike, spirits are clearly dwindling. We're all tired, cranky, and covered in sweat and muck.

"How much farther?" I call out, between gulps of water from my bright-pink bottle.

"About three minutes, then we'll just need to set up camp," Helen says, turning around and smiling broadly. I fight the urge to glare back at her.

"My legs feel like jelly," I whine.

"It'll be worse tomorrow," Maggie says. "Make sure you stretch tonight before bed, or you'll have awful cramps."

"Oh my god," I whimper. "I forgot that we had to do this again tomorrow."

Maggie laughs, but it's tired and breathy. "C'mon, you can't let us old folks outlast you."

Caleb has his head down, his shoulders hunched forward, and he's been eerily quiet. I decide to leave him to whatever dissociative survival mode he's fallen into. About an hour ago I began pretending I was in a fantasy novel, and this was my unlikely band of heroes on a righteous quest. But then my imagination got away from me and I almost made myself cry thinking about the love interest I lost in the war two years prior, who I'd sworn to avenge, so I had to come back to reality.

"Phil, hype me up," I request, locking my bottle to my pack with a carabiner. "It's the ninth quarter and we need one more point to win the game, c'mon."

"Pretty impressive that you're playing *nine* quarters."

"Prior to today the only physical activity I've partook in—is that a word?—*whatever*—I don't exercise. I don't know a single thing about sports. Please, humor me."

Phil laughs at my obvious desperation. "I usually tell my players to visualize themselves after the final buzzer, celebrating their win. So, imagine yourself at camp, changed into clean clothes, sitting next to a lovely campfire."

"Aah," I say, elongating the word, "bliss."

"After today it will feel like heaven," Maggie says, wiping sweat off her brow with a cloth discreetly handed to her by her husband.

"Just up ahead!" Yvonne says, spinning to speak to all of us from the top of a small incline, the light shining through the linen of her clothes as she practically twirls. "It's all ready for us!"

"What's all ready?" I ask.

"You'll see," Maggie says, smiling widely.

"Another surprise," Caleb grumbles. "Whoop-ee," he adds.

"Don't worry mate," Jai speaking over his shoulder. "It's a good one this time."

"How much are you loving him calling you mate?" I ask quietly, leaning toward my husband.

He laughs, though it doesn't mask his tiredness. "*Iloveitso-much,*" he says in one jumbled, whispered sequence. "I think I'll have to insist that Bo call me mate when we get back."

"Oh, you'll make him jealous if you tell him that you met someone new."

"What can I say?" Caleb breathes heavily as he finds his footing on a rock, then hoists himself up the final part of the path. "I'm a sucker for an accent," he whispers, grunting as he pulls me up after him by my hand.

Once over the ledge, the campsite is in view. I breathe a sigh of relief as Kieran and Henry lower themselves to the base of a tree, stretching their legs out in front of them. Jai and Nina have seemingly made up, sharing a quick kiss as they drop their bags to the ground.

"We did it," Caleb says, presenting his hand for a high five.

"We did it," I repeat, shuffling my bag off my back and letting it hit the ground behind me before meeting my palm with his.

Phil clasps my shoulder. "Good job, rookie," he says, walking toward Yvonne and Helen and . . . *oh my god* . . . "Yes," I say, falling to my knees dramatically at the sight before me.

There's a picnic. A luxurious one at that. There's a low table with a white linen tablecloth *covered* in delicious-looking sandwiches, meats, cheeses, and anything else that you could possibly want after a long day, surrounded by colorful floor cushions. They must have sent someone ahead to prepare this.

"Night one comes with real food," Maggie says, stopping next to us as I move to stand. "But it's only what you packed from home after this," she warns.

"Picture time," Jai says, pointing a small film camera toward us. "Get in there, Nina. I want one of all our first timers," he adds, gently pushing her our way. She squats in front of Caleb and me, presenting two thumbs-up. Caleb wraps his arm around me, and though I'm not so pleasantly greeted by the smell of him, I still lean into him and smile proudly, putting my two fingers up like bunny ears behind Nina's head.

"Perfect, just like that and . . ." *click,* "got it. Well done you three."

We survived the first hike.

Now, the real work can begin.

LIFE HAS BECOME INFINITELY BETTER SINCE I WON THE prize money from the short-story competition. I used three hundred of it to buy a used laptop from Caleb's older sister, about a hundred to pay our water bill that was long past due, and bought a few of Cecelia's books so I can get her to sign them next Friday when we meet up. The rest went toward a Blackberry and phone plan which means Caleb and I are *finally* texting like all the other couples at our school do. Mom was so proud of me for winning.

Caleb too. He's driving me to Toronto to meet Cecelia next week, though I told him I could take the bus. He insisted he wanted to be a part of it. "And miss my chance to be present at the start of Sarah Green's illustrious writing career? No chance . . ." I laughed him off, but I liked the sound of that very much.

"Did you come?" Caleb asks, his head still buried between my thighs, while he kneels on the floor of the backseat.

Oh, *shit*. I completely zoned out. "Yeah," I say, pitching my voice to what I *hope* is a seductive tone. "So-ooo good." He raises a brow as his eyes narrow onto my face. "Sorry," I admit, wincing down at him. "I got a little distracted."

He laughs dryly, licking his lips. "Let me guess," he uses his forearms placed on either side of my knees to lift himself up, then falls next to me on the seat as he pushes the hair away from his forehead. "You're thinking about your meeting next week."

I bite my bottom lip, smiling at him. "Maybe . . ." I whisper. "What do you think I should wear?"

He glances down at the flowy skirt bunched up around my hips. "Probably more than this." I laugh, fixing my skirt before I reach toward the front seat for my abandoned underwear. "It doesn't matter what you wear, Sar. You're always beautiful," he adds as I fall back in place next to him. "And I don't think Cecelia Floodgate will give a shit."

"I want to impress her."

"And you will. With that insane brain of yours."

"You think me insane?" I gasp, clutching my chest. "I'm wounded."

He smiles crookedly, his eyes piercing me in the best possible way. "I think you're overthinking it. You've already won. She obviously loved your work."

"Cecelia didn't have any say in who won." I bring my fingernail to my mouth, and Caleb pushes my hand down before I have the chance to bite it.

"Well then, she *will* love your work. She's reading it, right? That's part of the deal?"

I nod. But before I can explain, I'm interrupted by my phone's ringtone. I reach around to the front seat once more, pull my phone out of my purse, and hit accept call from a familiar number. "Mom?"

"Hi, hon. Can you come home early tonight? The doctor called and, well, we need to talk."

EIGHT

MY LEGS ARE SIMULTANEOUSLY NUMB *AND* ACHING, somehow. Once I had my fill of the gorgeous selection of meats, cheeses, crackers, fruits, and crudites, I'd fully intended to stand up, fetch some water to filter before bed, and tuck myself in for the night. But, it would seem, standing is not in the cards. I nearly buckled and face-planted trying to get up, and while I think no one witnessed it the first time, I may not be so lucky if I attempt it again.

Since I am too proud to admit my weak thighs are keeping me here, I am giving Nina a run for her money and putting on an Oscar-worthy acting performance, reacting to each of Helen's stories like they're pure fucking gold.

"No!" I cry out, though I've honestly lost track of this particular story's plotline and *why* Helen is nodding, smiling as if to say, *can you believe it?* "Seriously!" I add.

Caleb snickers next to me, his chin tucked against his chest as he uses Kieran's knife to whittle down a piece of wood. He's been in nature for two seconds and is crafting a weapon as if he's Bear Grylls himself. I'm oddly proud.

"Really!" Helen says, punctuated by a resigned laugh. "I couldn't believe it." She glances at the leftover scraps on the table. "Ah, well, we better get this all cleaned up. Big day tomorrow."

Shit, no, I'm not ready! "Well, while I have you both . . ." I say. Helen settles back against her cushion and Yvonne tilts her head toward me—her owl-like eyes unnervingly close. "What *is* happening tomorrow?"

"They went over all of that at dinner," Caleb reminds me, whisper quiet. Reminding me, of course, because I was most certainly listening. I was *definitely* paying attention and *not* gorging myself and singing a cheese-themed parody of "Sweet Dreams Are Made of This" by the Eurythmics in my head.

Sweet dreams are made of cheese, who am I to diss-a-brie.

"Sarah?" Helen says, getting my attention. I can tell it wasn't the first time she attempted to, based on the obvious concern in her tone.

"Sorry, I think I'm just a bit tired." I shake myself. "Caleb will fill me in later, sorry."

"Of course, don't apologize," she says warmly, reaching across the table and patting my arm. "I'm surprised you're even vertical right now. . . . Go, get some rest and we'll tidy up."

I look at Caleb with pleading eyes. "I can't feel my legs," I say behind gritted teeth as Phil and Maggie pass by, saying their goodnights to us all. "Have a good sleep!" I reply, totally cavalier. Yvonne walks toward them, sharing some hushed conversation as Helen disappears from the table to grab a trash bag.

Caleb leans in close. "What do you want me to do about it? Roll you?"

"Roll me to our tent?" I scoff. "You thought of rolling me before carrying me?"

"Carrying you would be a little obvious," he says, shrugging. "If you don't want people to notice."

"But *rolling* me wouldn't?!" I shriek, somehow still in a whisper. It's a great skill, the whisper-yell. I think I have perfected it.

"I don't know if I can, regardless. My back is wrecked after today. I'm sore all over and—"

"Okay, well . . ." I look between where I'm sitting and our little orange tent that Caleb set up earlier while I was listening to a story about a figure-skating competition that Helen once judged where a stray pigeon found its way onto the ice. That story, actually, was quite memorable. That little bird was on the ice for ten minutes before they rounded him up. When the pigeon was done, the judges all held up a perfect score. From then on, they called a perfect score a "pigeon."

"Sar?"

It's cute to imagine, a pigeon captivating everyone's attention like that. For some reason in my imagination, he has a top hat and a monocle. . . .

"Earth to Sarah!"

"Shit, sorry. I am . . . I am *really* tired."

"You look like you're about to fall asleep. . . . It's like twenty feet, surely you can make it if I help you up."

"I can't."

"You *probably* could."

Probably. "Just leave me here to die," I whine, throwing myself back onto the hard ground, my bum still nicely cushioned on the pillows set up around the table.

"Baby . . ." Caleb sighs. "C'mon." He stands up.

"Drag me," I beg.

"Seriously?" A low laugh escapes him as he looks down at me, shaking his head.

"It's that or you bring me my sleeping bag and I take my chances with the elements." My husband looks thoughtfully at the tent, seemingly weighing his options. "Seriously? You're considering that? There could be bears!"

"Fine." He steps around to the top of my head. I present my arms to him, and he grabs onto my wrists as I cling onto the fabric on his forearm. "Sit up so you don't bump your head, at least." I do as told, lifting slightly. "These leggings are going to be wrecked," he says, beginning to pull me in the direction of our tent.

"Ow, my butt!" I say, as a twig scrapes my left cheek.

"This was *your* idea," he points out.

"Only because you wouldn't carry me."

"I really hope no one sees this," he says, navigating me indelicately around a larger rock. "It looks very questionable."

I let my head hang back, staring up at him adoringly.

"What?" he asks, his tone suspicious.

"I forgot my water bottle at the table." I smile sweetly up at him, batting my eyelashes for good measure.

"I'll go back for it," he says with as much attitude as he can muster. But I see the hint of a smile forming. "Seriously though, this is very primitive." Caleb readjusts his grip. "Me-man. Drag pretty wo-man to cave."

"Aww, you think I'm pretty?" I ask, pitching my voice higher. We stop outside the tent, and Caleb drops his hold before turning to unzip the entrance. "I can take it from here," I say, rolling onto my stomach and army-crawling in.

"So . . . so pretty," Caleb says slowly, his voice laced with sarcasm.

"This really does it for you, huh?" I ask, maneuvering my top half into the tent.

"Take those off before you get into bed." I turn to waggle my eyebrows suggestively at him, then continue to crawl. "You're going to let all the bugs in." Before I can respond, Caleb's left to fetch my water bottle.

"Sarah, are you quite all right?" Yvonne asks from somewhere nearby.

"Oh, you know . . ." I say, not even bothering to look in the direction of her voice. Caleb's footfalls return just as I scoot myself all the way inside of the tent. "Thriving," I add with effort, though she may have walked away by now. I roll onto my back, squeezing myself into the narrow space between our sleeping mats.

Caleb lowers himself to one knee at the door of the tent and wordlessly begins untying my boots. He pulls one off, then the other, and places them outside before tearing off my socks, taking some blistered skin with it.

"Fuuuuck," I cry out.

"Shit," he hisses. "Sorry, baby."

"Not your fault," I grunt, grimacing as I let the wave of searing pain pass.

"I put some medical stuff in your kit. We'll let these breathe tonight but wrap you up before tomorrow's hike." He lowers my feet to the ground, scoots inside the tent, and zips it shut. "Do you need help taking off your pants?"

I nod pathetically. "And, yes, speaking of tomorrow . . . Can you fill me in? I zoned out."

Caleb begins tugging at my leggings as I prop myself up onto my elbows, bracing my weight on my forearms. "Camp is silent before seven. They expect everyone up and torn down before breakfast. After breakfast we clean up and clear out. Tomorrow's hike is less than two hours, depending on how many breaks we'll need. We're camping in that spot for two nights." He finishes, balling up my leggings into his fist. "Will you *ever* want to wear these again?"

"No, I'm pretty sure I peed on them earlier while squatting behind a tree. Plus, they're ripped now."

"One less item to carry," he says, forcing optimism. I mumble my agreement as I roll onto my mat and sit up to zip myself in for the night. I threw on a sweater earlier, so at least my top half will be warm.

"Did they mention anything about therapy? Journaling? The *inner work*?" I add a dramatic flair to those last words.

"Just that they'll make time for individual sessions tomorrow and go from there."

"Go from there," I repeat. "Ominous."

"This was your idea," he grumbles, undressing down to his boxers from a lying-down position.

"Oh my god it reeks in here," he says, scrunching up his face as he tears off his socks.

"It's my feet and your pits," I say, giggling. "Our smells melding together, as one," I add dramatically as I put my hands up in the air, interlocking my fingers. "Just like we will be after this."

Caleb shakes his head, laughing. "You're so weird."

"Can't you feel it? We're bonding."

"Oh, *definitely*," he says, pulling on basketball shorts and a sweater and collapsing onto his mat with a groan. "Your turn to drag me to bed tomorrow, okay?"

"That sore?" I ask, turning onto my side, my hip a far less successful layer between me and the rocky ground beneath my mat than my butt was. "How are your feet?"

"My feet are fine, but my back is fucked," he answers. "I hope we feel better by tomorrow or else we may have to get Phil and Jai to carry us."

"I'll let you have Jai."

"Kind of you," he says through a yawn as his eyes drift closed.

"All right . . . Well . . . Get some sleep," I say, fidgeting inside of my sleeping bag.

"Didn't you say you were tired?" He adorably opens only one eye to peer over at me.

"I think I'm a bit excited, is all. For tomorrow. To see what's next. Maybe it's the endorphins from today's hike. Exercise gives you those, I've heard."

Caleb yawns again. "Do you want your e-reader?"

"I didn't pack it. It would've only lasted a few days before the battery gave out anyways."

Caleb smiles knowingly, his face still tilted up to the ceiling. "I brought it and a solar charger. I didn't want you to lose your reading streak. Downloaded a couple of extra books too." I gasp. I actually, audibly gasp. I would have never admitted such a thing out loud, but I was *devastated* that upon our return my eBook reading streak would've been back to zero. "You're at what . . . a thousand days of reading all in a row?"

"One thousand, nine hundred and eighty-nine, but who's counting . . ." I say, my voice verging on tears. "Caleb, that's very, very thoughtful of you. Thank you."

"Want me to grab it? It's just in the outer pocket of—"

"No, I've got it," I say, unzipping my sleeping bag before crab-walking over to his bag.

"*Now* her legs work," Caleb mutters under his breath.

"I'm going to let that comment slide because this," I say, pulling out the e-reader from his pack and holding it to my chest, "is a very sweet gesture."

"Enjoy your smut," he says, yawning once more. "Turn out the lantern when you're . . ." he doesn't finish his sentence, his voice drifting off as he falls asleep. I've always envied Caleb's ability to pass out the instant his head hits a pillow as if there's no ruminating thoughts keeping him awake. Seemingly he has no regrets or embarrassing memories his psyche would like him to replay time and time again. No distractions are necessary for him to just blissfully stroll into the land of Nod.

But tonight, when his ferocious snoring begins, instead of lying bitterly awake and contemplating suffocating him, I feel happy that he's getting some much-needed rest. While I lie cozily tucked into my brand-new sleeping bag with crickets and the sounds of nature that I would normally have to play from an app surrounding me, and Caleb's sweet gesture in hand—in the form of a spicy second chance, best-friend's-brother vacation romance—I feel the most content I have in a while.

And, when sleep comes, giving relief to my tired body, I feel as if I've earned it.

"CAN I SLEEP IN YOUR BED TONIGHT?" WIN WHISPERS
into our darkened bedroom, from the bunk above mine.

"Sure," I say, sniffing back tears. Win comes down the ladder
and I lift the corner of my blanket up so she can slot herself in
next to me. For a while, we say nothing. I shuffle a hand under my
pillow and use the shoulder of my nightgown to wipe my tears.
Win sniffs too, then clears her throat which leads to a sputtering,
phlegmy cough. "Ew!" I laugh out. "That was fucking nasty, dude."

Win laughs too, near breathless. Her laughter, like always, is
contagious. After fits of giggles that are restarted by my inability
to stop a snort laugh from happening twice, we fall back into
deafening quiet. Then, Win throws her arms around my neck and
tucks herself in close against me. "She's going to be okay," she
whispers into my hair.

But she's not. Mom knows it. I know it. Aunt June knows it.
The doctor seems to know it. And I can tell Win does too. The
only one who seems not to know yet is Caleb, who, despite only
leaving our house two hours ago, has already sent me a research

paper discussing new and improved techniques for treating ALS and has asked his mother to contact a friend of a friend's husband who works out of some special research clinic in Toronto.

I wrap my hands around her waist. "It's never going to be the same again, though." Exhaustion settles heavy against my throat. "No matter what happens. Nothing is *ever* going to be the same."

Win lets that truth linger in the space between us for a minute before speaking. "Probably not."

"I'm scared," I admit. "I'm *so* scared," I whisper softly.

"I know . . . Me too." She holds me tighter. "But I've got you. No matter what, we will always have each other."

"I don't want to lose her," I choke out between tears. "I don't know . . . I don't know how I could—how I would—what it—"

"You won't." Win says it like a promise she has *no* business making. "There's still hope." It really, truly doesn't feel like it.

We spend the next hour taking turns crying and consoling. Each time we fall asleep, one of us wakes up startled—like the feeling of waking up when you dream you're falling and about to crash to the ground. Eventually, we give up on trying to sleep in our own beds and decide to go crawl into Mom's. When we enter, we find Aunt June already in bed with Mom. They've moved the television from the living room onto Mom's dresser and they've got their favorite telenovela playing from an old VCR tape.

"Hi, girls," Mom says softly, patting the bed next to her.

All four of us squeeze in and, at some unknown hour, I fall asleep to the sounds of an infomercial for an at-home perm solution, Aunt June loudly chewing popcorn, and my mother's soft snoring.

I wake up to a dozen texts from Caleb, sent all throughout the night, with a countless number of articles that had been behind paywalls, all pointing to hopes of a cure. He must have not slept.

I foolishly let hope creep in like the sunrise through my mother's blinds as I read them over and receive one more text from him.

> Caleb: My mom just heard back from her friend. Dr. Torres has agreed to meet with your mom.

NINE

DAY TWO OF REIGNITE

EVERY INCH OF MY BODY IS SORE BUT I'M VERTICAL AND choosing to ignore it to put one foot in front of the other. Thankfully, I slept well before the sun shining through our thinly walled tent woke me up at the ass crack of dawn. I tore down the tent while Caleb made our breakfast—apple cinnamon oatmeal from a packet—and Nina came over to chat while I finished packing up, offering extra coffee from her thermos before she went to find somewhere to relieve herself. I got great joy in imagining a stunning, elegant, giraffe-like woman such as her pissing behind a bush.

We're all equal in the woods, as Sondheim once wrote . . . *probably.*

When Caleb wandered back from the fire, holding two spoons and a small silver pot filled with our breakfast, we chose to sit on the ground next to our things and eat together.

"How're you feeling?" I ask, scooping oatmeal from the pot.

"Fine," he answers between chews, already reaching for more. "Tired. You?"

"Better, for sure."

"Good," he mumbles, his mouth full of food.

"Morning!" Helen chimes, wandering past us with a bell in hand, ready to wake the remaining campers. "You two are up and at 'em nice and early! I love to see it!"

I smile at her, but immediately realize there is oatmeal coating the outside of my teeth when her eyes dip down to them. "She's so peppy," Caleb says quietly, blinking his droopy eyes in Helen's direction.

I lick my teeth clean. "I prefer Mrs. Chipper over Madam Clairvoyant over there," I say, watching as Yvonne lays a hand on Kieran's shoulder. I can tell her eye contact with him is uncomfortably intense, even from a distance.

Caleb mumbles something incoherent, shoveling far too much oatmeal into his mouth.

"What?" I ask, smirking at him.

He swallows his spoonful. "I said: Please welcome to the stage, Claire Voyant," he announces proudly.

I laugh, barely swallowing my food before it sputters out. This is a bit we used to do but haven't in quite some time. Our first apartment was above a bar and they'd frequently have drag performers on Friday nights. We'd spend the night curled up in bed, listening to the performance below, giggling at each of the genius, punny names the performers had given themselves. My personal favorites were Lynn Gwistic and Penny Tration whereas Caleb favored the more sophisticated Dame Judi Bitch. We've been searching for Caleb's drag name ever since. Mine, if ever given the chance, will be Paige Turner.

"You could definitely be a Claire," I say. "It suits you. And, it fits in with your family's weird C-name thing . . ."

He smiles crookedly at me, bringing my attention to some oatmeal on the corner of his lip. I reach over to help him, taking the food away from his slowly forming mustache and onto my finger. He dips his lips around the tip of my finger and licks it clean, eliciting a giggly, warm response that is followed by a wave of electricity throughout all seven trillion nerve endings.

"Don't do that," I whisper, still holding up my finger between us like I'm scolding him. In reality, I can't seem to remember how to lower my arm.

There's something about Caleb out here. Something about being told *not* to have sex with my husband that makes me hot and bothered. Something about the early morning sunlight filtering through trees, the birds and echoes of nature closing us in some sort of bubble away from the outside world and all its realities . . . *and* him preventing my reading streak from ending.

I am a simple creature, at my core. Give me books, sunlight, water, and a handsome man looking at me like I'm some rare jewel, and I'm all set. Especially when it feels like a long time since I've shined for him.

"Or else?" he teases, a lopsided smirk ever-growing as he reaches for his water bottle.

"You're trouble, Linwood," I stammer, watching Caleb's Adam's apple bob as he gulps back water.

He lowers his bottle into his lap then leans in closer, his nose nearly bumping mine. "You know, I was thinking last night . . ."

"In the six seconds before you fell asleep?" I tease.

"Maybe we can't have sex . . ." He sighs wistfully from the hollow of his chest. "But they didn't say a single thing about touching ourselves."

I attempt to fight back a smile, but almost immediately lose. "That is an *excellent* point."

"No rule against watching, either," he says, voice low and as gravelly as the ground beneath us.

I nod, feeling heat pool in my belly. Suddenly, our parting kiss yesterday afternoon was a century ago and I miss his lips. "That is also a great point," I whisper, my voice unsteady. "Maybe, if you're not too tired after today's hike . . ."

"Too tired?" Caleb leans back, satisfyingly smug. "I would climb mountains for the chance to watch you come undone, baby."

I blink at him, slightly shocked but mostly turned on. Caleb's great in bed, sure, but he's not usually much of a dirty talker.

He holds out his water bottle toward me. "Here, take this. You look thirsty."

"Shut up," I say, snatching it from him.

Just then, a tent across from us begins opening in a manner that suggests the zipper is sticking. "Morning," I say to Libby as she stumbles out in her fuzzy purple pajamas. She glares my way but raises a palm before dramatically letting it drop to her side.

"Grandma H . . ." she grumbles, locking eyes with Helen. "My stupid tent is broken," she says, pointing limply.

"Yikes," Caleb says to me quietly, flaring his eyes. "Good morning, Little Miss Sunshine."

My eyes follow Libby as she dodges a hug from Helen, places her back against a large tree and crosses her arms, glaring at everything and nothing all at once. *Yikes is right*. But . . . "I don't know. Seems fair to me."

"Really?"

I keep my voice low. "I mean, she's not mad *at* Helen, she's just angry at the world. Which, I think, she has every right to be. Losing your mom is already hard enough but then being dragged on a weeklong hike with a bunch of adults you don't know the summer before the fifth grade sounds like one nightmare on top of another."

Caleb pouts, nodding softly. "Okay, that's fair."

"Plus, dead mom or not, I wouldn't wish being a ten-year-old girl on my *worst* enemy. It's lousy."

I remember it all too well. All the contradictory feelings of being trapped in that tedious prepubescent stage between girlhood and whatever mysteries lie beyond that feel out of reach. All the while becoming increasingly aware that there are secrets you must learn to transition into womanhood and wishing time would move faster as your body starts to shift and change. That growing awareness picks and chips away at childhood until you're suddenly twelve and crying in the bathroom because you got your first period and came to realize that everyone was right. You shouldn't have wanted to grow up. Womanhood is just a trap of a different making.

"But . . . I could be projecting," I add once I notice Caleb's obvious concern. "Still, she could be nicer to Helen, for sure."

He smiles softly, his head tilting *just* enough to the side to signal that he's thinking deeply. His eyes dancing over me in such a way that I know he's thinking about me. I don't pry into his thoughts. . . . I'm not sure how complimentary they'd be.

Caleb and I finish our breakfast and place our bags with everyone else's under a large oak tree, then, once everyone's ready, the group gathers for a morning meeting. Yvonne leads us through a brief sun-salutation stretch and then we are given some time to quietly disperse and write in our journals. We're encouraged to write our intention for the day, two things we wish we could change but can't, three things we can choose to accept, four things we can change for the better, and five things we're grateful for.

Afterward, we break off into two groups, separating from our partner, for the morning hike. Yvonne, Libby, Jai, Henry, Phil, and Caleb get a head start, setting off onto the trail before the rest of us.

"Distance *can* make the heart grow fonder," Helen says, clasping her water bottle to her shoulder strap. "But more importantly, it also gives us time to air our grievances to one another. Use your group as a sounding board this morning. Be honest with one another and be open to pushback. Remember, other perspectives can often bring clarity and resolution. We're all here to work, and many hands make a lighter load."

"Scheduled gossip time?" I ask Maggie quietly, smiling. She rolls her eyes affectionately as she grins back at me. "I love it," I add. "*This* is the shit they should put on their website."

"Thank *god*, because—" Nina struggles to clasp the buckle that connects her pack's straps across her chest. I walk over and assist her, then step back into position in this circle the five of us have formed. "Thank you," she says to me with a quick look my way as she stands straighter, lifting her chin defiantly. "I seriously cannot *believe* Jai didn't tell me he was engaged before. He completely blindsided me. And he did it when I didn't even have cell service to put his ass on blast."

We all nod passionately. "How long have you two been together?" I ask.

"Exclusive or . . ." Nina glances at Maggie, then Helen, and hesitantly mumbles, "sleeping together."

"Exclusive," Kieran answers. A grin pulls at his features as he hoists his bag up his back.

"Seven months," she answers. "I knew he had exes, I'm not like *delusional* but it bothers me that he was engaged, and I had no idea. We've never even talked about marriage, not that I want to. I get that he's twenty-eight and might be ready for that sort of thing but I'm only twenty-three. That is *way*, way too young to even consider getting married. I've always said that I'd get an Emmy, an Oscar, or a Tony before a husband. Preferably all three. I'd basically be a child-bride if I got married now."

I chuckle to myself. Except it wasn't to myself, I discover, when four sets of eyes turn toward me in confusion. Nina's perfectly plump lips fall into a frown.

"Oh, no, sorry, I'm not laughing at you, Nina!" I say in a quickened panic. "How you're feeling is extremely valid. I'm sure I'd feel the same. It's *definitely* not cool that Jai didn't tell you about his engagement before you got here. I only laughed because of that last thing you said . . ." I look around, making sure everyone can hear that I'm not being an asshole . . . *I'm not an asshole, right? Oh god, am I making it all about me? Why can't I ever shut up?*

"What thing?" Nina asks, her expression hard to read.

I swallow thickly. "About being a child-bride at twenty-three. It's just . . . I was only nineteen when Caleb and I got married. What you said reminded me how ridiculous that truly is, that's all. Anyways, ignore me, you were saying?" I clear my throat nervously. I attempt to take in all their expressions at once, but it takes me a minute to make it around the entire circle.

The group seems to have landed somewhere between politely shielded horror, confusion, and surprise. Other than Helen, that is, whose expression remains neutral in what seems to be a professionally trained manner. Her lack of surprise could *also* be because she already knew what age Caleb and I were married from the registration questionnaire. But then again, she called me Sierra yesterday so perhaps she didn't exactly put it to memory.

"Nineteen." Nina says the word as if it's foreign to her, an impossibility. I nod, feeling my lips pull into a tight-lipped smile. "Why?" she asks, then admonishes herself with a shake of her head. "Well, not *why*, but like . . . why *then*? Were you . . . knocked up or . . . ?"

I laugh weakly, rocking back on my heels. "Heh, no . . . My, uh . . ." Helen's words repeat in my head, *be honest, we're here to work, many hands make a lighter load.* "My mom was ill and, well,

Caleb and I knew we would probably get married eventually anyways. We both wanted her to be at our wedding and it was something she really wanted to be there for—obviously—so we . . . got
married." I say it in a lighthearted way that I'm sure is entirely
unconvincing, based on the hard lines between Kieran's brow,
Maggie's nervous glancing around, and the soft, lip-parted gri-
mace from Nina.

This is exactly why I never talk about it.

I've often found myself envying anyone who can fondly look
back over their wedding day. I'm jealous of my friends with stories that are only marred by rain, a broken heel, a drunken
groomsman, or a shitty DJ. Those who can recall every detail of
their "special day" and *actually* want to. I've never wanted to.

Recounting that day feels like picking at an old scab. Grief is
so deeply intertwined with our wedding, with that entire year,
that the day no longer feels like ours. It feels closer to a parting
gift. A checked-off item on Mom's bucket list. A memory we
could still share before it was too late.

We threw together a wedding in six weeks once Mom's condition began to worsen. We sent out email invitations—which
nearly put Caleb's mother in an early grave of her own—and gathered twenty of our nearest and dearest to a dimly lit, century-old
church, which neither Caleb nor I had ever stepped foot in before, that my mother picked out.

We sang songs none of us knew the melodies to, holding the
hymnal books loosely as we fought back laughter, desperately
trying not to sing out of place to an unpredictable rhythm set by
an organist who looked to be at least a hundred years old. We said
our vows in front of a priest who kept referencing my "sacred
maidenhood" and who, truthfully, smelled a bit dusty, as if his
robes had sat in a closet for far too long. I held a horrendously

ugly bouquet picked up from the supermarket and wore a dress that didn't quite fit.

Mom, Win, Aunt June, and I had gone to pick out my dress a month prior. It was on clearance, and it was a bit too long, but it was good enough and affordable. Lacy, modest, and relatively plain—the dress was nothing like what I'd imagined I might wear someday. I didn't have the heart to tell my mom that it wasn't the right fit—both literally and figuratively—when she said she loved it and began to tear up.

Mom had always been an incredible seamstress. I didn't want her to know that her daughter's wedding dress needed to be hemmed shorter just weeks after she'd lost all motion in her dominant hand. I knew alterations from anyone else would cost almost as much as the dress itself and my mother would have insisted on paying. So, I wore it as is. Impressively, I only tripped once and managed to not fall flat on my face.

"Is she okay now?" Maggie asks, her features softening into a concentrated, hopeful stare. "Your mother?"

I apologize to her with downcast eyes, wishing I had a happier answer for her sake as well as mine. "She passed away three months later." I keep my tone as even as possible. "She'd been sick for a while," I add for reassurance, as if to say *It was her time*—which has never once felt like the truth.

They all hum and tsk, making the appropriate, apologetic sounds that I've learned typically follow this conversation. I thank them with a wistful smile, hoping to get back to Jai's terrible timing and manners or quite literally *anything* else.

Anyone here ever run a marathon? You should talk about it at great length. Just how rigorous is that training process? Please, spare no details.

"Did you guys meet in college?" Nina asks, unknowingly diverting the topic away from my mom but onto an equally touchy subject.

"We started dating in the tenth grade. I never went to college, actually . . ." I feel myself disassociate a small amount, the trees and sky blurring into one in my line of vision. "I looked after Mom and then . . ." *She was gone.* "Caleb comes from a wealthy family so, uh, once he turned twenty-one, we got his trust fund. He started his company shortly thereafter."

Life kept going, the Earth kept spinning, everyone moved on, but I stayed still.

I leave out the time between my mother's death and Caleb's trust fund coming in out of embarrassment. I had given myself permission to wallow for those two years, believing I'd go to college once Caleb graduated and the heavy foot of grief stepped off my neck. We were scraping by just fine on the money Caleb was making from programming in his off time but, unlike his tuition, we would've had to pay for my education out of pocket or with loans—which the Linwood family decidedly did *not* do. So, it made sense to wait for Caleb's trust to come in and wait out my sabbatical of self-pity.

Whenever times got tight financially, usually when Caleb was working less due to exam season or internship programs, I would try to work. But I couldn't keep a job for very long. I was rightfully fired from two different retail gigs and one fast-food restaurant for my "bad attitude" before I admitted defeat. I simply cannot tell these near-perfect strangers all of that. It's far too humiliating.

"So," I say, picking up where I left off, looking around the circle of faces hanging off my every word. "I've been holding down the fort ever since." Although I *hate* how the phrase sounds every time the words seem to slip out of my mouth, *holding down the fort* has become my go-to cutesy explanation for my permanent stay-at-home-wife status. There's no saccharine way of saying *I do nothing for a living!* that doesn't make me feel like gagging on the size of my own privilege.

If my mother could hear me now, she'd roll in her urn . . . *That really doesn't have the same ring to it, does it?*

Once Caleb graduated, he immediately launched his company, Focal. He was working almost constantly to get it off the ground, and we realized that we'd never see each other if I enrolled for a fall semester. I had already given up on the possibility of being a writer at that point, so I'd decided a diploma in business management would be best. At least that way I could help at Focal or maybe Win's camp that she'd always dreamed of owning someday. But Caleb insisted that I should wait for his work to slow down first before enrolling.

He knew I was still, somehow, not up for the challenge. Though he never actually used those words.

Regardless, he was right. It would have been difficult for me to commit to a full schedule of classes. And doing so while he worked seventy-hour weeks? That could have ended us. And, though I'm not proud to admit it, I know it also could have ended *me.* I was clinging on to Caleb like a life raft in every spare moment during those days.

Shortly after my mom passed, Aunt June won ten thousand dollars on a scratch-off ticket and immediately fucked off to Florida to regroup. She'd planned on it being a three-week vacation, but a few days in she met a guy and decided to stay put, giving up the apartment we grew up in and closing that chapter of our lives, officially, forever. Win had left for university on a swimming scholarship the month after Mom died—which we'd all whole-heartedly encouraged her to do—but we barely saw each other during her four years of school. She was a six-hour drive away and dating a total dickwad who was far too controlling and wanted her all to himself.

At the time it felt like all my support systems had died with my mom. All but Caleb.

I felt alone, and sad, and constantly tired even though I couldn't bring myself to do much of anything around the house. Caleb, in his brief moments between work and sleep, was cradling my sanity in the palms of his hands.

When I could tell it was becoming too much for him to handle, I got nervous. I began worrying that he'd grow to resent me and decided to pour all the energy I had into the role of the level-headed, busy housewife. I convinced myself that it might begin to feel natural if I tried hard enough and Caleb seemed glad to see me step into the red-bottomed shoes.

After that, my days were filled with house decorating, baking, party planning, and various other superfluous things that, for a while, somewhat fulfilled me or at least kept my brain occupied enough to avoid slipping back into that dark place. And when reality crept in to an uncomfortable degree—I'd escape with books.

When Win moved back home after university, it gave me purpose. Not only did I have my best friend around again, but truthfully, I was also relieved to see that she was a bit of a wreck. Win was struggling after her tumultuous breakup and found herself in a post-graduation financial slump and I could help. I finally felt like myself again, having someone to look after.

Then, five years later, Bo showed up. And a short nine months later, baby August. I had a front row seat, watching as my best friend built a life worth envying . . . and it made me confront the fact that I didn't like mine all that much.

That's where the fundraiser came in. I'd decided to stop moping, take a page out of Win's book, and finally *do* something. No more words. No more excuses. But action. I'd help a cause near and dear to my heart and feel some sense of purpose.

Then, one half-baked comment from Caleb where he called it *our* event had me reeling and grasping for total control. It was as if I woke up out of a ten-year daze, looked around and saw Caleb's shadow in every single aspect of my life, and decided I had to do it all on my own.

But I couldn't. I failed.

Now, I've landed us here. Clinging onto a husband that I've started to resent, through no real fault of his own, other than his being a safety net I wish I'd never needed in the first place. And for what may *pathetically* be the first time, I'm considering whether I'm perhaps not even a fully realized person at all. That, most likely, I'm incapable of ever becoming a productive, helpful, functioning member of society because I can't seem to move past shit that happened over a decade ago.

It's not until Helen softly nods that I realize, mortifyingly, that I'd been talking out loud. I'm not sure for how long . . . and I'm not even totally sure what I said or didn't say. But panic creeps up just the same. "I guess I really had to get that off my chest." I attempt a joking tone, though it's clearly not effective. I paw at my chest, then lay a palm across my beating heart and will it to slow down. "Sorry," I add for good measure.

Maggie, Nina, and Kieran all avoid eye contact, though Maggie keeps failing, her eyes briefly catching mine with a comforting, quiet acknowledgment before she turns away.

If there is a saint of shutting the fuck up, my mother never introduced us. Ideally there would be a patron saint of reversing time who'd hear my plea. I could just try to pray to the Big Guy himself for a conveniently timed bolt of lightning to put me out of my misery . . . Or would that be Zeus? I'm not picky, I'll ask whomever.

I weigh my options and decide against seeking divine intervention. I got myself into this mess, and I intend to get myself out. Perhaps my newfound independence needs to apply to the supernatural as well.

Plus, Helen did ask us to be honest! I'm just doing as told! Hello, fellow hikers, here are all my cards laid out on the fucking table! What do you think of me now? Scared? Yeah, me too.

Oddly, it does feel good. My mouth got ahead of me, *sure,* but there's something freeing about having most of my crazy aired out in the open early on. I feel lighter for it. I'm an uncorked bottle of wine or toothpaste after it's squeezed out of the tube—there's simply no going back.

I tilt my head toward Helen, pleading. *Come on,* I say silently. *Fix me,* I implore. Do whatever you need to do. A lobotomy perhaps? I could go gather some sharp sticks. Seriously, I'll do anything. Just . . . help me. *Please . . .* Say *something!* Anything!

"How about you and me walk and talk for a while?" Helen suggests, gesturing for me to follow her, jutting her chin toward the trail. "It's about time we got going anyway."

I nod, then hang my head and pretend to adjust the straps of my pack as everyone gathers themselves to leave. I turn over my shoulder toward Nina once we all take to the trail. "Sorry I interrupted," I say softly. "I sort of lost my cool there," I add, in the understatement of the century.

"No, girl," she says reassuringly before blowing out a long breath. "You have *way* more going on than I do . . . You take Helen. I'll talk Kieran and Maggie's ears off."

I turn to face forward, pointing my blank smile at a tree branch as I pass under it, as if there's a hidden camera inside recording my own personal documentary. You know times are tough when one of the other members in *group* therapy decides you should take precedent.

Perhaps, instead of requesting lightning, I'll pray to be Nina's age again. Or, at the very least, I'll pray for the tits I had at twenty-three—when my nipples pointed out like perky headlights and not like Caleb's mother's ancient shih tzu with two lazy eyes pointing in slightly different directions, as they do now.

"What's on your mind?" Helen asks as we put distance between us and the rest of the group.

"I miss my tits," I answer, keeping this thin filter between my mouth and brain intact. "The way they used to be," I explain further, looking toward her as we keep walking the trail.

Helen studies me for a long, thoughtful moment, and then nods slowly as she looks down at her own chest, covered by a simple black T-shirt, and sighs. "Don't we all."

"I SHOULD NEVER HAVE WORN THIS," I SAY, FIDGETING in Caleb's front seat as I attempt to pull down my mother's black pencil skirt that I insisted on borrowing. I thought it would make me look mature. It does not. I look like I'm playing dress-up. "I feel like an idiot."

"You look great," Caleb says. He's hunched forward over the steering wheel, his eyes bulging out as he stares at the rearview mirror. This is his first time driving in Toronto and I think he's fighting off a panic attack as he parks outside the café. "Oh, sweet mercy," he whispers.

"Where are you going to go?" I say, nervously watching the intersection ahead where cars, cyclists, and pedestrians all seem to be making life-and-death decisions flippantly.

"In there." He points to a parking garage with a sign that says $20 TWO-HOUR PARKING. "I'm going to read my book, chill the fuck out, and pretend I don't have to drive us out of here after your meeting."

"I really appreciate you driving me," I say, brushing my hand over his cheek. "I'll cover the cost of parking. Thank you."

"No. Consider it an investment in your career." He leans in over the center console for a kiss. "I love you. You're going to be great. You deserve this meeting, and Cecelia is going to be your biggest fan. Just try to just put everything else that's going on to the back of your mind."

The *everything else* comes immediately rushing back into my thoughts, though they had momentarily been preoccupied by this stupid choice of skirt. Mom's *sick. Really* sick. *Forever* sick. "I love you too," I reply instinctively.

"You've got this," he says, nodding as if he wants me to say the same.

"I've got this," I repeat, grinning softly.

"You're the next big thing in writing," he says. I giggle, covering my face with both hands. "C'mon!" he jeers.

"I'm the next big thing in writing," I mumble.

"Nope! Louder!" he shouts, making my laughter build some more.

"I'm the next big thing in writing!" I yell back.

"There she is!" He leans over me and opens my door toward the bustling sidewalk, nearly taking out a mom with a stroller passing by. "Sorry!" he yells at her, wincing, then turns to me, his bewildered smile steadying on a sigh. "Kick ass, Green."

"I'll see you after, wonder boy," I say, unbuckling my seatbelt and stepping out onto the sidewalk. "Drive carefully!" I watch as he crosses himself, incorrectly despite my mother's best efforts, and then pulls away.

Twenty minutes later, I'm sitting across from my favorite author, fighting off tears . . . and not the good kind. "Shallow." The word sticks onto my tongue. "You thought my story was . . . shallow?"

"That might not be the right word," Cecelia says slowly, licking a crumb from her upper lip. Her voice is muffled by the food she's still sucking out of her teeth before she swallows. "Vapid, maybe?"

I huff out a wounded breath unintentionally, as if I'd been struck.

"Don't sweat it, though. Being a writer is not all it's cracked up to be, trust me." She laughs bitterly, digging around in her over-sized purse. "You're better off—" She curses under her breath, her eyebrows furrowing as she loses half her arm into the bag. "God dammit, where is it?" She seethes.

I'm slack-jawed, staring at the deep, heart-shaped scratch in the linoleum diner table between us. The space that seems to widen as the world ebbs out of focus.

"Ah, here." She taps a pen to the table where I'm stuck staring. "He-llo?" She laughs, short and cutting. "Anyone home?" I glance up to her face, feeling a potent mixture of confusion, embarrassment, and disbelief. "I found it," she says, gesturing with the pen, seemingly waiting for me to say something. "Didn't you have something you wanted signed?"

I look down to the tote bag at my feet, filled to the brim with Cecelia's books. The ones I spent part of my prize money to get just last week. *I should have given the money to Mom. She just quit her job. Trips to the clinic are going to be expensive.*

"No," I answer, tucking my foot against the bag, keeping it firmly in place and, hopefully, out of her view. Cecelia leans back in her chair, putting her pen away as her eyes find the star-shaped clock on the wall. "W-what—" I stutter, then stop myself, straightening in my chair. If I fake confidence, perhaps it'll find me. I am *not* a quitter. Us Green women do *not* quit. "What could I improve?"

Cecelia blows out a long breath. *That bad then.* "Well, you could start with writing what you know. Your piece lacked nuance. It had no real, individual perspective. I could tell you hadn't experienced half of what you wrote about."

I cross my arms as my cheeks begin heating. With wounded pride gathering in my throat, I scoff as if to clear it. "I'm seventeen. . . . It's not like I can travel or drink or—"

"Henry Thoreau said, 'How vain is it to sit down to write when you have not stood up to live.'" She stands, pulling her bag to her shoulder before she brings the sunglasses from the top of her head down to cover her eyes. "It's not your fault, honey. Plenty of kids your age think that being a writer is their ticket out of whatever pass-through town they had the misfortune of being born in. But the truth is there's no money in it. You're a pretty enough girl and you're clearly not an idiot. . . ." *It's sad that this is the closest thing to a compliment she's given me.* "So the good news is that you have time to find something else."

"But . . . What? I don't . . . I don't like anything else. I don't *want* to do anything else."

"I'm sure you'll find something." She drops a twenty-dollar bill onto the table then tilts her head in my direction. "And if you want me to sign those some other time," she says, pointing to the bag at my feet, "let me know."

I watch helplessly as Cecelia walks out of the café, feeling as if she's taken every semblance of hope for my future in writing I'd had with her.

TEN

HELEN AND I WALK FOR A WHILE IN COMPANIONABLE silence. My boots, which are rubbing against all the sorest parts of my feet, occasionally snap twigs along the path and the wind blows through the trees above. But other than that, it's perfectly quiet until Helen asks, "What did your mom have?"

"ALS," I answer, stepping over a shallow puddle left over from yesterday's rain. Where the trees are thick along the edge of our path and cast a heavy shadow from the sun, the ground is still wet. But for the most part, we've been out in the open, under a calm and white-wisped blue sky with dry earth below us.

"Brutal disease," she responds, and I nod, breathing deeply and then exhaling a word that's meant to sound like *yeah,* but doesn't quite make it. Silent moments pass as we make our way toward a split in the trail. The tree to the left has a small patch of blue paint as a trail marker and a tree to the right has a dot of yellow. Helen looks over her shoulder toward the approaching other members of our party and points toward the blue tree before we continue toward the left.

"Tell me about Caleb," she says, ducking under a low-hanging branch.

I laugh, uneasy in the vagueness of her demand. "What about him? Him as a person? Him as my husband? What I like about him or—"

"You love books, right?" *I guess she did read the questionnaire.* "Describe him as if he was a character from your latest read."

My throat tightens. "I am *no* writer," I say quickly, narrowly avoiding stepping into a patch of mud. "I tried to be, way back when, but—"

"Just give it a go," she says in a tone akin to *Humor me.*

"Well, he, *er,* he's . . ." I stop walking and brace myself with one hand grasped around the trunk of a smooth birch tree, then rest my hip on it as I fix the positioning of my foot inside of my boot.

Flashing images of Caleb play in my mind's eye, as if I've unconsciously created a *dead-wife* montage that you'd find at the beginning of a sad indie film. You know the ones . . . *Lens flare, she's running in between sheets hung on the laundry line. Lens flare, she's smiling at the beach as she splashes in the water. Lens flare, she winks at the camera playfully . . . Lens flare . . . Oh no—her tombstone—she's dead!*

"Sarah?"

"Sorry, uh . . . just thinking . . ." I answer, staring off into space.

Reality around me blurs and in its place, I see Caleb's subtle smile from across a crowded room. I see every time he has locked eyes with me instinctively when we both unexplainably look for each other at the same time when mingling with different groups of friends. Then, his lips trilling on the pillow next to mine as he snores. The immediate look of panic on his face when he distractedly rested his forearm on our flat stovetop and set his sleeve on fire a few months back. The moment he asked, "Can I kiss you?" for the first time, sitting on a park bench after dark with a streetlamp casting half of his face in a warm glow. His laughter with an undercurrent of annoyance as he chased me through the house, trying to get his briefcase back from me after I ran off with it before his first day at the new office. The first Halloween party we threw at our place when we dressed up as Elton John and Freddie Mercury. The tears I watched him wipe as we said our final goodbyes to Mom. His slack jaw and owl-eyes when Win told him she was pregnant. The tie around his head as he danced at Bo and Win's wedding reception, screaming the lyrics of *Dancing Queen* louder than anyone else. The hardened edge of his jaw when I confronted him at the fundraiser. The exhaustion on his face during the drive home that night.

"He is," I start slowly. "Intelligent, driven, nerdy, a *bit* of a workaholic . . . he's . . ." the right word is on the tip of my tongue, but it escapes me. "Soft" is what I land on. "He cares deeply. He protects out of love, not dominance. He's grumpy in the mornings. He talks in his sleep, and he also snores. He grew up well-off and it made him a little too laid back, in my opinion. He's great in bed," I add, for good measure as I continue to blankly look ahead.

Helen chuckles softly from ahead of me on the path, and I move to follow her.

"The day we met, before I learned his name, I called him *wonder boy*," I recall fondly. "I'd spent the morning trying to find the new kid but failed. Then, later on, he strolled into my math class with this outfit that I'm certain his mother had picked out. A maroon-and-navy-striped sweater with a white collared shirt poking out of the top and spilling out the bottom and a pair of classic blue jeans. He was different from every other guy my age. He had a carefree lightness about him that set him apart, but it was also the way he didn't have that prey or predator look in his eye that the rest of us did. He just sort of . . . floated above it all with this confidence that can't be faked. It made him seem so much older. It took me less than a day of shared classes to realize he was smart too. And only a week to toss a paper airplane at his head with my number on it."

"A paper airplane." Helen turns over her shoulder, smiling. "That's cute," she says, looking at the horizon as she sidesteps a burrow of some kind.

"Well, everyone was vying for the new kid's attention," I recall fondly. "I had to stand out."

"And? Did it work? Did he call?"

"No," I say, punctuated by a short laugh. "I didn't sign my name on the paper, and he had no clue who'd thrown it at him. Two days later I cornered him and asked if he wanted to eat lunch with me. We didn't talk about the airplane thing until a month later. Then, he asked me to be his girlfriend by leaving a paper airplane note on my locker."

Helen laughs, the sound fading to a contented sigh. "Oh, to be young and in love."

"Amen," I say, struggling to keep pace as we begin walking up a steep hill.

"You seem to really love him," she says, voice slightly strained. "That's a good place to start."

"No, yeah, he's great," I say between panted breaths.

"*So* . . ." Helen says, grabbing her hips as she stops, reaching the top of the hill. "Why are you here?"

"What?" I ask, bending at the waist to catch my breath.

"If you love him," she pauses to take a sip of water, "if you're happy with him . . . What made you decide to come? Your questionnaire was fairly . . . vague. Is this more of an adventure for you two or . . . ?"

Did you not hear my matinee monologue earlier? There'll be another show at seven. "I don't know if I'm happy," I answer, my tone defensive. "I don't *feel* happy."

"Well, why not?"

Isn't that your job, lady? "I . . . I don't know."

"You said earlier that you resent Caleb."

Did I? "I—"

"Why's that?"

"I—" I look around, then wipe sweat off my brow before dropping my hand to my hip. "I . . . because I— well, I never learned to survive on my own. I never had to provide for myself."

"So, you resent him looking after you?"

Well, when you word it like that. "No but . . ." God—I think I might. I am a proficient asshole. "I just wish that I'd met Caleb at twenty-five, you know?" Helen nods, waiting for me to go on, as we begin walking side by side. "Sometimes I fantasize about it. What it would've been like to meet him at a bar, or through a friend, or at some party . . ." I block the sun from my eyes with my hand until we're hidden under the shady canopy of the trees again.

"So even in your fantasies, it's still Caleb you end up with? Just, later on?"

"Yeah . . . Of course."

Helen smiles to herself, face pointed toward the ground. "In that case, you're better off than most of my married clients, I'll tell you that."

"It's Caleb," I say as justification. Who could *not* love Caleb?

"So, in this hypothetical where you meet later on, how do you think it would have all played out?"

"I don't know," I answer truthfully. "I've never really followed the thought that far."

"Do you think it would have been easier without him? Your early twenties?"

I instinctively shake my head no, then once I give it some thought, do so again. "I'll always be grateful that I had him through that time of my life. Losing my mom was the most painful experience I could ever imagine, and he supported me through it. But I went from someone's daughter to caretaker to someone's wife. I never got the chance to *exist* on my own. That was my decision too, so I don't think I resent Caleb as much as I just resent the circumstances in which we chose to get married. Still, I'll never regret marrying Caleb—I don't ever want to not be married to him—but I wish the timing was different, is all."

"I can see that," Helen says assuredly. "I think that makes a lot of sense."

My shoulders relax with those words. I hadn't realized I'd needed that validation, but it feels great to receive it. "I don't even know what I would have done if we'd not met when we did. I just know I would have *had* to do something with my life before he came along."

"Probably, yes," Helen says. "But then again, maybe not. Plenty of people who've had to pave their own way still consider themselves unsuccessful. Feeling inadequate tends to be a relatively common experience when we struggle with our self-esteem. You could have been miserable all the same, even if the timing were different or with a degree or career you felt proud of."

I snort. "Maybe." I'd actually not really considered that before.

"Often, we can find ourselves playing *what-if* instead of recognizing what we can do *now* to build the life we want. The truth is the past is one of the only things as stubborn as us humans. Unfortunately, it won't change no matter how much you ask it to."

She gives that wisdom space to breathe, and I appreciate it. I feel the weight of her words settle under my skin.

"I want you and Caleb to find some time together away from everyone else and write out a list of what you want your life to look like ten years from now. Tomorrow evening we'll start discussing ways to get you both there, together."

I nod. "Okay," I say, my voice quiet yet determined. "Yeah, that actually sounds really great."

"Until then," Helen says, looking over her shoulder toward the group behind us. "Go jump back in with them. I think you have an interesting perspective that they may need to hear."

WHEN I REJOINED the group, Nina had already concluded that she wants to confront Jai. From the sound of it, she's willing to move past this with him but needs to know if there's any other skeletons in his closet *and* to clarify that she is in a stage of her life where her career goals come first. Maggie and Phil are somewhat less interesting. They come up every year as a sort of maintenance check, like getting the oil changed on your car, she'd said, and had no real issues to discuss. Though she does feel like they need to have more sex. *Rock on, sister.*

Kieran and Henry came for the first time last year after opening a retail store together and hitting a bump in their marriage. Kieran is a talker and Henry, apparently, is more of a dweller, ruminating on his feelings until they eventually bubble up and come out with anger. He's not violent, but he's got a nasty habit of slamming doors and raising his voice that makes Kieran uncomfortable. Kieran also expressed that he is guilty of trying to get a rise out of Henry sometimes too, which I thought was brave of him to admit.

Afterward, I understood why Helen would want us to have this time as a group. There's something very humbling about it. Putting your ego aside to talk about the most difficult aspects of your relationship and where growth can happen, as couples and individuals, was a painful yet necessary exercise.

Before I had the chance to share, the sky opened and rain began to pour, making the final hour of our hike less enjoyable.

We all walked with our heads down, trying our best not to slip, and the conversation was forced to end when the rain got so loud, we couldn't hear one another.

That is when my thoughts grew impossible to ignore.

I spent the last portion of our hike imagining what Caleb's group may have discussed. The flip side to these problems. Then, I mostly wondered what Caleb could have said about our relationship. About me. From there, I listed each of my greatest insecurities and imagined them pouring from Caleb's lips.

I drink too much. I tease too much. I spend too much. I'm clingy, ungrateful, lazy, dependent, judgmental, harsh, critical, brash, needy, unaccomplished . . . all the ways I don't measure up to my potential. The potential he saw in me before I saw it in myself. That he has, no doubt, painfully watched go to waste over the years.

By the time we reach camp, my self-esteem is at an all-time low.

"I DON'T KNOW," CALEB SAYS TENSELY, FIXING HIS HOLD on my hair as he moves to tuck his phone against his shoulder. "She wouldn't tell me what happened. She was crying, and she asked me to drive her to this party, and—" He's interrupted by the sound of me puking into the toilet. "She drank . . . a lot."

"Who are you talking to?" I ask, dropping my clammy cheek against my forearm as tears well in my eyes. My voice doesn't sound right, all slurred and wet. Nothing feels right. This was not supposed to happen. My mother was never meant to be sick. Cecelia was never supposed to hate me. And I was never, *ever* going to throw up in the basement of some jock's lame high school party. I gag again, but don't bother to move and aim for the bowl. I don't think there could possibly be *anything* left inside of me to puke up.

"She won't leave." Caleb seethes. "She just keeps saying that she wants you and, well, honestly, she's been kind of mean."

I *do* have a vague memory of telling him to put on sandals and kick rocks when he suggested I switch to water at some point. So, he may have an argument there.

Adults always say that drinking is dangerous because if you drink too much, you'll black out and forget everything. Turns out, they lied. I want to forget so badly . . .

"I can try that, but I don't think she'll listen." The room tilts lopsided in my vision, and I shut my eyes tight. *I want my mom.* I think maybe I said it out loud that time because Caleb rubs my back and says, "I know," quietly, just for me to hear. "Okay, yeah," he speaks into the phone. "191 Lambro, near the . . . Yeah, exactly. Thank you. See you soon, Marcie." Then Caleb drops his phone to the floor.

Those are the most sobering words I've ever heard. "My mom?" I sit up, though the room continues to spin, hideous yellow tile and awful fluorescent lighting dance around my head. "Did you seriously call my fucking mom?" My eyelids are hooded as I fight back the dizziness. "She'll kill me!"

"You haven't stopped asking for her all night, Sarah."

"I'm drunk, you idiot. People say stupid things when they drink."

"Yeah, and I'm really fucking unsure why you're acting like this. Why are we here, Sar? What happened? Why won't you just talk to me?"

I feel rage bubble up inside of me, and I'm ready to unleash it all on someone I know doesn't deserve it, as that same person pulls me into his lap and wraps me tightly in his arms.

"Tomorrow," Caleb whispers into my hair, "when you're nice again, you'll thank me for calling her. Then, you can tell me whatever Cecelia did or said to make you *this* upset. And, after that, you can apologize for calling me a douche in front of half of our grade . . . and an idiot just now."

138   HANNAH BONAM-YOUNG

"I'm sorry," I choke out, crying into his shoulder. Tears stream down my face, blotting into the soft material of his sweater. "Everything is so fucked up. I don't know what to do anymore."

He shushes me, rocking me back and forth as I continue to sob against him. "Don't cry, baby." *He's never called me that before.* "Whatever it is, we'll figure it out. Together."

At some point, I'm ushered into a car by Aunt June who silently drives me home as I lie down across her backseat, a puke bag in hand. I don't remember getting in bed *or* my mother lying down next to me, but I can feel her weight on the mattress behind my back, and smell her familiar perfume.

I roll over to face her, my blanket pulled up to my nose, and watch as she nervously assesses me.

"Hi," I whisper.

"Hi." She sighs, her demeanor shifting from concern to exasperation.

I start crying almost immediately. "I'm so sorry, Mommy."

"Darling," she coos, wiping a tear from my cheek. "What on *earth* happened today? This isn't like you. . . ."

"She hated me," I say through a wet sob. "Cecelia *hated* me."

Mom blinks rapidly, her head beginning to shake. "There's no way."

"She called my writing shallow . . . a-and," I stutter, struggling to catch my breath. "Sh-she—"

"Breathe." Mom rubs her hand over my shoulder. "Breathe, Sarah."

"I'm sorry," I burst out. Mom moves to hold me as I sit up and cry against her shoulder. "I'm sorry, I'm sorry, I'm—" Mom shushes me, over and over, as I shake against her, apologizing a hundred times for *everything* that's happened in the last week, for not having good news amid this shitstorm. For failing her when she needed me to succeed the most. It keeps coming out in those same two words. *I'm sorry.*

I don't remember falling asleep, or what Mom did to get me to calm me down, but when I wake up in the dead of night in a cold sweat, she pulls me into her chest and cradles me back to sleep without a word.

ELEVEN

"YOU ALL RIGHT?" CALEB ASKS, HIS EYES NARROWING on me. "You've barely touched your . . . *mush*," he whispers as to avoid interrupting the group's discussion. We're sitting around a campfire that Kieran and Henry are desperately trying to keep ablaze even though everything surrounding us is wet—the ground, our packs, our tents, our clothes—but the fire is helping. I don't even know how they found wood dry enough to burn, but based on the thickness of the smoke wafting around us, it's still partially damp too. Even our food packet, which I *think* is supposed to be some sort of rice and chicken combination, tastes wet.

"I'm fine," I reply with a tight-lipped smile. It's a lie. I've been paranoid since we arrived, second-guessing any comments or glances or conversations from Caleb's company this morning. I try, and fail, to tell myself that he deserves the chance to talk about whatever is weighing him down. That any issues we have are his to freely discuss. That I shouldn't care what these people think. "Promise," I add when Caleb doesn't look convinced.

Caleb nods slowly, then turns his attention back to Phil who's waxing poetic about his many years spent teaching and the ne-farious habits of teenagers in locker rooms that he's had to deal with. "But have you ever deliberately sat students next to each other? To set them up?" Kieran asks, stoking the fire.

Phil's laugh is hearty and boisterous. "I teach gym, so there isn't a whole lot of sitting involved. And the last thing I'd want to do is sit potential couples next to one another during health class. They may never look each other in the eye after that."

"I have," Maggie says cheerfully. "I've been invited to two dif-ferent weddings of students I had a hand in setting up. One cou-ple was from my yearbook class; I kept assigning them the same projects. The other were just two frequent flyers at the library who kept checking out the same books after each other and I suggested they start a book club. It's been one of the major perks of teaching. I *love* playing matchmaker."

Caleb grins at me over his shoulder under a cast of orange light as if to affectionately say, *Sounds like you.* The flickers of flame play against his skin, reflect in his glasses, and illuminate all his best features. His nose casts a sharp shadow across his cheek, high-lighting his cheekbones and the facial hair that he never normally allows to grow. It is so foolish of me to not spend time seeing him under all the layers of familiarity. I can't even remember the last time I gave him an unrequited compliment.

"You're beautiful," I say, for his ears only.

He turns toward me, his head tilted in confusion as if I mis-spoke. So, I repeat myself. "You're *beautiful*," I emphasize.

"Thank you . . ." he says, lips turning downward into a senti-mental frown. He studies me for two long beats, his eyes creasing at the sides as he brings a thumb to my chin. I think we're sec-onds away from a kiss until he swipes his thumb over something unmistakably sticky and flicks it off his fingertip. "You had a dead mosquito on your chin," he explains.

And they say romance is dead. *Clearly, they haven't met my husband.* My shoulders fall and I give him a sad sort of smirk before drifting my gaze back to the fire. "Sounds about right."

He laughs weakly. "Sorry . . . I ruined the moment, didn't I?"

"A little," I say, matching his weary grin. "But that's okay. I'd rather be bug-free."

"You're beautiful, baby. Dead bugs and all."

A coy smile tugs at my lips. "Even when my hair smells like smoke?" I ask flirtatiously, knowing he *loves* the scent. When we decided to buy a house, Caleb had three requirements:

1. A garage so he didn't have to clear the snow off his car every morning before work in the winter.
2. A shower that was big enough for two.
3. A wood-burning fireplace.

That last one was hard to find, but after some searching, he got all three. I asked for a bathtub, so Win would want to come stay with us, an office for Caleb, in the hopes that he'd work from home more often, and a room that could fit all my and my mother's books. I *also* got all three.

Caleb leans in close and deeply inhales next to my neck, his chin brushing the strands that have broken free of my pigtail next to my ear. "Mm-hmm," he hums. "*Especially* that."

The tiny hairs on the back of my neck rise at his proximity and the hushed, hungry tone of his voice. "I missed you today," I whisper into his ear, tempted to plant a kiss on his soot-covered cheek and ask if he's ready to go to bed and push the rules ever so slightly. But my anxiety breeds curiosity and I let both get the better of me. "What did you talk about with your group earlier?"

Caleb leans back, his thumb and finger pinching the tip of his nose. He drops his hand to his lap and rubs his thumb along the tendon of his opposite hand as if he's trying to massage out a sore muscle. He glares at the fire in front of him for a while and then clears his throat. He might as well be holding up a giant, flashing neon sign that says: *I talked shit about you, so please don't ask me that.*

"Got it," I say snidely, looking up to the night sky dotted with stars.

Caleb sighs, letting his head fall backward as if he hasn't got the energy to deal with my bullshit *and* the weight of his brain as he attempts to think his way out of this.

"Only good things, then," I say sarcastically, my hurt obvious as I pick at my nail beds.

"Wasn't that the point?" he asks, his tone indignant. "I'm sure it wasn't exactly sunshine and rainbows over in your group either."

No, it wasn't. . . . "I actually talked about how wonderful you are," I argue, crossing my arms. Thank god everyone is enraptured in Helen's story about the skating pigeon that I've already heard and *not* paying attention to our hushed bickering. "I told Helen all about the day we met and what I love about you and—" I quickly come to the realization that we're heading into full-blown argument territory and want to retreat. I can't do this here. Not in front of all these people but also, I'm tired. It's been a long two days and I know I'm not thinking straight.

So, I pull an emergency ripcord and pout at him exaggeratedly, in a particular way that I haven't since we were dating. I suppose that was the last time things felt *this* precarious between us, before we had years of commitment and paperwork binding us together. The spoiled-princess-pout that says: *I'm upset but you don't have to take me seriously.*

It makes me feel nauseous, behaving this childishly. A sick-to-my-stomach sort of embarrassment for my past and present self who finds this worthwhile.

The reality is that if Caleb did think of several *negative* things to say about me when I wasn't around, it will only magnify my hurt feelings over him not being able to think of *one,* single positive thing to say about me when I asked him on the night of the fundraiser. He hasn't tried to amend his nonanswer either. I've thought about it almost constantly since. Visualizing his silence as if it is now a third member of our marriage, sitting between us.

Caleb takes the bait, laughing softly at my petulant expression. He bumps his shoulder against mine, mimicking my features in a teasing manner as his frown turns to a grin. I *hate* that it worked, but I suppose old habits die hard for us both. "I'm sure you shared other things too, baby. And, for the record, I talked about how we met as well," he says fondly. "I also said many, many positive things."

"You did?" What I mean is: *I'd like to hear them, please.*

He nods. A lackluster response, but it sets me at ease enough to try and drop the subject. I don't want to fight tonight. Not before we can talk about our ideal future and how we can get there together. So, I swallow my pride and decide to apologize. "Sorry," I say, dropping my gaze from his. "I'm just feeling self-conscious. I don't want people here to think I'm this . . . terrible person. But you have every right to share what's on your mind."

"You don't need to worry about that, I promise. You're the farthest thing from a terrible person." He tucks a loose hair behind my ear. "And, because I forgot to say it before, I missed you today too."

"You don't think anyone here thinks I'm terrible?" *Not even you?*

"Of course not."

"Well, I feel pretty terrible after today," I whisper even quieter, leaning in close, resting my forehead on his chin. "Nina is eight years younger than me and has accomplished so much already.

Hell, if we play our cards right, we could be friends with a future EGOT winner. Kieran owns his own store and is looking to open a second location since it's been so successful. Maggie has been teaching and happily married for over twenty years. . . . I want—" I sit up to look at him. "I want to be proud of me. I want *you* to be proud of me."

He nods thoughtfully, a few breaths passing between us as the rest of the group laughs and the fire continues to roar. "You know what I took away from today?" Caleb asks, smiling softly as his eyes wander around the campfire and the newly familiar faces circling it. "That everyone is a bit of a mess. Here or anywhere." He shrugs one shoulder. "Anyone who says any differently is faking it or trying to sell something."

"*You're* not a mess," I say defiantly.

He pushes his tongue against the inside of his cheek and breathes out a laugh. "Well, I guess I'm good at faking it then."

"You don't have to," I offer, my instincts telling me that's what he needs to hear. "Not with me," I add.

His eyes hold on mine, filling with emotion I don't recognize— which frightens me. It's been a very, very long time since Caleb's expressions were hard for me to read. I begin wondering what is worse: being overly familiar with each other *or* fading into strangers who *used* to know it all. I think it's definitely the latter.

"Promise?" he asks, turning to straddle the log underneath us. He places his elbows on his knees and focuses on me with undivided attention, our eyes meeting as I nod cautiously.

"Yes," I say. I desperately want to know whatever is causing that line in the center of his forehead and the tension in his jaw, under his ear, as his molars seem to grind together. Is it anger? Hurt? Worry? All the above? "I can take it," I promise him, though I'm not sure it's true.

The moment those words leave my mouth, it's as if a dam

breaks loose over Caleb's tongue. He'd been waiting for that permission, it would seem.

"I'm scared," he says, keeping his voice low. His nose twitches and nostrils flare, as if he's holding back tears. But it appears to be something closer to anger. I wait for him to go on.

"Ever since the fundraiser it's been like one shitty revelation after the next as to how miserable you are. I guess I've been naïve," he says, licking his lips as his eyes hold on the fire. "But it doesn't feel like so long ago that you and I were this unbreakable, undoubtable thing. I put so much stock in that. Maybe it means I was lazy, or it means that I haven't been paying enough attention to you but—*god, Sarah*—I miss feeling settled, don't you?" he asks raggedly, a shaky breath passing through his lips. "I miss not having to overthink everything I say or do around you. You keep saying that you want things to change, that you need change, but that sounds awful to me. I liked our life. No, actually, I *loved* our life. I miss the comfort. I miss the assuredness. I miss being ignorant to all of these . . ." He pauses, wiping a hand through his hair and down his neck. "Problems," he finishes, hanging his head between us.

"Caleb," I say. What I mean is *Look at me.* He doesn't.

"I never thought we'd have to start again." He speaks toward the hollow space between us. "I never *wanted* to start again. It's scary and frustrating and uncomfortable and to be honest . . . I'm fucking annoyed. I'm annoyed that we're here. I'm annoyed that our life wasn't good enough for you. I'm annoyed at myself for not figuring all of this out sooner, before we needed to drag our asses out into the woods." He straightens, and I immediately notice that his eyes are wet with the hint of tears to come. "I'm second-guessing everything and . . . I hate it. I thought we were good, baby. I thought we were the lucky ones."

"We are the lucky ones," I say defensively. "But we—"

"I know," he says, interrupting me as he scrapes the toe of his boot against the gravel. "But we've *changed*." The last word is shrouded in disappointment.

"No," I say. "I don't think *we* have changed . . . I think that's the problem."

"And is that so bad?" he asks, eyes searching. "What *truly* needs to change? What is *so* terrible about our life as it is?"

"Do you really want to be exactly as we are ten years from now? Twenty years? Thirty?"

Caleb's jaw slackens, his eyebrows rising as he huffs out a forceful breath.

"Oh my god, you do . . ." I whisper. "You—"

"Fuck me for being happy, I guess," he says exasperatedly, standing up in a fury. He paces as if he's intending to walk away but turns back around to say one last thing. "This has always been enough for me, Sarah. *You* have always been enough. But I guess I know where I stand. I'm not enough for you. Clearly *nothing* ever will be."

"I didn't—" I say, my gaze quickly darting around to the many sets of eyes now watching us. "You're—"

"I'm going to bed, please give me some time before you come in," Caleb says before he's out of sight.

I delay it as long as I can, watching Caleb's back until he disappears into our tent and holding for a while after that too, but eventually I turn my body toward the group. I keep my head low, my shoulders hunched and tense as I try to hide my face from the other campers.

"Draa-maa," Libby singsongs, loud enough for me to hear her on the opposite side of the circle.

"Libby!" Helen chastises. "That is *not* helpful."

My throat has gone dry, but I try to speak, nevertheless. "I'm . . . sorry." Still, I don't look up, intently watching my hands wringing in my lap.

You wanted him to be mad, didn't you? I hear that cruel part of my psyche mock once more. *Well, look at you now. Got what you wanted. Just like you always do.*

"Honey, what do you think we're here for?" Maggie says, patting my thigh.

"We've all had our not-so-private arguments, and we all will again. No sweat," Phil adds.

The fire cracks and sparks fly as another log breaks in two, but otherwise the awkward silence persists until Kieran speaks. "All right . . ." He claps his hands together, then rubs them eagerly. "Who wants a roasted marshmallow?"

I lift my head timorously, relieved to find that no one is looking at me, other than Yvonne. She's studying me, as she so often seems to be, but this time with a softness I've not received before. A gentle smile that doesn't feel particularly earned but *does* feel comforting.

"You packed marshmallows?" Henry asks, his tone disbelieving as he sets another log onto the fire. "What happened to only bringing the necessities?"

"Those *are* necessities," Jai argues, voice slow and relaxed as he eagerly looks toward Kieran. If the faint smell on him and his frequent disappearing acts are anything to go off of, Jai has been sneaking away to smoke joints here and there. I wonder if Nina would sneak one to me if I asked nicely. I could *really* use it.

"Exactly." Kieran points to Jai. "I'll go get them," he says as he moves to stand.

"Sarah and I will find roasting sticks," Nina says, standing and signaling with a nod for me to do the same. I smile appreciatively at her as she makes her way over to my side of the campfire.

"C'mon," she says, looping her arm through mine as I stand. "Let's get some air."

We're literally out in the open air, I think to myself. But the sentiment is kind all the same. Still, I don't think there's a place in this world where I won't feel suffocated by embarrassment right now. Or by my wounded pride. Or by the deep, aching fear that I've hurt Caleb in an unrepairable way. Or . . . my increasing worry that it's only going to get worse the more we open up to each other. Perhaps ignorance *was* bliss. Perhaps I've unraveled us beyond repair.

As Nina and I walk toward the thick grouping of trees that line the perimeter of the campsite, I notice the lantern inside of our tent turn off.

Don't go to bed angry, my mother had told Win and me after a stupid fight we'd once had over a borrowed and *then* misplaced blouse. *That is, unless you're going to rip each other's heads off,* my aunt June had added. They often spoke in tandem like that, piggybacking off each other's tidbits of advice. I wish my mother were here now to bestow some half-baked platitude. Hell, I'd even settle for some of Aunt June's less sentimental words of wisdom.

"Do you want a hug?" Nina asks, once we're out of sight. Her body is dimly lit by moonlight, but I find my eyes adjusting to see her as she reaches out her arms.

"Yes, please," I answer, already moving toward her. She curls her lean, long body around me and squeezes tightly. She is a surprisingly good hugger and doesn't rush me out of her hold until I'm ready.

"I know I don't know you very well," Nina says as we part. "Or like *at all,* really. But I can tell you and Caleb will be totally fine. You're good people. You're good to each other."

I sigh, not sure of what to say. She's right, she doesn't know me well enough, clearly.

"You two remind me a lot of my parents," she says sweetly. I whine, mimicking taking an arrow to the chest. "Not in age!" She shoves my shoulder lightly as she giggles. "Just that—they've been married for almost thirty years, and they look at each other the same way you two do. Like they've got the other person memorized. Inside and out."

"That's sweet. Thank you," I say, diverting my eyes from her focused gaze. "We should probably find some sticks and get back."

Nina scoffs, rolling her eyes. "Oh, no, Jai has that covered. I've just snuck you away so I could give you this." She pulls a joint out of her jacket's pocket. "But . . . I *was* hoping we could share it instead?"

I gasp, taking it from her. "Yes, please!"

"Jai might not be the best at words . . . *or* the truth . . . but he rolls a *very* good joint."

"And what more do you really need?" I ask, taking it from her as she holds it out to me. "Seriously, thank you."

"C'mon, there's a good spot over here where Jai's been hiding out," Nina says, walking farther into the tree line.

TWELVE

THAT WAS PROBABLY THE WORST NIGHT'S SLEEP OF MY life. In between his fits of snoring, Caleb was fighting with me in his dream. Not that he was saying many *actual* words—but I could tell by his urgent tone and the frequent uses of my name, muttered disgruntledly. When I did finally fall asleep it was already dawn. I woke up shortly after to the sun filtering in much too brightly for tired eyes and the sounds of Caleb zipping the door closed, followed by the squelching of his boots in the dewy morning grass outside of the tent as he walked away from me *again*.

"Guess I'm awake," I say to myself, my voice groggy as I sit up, still inside of my sleeping bag. I attempt to open it and free myself but quickly realize the zipper's stuck on the inside lining, and I end up having to awkwardly maneuver my body out like an uncoordinated snake shedding its skin. "A brilliant start . . ." I reach for my water bottle and immediately notice it had tipped over, not *entirely* sealed, and had spilled onto the floor between our sleeping mats. At least we don't have to pack up and move to a new site this morning because today is clearly not my friend. "It'll only get better from here," I whisper to myself, forcing optimism from behind gritted teeth.

I take the towel out of my pack and lay it onto the mess, letting it absorb the water. Then, I make my way outside to wring out the cloth and hang it on the tent's guy line to dry.

"Happy morning, Sarah!" Helen says from somewhere behind me.

"Morning," I reply cheerfully, despite how I feel, waving a hand over my shoulder as I slip my feet into my boots.

"Hello," Yvonne's low, unmistakable voice says from *right* beside me.

"Oh my god!" I jump, clasping my chest. "Fuck, sorry, Yvonne," I say, desperately trying to catch my breath. "You . . . you scared me." I swallow, blinking at her as I adjust to her looming proximity. She's worn pretty much the same outfit since we arrived, all linen, always billowy, always see-through *enough* that you have to avoid looking down to not get an eyeful. Though, I've got to give it to her, Yvonne's body *is* banging. "Morning," I add, settling some.

Her mouth puckers, but the corners of her lips turn upward some. "I was hoping that you and I could go for a walk," she says. Is it possible that she sounds *more* British today? Her accent seems thicker to me. Perhaps it's the fresh air clearing out her windpipe. "After lunch?"

"Oh, yeah, sure," I say, smiling tightly, glancing over her shoulder toward Caleb who is wandering back from wherever he must have taken his routine morning dump. He looks miserable, but then again, I'd be inclined to judge him if he looked perky following taking a shit in the woods *or* after our fight last night.

"He'll manage for a few hours without you," Yvonne says. "Probably best to take some time apart until tensions ebb. Helen has a plan for the group this morning, but we'll head out after that." In my peripheral vision I see her angle her head toward me, as if she's trying to get my attention.

I turn to face her, realizing Caleb isn't looking my way regardless, then nod. "Sounds good." It in fact does *not* sound good. I'm being separated from the class. Singled out. I am the *worst* one here. I am lower on the scoreboard than had-a-secret-fiancé Jai. Fuck, Caleb was dead wrong—we are *not* winning this. I will bring down our team's average, as per usual.

"Don't worry." She pats my arm as she steps around me, headed toward the neighboring tent where Kieran is stretching after crawling out and greeting the sun. "I don't bite," she calls over her shoulder. She chuckles as she rubs Kieran's back in a silent greeting then continues wandering aimlessly away from camp as if she can hear a siren's call the rest of us cannot.

"What was that about?" Kieran asks, flashing his eyes at me and jutting his chin toward where Yvonne had just stood.

"I think I'm being put on time-out," I say, wincing as I walk over to him. "She wants a one-on-one with me after lunch."

"If it helps, she eventually corners everyone."

"But I'm *first,*" I point out, leaning closer as I cross my arms in front of my chest.

He smiles, shaking his head. "It's all a part of the experience. . . . At least you won't miss Helen's morning exercise."

"Which is?" I ask, smiling back at his wide, cheeky grin.

"Screaming off a cliffside," he answers, tugging at his hair to tie it up into a topknot. "Or somatic body movements. Stomping, pushing at trees, tapping your shoulders—shit like that. Or, that's what it was last year."

"That does sound nice," I say genuinely. "I actually think I'd *love* to scream out shit over a cliff."

"See, the day's already turning around." His eyes flick over my shoulder as someone approaches from behind. It's almost embarrassing to admit that I can tell it's Caleb based on the sound of his footfalls, but I know it's him. "Good morning," Kieran hums out, his forever-amused tone remaining in check.

"Hey," Caleb says, stopping next to us, his expression of exhaustion not helped by the two-day scruff that has crossed into full-fledged beard territory. I look at him, unsure of what to say or do or even think in his presence. And he stares blankly ahead, blinking like a newborn as he yawns and lifts the hood of his sweater up. I don't think he's intentionally blocking me out, he just seems tired, but I can't stand here in awkward silence with Kieran as witness a moment longer.

"I'll get started on breakfast," I say, waving as I step away like a total idiot. *We're not usually this way!* I want to shout while laughing hysterically. *I swear we are totally going to be fine!*

God, I hope that's at least a little bit true.

"WELCOME TO DAY three." Helen projects her voice, her water bottle in the crook of her arm as she holds a clipboard. She hasn't told us what we're doing this morning, but we've followed her to an open field far away from camp and those of us with long hair have been instructed to tie it up. So, wrestling, I can only presume. In which case, I'm fucked because we've been partnered up alphabetically so I'm with Phil who's got about a hundred and fifty pounds on me at least.

Despite his ability to undoubtedly kick my ass if Helen decides to create her own sort of *Hunger Games* situation, Phil is a great walking partner.

One thing about me is that the more I feel ignored by a person in my life (see: Caleb), the more I'm going to talk to just about *anyone* else. It's a chronic condition. Therefore, I blabbed to Phil about pretty much every available topic under the sun in the twenty minutes it took for our group to make it to this field, and he obliged so politely I do think a statue should be built in his honor.

"We're going to do a few different communication exercises today," Helen says. Which is great and all, but it's not exactly Phil that I struggle to communicate with, so . . . why is *he* my partner? Wouldn't it be better if Caleb and I were teamed up for this? *Oh* . . . are couples *normally* teamed up for this? Did Caleb and I break the status quo by fighting in front of everyone last night? Oh god. Have *we* caused this untimely divide?

"Phil," I whisper, staring up at his profile. He subtly looks toward me, as if he's trying not to divert his attention fully away from Helen as she shares instructions for today's activity. I'm being rude by interrupting his focus and speaking over her, I know. But I'm running on paranoia, no sleep, a cup of lackluster oatmeal, and the weakening effects of half of a joint from last night, so I give myself permission to spiral a little bit. "Is it usually the couples that are partnered up or . . . ?"

"We've never done this before," Phil whispers back.

Oh my god, it's even worse than I'd imagined. We've changed the curriculum entirely. Helen is bringing out the big guns because Caleb and I have fucked up the system.

"You okay?" Phil asks, eyeing me suspiciously.

"Totally," I say, glancing toward my husband whose stern expression is locked on Helen. His arms are folded in front of his chest, his forearms doing that tendon-flexing thing that both turns me on and makes me eerily aware of the tension flooding his system. I should have pulled him aside to talk this morning. This is far too strange. We came here to stop avoiding talking to each other and yet, here we are, doing just that. What if—

"All right, got it?" Helen asks, interrupting my train of thought. Everyone else nods as I blink back into reality. "Great, let's get into positions."

Shitting fuck . . . I didn't catch a word of what we're doing. I copy everyone's movement as they all step closer together, shoulder to shoulder, forming a small circle.

We're going to sacrifice someone, my sleep-deprived brain suggests. *I volunteer,* I think to myself as I feel a new wave of exhaustion wash over me.

"Sarah," Nina says, outstretching her hand toward mine. I take it hesitantly, side-eyeing Phil as Maggie reaches out her hand toward him to take it. When it was my turn, I offered my free hand to Caleb, who took it rather begrudgingly. Eventually, we're all holding hands, a messily tied knot of limbs between us.

"Okay," Helen says from outside of the circle. "You can begin," she says.

It doesn't take me long to guess, based on Kieran's directions, that we're supposed to untangle ourselves without letting go of one another. But as time ticks on, and I perform my tenth squat to allow someone to step over my and Nina's hold, the group grows sweaty, impatient, and a little hostile. Caleb and I, for the most part, remain silent. I believe we've both decided that we've embarrassed ourselves enough for the time being after last night's performance. Still, our hands remain firmly grasped.

And, when he squeezes my hand twice rhythmically, I look up to find him smiling at me. "Hey," he mouths.

"Hi," I reply silently, feeling a twisting in my gut as his mask slips away and I see the sadness behind his eyes return. I hurt him. I hate that I hurt him.

"Jai!" Nina snaps as Jai *once again* drops her hand to maneuver himself into a more desirable position. "Stop cheating!"

"I have to take a piss," he seethes. "And it's fucking hot as balls out here!"

He has a point. About the heat, I mean. I peed before I left, like a good girl.

"Why do you feel entitled to break the rules when no one else is?"

"I didn't say no one else couldn't," he fires back. "And I didn't make the rules so why should I follow them?"

"You're infuriating."

"Can someone move please?" Henry says, his voice shaking as he holds his crouched position between all of us. "It smells like old boots down here."

"No one asked you to get in such an uncomfortable position this early on," Kieran mutters, spinning with Maggie as he over-steps Caleb's arm.

"Someone had to," Henry replies, glaring up at his husband.

"Then, that *someone* shouldn't complain then."

"Here," I say, curling myself under Phil's arm and ducking underneath Jai and Nina's arms. "Everyone, follow through that hole." I use my chin to point to the circle of limbs I just passed through.

"No," Caleb says firmly. I turn my attention toward him, waiting for him to explain as my thighs start to burn from this squatting position. "That'll make it worse."

"No . . ." I argue, "It won't."

"Okay," he says, and I can *hear* the rolling of his eyes before I catch a glimpse of it. "Let's try it then."

"Well, if you have a *better* plan, please share it," I snap. Though, if I'm entirely honest, a part of me knows that if Caleb has his doubts in my plan—it's for good reason. And the only thing *worse* than being wrong is being stubborn and then *proven* wrong.

"Maggie and Phil, you need to switch positions. Then, Jai needs to crouch down so we can all step over him and Henry. After that we'll just need them to go under you and me and then we should be set," Caleb says, in an absentminded tone that I don't think is intentional but speaks of boredom all the same. As if he's known the solution all along and was waiting for the rest of us to catch up.

But . . . Now that I look at it . . . his plan does seem to make sense. I bite my tongue, *hard,* but I pass back through where I'd crossed and stand in position next to Phil as he and Maggie attempt to swap places. After a few near collapses and an awkward sweat-filled five minutes—we're standing in a perfect, untangled circle. Everyone begins praising Caleb as we drop hands and step away from one another, our first task completed. He smiles as he nods, his humble shyness far from boastful . . . which is somehow more agitating.

"Great work," I say, less than genuine before I begin gulping back water, feeling it dribble down my chin.

He just sighs as he walks away from me toward the next two activities he easily masters and guides us all through, so fast that Jai misses one of them altogether while he was peeing.

"That vein in your forehead is going to pop soon," Nina warns, picking up her water bottle from near my feet. "What's got you so mad?"

"Would you judge me if I said I'm angry we're doing so well at these?"

She sips loudly, then ponders for a split second, her eyes up to the sky. "A little . . ."

"Well . . . then judge away."

"Helen really knew what she was doing today," she says against her straw as it pulls at her bottom lip.

"What do you mean?" I ask.

"I feel like I've learned more about our communication styles in the past hour than I have the rest of the trip so far." I stare blankly at her, so she continues on. "Me and Jai disagree because we have different expectations for ourselves . . . Kieran and Henry disagree because Henry often will play the victim . . . Maggie and Phil *don't* communicate really, which seems to weirdly work for them . . . and you guys . . . well you don't like being told what to do and Caleb doesn't like feeling unappreciated."

"I don't mind being told what to do!" I argue.

She quirks a brow.

"I just . . . I don't like being dismissed."

"Even when you're wrong?"

Especially when I'm wrong. I change tactics to deflect with humor. Clearly, Nina's seeing right through me and that must be stopped. "I am actually *great* at being told what to do," I waggle my eyebrows suggestively.

"I bet." She backs away, smirking as she continues to sip water.

"Sarah?" Helen calls out, lifting her walkie-talkie away from her face. "Yvonne's wondering if you're free to meet with her now?"

I force a thin-lipped smile and nod. *Why the fuck not.*

THIRTEEN

AFTER I MET YVONNE BACK AT CAMP, SHE ASKED ME TO fetch my journal and follow her. Neither of us spoke until we reached the bottom of a hill, at least a solid five-minute walk away from the campsite and in the opposite direction of the field.

"So . . ." I say, admiring the sunlight as it filters through the canopy of trees above. I search my mind for a safe topic to start us off with, having already had my fill of uncomfortable quiet today. "Libby is great." I aggressively swat a bug away and nearly lose my balance but regain it before falling.

Sarah 1—Nature 0

Unless you count the many, many bug bites on my butt. Then it's more like, Sarah 1—Nature 8. That's on me for having such a juicy ass, as Win would lovingly point out.

"She's quite fond of you as well," Yvonne says, not turning from the path ahead. Not that we're really *on* much of a path at the moment. I'm fairly certain we started walking on untouched ground around the two-minute mark, once I started having to pull thorny bramble stems off my pants and sidestep to avoid what must be decades-old spiderweb colonies. I'm not a fan of bugs—but I don't plan on being the Godzilla to their metropolis any time soon. "Libby rarely likes people so if I were you, I'd let it go to your head," Yvonne adds, admiring a flower in her grasp before leaving it be.

The compliment immediately lifts my spirits. I was being polite and, for the most part, trying to start a conversation when I said Libby was great. But it wasn't a lie. I do like Libby. I just didn't expect her to have any sort of thoughts or feelings toward me. Especially positive ones, that is. We've hardly interacted. Still, it's nice to hear. I'll make a point to find her later. Maybe she's into books. I try to recall what I was into at her age . . . Percy Jackson, probably. Ten would have been *after* my hardcore Anne of Green Gables phase, most likely. Had I ventured to Narnia yet or—

"Don't tell her I said that," Yvonne says, turning over her shoulder only briefly enough to roll her eyes. "She would hate it if I paid anyone a free compliment on her behalf."

I chuckle, smiling to myself. "She's at a difficult age," I say, surprisingly defensive.

"Well, yes, and she's had a difficult year," Yvonne adds. "But then again, we all have." She turns to duck under a branch. "And yet you don't see *me* in a tizzy near constantly."

I nod as if I have *any* understanding as to what a tizzy is. A bad mood, I'd wager to guess. "I was very sorry to hear about your daughter's passing," I reply somberly. The moment the words have left my mouth, I realize that I was perhaps not *meant* to know the reason for her "difficult year" and cringe.

"Ah, well." Yvonne says it like it's a complete sentence. To me, it is. I hear the emptiness that follows. The quiet, bitter resolve that only those who've known great loss can recognize.

"Thank you," she says softly.

I choose not to press the subject. I've heard from Win, in her most recent experiences of therapy, that you're apparently not meant to treat a counselor like your friend. So, I don't pry, though every part of me instinctually wants to let her know that she could talk about it, if she'd like to.

"It is *gorgeous* today, isn't it? That is one thing I certainly do prefer about Ontario over my hometown back in England: the weather."

"Even the snow?"

She stops, considering. "I suppose not *all* of the weather."

I huff out a laugh as we approach a moss-covered, rocky ledge that overlooks a valley. A stream below carves its path through undisturbed nature, and the treetops blow gently in the breeze like a rolling tide in stunning, varying shades of green. It is breathtaking.

As I consider whether it's safe to go onto the jagged platform carved from stone, Yvonne jumps down onto it and sits on its mossy surface. By the time I hesitantly step out next to her and lower myself to sit, she's already pulled her thermos out of her small crossbody bag. She takes a swig, sucking a breath through her teeth as the hot liquid hits the back of her throat.

"Tea's still hot," she says, sucking in air. I shuffle over to hide from the glare of the sun, careful as to avoid getting too close to the edge. "You know . . . Helen has made me this exact blend of herbal tea every morning for the past nineteen years without fail."

"That's very sweet," I say, looking at the green thermos in her hands. The vessel reminds me of Helen, oddly enough. Sturdy, army-green, like it's built strong and reliable. It looks out of place in Yvonne's long, almost ethereal hands.

"It's horrendous," she says, turning to me with a stone-cold expression. "Like ground up dirt with a pinch of cinnamon."

My surprised laugh falls out of me. "Seriously?"

She holds the tea out to me in offering, her grin mischievous. I take it from her, and sniff—noting that hint of cinnamon she mentioned but not much else. I take a small sip and gag as it dribbles out of my mouth and onto my chin as if my body is refusing to accept it.

"Oh my god!" I say, though with my tongue sticking out it sounds more like *aumagad*. I reach for my own bottle and drink water until my mouth feels properly cleansed and wipe myself clean, tea stains now blotching my white long sleeve shirt. "That is *awful*," I say with a breathy laugh.

Yvonne smiles knowingly, holding eye contact with me, then takes a long, gulping sip from her thermos.

"Stop!" I say, giggling. "You cannot drink that! You have to tell her."

"I won't," she says adamantly. For some reason those two words seem to hold a lot of weight, making my response come slower.

"Why?" I ask softly.

"She means well," she says, looking off into the distance toward the different species of trees scattered throughout our line of vision.

I do the same, bringing my knees to my chest as I take in the melody of birdsong around us. There's a slight echo, the sounds of nature reverberating off the side of the cliff we're sitting on. I can hear the hint of the stream below, and the subtle creaking of tree branches nearby. For an indiscernible amount of time, I get lost in it all.

"It really is beautiful up here," I whisper, taking my first deep breath since last night.

"It's certainly peaceful," Yvonne agrees, setting her thermos down between us. "Not afraid of heights, then?"

I shake my head. "When I was a kid," I say, resting my chin on top of my knee, "I loved climbing things. My mother said I almost gave her a heart attack every time we left the house. She'd blink and suddenly I'd be up a tree, or on top of the playground, a gentle breeze away from breaking an arm or a leg or worse . . ."

"I can imagine! Your poor mother."

"But I loved being up high. I couldn't get enough of it. My favorite part of the year was the carnival that came into town during the last week of summer vacation. I'd save everything I could during the year and spend it all on tickets to ride the Ferris wheel for hours. Whenever my carriage reached the top, I could look over our neighborhood and it was like . . ." My words fall off, as I close my eyes and feel the breeze on my skin, just as I had back then. "Everything suddenly felt small, you know? And I felt bigger. Older. Not so afraid."

"And what about now? Up here . . . Do you feel bigger? Older? Not so afraid?" She repeats, lightly teasing.

I shake my head, forcing a soft laugh. "I feel . . . heavy."

"This high up?" Yvonne tsks. "Well, it must be dire, then." We exchange timid smiles.

I'm grateful for her levity, otherwise this would be entirely too awkward. "I think when a new perspective helps, it's for external problems. Looking down and realizing nothing is *that* significant in the grand scheme of things. But this—these feelings— they're . . . more internal. I'm not really sure what to do."

Yvonne nods thoughtfully. "Well, I'd like to hear more about these feelings if you're up for it. What is bothering you?"

"My identity, I guess?" I ask in case I'm wrong, which, maybe I am. "What to do, who I am, where I'm going. Your average existential crisis, I suppose." I chuckle halfheartedly, but Yvonne doesn't grin—not this time. I take it as my cue to really dig deep.

"I feel like I'm in some sort of vise half the time . . . being pushed on by the past and future."

"Elaborate on that," Yvonne says, shifting to face me. "A vise is an awfully powerful image."

"I guess it's a bit dramatic," I say, looking away from her.

"No, no, none of that. We *should* use powerful imagery for powerful feelings."

I take a deep breath. "I have a hard time being present," I admit. "I'm usually either dwelling on the past or worrying about the future."

"And how would you say that affects your daily life?"

"Well, I have a hard time concentrating. I think—" I pause, blinking rapidly as I lean back onto my palms spread out behind my back, turning up to face the sky. "It can sometimes be difficult for me to feel grateful for what I have because I'm thinking about what I've lost or what I *could* lose. I feel directionless, because I don't really *know* my own feelings or wants or desires. I just sort of live in some . . . middle. Not really pleasing myself or performing what is expected of me."

"What do you feel is expected of you? Are these self-imposed expectations or do you feel that they're external?"

"Definitely self-imposed. I think sometimes my issue *is* that other people expect so little of me." Caleb, for one.

"And what expectations do you feel that you need to meet?"

I feel my eyebrows push together, as I close my eyes and search inwardly for an answer. I come up disappointingly empty. "I don't know, really. Whatever they are, I think I'm failing."

"Often, we measure ourselves against what we had envisioned as our future. What did you want your life to look like when you were younger?"

"I wanted to be an author," I answer truthfully, feeling a sense of embarrassment as I imagine that sixteen-year-old girl with such *hunger* seeing me now, aimless. "I dreamed of writing in muggy cafés, fingertips sore from typing, and ink smudged on the side of my hand."

"You know, most young girls dream of marrying Prince Charming or having a pet pony . . ."

"Oh, so younger then?" I ask, grinning. Yvonne nods. "Well, I remember wanting to marry Lance Bass . . . Mostly because my best friend called dibs on JC."

"Oh, well, best not to tell *little you* about Lance's proclivities then."

"Twelve-year-old me was devastated . . ." I breathe out a laugh. "But no, little me didn't really want much else," I say, then sigh. "She was content. I suppose she imagined that she'd build a simple life for herself, stick by her best friend, and get by, like Mom had. The older version of me demands quite a lot, however."

"Oh, she does, does she?" Yvonne pouts her bottom lip, nodding. "What does *she* want?"

"Mostly for me to get my shit together."

"So younger you has simple dreams and older you has demands. Where do you slot in? The Sarah I get the pleasure of speaking with right now . . . What does *she* want?"

"Like I said, it feels like I'm between them. These two versions of myself closing in on either side and I'm stuck in the middle, not satisfying either of them . . . I . . . I just don't know."

"Interesting . . ."

"Will the men in the white coats be here soon to whisk me away?" I joke, scrunching my face up as I turn to face her.

Yvonne laughs and it's surprisingly loud, unlike her naturally level voice. "They'd have to take both of us, then."

I pause, my eyes flicking to her. "Really?"

"Yes," she laughs, shaking her head as if it's obvious—the insinuation of which sets me at ease. "I remember feeling it far more at your age, but I still have my moments. My god, I was a *mess* in my early thirties."

"I can't imagine that."

"Oh, I absolutely was. I was traveling without a penny to my name, crashing on couches or staying in hostels. I had a slew of terrible breakups that almost destroyed me. I was convinced that I was going to be an artist but didn't bother to pick up a brush. I never stayed still, never got a full night's rest, never felt quite right in my body."

"That first part sounds exciting though."

"It was. It was also lonely," Yvonne says, her voice low. She studies me, and I watch as her chest and shoulders rise on a slow, long breath while her eyes scan my features. "It's not a surprise to me that you feel all this pressure. You had to grow up fast, Sarah. You were thrust into adulthood very young and tried your best to play catch-up. You had a lot on your plate and more responsibility than many of your peers. It's natural that you still expect yourself to excel—you were used to being ahead of the curve. But you don't have to be ahead. You don't have to be extraordinary. You don't have to *do* anything. There's no shame in living a carefree existence."

"I *want* to do something though," I say, the threat of tears suddenly stinging my eyes and catching me by surprise. "I want to have something to look back on when I'm old. I want to make my life worthwhile. I want to be *great*."

"Great for whom? By whose standards?"

I instinctively go to answer but stop myself. *My mom,* I almost say. Because what was the point of all of Mom's sacrifices if the only piece of her left in this world fails to leave a mark? She helped people, sure, but those memories will die with them. She never left her hometown. Hell, she didn't even own a passport. If I wanted kids, maybe I could cross my fingers and hope that they'd go on to do great things—but I don't.

"You have time," Yvonne says—so simple I *almost* believe her. "You're young," she adds, in a tone that has a slight tinge of affectionate jealousy to it as she shoves my knee playfully. "Van Gogh didn't attend art school until he'd failed at being a missionary at age twenty-seven. Harrison Ford was still a carpenter at thirty. Julia Child released her first cookbook at thirty-nine. Vera Wang didn't design a single dress until she was forty."

"But I'm none of those people," I protest, my voice quiet.

"They weren't *those people,* until they were. And, if I'd wager to guess, they probably still felt lost at times, even after all of their accomplishments. Humans are typically just stumbling through this life, making mistakes and trying again. Anyone who says anything different is trying to sell something."

My ears perk up. "Caleb said that to me yesterday, actually—the selling something part."

"I may be recycling some of the same ramblings I shared with him. He and I had quite a lot of time to chat yesterday on our hike."

I scoff as if to say, *So you see what I mean then.* "Cay is so together. He's like the most stable, steady, consistent person alive."

"Well, he's had to be."

Those five words hit like five swift punches to my gut. "True," I squeak, blowing out a short breath.

"That seems to be in his nature as well," Yvonne says, dusting the dirt off her hands when she changes sitting positions, "to be a helper."

"It is," I reply. For me, for Win, for anyone he cares about—

Caleb will show up to help however he can. The night of the fundraiser plays in my mind, the six words that followed my frustration . . . *I was just trying to help.* He was, I know that. Caleb was following our pattern. He hadn't known differently, and I'd not asked him to treat me any differently either. "I worry that I've relied on him too much. He was so young when my mom got sick, and it would have wrecked me at the time but sometimes I wish he'd have called things off between us instead of having to grow up so fast."

"But you were both young and in love. You didn't know any better than to rely on him and he didn't know any better than to stand by you," Yvonne replies. "Do you believe he regrets it? That he'd change it, if he could?"

I shake my head *no*.

"A lot of people will say relationships are fifty-fifty, but I think that's a load of rubbish. We all have seasons and periods where we require more from our partner. The trick to a long, lasting relationship in my professional experience is not getting stuck at a set percentage."

I nod enthusiastically, though my expression remains somber. "I think that's . . . I think that's exactly how I feel. Like we're stuck in these roles. The helper and the helped. The giver and the taker. The hero and the damsel in distress. I want to feel reliable. I want to give as much as I take."

"And it's the goodness in your heart that makes you want to break free of that. And the fact that you feel capable to take more on shows that you're healing, Sarah." She punctuates with my name as if she *really* wants me to hear her.

"It doesn't feel like I'm healing . . . I kind of feel like I'm breaking open more than ever."

"Often it's darkest before dawn, my dear. You're doing the work and that is *hard*. You're here, aren't you? Trying?"

I smile shyly, feeling some heaviness lift off me, like dropping my pack after yesterday's hike. "I guess so."

"When our perceptions begin to shift it is usually because we're ready for something new."

"But Caleb doesn't *want* anything new," I protest. "And I don't know how to change when the person I love most wants things to stay the same."

Yvonne nods thoughtfully. "Do you think Caleb is truly afraid of change or is he possibly afraid of what will happen if you don't need him anymore? He's found security in these roles, just as you once had."

"Right . . ." I blink rapidly, absorbing her insight.

"Caleb briefly shared yesterday that you two aren't planning on having children. Has that been a point of contention between you?"

"No," I answer. "Before Caleb and I got engaged he'd asked me if I saw myself as a parent and was relieved that I felt the same as he did. It's just not something I'd ever really wanted for myself. We've revisited the conversation a few times but have never contemplated it for long. I love hanging out with my niece, and I like being around kids, but I also enjoy going home to have a full night's sleep in a tidy house with a white couch and breakable shit everywhere."

Yvonne laughs dryly. "I can't even imagine what a toddler would do to a white settee."

"Truthfully, sometimes, in my most insecure moments, I've thought about having kids just to have something to fill my time or give me purpose."

"I think far more people than we'd prefer to have done just that. I actually think it is quite impressive you've held true to your convictions in that regard."

"Yes," I say with mock pridefulness to my tone. "My IUD and convictions remain firmly in place."

Yvonne laughs softly. "Glad to hear it." She bends down and removes her shoes and socks, pressing her feet into the mossy earth below. After she seems to take some grounding deep breaths, she turns toward me. The corner of her lip twitches upward as she takes in what must be my skeptical expression. "I'd like us to try something together." She stands up and offers me a hand to do the same.

I take her hand and lift off the ground, hesitant with my smile until she confirms whether I can keep my shoes on.

"Trust me?" she asks, voice teasing but assured.

I think I surprise us both when I take a deep breath of my own and say "Yes."

FOURTEEN

THE FIRE IS NEARLY OUT WHEN YVONNE AND I MAKE IT
back to camp, the logs red and glowing but no flames flickering
above them. The afternoon sun sits right above us in the sky,
helping everything dry again after yesterday's rain.

"They should be back soon," Yvonne says, walking over to the
fire and picking up some kindling. "I'm going to make some
lunch; would you like some?"

I shake my head softly. "I'm going to lie down until everyone's
back." My body needs the rest, and my mind needs a private moment to reflect. I feel emptied out following Yvonne's exercise—
and while I feel inextricably different about her, I still am
desperate for some alone time before whatever the rest of the day
holds.

I climb into our tent and find my sleeping bag neatly laid out
over my mat. Folded nicely on top of it is a fresh change of clothes,
my e-reader, and a small bundle of yellow cornflowers. It's the last
thing I expected to see. So much so, that I nearly tear up at the
sight of it.

I sit on Caleb's mat, so as to not disturb his peace offering, and curl into myself—hugging my knees and grasping at my elbows. I sway, studying each petal attentively, noticing the dusting of pollen. Caleb has bought me many extravagant presents over the years—but none compare to this. My heart swells and sings as I take it in.

Folded clothes, a piece of comfort, and a sweet gesture. Simple, as things used to be between us.

Eventually, I move to lie on my side, and breathe in the scent of Caleb from his sleeping bag. The faint remnants of his eucalyptus deodorant mixed with sweat and dirt and grime. I find it oddly comforting.

I lie awake, with one thought persisting that I cannot shake. *He deserves a gesture of his own.* So, I get up, throw on my boots, and head toward the path where I'd seen some aster flowers earlier with Caleb's multitool in hand. I cut a dozen or so flowers, praying the local bee population forgives me, and use a long weed to tie them off into a bouquet. I make my way back toward the tent, climb in, and place the flowers on Caleb's bed. I pull out his last clean pair of socks—because he's already worn all his other clothes somehow—and ceremoniously lay them next to the flowers.

But something is missing. Something to bring him comfort. With limited resources, I pull out my journal and pen, tear out a page. *I love you so much,* I write onto a blank page before folding it into a paper airplane.

However, as soon as it's folded, I realize I have more to say. So, I tear out another page. *You've always been enough,* I write on this one, then fold.

Then, again, I realize I'm still not quite done.

You don't have to fake it anymore.

Tear, write, fold.

I am sorry for not telling you how I've been feeling.

Tear, write, fold.

I am grateful for you, I promise.

Tear, write, fold.

I want us to grow together.

Tear, write, fold.

I want us to change for the better.

I keep going until Caleb's bed is covered in at least two dozen paper airplanes. When I've finally poured out every thought and see the mess that I've left, I gently move my nicely folded clothes off my bed, tucking them at the end of my mat, place the flowers next to my water bottle between where we sleep, and lie down to read.

"SAR," I HEAR gently in my ear. "Sar-ah," someone sings out. "Baby—"

I blink awake, yawning as I do. "I fell asleep," I say, though it sounds more like *ahfeyelasweep*. Caleb's kneeling next to my mat, smiling down at me as he softly tugs a strand of hair away from my mouth. I feel it peel away like it had been stuck on my chin by drool.

"You were out cold," he says with a timid laugh. "I see you've had a big day . . ." He gestures to his bed with a thumb over his shoulder.

"You left me flowers," I say with another yawn, then shake myself. "That was really nice." I move to sit up, stretching out my neck—feeling stiff after a few nights' sleep without my beloved Tempur-Pedic mattress and memory-foam pillows.

"I see I got some flowers too." Caleb's smile is hesitant, but bright nonetheless—I think he's feeling the same sense of precariousness as I am. We both know this isn't a clean slate situation. We have to talk about what happened. But it is nice to see that we're both trying to lead with kindness.

"Do you like them?" I ask.

He grins, nodding. "Of course, and the planes too. Thank you, baby."

"I'm sorry for fighting," I say alongside a soft sigh.

"I'm sorry too," Caleb says, his head hanging in the space between us. "Really sorry. I hate that I made a scene in front of everyone."

"At first I was embarrassed because they were all looking," I admit, reaching to tilt his chin up to see me. I stroke his jaw with a bent finger before dropping my hand back to my lap. "But then, after you went to bed, I got a little bit high—" Caleb's face crumples into an amused look of confusion. "More on that later," I interject. "And I realized I was actually feeling relieved. You got angry with me for real. Of course, it didn't feel great in the moment but I'm glad that you expressed yourself instead of sitting with it alone. You trusted me to see your anger and not shield me from it." I pause, turning to sit cross-legged across from him as he moves to do the same, shuffling some planes off his mat to make room. "I know it might sound strange but I'm grateful. I'm glad you see me as capable of handling the good and the bad emotions. Because I *am*," I emphasize. "I'm capable of seeing you at your worst. At your angriest. At your lowest. At your meanest . . . and *still* loving you. What I want most is for you to stop taking care of me so much so I can finally start taking care of myself . . . and you kind of did that."

Caleb nods slowly, his nostrils flaring on a long sigh out through his nose.

"Sorry, that was a lot at once, huh?"

"Y-yeah, no, well, yes, but . . . Good," he stutters out.

"I'll give you a minute," I say with a bashful smile.

After a long beat, Caleb nods to himself as if he has internally processed it and is now prepared to speak. "I think sometimes I do want to protect your feelings instead of expressing mine. I'm definitely guilty of telling white lies just to avoid any sort of conflict. It's not that I don't trust that you can handle yourself—I just don't want to see you experience any more hardship than you already have." He nervously chews at his bottom lip, then drops his hands into his lap. "It's so strange because I see you as this confident, funny, smart, spontaneous, sexy, slightly intimidating woman and there's this part of me that thinks . . . 'How'd I get so lucky.' But then, I'm the only one who gets to see the softer, emotional, grieving, hurt person underneath . . . and I wonder who I'm supposed to be married to sometimes. And playing it safe means treating you like some wounded bird instead of the courageous, brave woman you are."

I blink, slightly stunned.

"A lot at once, right?"

I nod, that same wistful smile returning. "I'm ready to not be wounded anymore," I say. "Are you ready to let me have all of you? Good and bad? Safe and vulnerable? Do you trust me?"

"I am . . . I do," he responds, reaching for me. I take his hand in both of mine and begin stroking my thumbs along his palm, tracing the lines and scars and edges of him. "And . . ." His chest rises on a deep breath. "I'm sorry about the fundraiser. I get it now. Why you'd want it to succeed or fail all on your own. I get that I overstepped. I—"

"You were just following our pattern," I interrupt, my eyes not leaving his hand. "I know your intentions were good."

"But next time," he says quietly, "I won't intervene."

"Thank you," I say, a slight hitch to my voice. "I appreciate that . . . And I'm sorry for how I reacted."

"It was a difficult night for you," he says softly.

"Still . . ."

"I really don't like change," he admits, his hesitant gaze falling to the space between us.

"I know, love."

"I don't want to risk losing you." I trace the scar on his hand, thinking of all the hundreds of times I've done it before.

"You won't."

"Promise?"

I look up to find his eyes, searching for mine. "If you give me the space to grow, I'll plant myself next to you. Always."

"You've always been a lot better with words than I am . . ." His eyes shift to my journal, and the airplanes around him. "And that probably *won't* change. . . . But earlier this morning I woke up and couldn't get back to sleep. I wrote something and I want you to hear it. It feels a little vulnerable but . . ."

"If you're comfortable," I say, nodding. "But if it's just for you, that's okay too."

He removes his hand from mine, then reaches to pull his journal out of his pack. "I kind of wrote it like a letter. And, obviously, it was before we got the chance to talk." He clears his throat, opening the journal and holding it open in one hand as the other tightens and flexes across his knee. "Sarah," he reads. "I don't think I felt you slipping away until it was too late, so I gripped on too tightly, afraid to let you go. Then, after the fundraiser, it felt like you were halfway out the door and I didn't want to spook you so I kept my distance, trying to figure out how we could best move forward. I spend my days solving problems and compiling data and you feel like the one piece of my life I cannot solve. And, maybe, I should stop trying to. You're my wife, after all, not a mathematical equation or an algorithm. But just like you turn to prayer when you're most afraid—I turn to logic. To facts. To what I know to be true. Clearly, that's not doing me any favors. So, here's what I know to be true that logic cannot confirm . . ." He flips the page, then taps at the top left corner of the journal with his forefinger.

"I can feel you when I'm alone. I can sense your presence like a second nature and can anticipate your random visits to the office based on some sort of intuition or connection between us. And, when you're not near, you occupy every corner of my life. Half of my thoughts are about you. All of my dreams involve you. My hopes and fears and purpose revolve around you. I just want you to be at peace. That is all I have ever wanted from the first moment I saw you cry and had the privilege of being the arms you ran to. And, if your future peace means leaving, so be it. But don't think for a single second you could ever truly leave me. You can go as far as you need to, but you'll always be a part of me. You will always be the second voice in my head. The force that surrounds me. The source I pull inspiration from. I am sorry if it's too late. Sorry for myself that I'll have to go on as half of a whole. And I hope that if you have to rewrite your life, you won't erase my part in it, that you'll let me stay a part of your story." He looks up with tears in his eyes, "Always yours," he pauses awkwardly, "Caleb."

I dive at him, grasping onto the extra fabric of his shirt as I pull him to me. "Never," I promise as a sob wracks me. "I would *never* erase you from my life, Caleb." I lean back, tears falling off my chin as I desperately try to clear my eyes enough to look into his. "It's *our* new chapter, okay? For both of us. Together."

"Together," Caleb says like a vow. "Okay," he says, letting his forehead fall against my neck. "Thank god," he whispers, so quietly it's as if he didn't mean for me to hear it.

Neither of us moves for a long while. We stay tucked around each other, letting our breathing slow and hearts rest in each other's safekeeping. Then, Caleb leans back to wipe his nose and face with his sleeve. An embarrassed sort of laugh escapes him as he does, his sweet smile in stark contrast to his red-rimmed eyes.

"Helen gave us some homework to do."

"I just got a vivid flashback of you asking me to help you 'study.'" He throws up quotation marks over that last word.

"Well, we'll *actually* be doing the work this time and not groping each other between the school's library shelves."

"Less fun but understood. What sort of homework?"

"Well, more like *tent-work,* I guess," I say, rolling my eyes at my own stupid joke. "We have to write down where we want to be ten years from now. Like, metaphorically speaking. Then, later, we can chat through it with her."

"Okay," Caleb says decidedly, nodding. "But does this tent-work actually have to be done here or . . . ?"

I shrug. "No, I guess not. Why?"

"We passed a pretty cool spot earlier and I wanted to show it to you," he says, looking me up and down appreciatively. "Did you pack your bathing suit?"

I nod excitedly, eyeing him with eager suspicion.

"Perfect, change into it and meet me outside." Caleb makes his way outside the tent, practically diving at the door's zipper.

"You can stay here while I change, Cay . . ." I reach into the bottom of my pack for my swimsuit. "Nothing you haven't seen before," I tease.

Caleb raises a brow in my direction, then shakes his head as if I cluelessly misspoke. "You have no idea, do you?"

"What?" I half-say, half-scoff.

He drops his hand from the zipper's pull and places his forearm over his bent knee before he flexes his fingers. *God, I love his hands.* "I'm trying to be a good boy, Linwood."

"Linwood, huh? Been a long time since I got referred to by my last name. . . . And what does staying in here with me have to do with you being a good boy?"

"Because you changing clothes requires that you first get naked. And if you get naked, I'm going to forget the rules. And if I forget the rules we're not going to get our homework done. Thereby, proving the point of said rules in the first place . . ."

"You always were such a teacher's pet," I whisper, my cheeks heating as I reach for the hem of my shirt.

"Be *good*," he warns.

"Always am," I reply, my grin turning to a devilish smirk as I pull my shirt off over my head.

"Such a fucking tease," he says, hungry eyes on my bare tits as he wets his lips.

"Go on then," I say, shoo-ing him with one hand as I place the other arm across my chest, feigning modesty. "Go and be a *good* boy."

He groans, but does as told, leaving the tent and quickly closing the entrance behind him. Then, I hear him sigh, just outside the door—and realize immediately what he's forgotten.

"Need your bathing suit?" I call out.

"Heh, yeah . . ."

I smile to myself, rifling through his bag, then unzip just enough of the tent to present it to him.

"I'll be back after I change," he mumbles before he starts walking away. "I love being butt-ass naked in the woods." I hear him grumble some more just before his footfalls grow too far away to hear.

I smile to myself, gripping the bathing suit to my chest.

Hope, in my experience, is a dangerous feeling, but I'll choose to feel it anyways.

MOM HAS BEEN IN BED A LOT LATELY. WHICH MEANS I have been in Mom's bed a lot lately. We watch telenovelas as I paint her nails. We rest together. She reads to me as I brush her hair or fold her laundry. I fetch her medicine. I bring her food and fresh water. I avoid school on the days she's too tired to push me out the door.

Today, once I was done combing her hair, I wasn't ready for her to stop reading to me. Hoping she'd continue, I began braiding her a crown, starting from the center of her forehead and making my way around her head. My outstretched legs are acting as arm rests for her as she holds her tattered copy of *Life's Poems and Essays* and reads from it out loud.

"Ah, here . . . *This* is the one I wanted to read you," she says, flicking to the next page. I lean over her shoulder to read the title, "Fig Tree" by Sylvia Plath, an excerpt from her novel *The Bell Jar*.

When out of bed, Mom's breathing has become noticeably labored, robbing her of the booming, confident voice that she's always had. But while in bed resting, Mom's voice still commands the room with her steady and thoughtful narration.

She reads it to me, and I find my hands moving at their own accord as I focus on each of her tender words, feeling them burrow into my chest and make themselves at home. The author describes a tree, filled with delicious figs ready to be picked. "One fig was a husband and a happy home and children, and another fig was a famous poet and another fig was a brilliant professor . . ." The author goes on to describe each of the possible futures she could imagine for herself, how appealing they all are, but the fruit rots as she sits there, trying to make a choice and failing. "I wanted each and every one of them, but choosing one meant losing all the rest, and, as I sat there, unable to decide, the figs began to wrinkle and go black, and, one by one, they plopped to the ground."

Cheery book you got there, Mom.

"This meant a lot to me when I was your age . . ." she says, bringing her hand slowly to cover mine as I finish fastening her crown in place. I pause, my heart reaching for hers as it always does when I imagine her younger, full of potential that my unexpected arrival robbed from her. "I want you to understand that you can be *anything* but not *everything.* And, sometimes, you have to make a choice for yourself, right or wrong, before life makes it for you. I don't want you to let *anyone* tell you not to try just because you might fail. Failure is simply an opportunity for those who have time. And you will have *so* much time. Okay, baby?"

I loop my arms around her from behind, curling my face into the back of her neck, breathing in her familiar, comforting smell.

I know Mom means well. I also know, despite her not saying anything directly, she's noticed my grades slipping and my attitude about school growing more indifferent day by day. I've even heard her and Caleb whispering about missed classes and late assignments.

I don't understand how she, or my aunt, or Caleb, or any of my teachers could expect me to care about anything outside of this bedroom. What is the point of dreaming or imagining a future when that doesn't include my mom? I'd rather not think about that at all.

And as for my potential . . . I know now that Cecelia had the guts to tell me what no one else in my life would. I can't say all of this to Mom, however, without causing her more worry—and that's the last thing she needs. I have to be strong for her.

"Okay, Mom," I mumble against her.

FIFTEEN

SUNLIGHT SHINES THROUGH CALEB'S HAIR, CASTING him in a halo of golden light as we stare at each other in our own little bubble of intoxicating anticipation. We're about eight feet above the water's surface, standing on top of a large grouping of boulders. The crystal-clear waterhole is probably a good twenty feet wide, fed by a creek and pouring out in the opposite direction downhill. Surrounded by old pines and birch trees and flattened stone, it is a near-perfect oasis.

The only thing that would make it *truly* perfect is the guarantee that there are no fish in there wanting to nibble at our feet. Because I will absolutely lose my shit if that happens. Caleb did *not* provide me with any guarantees as to the lack of marine life below when prompted.

"We doing this, Linwood?"

I shriek nervously, laughing nearly hysterically as I look over the edge and take a few steps back.

Caleb's cocky grin spreads as his eyes dip down to the tie of my bikini string resting on my hip. "C'mon, gorgeous, are you in or out?"

"Ah, yes, okay! Fine!"

"One . . ." Caleb says as he bends into a running ready position. A boyish smile overtakes his face. "Two . . ." He turns to me expectantly, flashing his eyes right before . . . "Three!" We say it together.

Then, we both jump.

It's a thrilling millisecond before I hear Caleb's splash and then land myself. The water is colder than I was expecting, but my body has no choice but to adapt as I float up to the surface, smiling at the rush of it all.

"Woo!" Caleb shouts. I spin toward him, slicking my hair back. I watch as he shakes his head like a puppy, his hair sending droplets of water everywhere around him. "A bit nippy," he says in a god-awful British accent, attempting something similar to Jai's.

"Just a bit," I return, in the same accent. I flutter my legs under the water to stay afloat and watch as Caleb dips back under and attempts a handstand, despite the fact that the water is at least twelve feet deep. "I can't believe you found this spot," I say when his head pops back up above the surface. "Who knew the outdoors had so much to offer?"

"Don't tell Win about your newfound appreciation, she'll never let it go."

"Oh, never," I say, giggling just before he dives back into the water, as if he's attempting to retrieve something from below.

I swim over to where I suspect he'll surface. When he does, his back facing me, I press myself against him, feeling the warmth of his torso all over my chilled skin. "Hi," I say softly, wrapping my legs and arms around his shoulders and hips. He rotates within my hold, moving to bring us face-to-face.

"Hi, yourself," he says as he adjusts me, hoisting my thighs up to rest around his waist instead of his hips. He looks up at me with an innocent, dazed type of grin. It reminds me of the smile he had on the very first morning we woke up in the same bed when his parents were out of town. Some newness. Some hopefulness. Mostly, contentment.

I cannot help but smile at him in return, rubbing my thumb along the deepened lines next to his eyes before tucking a strand of his hair that had fallen against his temple. I admire the tanned skin across his forehead and the faded sunburn along the bridge of his nose that has revealed freckles underneath. I don't usually see those until late August, and their early appearance is a welcome surprise. Without his glasses on, his eyes appear larger. More vivid as they soften, silently looking up at me like I'm about to reveal the secrets of the universe to him.

It's been a long time since he has looked at me like that.

Or, maybe, since you've noticed, a kind part of my mind tells me.

I place my hand against his cheek, wondering, as it tickles against my palm, how his coarse facial hair would feel against the softest spots of my skin. In an instant, I'm flooded with desire. I long to feel it drag from one hip to the other as he presses kisses along my abdomen. I can't help but imagine how it would feel lower, too. Along the sensitive patch of skin where my thigh creases and meets the spot where I want him most. I know we have a lot of work we *should* be doing, but the only thing I'm remotely interested in right now is lying out naked on a rock like a lizard warming in the sun as Caleb devours me.

"Dangerous," Caleb says, a crooked smirk appearing as he takes hold of my thighs and tugs me up to his hips again, away from where his bathing suit was growing a little too tight.

"You're just keeping me afloat," I answer, wearing a mischievous smile. I tighten my thighs along his side to hold myself in place, in hopes of relieving some tension. Our intertwined bodies drift around the swimming hole until Caleb's back finds the rocky edge. He looks over his shoulder, notices the layers of sediment behind him, and rests an elbow on one of the stone platforms, using his purchase on the ledge as an anchor for us both. His biceps flexes as he adjusts his weight and I feel my lower belly coil in response. *God*, he looks good out here. So relaxed. So carefree. So sexy.

"Careful, baby," he coos.

"Hmm?" I *think* I say, looking at his collarbone where a pool of water has collected. Suddenly, I'm thirsty, and that is the *only* vessel I'm interested in drinking from.

"That look on your face," he says, nearly laughing. "You're looking at me like I'm your next meal."

I bite down on a grin. "D'ya want to be?"

"This was a bad idea," Caleb says as if he *just* realized he brought his wife to a remote, romantic spot far away from company when there's a no-sex-rule in place. He's always been a bit endearingly clueless—and it still charms me when I catch the moment he glances suggestively down my body, then checks that no one has decided to follow us out here. I watch the balancing scale in his conscience begin weighing the pros and cons, his eyes shifting side to side as if he's fighting a losing battle.

It's nice to be back in his head again. It's so much quieter there than in my own.

"We're alone," I say, pressing my chest harder against him. "And, when's the last time we fucked like this? Outside . . ." I whisper, tasting a droplet of water off his throat. "In the water . . ." I kiss that same spot. "It'll be fuuun," I elongate the word, dragging my teeth against him.

"The hot tub on Christmas Eve," he answers without missing a beat. "I thought I was going to pass out."

I roll my eyes, huffing a laugh. "Right, but . . . in a good way?" I ask.

"The rules," he says, turning toward his rested arm, as if he can't look at me, or the tits I've purposefully squished against his chest. "We shouldn't even be doing *this,*" he says, looking down at the minuscule amount of space left between us. "This feels like sex."

It's an oddly sweet sentiment that wrapped up in each other still somewhat clothed, could feel like sex to him after all this time and *all* the ways we've experienced each other's bodies. "It isn't, though," I say coyly as I bring one hand from his shoulder, up his neck, to the base of his hair. I thread my fingers through it, digging into his scalp with my nails in a circular motion until his eyes roll back into his head. "But it could be . . ."

"You're playing dirty." His voice is gruff as he relaxes into my hold.

"What about this . . . ," I say softly, leaning in to whisper just to see the goosebumps appear across his neck. "We fuck *really* quick and then do our homework. Just like old times."

Caleb's nostrils flare as he opens his eyes on me, an unmistakable look of guilty wanting in his eye. "As you *probably* recall," he says, turning us so *my* ass hits the rock, pinning me there with his hips and *hello,* his rock-hard dick. "I always made you finish your homework first. And . . ." He leans in until his beard grazes my neck, and a small moan escapes my lips. "It's been a *very* long time since I fucked you quickly, baby. I'm grown now. And a grown man knows how to take his time."

"I'd be willing to settle for a nice, long fuck," I tease. "If that's what you'd prefer."

"We make our list first," he says, as he tilts his hips against me *exactly* where I want him. "Then, if you're *good,* we'll take care of it." He groans, feeling the way my thighs tense around him as I use the heels of my feet to bring him closer toward me. We're playing tug-of-war with who's in charge here, and I plan on winning.

"Take care of *what*?" I ask, feigning confusion.

"Baby," he says, his tongue pushing against his cheek and eyes drifting shut as if he's about to lose control.

"I'm listening," I say, rubbing against his hardness where I need him most. It feels *good,* but not good enough. I arch my back, exposing my tits to the cool air above the surface. My nipples harden against the flimsy material of my bathing suit top, and as I tilt my head to proudly watch Caleb's resolve slip away, his face only hardens. He glares at my breasts as if he's offended by them, the muscle in his chin flexing.

Some men are boob guys, and some are ass guys. Then there are men like Caleb, who are whatever-is-closest-to-my-face guys. Even still, two firm hands find my knees and pry them apart. "No, no, nope, nuh-uh . . ." His voice's pitch starts low and ends high. Caleb backstrokes away, leaving me alone and wanting.

"Seriously?!" I call out after him, shaking my head as my smile grows.

"C'mon, trouble," he says, before turning onto his stomach to swim a breaststroke toward shore.

I wish he was stroking my breast, but whatever.

And despite my wounded pride, I'm actually a little impressed at his newfound level of self-control. In high school I could get him to break with just a bite of my pouted bottom lip. It weirdly turns me on more to have to work for it. "But later?" I ask, embarrassingly aware that I just held up a white flag in our little back-and-forth.

I watch the muscles in his back flex as he lifts himself onto the edge. It feels like a taunt. A cruel, muscular taunt. He turns and sits, his legs spread wide, as his feet rest below the water—the picture of collected confidence.

"What has gotten into you?" I ask, beginning to slowly make my way to shore.

He smiles back at me like a warning. A red flashing sign that says he's got *plans* for me. I feel the look settle between my legs and tighten my throat, forcing me to swallow. "Maybe," he says with a throwaway shrug, "I'm not as easily influenced to break the rules as I once was. Maybe you will have to beg for it."

I lift a brow in challenge toward him before I start to swim. He's got another thing coming if he thinks *I'm* going to be the one begging.

I'll have him on his knees soon enough.

MY BOTTOM HALF is wrapped in my towel and my top half is covered by Caleb's zip-up sweater that he forced me to put on after my attempt to sway him by going topless failed. He put *his* shirt back on after I claimed his naked torso was equally distracting and creating unproductive working conditions. He's lounging on top of his towel with his legs out in front of him with the journal on his lap as I sit cross-legged facing him.

We agreed to sit in quiet contemplation for a little while, only breaking the silence to point out a flock of birds in a perfect triangular formation and a cloud drifting overhead that looked *distinctly* like an old man holding a smoking pipe.

Caleb writes *Ten years from now* at the top of the page, then looks at me expectantly. There's a hint of fear in his expression that most people wouldn't be able to pick up on unless they knew him as well as I did. Which, I'd like to think, no one does.

"Together," I say, and he writes down *still very much married* next to a bullet point.

"Same house?" he asks.

I nod, shrugging at the same time. I wouldn't want to move away from Win, Bo, and August. I also like that we're not *too* far from Caleb's office. His commute is short but it's just far enough that he's not running into the office in every spare moment.

"I was actually thinking that we should get something smaller," Caleb says. "There are too many rooms at our place. Too many places to hide from each other."

I conceal a shy smile instinctively but force my hand into my lap and let him see it. "Okay, yeah. But I'd want to stay in the same neighborhood. I'd hate to be farther from Gus."

"She'll be eleven in ten years, almost twelve," Caleb says, tapping his pencil against the page. We both shudder at the thought of our sweet baby niece being so much older.

"So, she'll *definitely* need a second home nearby," I add, laughing halfheartedly. "She lucked out in the parents' department, sure, but no eleven-year-old likes their parents *all* of the time."

Caleb writes *smaller house, same neighborhood* on one line, and then, *be present for Gus and any future nieces or nephews* underneath.

I like that he gave them their own line almost as much as I like the idea of us downsizing to be in closer quarters. We sit in silence for a few more moments as I imagine all the different avenues I could take, if I would just start walking one. I think of the passage Mom read me so long ago, with the fig tree and the limitless choices. What Mom said afterward, about letting myself fail. The words closer and finally louder than those from a woman who'd not known me at all, spoken across a café's table. I think about what Win said, her hopes for me. Mom's hopes. I think about those two versions of me that Yvonne and I had discussed, and how to satisfy them both.

"I want to go to school . . . I know that I may not ever be *the best* or even halfway good enough but . . . I still want to try. I want to be a writer."

The corner of Caleb's lip tips upward as he swallows, as if he's holding himself back from reacting more. "Yeah?" His voice is so filled with hope, it spurs me on.

"I think so . . ." I say shyly. "I've been thinking a lot about it. About what I wanted before . . ." *Before Mom got sick. Before the Cecelia incident. Before life started making decisions for me.*

"I miss writing . . . I miss that version of me. I think it's worth trying, even if I fail."

"That's great," he says, writing down *Sarah wants to write again.* "That's so, so great, baby."

"What about you, wonder boy?" I ask, smiling back at him. "Any big plans of your own?"

"Actually . . . yeah." He moves the journal into the space between us and sits up straighter. "I've been thinking a lot about the company and, well, when I thought about ten years from now I started thinking about what my dad always says . . . about leaving a legacy."

Yikes. Legacy, in Cyrus's dictionary, is code for exorbitant, generational wealth. Hoarding, in other words. I tell myself to keep my expression neutral. To let Caleb finish before pushing back. But are we really that unaligned? I thought, if anything, being away from work would—

"I'd like to set up a charity fund that funnels out of Focal's profits," he says confidently. "Also, I was chatting with Henry the other day about their business structure, and it inspired me to make some changes. They profit-share among their staff, so everyone earns about the same from new hires all the way up to owners. It would have to be scaled differently at Focal, given that we're a team of over fifty, but I think we'd be able to get close to that within ten years' time if not a hell of a lot sooner."

I blink at him silently, processing. I don't think I've ever been more in love. "Your dad would lose his ever-loving mind if he found that out. You know that, right?" I ask, my pride blatant. "When you said legacy I thought—"

"How else would I know that I'm doing something right?" he asks, his tone lighthearted but his expression anything but. Caleb, despite years' worth of reasons to, rarely says *anything* remotely negative about his father or his business practices.

"That's a pretty loaded statement," I say, approaching the subject as gently as I can. "Want to walk me through it?"

Caleb nods, blowing out a long breath. "I've spent so long trying to impress a man I don't want to be like . . ." His head tilts slightly as his eyes lock on something in the distance. "Being away from work for a few days—being unreachable—has made me recognize how much time I spend caring about shit that just *does not matter.*" He says the last few words as if they exhaust him. "I don't want to look back on my life some day and realize that I prioritized money over people. Or . . ." He sighs.

"Or?" I ask, after a long, lingering silence.

"Do you remember when my dad missed our graduation?" he asks abruptly.

"Of course," I answer.

"Well, when my mom told him I was upset, he didn't call . . . or text . . . or even email. He just gave me a thousand dollars without so much as a memo on the check."

I wince, not having heard that part of the story before. "I'm sorry, Cay."

"But . . ." he says, his voice somewhat distant. "Your mom and Aunt June were there. Aunt June switched her shift at work and your mom fought through her pain to climb up the stairs to the auditorium. They brought me flowers like yours and Win's as if I was theirs too. They cheered when I crossed the stage and applauded louder than anyone else when I finished my valedictorian speech."

I smile, remembering it fondly. "They were *so* proud of you," I say. "I'm pretty sure my mom told everyone within earshot she helped you write your speech."

Caleb turns to face me, wearing a weary smile. "That meant a lot more than a thousand dollars." I almost say *Of course it did,* but I stop myself. I'm in no position to point out a late-blooming realization. . . . We're both here to learn.

"But even knowing that, it never made me think twice about throwing money at a problem. Just like my father." He stares at me with an unspoken apology. "At the fundraiser . . . I knew, deep down, that it wouldn't make you feel better, but I did it anyway because—because I wasn't prioritizing you or *your* needs. On some level I thought that I could quietly solve the issue. . . . I thought that would make you move past it. I justified it, just like he did."

It's a confirmation of my feelings, but it stings all the same. I look at the boulder's surface between us as I hear him inhale a shaky breath. "I hate that I did that, Sar," he says slowly. When I look up, his expression is disgruntled as if he's disgusted with himself. "I *never* wanted to be that guy. Where work takes priority. Where money is the answer. Where people and their feelings are easily paid off. I *do* not want to be that guy and I am so, so sorry."

"You're not that guy," I say simply. "You acted out of character, yes, but . . . that's not you."

"Not anymore," he vows. "Where *I* want to be ten years from now is content. Not striving for more. Not trying to fill a bank account in an endless cycle. Not prioritizing anything above you or our life together. I want to restructure the business, downsize our life, and help you figure out what you can do with that brilliant, generous, kind, sharp mind of yours. The legacy I want is that I was the type of guy who would show up for people, cheer people on. The guy who was . . . present."

I stare at him, my lips parted, and the breath stolen from my lungs. *These* are the words I have wanted so badly to hear. *This* is why we came here. Finally, finally, *finally,* we're on the same page.

"And," he says decidedly, followed by a deep breath, "I want a dog. Something not too active and that doesn't shed much but . . . yeah, I want a dog."

I laugh, partially in disbelief but mostly amazement. "Okay," I say in a breathy voice, "write it all down."

And so, he does.

WE'RE SITTING IN THE PARKING LOT OF THE FANCY French restaurant that Caleb had booked for our anniversary dinner, missing our reservation. I borrowed one of Aunt June's more subtle dresses and took the time to do my hair and makeup, which I haven't in some time, and Caleb's in his suit that I haven't seen since our high school graduation. We look good. Too good to be crying and missing the appetizer portion of our rigidly scheduled, already paid for, five-course dining experience.

But that's what happens when you get a call from your mom relaying the words from her doctor on the way here. Those six awful, terrible, no-good words. *We've done all that we can.*

"Fuck, I'm sorry," I say, sniffling. "I really wanted tonight to be nice."

Caleb lifts his glasses off with one hand as he uses the sleeve of his jacket to wipe his eyes. "What do you mean? This isn't nice? I'm having a great time," he jokes halfheartedly.

I knew Mom wasn't getting better, I see it every day. She's frustrated by the growing weakness in her limbs that keeps her in her chair or bed. There's nothing worse, she says, than the combination of exhaustion and restlessness. She jokes with her physical therapist that the only thing getting stronger are her prescriptions. Still, when we're alone, she asks me to pray with her. I don't believe in miracles, and I can see her struggling with my own eyes, but I didn't think we'd be approaching there's-nothing-left-to-do territory just yet. I thought we'd have more time.

"Let's forget dinner," Caleb says at the exact same time I say, "We should go in." His kindness only brings on more tears, proving that he probably presented the better option. Seconds later he's out of his seat. I watch as he walks around the front of his car and then opens my door. He awkwardly maneuvers himself in next to me, lifts me across his lap, and then shuts the door behind him as I curl my face into the space where his shoulder meets his neck. He holds me like I'm a treasured, precious, delicate thing, drifting his hands up and down my back in slow comfort.

Eventually, when I've stopped crying, I sit up and begin playing with the collar of his crisp white dress shirt as a mindless distraction. "Sarah." Caleb says my name softly, wiping a rogue tear from my cheek with his thumb. "Can I ask you something?"

"Mm-hmm," I say, my voice low and far off.

"I had planned to do this inside," he says, tucking a strand of hair away from my face after threading it between his fingers. "But I don't want to wait anymore." I look down as Caleb reaches into his glove compartment and pulls out a small blue box. "I want you to know, that no matter what, you will *never* be alone. That you will always have me. Sarah Abilene Green, will you marry me?"

He opens the ring box, and my ears fill with water. Or, my lungs. Or, the entire car? Inside is a white gold, solitaire ring with a square-cut diamond in the center that probably cost more than his tuition. "W-what?" I stutter. "Caleb," I laugh nervously, "are you proposing?"

He nods eagerly, his tight-lipped smile thin as he swallows. "I sure hope so."

"But we're eighteen . . ."

"Just for a few more months," he counters, his typical crooked smirk in place.

"You just started school and there's no way your parents are okay with— How did you even afford this?"

"I don't need my parents' permission to marry the love of my life." He says it so defiantly, in total contrast to his normal perfect son routine, that it admittedly turns me on a little. "And, I saved half and borrowed the rest from Opa. I'm going to pay him back."

"I'm the only girl you've ever dated," I say, giving him one last reason. "And I'm not easy." *Okay, two.*

"I don't want easy. I don't want *anyone* else. I want you, Sar. I want to be the only man lucky enough to be loved by you."

"Caleb, I—" I cannot help but smile, and when I do, he does too, joy in his features besides the remnants of the heartache we're both still feeling. I cannot help but wonder if he's asking me because of today's news and, if that's the case, I can't say yes. "When did you get the ring?"

"Six months ago . . . and I've been waiting for the right time since. It's been in the glove box for a while."

"You're so lucky your car didn't get broken into . . ." I pause, studying his handsome face as my features are overtaken by joyful bewilderment. "Are you *absolutely* sure?"

He playfully rolls his eyes, his confidence growing as he senses my nearing resolve. "Yes, baby. It doesn't matter if it's tomorrow, five, ten, or twenty years from now—you're going to be my wife. So why *not* do it now?" His smile fades as his eyes well with tears.

He sighs, like every part of him needs relaxing. "It wouldn't be right for Marcie to not be there." He chews at his lip, staring off briefly. "Don't you think?"

"Yes," I say, answering both questions at once, smiling.

He grins but tilts his head curiously, like a puppy, waiting to be sure. "Was that?"

"Yes, Caleb, I will marry you."

His grin blooms as he dives at me, kissing me senseless until I manage to break free, giggling and begging for him to put the ring on my finger. After he does, I use that hand to hold his cheek, and we do nothing but smile like total idiots at each other.

I didn't know I could feel so many opposing emotions at once, but I do. Gratitude melds with bitterness. Fear and joy. Excitement and despair. They are all floating around in this old car, contrasting and overwhelming just the same.

No matter what the future brings . . . Caleb will be there.

There's hope in that.

And I need some hope.

SIXTEEN

THE AFTERNOON FADES AWAY AS WE WRITE DOWN EVERY thought that comes to mind for what we'd like the next stage of our married life to look like. Items on the list vary from quite serious—we want to find a therapist back home for monthly, if not more frequent, sessions as a couple and individually as well—to somewhat silly. For example, Caleb wants to find his signature uniform à la Steve Jobs's black turtleneck, whereas *I* want to burn every turtleneck that could ever potentially enter our home.

Overall, it's good.

It's *so* good.

It's more than good. It's great.

Great to be on the same page. Great to laugh together. Great to romanticize a quiet, less busy, more present life. Great to imagine a future that prioritizes connection over profit and communication over avoiding conflict. Great to be together without distraction.

It's a type of comfort that serves as a relief *and* a reminder. We're going to be okay, and we have been before.

"God . . . I love you," Caleb says, his voice breathy as he winds down from a fit of laughter, reacting to my ridiculous suggestions for names we could give our dog.

I feel myself blush from his confession, which is *so* asinine. But I cover my smile all the same. "I love you too," I say, rolling my eyes. "Are we going to be this lovey-dovey from now on? It's freaking me out."

"You like it," Caleb says, a crooked grin in full, destabilizing force. "And I like you."

"I like you too," I say in my best teenager tone as I smile brightly at him. A bird above us sings out, and with a quick glance to the sky I realize we've been away from camp for at least a few hours now and the afternoon sun has cooled to a pink and golden evening sky. "Should we be getting back?"

"Do we have to?" Caleb asks, his smile fading slightly.

"The bugs will be awful soon."

"Ah, yes. They attack at dusk," Caleb concludes dramatically. "But what about your reward?" He waggles his eyebrows suggestively, the same way I frequently do. *Dork.*

I fight the smile as he plays *right* into my hands. "Oh, that, right. Nah. Moment's passed." I make my way to stand, then shake off the debris that has stuck to my towel with a flourish. "You were right, rules are there for a reason. I mean, just *look* at how productive we were," I say sweetly.

Caleb eyes me suspiciously. "Glad we're on the same page then." He nods, then stands as well—crossing his arms and squaring his body off with mine as he stands on top of his towel. "Okay, trouble," he says, with a devious smile. "Let's get you back to camp."

"Don't even *think* about holding my hand on the walk back, Linwood . . . We all know handholding is a gateway aphrodisiac."

"Wouldn't dream of it," he quips back, picking up his towel.

"If I trip, don't help me up. Even if I'm hanging off a cliff, don't offer your hand."

"Of course not," he says, brows furrowed as he folds his towel over his arm. "I wouldn't dare."

"Good," I say, shrugging one shoulder as I finish bunching up my towel and toss it over my shoulder.

"After you." He holds out a hand toward the path. "Lead the way."

"Don't think for a second that I don't know letting me walk in front is simply a ploy to look at my ass," I say, walking ahead with a purposeful sultry sway.

"I plan on switching between your hips and your ass."

I make a point to hike up my bikini bottoms before I bend over to pick up my discarded clothes. I'd eagerly ditched my T-shirt and shorts as soon as the water came into view from the path earlier . . . but I don't think I'll put them back on just yet. I will, however, take my sweet time bent over to retrieve and fold them nicely.

"Cruel woman," my husband grumbles from behind me. I don't even know what game we're playing at this point, or which team I'm on, but I do know that it's fun either way.

We make it up the rocky, steep path that leads down to the water and onto more even ground.

"Left; right," Caleb half speaks, half sighs torturedly, keeping time with the sway of my hips. "Left; right," he repeats a few more times until I laugh. "So; hot," he says in rhythm. "Kill; me."

I turn around to wink at him, but in doing so I miss my next step and trip over a rock, falling ungracefully to the dirt with a groan and a stinged hiss.

"Shit," Caleb says, appearing at my side.

I roll onto my back, my ass cheeks punctured by the gravel below. When I open my eyes, he's looking down at me, trying not to look *too* pleased. "I fell," I explain, in case he missed it.

"Oh?" he asks, scanning me head to toe, then focusing on my knee—which I can already tell is pretty banged up without having looked yet. "I thought you were taking an oddly located rest."

"Is it bleeding?" I ask.

"Yeah, a little," he answers, locking eyes with mine as he scratches the top of his head. "Don't look, okay?"

Caleb knows that I *hate* the sight of blood. Mine or anyone else's. Win had a nosebleed in the summer between eighth and ninth grade and she *still* holds it over my head that I nearly passed out at the sight of her. Apparently, she'd never seen a human turn green with nausea before then. She had a red snot bubble for fuck's sake . . . whose stomach wouldn't turn at that? No, I can't think of it right now. I *refuse* to throw up. I will *not* let these woods get every possible bodily fluid from me.

"All right," Caleb says, ripping off his T-shirt. "Give me a second."

"That's very sweet, love, but I don't think a striptease is exactly what I need right now," I say, consciously trying to avoid looking down. He levels me with an amused but stern stare before he bends to one knee in front of me. I turn my face up toward the sky to avoid seeing what he's doing with my leg as he twists it to and fro in his hands.

"It's not that bad, I promise," he says, lifting my thigh with a grip and placing my ankle across his bent knee.

"What if a bear smells the blood and hunts us down?" I say. "You should save yourself."

"I believe you're thinking of sharks, not bears. Neither of which are on this trail."

"Everyone keeps saying that there are no bears here but that just doesn't make any fucking sense to me. How could we possibly know where all the bears are?" I ask, throwing my arms out to the side as if I'm going to attempt a snow angel. "They're wild animals, for fuck's sake! They can be anywhere they damn well please and I'm pretty sure they don't have to register their location." I feel the soft cotton of Caleb's shirt against the back of my thigh and then he ties it, like a giant Band-Aid, across my knee. "Well, Doc?"

"I don't know how they track bears; I've not really thought about it that much."

"Not the bears, the leg. Is it okay?"

"Oh . . . yeah, all good to go. Can I offer you help to stand or were you serious before about not touching even if you eat shit?"

"I didn't eat shit," I say, holding out my hand for him to take hold. He pulls me to stand, and I try to put weight on my knee before a quick sting of pain runs through me. "And, I was *obviously* joking," I say, leaning on him as I squint my eyes toward the direction of camp. "How far is it?" I ask. "Ten minutes?"

"About that."

"All right . . ." I say, wiping dirt off the back of my legs and butt. "I'll hobble." I nod at him like a soldier taking orders.

He rolls his eyes in response, immediately bending down to quite literally sweep me off my feet.

I'm woman enough to admit that the noise that came out of my mouth in response was deeply embarrassing, entirely involuntary, and downright orgasmic. I'd be mortified if I wasn't only able to focus on the warmth and firmness of his grip on the backs of my thighs instead.

Caleb raises a brow at me, tucking me against his chest as if I am an overgrown baby. "What was *that*?" he asks in a disturbed, yet comical tone. "Did you just . . . fawn? Isn't that how they describe it in your books? Or wait, no, it's—"

"Swoon," I answer curtly before pushing my lips together, afraid of what other sounds could escape past them. "I swooned," I add excitedly, then shut my mouth tight before another giggle has the chance to fall out. *It's not my fault, dammit!* There is a shirtless, hairy lumberjack carrying me through the woods who *distinctly* resembles my husband. It's like seven of my favorite horny book scenes all rolled into one. I am wetter than the bottom of a canoe right now.

Caleb lifts his chin, his lips curled into an upside-down smile. If I could translate the look I'd say it is something along the lines of: *I've still got it.*

And yes, he most certainly does.

"You okay?" he asks, his voice a touch too strained for my liking as he adjusts his hold. I am *not* light as a feather by any means but show me a lady who wants to hear her man *groan* when he lifts her, and I will show you a liar.

I nod slowly, my dopey smile spreading wider across my face as I choose to ignore the sounds of him hauling me like a yoked mule. "Loving the view," I say.

"Well, that's good. I did mean your knee, though."

"Right, no, that hurts like hell." Honestly, it's not that bad . . . But I'd have to be an idiot to shut this down and my mother didn't raise a fool. I hope.

"All right," Caleb mumbles, turning sideways as he guides us through a narrow passage between trees. He turns a little bit too early after passing through and, in doing so, my head whacks the side of a bush. "Shit, sorry . . ."

"It's fine, I needed a reason to brush my hair," I say, laughing softly. "Would it be better if we did a piggyback sort of situation?"

I ask a few minutes later when I barely avoid getting sideswept by a low-hanging branch. "This is romantic and all, but I *would* like to keep my face intact."

"We're almost there," he says, hoisting me up as we get onto the main trail.

"Hello, hello," Jai's familiar voice echoes from somewhere nearby. Caleb swings me around like a rag doll in his arms turning to find Jai. I always suspected that one of his bromances could cause my untimely death. But I had thought it would be Bo at the helm. "Oh, shit. What happened?"

"I fell," I say, pouting dramatically. "Where's Nina?" I ask. I haven't seen that beautiful critter since last night and I miss her.

"Ah, she's"—Jai waves a hand over his shoulder—"around here somewhere. . . ."

I turn my head toward Caleb's chest. "Suspicious," I whisper.

"She's probably using the bathroom and he's being polite," Caleb says quietly.

"There was a bathroom this whole time?" I ask sarcastically.

"You know what I meant," Caleb fires back.

"Say it," I grin mischievously. "Nina's shitting in the woods."

"You're so fucking weird," he says, though I notice he still smiles as he shakes his head.

"You know it's off-putting when you two start whispering between yourselves," Jai says in his usual, booming voice.

"Sorry," we respond in near-perfect unison as we turn back toward him.

"All right, well . . . I'll catch you later, ya?"

"Where're you headed?" Caleb asks.

"There's a bit of water down that way and . . ." Jai's face scrunches to the side. "We're gonna swim, I guess . . . I don't know." Jai licks his lips, swaying side to side, as a grin overtakes his features.

"They're going to fuck at our swimming spot!" I gasp. "No! We were supposed to do that first!"

"I didn't stop you," Jai says defensively, laughing. "Gravity maybe did," he says, pointing to my knee. "But not me."

"No, he did," I point up to Caleb flippantly. "He turned me down."

"*He* would like to remind you that *he* is carrying you right now," Caleb mutters under his breath.

"Cay, bruv, that's cold."

"Has no one here heard of building anticipation?" Caleb asks, his voice pitching up. "The rules are in place for a reason!"

I stop myself from laughing at Caleb's *hint* of a meltdown by biting down on my lips. Jai looks at him dumbfounded, if a little amused. "A'ight, well . . . I'm going to go 'build anticipation' that way with my missus and, er, you two have fun playing doctor, okay?"

"Have fun!" I shout over Caleb's shoulder toward Jai. "It would be wrong to go watch them, right?"

"Yes," Caleb says exasperatedly. "And I am *not* carrying you back there regardless."

"He called her his missus, that's cute."

"I think it's a British thing."

"So? Still cute," I say.

"Okay, missus."

"Hmm, you're right . . . It's definitely a British thing."

Caleb scoffs, but nothing seems to be wiping that smile off his face. *Good,* I think. Let's keep it there forever. "Hey," I say softly as we reach the clearing before camp. I watch the trees gently sway above his head as the sunlight once again casts him in a golden light. "Thank you. I love you."

He stops, lowering me to stand on one leg with his arm firmly wrapped around my back, supporting my weight. He pulls me to his chest and tucks my hair back behind my shoulder then places his hand on the side of my neck, his thumb just under where my jaw meets my ear. "I love you too."

God, I feel fifteen years old again. In more ways than one. In the giddy, excited, new beginning ways but also the begging-the-cute-guy-to-touch-me way that we'd had going on back then. "I'm just teasing about the rules, you know that, right?" I ask. "If you want to wait or—"

The words die on my lips as Caleb's mouth finds mine in a kiss. His lips move feverishly against mine as he drags his hand up to my cheek, holding forcefully with his thumb on my cheekbone. He molds my face in his grasp, making me open my lips in tandem with the slide of his tongue against mine. I *love* it—being manipulated to let him in so he can steal my breath. His hand on my lower back tightens, not letting me fall as I balance on one leg, even though *everything* feels like it's spinning with this heady, dizzying lust.

Then, he ends the kiss as shockingly abruptly as he started it.

"Understood?" he says, straightening to his full height so I can no longer reach his mouth. And it's cruel, how I can't strain to reach him or climb him like a tree right now.

"Yes, *daddy*."

His brow quirks, but he attempts to hide any sort of further reaction under a stern expression. "We have the *rest* of our lives to fuck each other's brains out. I'm here to get your heart back first." He lays his palm over my chest, right above my rapidly beating organ. "I know that your body is *always* mine but *this,* this is what I want most."

It happens again. The humiliating, stupid, uncontrollable giggle of a woman clearly coming unglued. I cannot help it. I don't even fight it this time. Because *what the fuck?!* Who is this bodice-ripper and what has he done with my soft-spoken, gentle, nerdy-ass husband?

"You're insane if you think you've ever lost it," I say, placing my hand over his. "All of me is and will *always* be yours."

His smile unfurls slowly as his eyes linger on our hands. "Me too," he says, his voice slightly choked.

I smile back at him, a warmth in our newfound understanding. A piece of comfort sliding back between us. The quietest reunion there has maybe ever been. I unbend my knee and put some weight on my right leg. It hurts, but not more than that first morning after day one's hike. "Huh," I say, looking down. "Would you look at that?" I fight back a grin. "All better."

Caleb's laugh tilts his face up to the sky, his smile the biggest I've ever seen.

"MY HANDS ARE FULL," CALEB SAYS AS WE REACH THE front door, holding up the bottle of wine and flowers he's bringing to his parents. He called them *softening-up* gifts. When we are let inside, Caleb's dad is on a call and Chellie invites us to sit with her in the *lounge*.

We do not lounge. We sit straight and rigid, Caleb's hand covering my left hand from his mom's view until the time is right.

When Cyrus graces us with his presence, I stay perfectly quiet while Caleb begins giving context for the news we're about to share. Justifications about the timing, my mother's illness, financial and taxation benefits. Hell, he even throws some vaguely conservative and/or religious reasoning behind it about it being the *proper* thing to do.

So, so romantic.

Then, after what feels like a business proposition and less of a love confession, Caleb holds up my newly adorned left hand.

His parents both go wide-eyed and nod, plastered polite smiles falling rapidly into place. Cyrus is the first to speak, as he usually is. He pointedly congratulates me, and not his own son. As if I'd outsmarted him—tricked him. As if *this* life—his parents' life—would ever be what I wanted.

We sit through an awkward lunch while Chellie imagines a wedding that I could never afford, and his dad asks who will walk me down the aisle two times before I have to excuse myself to go cool off in their wall-to-wall Italian-marble powder room.

I can see it in both of their faces. Cyrus and Chellie both want to scream at the top of their lungs: *You do not belong here.*

I want to yell back: *I know, I told him that too. Too fucking bad.* He chose me.

SEVENTEEN

"OH, HI," I SAY SWEETLY TO NINA AS I CONTINUE STIR-ring my pot of noodles over our small camping stove. "Welcome back . . ."

She giggles as she drops next to me, wearing Jai's oversized hoodie and bike shorts. "Hey," she says, leaning into my side. "Oooh, that smells good."

"Want some?" I offer. "Caleb ate half of Kieran and Henry's dinner before they went off to collect firewood."

"Yes, please!" She rolls her shoulders back as she points her face toward the sky, grinning ear to ear.

"You seem happy," I say, prodding gently. "Good day?"

"Very." She bites her lip and flashes her eyes at me in that I-got-dicked-down way that every woman could immediately clock. "What about you?" She turns toward me. "Wait, weren't you hurt earlier? Jai said—"

"I may have been a little dramatic," I say, lifting my pants to show her the two Hello Kitty Band-Aids that Helen deemed most appropriate for my wound when choosing from her medical kit. "I did get a free ride back to camp out of it though." I cannot help but smile, thinking of my hot mountain-man escort.

Nina laughs, waving at Libby as she turns away from her tent and looks around for her grandmothers, presumably.

"I think they're resting," I tell her, jutting my chin toward Helen and Yvonne's tent. "You're welcome to join us, though. Are you hungry? I've got noodles," I singsong.

Surprisingly, she walks over and plops herself next to me. "No . . . Thanks."

I glance toward Nina, and we share a brief giddy smile, having finally gotten Libby to come out of her shell even a little bit.

"So, what sort of things are you into?" I ask as I turn off the burner and hand Nina a fork from our cooking bag. "It's hot," I warn, seeing her immediately scoop up the ramen noodles. "Books? Movies? British history between the years 1509 and 1547?"

Libby laughs, shaking her head a teensy bit with a perplexed expression. "What?"

"The reign of Henry the eighth, of course," Nina answers, slurping back noodles that *must* be burning her mouth. *I knew I liked her.*

"Is that the king who had a bunch of wives?"

I nod enthusiastically. "Yes, ma'am."

"My dance group did a performance to one of the songs about him, from the musical."

"I auditioned for Anne Boleyn," Nina says.

"Really?" Both Libby and I ask at the same time.

"Yeah, not for the musical though. It was a live reenactment gig. I was studying in London at the time," she explains. "I didn't get it."

I scoff. "Their loss."

"I think maybe my accent wasn't convincing . . ." She drops the fork into the pot and then shuffles over on her hands and knees in

front of us. She then reaches up to clutch her neck, forcing a dramatically anguished expression. "No! Please! Don't kill me! I
have such a beautiful neck!" she says before mimicking her head
being cut off and falling to the ground.

Libby giggles uncertainly but when Nina twitches her body on
the ground, making all sorts of weird gushing and squelching
sounds, Libby's timid giggle transforms into a full-blown belly
laugh.

It's not that I think we should be talking about beheadings
with a ten-year-old—and boy, did we somehow find ourselves on
this topic quickly—but I laugh too. Especially when Nina sits up,
crooks one eye open, and then throws herself back to the ground
for more.

"You guys are weird," Libby says as she reaches into my cooking bag and removes another fork, apparently having changed
her mind about the food.

"Hey, what did I do?" I say, holding the pot's handle still as she
twirls some noodles around her fork.

"Why, thank you!" Nina says, sitting up and getting back into
place around our communal pot. "My nana used to say that
weirder people live longer."

"So, if not specific eras of British history, what *are* you into?" I ask.

"Dance," Libby says between mouthfuls. "I'm going out for
dance captain this year."

"Seriously? You should show us," I say enthusiastically, taking
the fork from Nina. "After we eat though because this shiii—stuff
is good."

"Smooth save," Nina says mockingly.

"FIVE, SIX, SEVEN, eight!" Libby says while clapping her hands
in time, leading us into the beginning of our performance.

Nina and I have spent the last few hours learning one of Libby's dance routines from her upcoming recital. Nina has natural talent. I, however, am mostly contributing enthusiasm to the group. But Libby requested we gather everyone at the campfire to watch, and dammit if I'm not going to help put on one hell of a show if she wishes me to. Without music it's certainly hard to keep time but Libby whispers the counts under her breath as we go.

And we're fucking nailing it.

Well, the two of them are.

I'm at least half a step behind, watching Caleb's smirk from across the fire that blooms into a megawatt smile as he watches my uncoordinated limbs dart out in all directions. I know we're nearing the end when we start the twirling portion. And it's one of those moments in life where time seems to slow. I'm spinning by a campfire, under a gorgeous sky of stars, feeling young and carefree and weightless. I tilt my head back and revel in the bittersweet remaining seconds, knowing it's almost over. When we hit our final pose, arms outstretched to the sky, chests heaving, and minds dizzy, the camp erupts with a boisterous standing ovation.

We bow together, then Nina and I step back to applaud Libby as she curtsies like the leading lady she so *obviously* was born to be.

"Brava!" Jai shouts.

Caleb puts two fingers into his mouth and whistles loudly before going back to clapping.

Nina wraps Libby and me up into a hug. "We did it!" she squeals, jumping.

Libby fixes her hair when we step back but smiles up at us both shyly. "That was fun."

"It really was," I say to her.

"I am ready for bed after just *watching* you girls." Maggie smiles warmly as she places her palm inside of her husband's. "Very well done," she whispers as she passes us.

"Aw, well, we'd be nothing without our fearless leader," I say, placing a hand on top of Libby's head and patting her.

"All right, *you,* time for bed," Yvonne says, waving Libby over. She gives her a tight hug before guiding her toward her small pink tent. Libby turns and walks backward a few steps, presenting two thumbs-up toward Nina and me before she heads off.

"Thank you," Helen says softly, approaching us from the other side of the fire. "She needed that."

"It was fun," I say truthfully.

"I'll see you both in the morning," Helen says, patting our shoulders before following after her wife and granddaughter.

"I see the knee's holding up," Caleb teases as I make my way toward him.

"Must be the air out here," I say, looping my arms over his neck. "Some sort of magical forest healing."

"You guys were great."

"Thank you." I dip my head in a bow once again. "I had an excellent teacher."

"I've heard she's a ten-ured professor." Caleb smiles following his dumb joke. I do too.

"Mm-hmm," I answer, looking up at him. "You ready for bed?"

"Let's wait out the fire." He tucks a stray hair back over my ear and rubs the pulse point on my neck he seems to instinctually find every time. "It's been such a good day," he says thoughtfully. "I'm not ready for it to end just yet."

I nod, tilting my head toward his hold. "Well . . . We could always end it with a bang," I suggest, leaning forward as I whisper mischievously.

He laughs dryly in response, dropping his hand to my chest, as he'd done earlier. After a long, quiet moment he sighs, really, really looking at me. "Your heart," he says solemnly.

"Yes . . ." *We've been over this,* I think. It's his . . . Does he not believe me? "I told you—"

"Something that's all yours," he interrupts. "Something you should be proud of," he says, pressing his forehead to mine. "That is what I should have said on the night of the fundraiser when you asked."

"Oh . . . I—"

"It's how you show up for people, the way you give them your all . . . You made Libby feel like she was the most special person in the world tonight. You make *everyone* around you feel that way. Me, Win, Bo, August. You love so deeply, it's hard for me to understand. It seems exhausting, but you do it anyways. You leave yourself open for anyone who needs a safe place to land, even near-perfect strangers. That is all, uniquely, individually, perfectly you. Something to be proud of that is all yours."

"I think that's my mom's, actually," I whisper, tears forming in my eyes as our noses softly rub together. "And I distinctly remember telling you that my heart was *yours . . . so . . .*"

"No." He taps my chest with the tips of his fingers, his voice heavy with emotion. "You inherited Marcie's heart, sure, but . . . you use it well. It suits you. It *is* you. And your heart is *mine* in the way that our home or our neighborhood or my favorite movie is mine. Mine but not for me alone. Your heart is mine to care for, to treasure. But it will never be just mine."

I inhale deeply, letting those words rest against my weary soul. And, honestly, I'm at a loss for words. Which, admittedly, is a relatively new experience for me.

"But partial ownership of something doesn't necessarily always mean collaboration, I know that now. You have to shine on your own. And you will, baby. I *know* you will. Because you shine brighter than anyone I've ever known." His lips twitch, but don't quite form a smile. His eyes are heavy under furrowed brows.

A disbelieving laugh rolls out of me as I stare at my husband in surprise. "Cay . . ." I start, still somewhat speechless.

"Sorry." He scratches above his eyebrow, laughing nervously. "I've had a few hours to myself."

"And you came up with all that in just a few hours?"

He shakes his head, his eyes finding mine and holding steady. "No . . . That was just from watching you dance."

"Never have such beautiful words been inspired by such terrible dancing."

Caleb pulls me tight to his chest, wrapping his arms around my shoulders and squeezing me to him. "You looked so carefree up there. Like . . ." His voice falls away on a whisper.

I relax into him, inhaling the smell of his campfire-scented clothing and the familiarity of him rolled into one. "Like I used to?" I finish for him. "Before?"

"Yes." He kisses the top of my head. "Exactly."

EIGHTEEN

"I'LL BE BACK IN A FEW MINUTES," CALEB SAYS, TAKING a flashlight with him as he exits the tent. I make quick work of grabbing the baby wipes the moment the tent's entrance zips shut.

I strip off my clothes and toss them into the corner. I wipe every surface of my body, paying extra-special attention to my armpits and the space between my legs. I tell myself that after our swim earlier and this quick refresh, I'm probably not *as* grimy as I feel. But after four days of not showering I'll settle for a neutral, if a tad baby-powdery, smell.

Caleb and I sat by the fire for hours, even staying long after Jai and Nina eventually went to bed, talking about nothing in particular. Conversation flowed and ebbed as we bounced from one meaningless topic to the next—in no rush to leave each other's company. Tomorrow isn't the last day of Reignite, but as we begin our return to where we began the hike four days ago, it certainly feels like the beginning of the end. I think we both wanted to hold onto this night as long as possible.

And . . . I don't plan on letting it go just yet.

I hide the used wipes under my clothes, deciding to deal with it in the morning when we pack up to leave the site tomorrow. I unzip my sleeping bag to reveal the fleece interior and lay it out flat across the floor of the tent, cozy side up. As I hear Caleb's footfalls approach, I throw my hair back into a tight, high pony and lie down on my stomach, reaching for my e-reader as I prop myself up on my elbows and cross my ankles to perk up my ass.

Oh, hi, love, didn't see you there. Welcome back. Me? Oh, this is just how I read, silly . . . My nude body cast in warm light from the lantern's delicate glow, my ass on show for you, my pussy playing hide-and-seek between my tightly shut thighs. Innocent, sweet, me.

The tent unzips and my smirk grows, though I do my best to focus on the page in front of me—but the words all blur and jumble like alphabet soup. "Hey, you." I try my best to project a relaxed tone, hitting the button to turn to the next page despite not having read a word.

He gives me no verbal response. Instead, I hear his flashlight hit the ground and a low, familiar, *needy,* anguished growl. I fight a laugh, tugging my bottom lip between my teeth. "See something you like?" I ask, leisurely turning to look over my shoulder.

My husband is on his knees at the entrance of the tent—which is half open between us—looking tortured. The lantern I've left to the side of the door casts him in the same softened glow, illuminating the desire in his eyes that threatens to burn me alive.

I let out a breathy giggle, half nerves, half excitement. The last time he looked this struck by lust, he fucked me so hard that I had bruises from his fingertips on my hips for days. I admired them in the mirror like a badge of honor. He apologized daily, whispering his regrets with kisses onto my skin until the marks faded to nothing but a memory.

"Baby," he whimpers low, leaning forward on a breath that

flares his nostrils. His eyes drift down the slope of my back toward the swell of my ass. "Fuuuck," he draws out, crawling through the opening and over to me.

"I love to see you crawl, love . . . but the door," I say, placing my e-reader aside as I smoothly roll onto my back, arching to prop up my chest.

He doesn't seem to hear me as he crowds me, his mouth just above my tits as he clenches his teeth, his eyes darkened. We both watch as my nipples harden and goosebumps spread across my skin with each of his warm breaths, tantalizingly close but somehow, simultaneously, too far.

"Close the door," I whisper, tilting my chin toward him, "so I can open my legs." I rub my knees together, desperate for any sort of friction.

Caleb's gaze slides down my belly toward the crest of my tightly closed thighs. He nods slowly as he backs away without taking his eyes from me. His chest heaves as he blindly reaches for the zipper.

"Good boy," I whisper, pushing out my lips as I speak. I guide my tongue across my top lip as I curve my mouth into a devilish grin. He's *absolutely* going to give in. I can *feel* his will breaking like a tether between us pulling too tight—about to snap.

When the zipper reaches the end of the track, securing us inside, tensions multiply tenfold.

"Open," he says before taking his shirt off with one hand grasping the fabric over his shoulder.

Instead of doing as told, I admire him, enjoying the hard edges of his chest and stomach and the trail of hair that disappears below his jeans.

"I said . . ." Caleb crawls over to me again then holds his half-naked body above mine. I let out a soft moan as he leans down until our lips *nearly* brush. "Open," he repeats, hovering above me. His minty breath has me unconsciously lifting up to kiss him as my eyes close. But, *rudely,* he pulls back.

I glare at him, lying down, resting on my elbows and forearms. He seems to enjoy my annoyance, the corners of his eyes creasing as a grin grows. It would seem we are *both* playing for control tonight. "Take off your pants," I command.

He listens immediately, moving to lie back on his sleeping mat. He tears off his jeans and tosses them aside, revealing black boxer briefs underneath that do *nothing* to hide his erection. He sits across from me, the shape of his legs creating a *V* as he gets comfortable with bent knees spread wide and feet touching in front of him. His forearms casually rest across each knee, his hands meeting in the middle and his fingers intertwining. "Your turn," he says, swallowing heavily.

We make eye contact so intense that it causes a thrill to course through me, forcing me to take in a sharp gasp of air. I tilt my head back as I lower my shoulder to the cushioning below and snake a hand over my ribs and down the center of my belly, toward the apex of my thighs. Still, I keep my eyes on him.

"That's it . . ." Caleb says, leaning forward with hooded eyes.

I watch him as I part my legs, bending my knees to the sides. I guide my hand down the sensitive skin of my inner thigh and his eyes trace the movement of my fingers as if he's stalking prey. Bringing my hand back toward my needy center, I caress the responsive flesh with a featherlight touch.

With a wistful sigh, I let my eyes close as I press my clit between two fingers and begin moving in agonizingly slow circles. I feel my nipples peak and harden again, and it sends a shiver across my skin that makes my back curl.

I hear Caleb move and feel the coarse hair of his thigh brush against my left knee, his warmth teasingly close. When I open my eyes, he doesn't notice. His stare is locked on the hand moving against my pussy. His lips rubbing together as if he's dying to put his mouth on me.

"Touch me," I say breathlessly.

He shakes his head, not losing his weighted gaze as I rub one finger down my slit and back. "No," he says, his voice low. "Make me pay for it, baby." Caleb drops down to lie on his stomach, resting his chin against the side of my bent knee. "Show me what I've been missing."

"Please," I say, desperately tilting my hips as if my body and my fingers are fighting for more and less. "This isn't fun anymore. I want you."

"It can be fun if you want it to be." He smiles up at me, his gaze flicking to my face. "I won't touch you tonight. I want you to feel good. I want you to come undone and I want to watch . . . but I don't want to break the rules. Not yet."

I bring two fingers through the slickness dripping from my entrance and then hold them out to him like an offering as I test my abdominal strength, sitting up slightly. "How about your mouth?" I ask. "Can I have that?" I say, coating his bottom lip with my wetness as he smiles for me.

He lifts his chin off my knee to shake his head no, but I watch as his tongue darts out to lick the taste of me off his lip, nevertheless. "Fuck, baby, you taste so damn good. . . ."

I lower myself back down and angle my hips toward him, so he can see all of me as I push two fingers into my entrance and curl them to *exactly* the right spot. The spot I didn't know existed before him.

"That's it, baby. Make it so good that I suffer. Make me jealous."

I don't even have to exaggerate my sounds to add to his suffering. I've been so *not* in the right mind space to touch myself for so long that my body is immediately brought back to life, panting and moaning, tensing, and heaving for every touch, tap, and movement.

"God dammit," Caleb grits out, his teeth bared.

"Having regrets?" I reply, my voice wavering with a cruel sort of laugh.

"So, so many." He tilts his mouth against my knee, not in a kiss so much as a muzzle, or a gag. It's as if he's keeping his mouth from moving or speaking by pressing himself into me to the point of what must be causing him pain—his bottom teeth digging into the inside of his lip. I lift my neck, wondering if he's shut his eyes or if he's taking this so-called punishment well.

Caleb's eyes remain transfixed though they're weary, pained, even, with a seemingly desperate amount of need.

I *think* I can get him to give us both what we want with one more push. "I need your help," I whisper. His stare quirks sharply to my face, the corner of his smile barely in view as he presses his face into the soft flesh of my thigh. "Do you want to help? Without breaking the rules?" He nods, like a man possessed as I shift my hand to my hip bone, allowing him a full view. "Be a good boy and spit on it," I demand.

Caleb lifts himself up urgently, the muscles in his upper body flexing deliciously taut as he moves into position between my legs. On bended knees, as if he's about to pray, Caleb bows his head, puckers his lips, glances up to me for approval, and then spits on my pussy. Not once. Not twice. But *three* times.

Everything inside of me tightens and coils, forcing a whimpering cry from my chest to escape past my lips.

I gasp as he falls forward, propping his hands on either side of my hips as he stalks above my lower belly. He groans, inhaling deeply as he brushes his nose dangerously close to my skin.

"I see you're putting all of your *other* senses to good use," I tease, though my voice is frail.

"You smell like sex." He bends his elbows and his beard skates across my hip. "Our sex."

I hiss, my toes curling at the sensation I had imagined earlier today, his coarse hair acting like a tripwire warning to my most ticklish, sensitive skin. "Fuck you," I groan, fighting the urge to press that beard exactly where I want it.

"Sorry." He lifts off me, going back to the praying position between my thighs, holding my legs open for him. "Continue," he orders, his fingers flexing over the top of my knees.

Try as I might to be a brat, I cannot find the willpower. So, I do as I'm told. I mix his saliva with my own wetness, coating myself until my slippery fingers can eagerly toy with my clit, increasing the speed until moans are spilling past my lips like incantations in long lost languages.

"That's it, baby," he tells me. "Feel it. Feel everything."

"I'm close," I tell him.

"Good, I want you to come. I want you to feel so, so good, baby."

"Not . . . good enough . . . without you . . ." I strain, sucking in sharp breaths between each other word.

"Yes, it is. Tell yourself how good you can make yourself feel. You own this pussy, right?"

"Yes," I reply, pushing my lips tightly together as I near what promises to be a deeply rewarding finish.

"Say it," Caleb says.

"Fuck," I groan out, beginning to shudder as the peak of my climax moves higher and further away.

"Tell me who owns this pussy," Caleb says, loud enough to hear over both of our panted breaths.

"I do," I answer, my lower belly coiling impossibly tight. "I own this pussy."

"Until tomorrow," he says just as I arrive, falling apart as he gently caresses the inside of my knee with his thumb. "Then, I'm going to have my turn with it," Caleb promises.

I cry out with a fluttering, helpless whine as I luxuriate in every second of my orgasm, each muscle and tendon throughout my body tensing before relaxing like putty against the blanket below.

"That's my good wife," Caleb says, moving to my side. My eyes drift closed but I hear him as he reaches into my pack, finds the crinkling plastic of the wet wipes, and then I feel him as he brushes the cool cloth along my inner thighs and core, wiping me clean.

It's indubitably cruel, that it's the most intimate way he's touched me in weeks. But it's equally thoughtful and kind.

"How do you feel?" he asks me, his voice in a whisper. "What do you need?"

"Perfect," I mumble. "Blanket . . ." I say with a wistful sigh.

With that, Caleb folds my sleeping bag over me and zips me into it, cocooning me in perfect warmth that I find myself wishing was his body instead. With a gentle kiss to my forehead, he turns off the lantern and, for what may be the very first time in our marriage, I think I fall asleep before Caleb does.

"HI, MAMA . . ." I DROP MY BAG NEXT TO THE HOSPITAL'S visitor's chair that has become my second home. I brought in cookies for the nurses on Mom's floor. Partially, because I bake when I'm stressed, and because I hope it softens the blow of when I'm particularly grouchy with them. I cannot help it. I'm running on next to no sleep, shitty hospital cafeteria food, and I'm furious that hospital visiting hours are keeping me away from her for fifteen hours a day . . . and that they only let me bend those rules half the time.

I know none of that is the nurses' fault. Hence, the cookies. Yesterday it was brownies. The day before that, shortbread.

Mom's asleep when I arrive so I pull out the book I brought from her collection and begin reading it to her. Today's pick is *Anne of Green Gables,* the first book she ever read to me.

An hour later, Mom wakes with a murmur and a cough. I reach for her cup of water and hold the straw to her so she can sip. It dribbles out the side of her mouth a little bit, but I clean it up with my sleeve. "We got our wedding photos back," I tell her, lowering into my chair.

Mom attempts to lift her eyes, but her abilities are sedated by both the drugs and the partial paralysis. She'd refused everything else other than the pain medication and a feeding tube, insisting that she'd not let a machine breathe for her. I had wanted to fight her on it, but she'd already had so many choices stolen away from her, it didn't feel right to take another. It was impossible, though, to accept the nearing end. That there'd be no miracle.

"Do you want to see?" I ask, already reaching for my bag. I pull out the white cloth album and flip through it, showing her each page, getting as close to lying in bed next to her as I can without breaking any more of the hospital's rules.

Mom hums when she sees the photo of her sitting in the front pew staring up at Caleb and me with so much pride.

"I like that one too," I tell her, looking between the woman in the photo and the woman lying next to me today. I hadn't fully realized how much Mom has changed in these last three months . . . how quickly she's faded. "You look beautiful, Mom." I drop the album to my lap and hold her hand. "So, so beautiful."

I don't know if I'd change them, if I'd somehow known, but those were the last words I said to my mother before she fell asleep and never woke up.

She passed later that afternoon, surrounded by all of us who loved her best.

And though I told her how much I love her and how much I was going to miss her, how grateful I am that she was my mom over and over again as she slipped away, I'm glad the last words she might have heard were someone calling her beautiful. Because she was. She really, really was.

NINETEEN

IT'S BEEN A MUCH MORE RELAXING HIKE TODAY THAN the rest of the week so far. We're walking downhill with lower temperatures and under overcast skies, keeping most of the bugs at bay—and the sweat too. Before we set off this morning, Caleb had asked if I'd mind him ditching me to walk with Kieran and Henry since he wanted to pick their brains about their business some more. Since I'm totally in favor of Caleb making some changes at Focal, I agreed. I'd walk with Nina, but she is with Helen for a one-on-one session. Jai is talking sports with Phil while Maggie and Yvonne chat up ahead, their expressions concentrated and somber. So, that leaves me in the company of my favorite ten-year-old.

"Are you excited to go home soon, or will you miss it out here?" I ask Libby, sidestepping some particularly dense moss that looks as if it could be supporting an entire fairy colony.

She levels me with a scowl-like stare but there's a hint of an *almost* smile. "You've got to be joking . . ."

"C'mon, it's not *that* bad."

"Well, I'm not going to miss the bugs," she answers, swatting away a blackfly with a disgusted frown. "But it's been better than I thought it would be . . . I guess. I miss my friends though."

"I've missed my bed," I say longingly. "It is pretty much my favorite place on earth."

Her laugh is bittersweet. "My mom used to say that all the time."

I instinctively turn toward her, wanting to read her expression. This is the first time Libby's brought up her mother in the past week and I'd begun to wonder if she ever would. I do my best to not fumble my words or act *overly* interested, but I've never been known to play it cool. "Yeah?"

"She had this humongous bed. Like I could lay sideways on it and stretch out my hands above my head and not even touch the sides. She named her bed Clive and said he was the only man she'd ever truly loved."

I immediately decide that I would have gotten along with Libby's mom. "Humongous . . . that's a great word. And your mom sounds very funny."

"I miss her bed," she says, shortly followed by a rueful sigh.

A memory of one Christmas morning plays in my mind as Libby's words settle in the warm morning air between us. I was probably six or maybe seven. I'd woken up, unsure of the time but knowing it was too early for presents and drifted toward my mom's bedroom. The hallway was dimly lit by the light of the Christmas tree and the moon coming through broken kitchen blinds. My mom was half-awake when she smiled toward me and lifted her blankets so I could slot myself under them to cuddle in next to her.

Without a word spoken between us, we ended up wrapped around one another, our matching fuzzy-pajamaed limbs all tangled together. I remember thinking that she was so warm and comforting, like a towel fresh from the dryer after a bath. I burrowed into her chest and breathed in the familiar lavender scent that she'd always spray on her pillows before going to bed. We slept like that, completely intertwined, until Win eventually woke up and came to jump on us both, yelling that she couldn't wait another minute to open gifts. I hopped out of bed to help her wake up Aunt June, bursting with my own excitement and leaving my mom's embrace without a second thought.

I wish I could tell that little girl that there was not a single gift under *any* tree that would ever be as good as lying next to her mom that morning.

"I miss my mom's bed too," I say, my words coming in slow.

"Grandma told me that your mom died," Libby says matter-of-factly, catching me off guard. "She said maybe I could talk to you about it . . . if I wanted to."

"Do you want to?" I ask.

"I don't know anyone else with a dead mom."

"Okay, well, we can talk about it if you'd like . . . but I can sometimes get emotional about it. As long as that's okay with you."

Libby nods. "Were you a kid when she died?"

Yes, is my gut reaction, though it's not entirely accurate. Or, at *all* accurate. "I was nineteen but she had been sick for a while before then."

"My mom wasn't sick."

"No?" I ask. "It must have been pretty sudden, then."

"She had an accident at work."

"That's so hard," I say, coming to the disheartening realization that, despite my desperation to help somehow, there isn't much else I can say. You'd think I'd have some sort of comforting words of wisdom to share after all these years, but is there anything you could say to a young girl who lost their mother that would *truly* help? "I imagine it would feel very scary that way . . . to lose someone without warning like that."

"Grandma H told me that when people die unexpectedly, we have a hard time believing it happened. Like, our brains tell us that they'll come back or something."

"Is that how you feel?" I ask.

"Not really . . ." she says, her eyebrows twisting together. "I know she's not coming back because everything changed so fast. I came home from school the day she died, and it was like my whole life was different. I moved in with my grandmas and had to change schools and switched dance teams and . . . I don't know. I just know she's not here. But sometimes, when I first wake up in the morning, I'll forget that she's not—" Her voice breaks the tiniest amount before it drifts off entirely.

"I love when I dream about my mom, but it hurts waking up and realizing she's still gone," I say, hoping that she hears my meaning. *I understand, I know how hard it is to lose her over and over again.*

"Does it hurt less? After time?" Libby asks, her normally cynical eyes searching mine with a youthfulness I'd yet to see from her. I slow my steps, looking down at her with a wistful smile as I pull together my best answer. I don't want to lie to her, but I don't want to scare her either.

"Yeah, I think so. Not because the pain changes. We just get stronger, I think. We have to keep *trying* to get stronger, at least." That last part is an in-the-moment realization. In the same way I'd not properly prepared my body for this hike, I'd also not been giving my brain what it needed to strengthen over the past decade. That is what I'm going to do differently from now on.

"But it still hurts?" Libby asks, her lips twitching into a frown. "Even though you're old?"

Well, first of all, I'm young according to your grandmother and when measured against Vera Wang or Julia Child or . . . I scrunch up my nose and nod, my crooked smile acting as an unspoken apology.

"That sucks."

It most certainly does. "You're already very, very strong, Libby."

"I know," she says quietly, stepping over a fallen branch.

I smile to myself, happy to hear her confidence, even if it's softly spoken. I'm glad to know that the two women charged with raising her from now on will stoke that strength and confidence as she continues to grow. That, perhaps, she won't find herself at thirty-one filled with regrets and missed opportunities because of a festering, internal wound she never found the strength to face.

But, a kinder, newer part of my psyche whispers, *it would be okay if she did . . . Because she doesn't have to be all right. She just has to try again tomorrow.*

And the new, kind voice soothes me some. I invite it to stay a while.

"What do you miss most about her?" I ask, stepping onto a footbridge over a gently flowing creek.

"I don't know. . . ." Libby says, a touch sassy as if she'd intended to throw the word *duh* in there but forgot at the last possible second. "She was my mom."

Those four simple words from a child's point of view encapsulate perfectly the feelings I've spent most of my adult life wrestling with. "So . . . everything?" I ask, smiling softly.

"Yeah," Libby says, or, rather, she sighs. "She was my best friend. I didn't really know that before."

My heart squeezes as if there's a fist tightening around it and threatening to tug it out. She is too young—*far* too young—to know this kind of loss. Ten-year-olds shouldn't have any regrets other than accidentally calling their principal Dad or sitting on someone's lap on the bus by accident . . . not that I did either of those things. . . . "What was your mom's name?" I ask.

"Everyone called her Gin . . . but her real name was Virginia."

"Gin is a pretty badass name," I say, smirking in the way my aunt used to after swearing or telling me something she really shouldn't have when I was a kid. The smirk that made me feel *so* special, and cool, and adult-like. "Would you want to tell me about her?"

Libby smiles shyly, but without any hesitation, begins talking a mile a minute, as if she's been not-so-patiently waiting for the chance to answer that exact question.

For the next hour of our hike, Libby tells me about her mom, and, when she asks, I tell her about mine too. I share a story about my mom accidentally cutting three eyes into a sheet for a last-minute ghost costume for Win. How I adopted my mom's love for Halloween and how throwing a party every year has become a way for me to feel close to her. Libby tells me she and her mother loved going to the movies together. That they'd always race to finish their popcorn before the movie started in order to get a free refill without missing any of the show.

I suggested that maybe *her* special way of remembering her mom could be going to the movies and stuffing her face with popcorn. She liked that idea.

Our conversation came to a natural end as we reached the campsite. Libby hugged me before running off in search of her grandmother to tell her about the popcorn and movie idea. Despite the hug being one of the shortest I've ever received, it was also one of the best I've ever gotten.

We hugged without resolution. There was no bow tied neatly around our conversation. No clean-cut answers. Just a mutual understanding that the pain would always exist but that we'd be a little stronger tomorrow. That, maybe, I'd helped her some.

"OKAY, LET'S GO around the circle and share what we wrote down," Helen says, smiling as she sits cross-legged in the crotch of a giant maple tree with the rest of us in a U formation around her.

This afternoon's journal prompt was "What is the hill you will die on?" Meaning, what are we unwilling to compromise on in our relationship moving forward.

Caleb is to my left with his hand resting on my thigh. He's not been able to keep his eyes or hands off of me since last night and I feel lit up from the inside out, basking in the warmth of his attention.

One by one, we go around the circle. With every answer, I notice Caleb becoming more and more agitated. Just at the point where I'm starting to get concerned enough to check in with him, I notice that he's dropped his hand and is tapping the pen against his journal page. A *fresh* journal page. Is he changing his answer? Had he not written anything down?

"Are you okay?" I whisper.

"Sarah," Helen says, nodding at me with a warm smile. "Would you like to share next?"

I glance between Helen and Caleb, both to my left. Caleb is blushing and I'm not sure how to help, other than take the attention off him.

"Yeah, sure, yes . . ." I look down at my journal. "I think, for me, the only thing I'd ever be unwilling to compromise on moving forward is kids. I don't want to have children . . . and that would be an automatic end for me, if my partner felt otherwise. Anything else . . . I think I'd be willing to have a conversation about."

"Okay, thank you," Helen says, then turns her face to Caleb, studying his nervous expression. "As a reminder, we *can* keep our answers private. . . ." My husband would *perhaps* keep his answer private if someone else had also asked but since he is last to go and *every* other person took their turn—he'll feel obligated to as well. "Caleb?"

"Sorry, right, uh . . ." Caleb laughs disjointedly, his thumb scratching at his hairline. "I think I maybe . . . Well, actually, I *definitely* misunderstood the assignment," he says, his eyes flicking to mine with a weary, self-deprecating glance.

I reach over into his lap, curiosity getting the better of me, and turn the page back one to find his list. His *long* list. But thankfully for my nerves, it isn't much to do with our relationship at all.

What I find instead is . . . well, it's *very* Caleb. I cannot help but laugh, though I attempt to stifle it with my forearm, faking a cough.

"Some help you are," Caleb whispers out of the side of his mouth.

My quiet giggling turns to breathless laughter. "I can't—" I reply, struggling. "You're on your own with this. . . ."

Helen, visibly confused, leans toward Caleb's journal and takes a peek for herself at the very full page. "Oh," she says, pushing her lips together to prevent a smile from growing. "That's all right, Caleb." She croons his name sweetly.

"I'm sorry, I was a little"—Caleb's heated gaze lands on my thighs as his cheeks continue to redden—"distracted."

Despite my bubbling laughter, my chin lifts with pride from being a *distraction*. This is just like chemistry class and the Bunsen burner all over again. Except this time, no one will leave with a scar . . . I hope.

"Put us out of our misery, mate," Jai says, grinning.

"All right," Caleb answers, then clears his throat. "For the record, I agree with my wife. On the kids thing . . . But I thought this was more of a general prompt. More like—"

"What hill would you die on?" I interrupt, reading the heading from the top of Caleb's page. "Number one," I read.

"Number one," Caleb repeats, loudly, tilting his journal away from my view. "*Deep Space Nine* is the superior Star Trek series."

"Oh, honey . . ." Maggie says softly, bringing a hand to her face to cover her laugh.

"Number two. If you put Kelly Clarkson on any season of *American Idol,* she'd still have won." That one gets Phil going. He buries his face in his hands as his shoulders start shaking with laughter.

"Number three—"

"I don't think you need to—" Helen interrupts.

"Please, Helen, he's doing *the work,*" Jai says in fake earnest, a hand splayed across his chest.

"Number three," Caleb repeats, beginning to smile. "There are so many things we could have gotten rid of to help the environment *before* ousting plastic straws. Paper straws are a sensory nightmare."

"That was a passionate one," Phil says between boisterous chuckles, nodding. "Really getting fired up now," he adds.

Caleb shakes his head with a dry laugh and closes the journal. "Uh-uh! Not so fast! Number four," I say, taking his journal, forcing a steady breath as I fight off another wave of laughter. "It's fucked up that people keep birds as pets."

"So true," Nina says, snapping her fingers. Jai, however, somberly whispers, "My nan kept birds . . . I loved them."

"Okay, okay," Caleb says, snatching his journal back. "That's enough."

I bite my lip as he glares at me playfully, chewing his tongue as it presses against the inside of his cheek. It's a look that, if I'm not mistaken, says *You're gonna get it*. And *god* I hope that's true.

"Now that we've had our fun . . ." Helen says, looking our way with a warm smile, "I think we should end our morning with some breathing exercises before we go spend quality time with our partners."

After Helen guides us through a few quick meditations we all go our separate ways. I slip my hand into Caleb's as we head toward our tent. "Let's ditch these and go for a walk?" I ask, holding my journal out in front of us. "Or should we keep reading about these hills of yours?"

Caleb's jaw ticks, a wicked smirk appearing. "If you think for a *second* that you're getting away with that . . ."

I melt at the sternness in his tone, my thighs going wobbly for a split second. "Oh, are we fighting again?" I feign disappointment as we reach the tent's entrance. "Such a shame. We were doing so well . . ." Caleb bends forward to unzip it, snatches my journal from my hand, and carelessly tosses both of our books inside without a second glance. "It's not my fault you couldn't—"

"Couldn't focus?" he says, cutting me off as he stands far too close and *far* too tall over me. Caleb moves his hand to my wrist, tightening his hold before tugging me closer. He keeps his face straight, as if he's looking over my shoulder. His chin next to the space above my ear, he whispers, "It is *precisely* your fault that I couldn't focus, and you know it. You put on those shorts to torture me, so don't pretend otherwise."

"And?" I whisper. "What are you going to do about it?"

He steps away, shrugging a shoulder and smiling coolly as if he didn't just whisper me to half an orgasm. "Let's go for a walk," he says, innocently enough, as he lowers his hand to mine and begins pulling me away from camp.

TWENTY

"WE'VE PASSED THIS TREE AT LEAST THREE TIMES," I complain, reaching up to tighten my ponytail before bringing my forearm across my chin to dab the sweat away.

"We're in the woods, Sar. A tree is a tree is a tree."

"No, *Cay*," I throw back at him. "We've passed *this specific* tree. It has a nasty-looking orange mushroom at the base of it and the lowest branch looks like the letter *W*," I say, pointing. "I know this tree and, at this rate, this tree knows us. We are going around in circles."

Caleb studies the large oak, his eyebrows twisting together as he blows out a long breath and holds up his compass *again*. "Yvonne said to head northeast . . ." he mumbles.

"Admit it, we're lost."

"'Not all those who wander are lost,'" he says absentmindedly as he turns his body abruptly to the right, seemingly testing the compass's capabilities.

"That's nice and all, master Tolkien, but *we* definitely are."

My husband throws me the proudest smile I have ever seen

from him. "This stupid thing is broken," he whispers, spinning on his heels again. "It's stuck pointing north."

"We have been walking for a biblical amount of time now . . ." I complain, mostly to myself as Caleb starts hitting the compass against his palm, glaring at it with all of his might. "Forty days and forty nights . . ." I add, falling back onto a large boulder as if it was a fainting chair. "I was warned about following strange men around the woods, but I didn't listen." Caleb seems to be looking for something to open the back of the compass with. As if a screwdriver will be conveniently under a nearby rock or leaf. "We're running out of daylight."

"It's been less than thirty minutes," Caleb replies dryly.

Oh, so he *can* hear me. "We could have done a *lot* in thirty minutes."

That gets his attention . . . or, at least, half of it. "Patience, baby," he coos.

"What is it, *exactly,* we're looking for?"

"A waterfall."

Okay, a waterfall *would* be nice . . . I'll admit. To myself, that is.

"Exactly. Which is why I'm trying to get this"—he grunts, shaking the compass—"stupid thing to work."

"I didn't say anything," I respond.

When he looks up at me, smugness *radiates* from him like steam wafting off of hot cement. "Nine times out of ten you say a *lot* more by saying nothing at all," he says from a crooked mouth.

I can think of a lot better uses for that mouth.

"You don't know me," I argue mockingly, swallowing heavily in consequence to that *look* in his eye. The one that says if I keep acting up, I'll get punished. This waiting isn't *exactly* the punishment I had in mind, but who am I to criticize his tactics? Just kidding, I love to criticize and this is straight-up edging *and* stupid. "Now hush and get us where we need to be before I go rogue."

I lie back onto the rock, tilting to face him as I cushion my head with my forearm.

"Working on it . . ." he says, his eyes carving intention against every inch of my uncovered skin before he manages to pop the compass's clear case off, revealing the instrument underneath. I close my eyes, listening to the sound of nature as I've become accustomed to doing over the past five days, allowing the sun's glow to suffuse my body in its comforting warmth.

If I am not going to get laid, I may as well get a tan.

But after a minute—or possibly less—I cave. "You know, *here* would be just fine." I open my eyes, peeking at my husband who's, evidently, back in his little fix-it universe. "Or, anywhere . . ." I say, twisting in the opposite direction. "Actually, that tree *does* offer quite a lot of privacy."

"I think it's busted," he declares, glaring at the compass in his hand before shoving it into his shorts pocket.

Yeah, sweetheart, I could've told you that. I prop myself up onto my elbows, determined to take matters into my own hands. And, by *matters,* I mean Caleb.

"So, I guess it's time for a new plan," I say, sitting up and twisting to place my feet back on the ground before walking over to him with *one* clear intention, easily communicated by the exaggerated sway of my hips and a devilish smirk. "How would you like to have your wife up against a tree?" I fist his T-shirt in my hand and tug his face nearer to mine.

"You wanted water . . ." His mouth barely brushes mine and yet it sends a shiver down my spine. Without conscious thought I find myself straining to reach him—my body seeking his without permission. "It's more romantic that way," he says, pressing his forehead against mine.

"What if I told you that I don't want romantic?"

"What do you want?" he asks, toying with me as the tip of his nose traces my eyebrow in a path to find my hairline. He buries his face into the side of my neck, breathing me in with a low growl of appreciation from the back of his throat.

Campfire, I think to myself. His kryptonite.

"Honestly . . ." I whisper dryly, "I would take a dirty roadside motel at this point, love."

"Hot." He breathes out a laugh against my cheek, tilting my mouth toward his with the push of his jaw against mine.

"You know it," I say, narrowly avoiding his kiss by ducking to the left. "But we have to get off this trail first . . ." I look toward the clearing behind a large tree nestled against a moss- and rock-covered cliffside. "Unless you're suddenly into voyeurism."

I inhale sharply when Caleb reaches for my tank top's strap and hauls me back to his chest. His knuckles press into my collarbone as he tightens his hold. His laugh, in reaction to my involuntary gasp, is low and falls heavy against my skin. Goosebumps follow as I blink up toward him, finding a matching, weighted heat behind his eyes that pins my feet to the ground.

"I think you meant exhibitionism . . . and *no,* I'm not. Trust me when I say that the way I'm feeling right now"—his other hand moves to grip my hip, his fingers flexing as if he's restraining himself from burying them into my flesh—"let's just say I'd not be up for sharing."

I giggle nervously as I slowly begin walking backward, guiding him toward the clearing with his hand wrapped around my shirt's strap acting like a leash. We make it as far as the boulder I'd been lounging on before I trip, the back of my foot catching on a tree root, and almost fall backward. Caleb uses his hold on my shirt to catch me, quickly throwing his other arm around my lower back. "Careful," he whispers, his heated gaze slipping for a second as a teasing grin takes its place.

I'm hanging in his arms like he's about to dip me amidst a ballroom dance, hot and *all* kinds of bothered, yet all I can muster is another, uneasy, girlish giggle. I wish I could astral project out of my body and physically shake myself. I've read enough romance books to build my own library and yet all those clever quips, witty comebacks, and kiss-me-why-don't-you phrases are evading me entirely.

"I—" Caleb says, his eyes held on me in earnest, cradling me like I'm something precious. "You—" He subtly shakes himself, his nostrils flaring slightly as he seems to center himself. "I love you so much." The words are whispered but far from soft. "I love you," he repeats, his chest rising as if he can't catch his breath.

Caleb moves so fast; I blink and nearly miss it.

The moment he straightens so I can stand on my own two feet, he instantly bends down to pick me up, pulling my legs to wrap around his back and supporting my weight with his hold on the backs of my thighs. Then, finally, our mouths collide.

Our kiss is downright violent. Tugging teeth, fighting tongues, and shared, breathless gasps. Caleb bends down, balancing me on his legs as he readjusts his hold on me. His palms find my ass cheeks and squeeze to the point of *near* pain as his thumbs pull the material of my shorts into a makeshift thong.

"And . . . fuck you for these," he says, bared teeth at my jaw as he walks us into the darkened shade of the oak tree. "I should spank you for even wearing these in front of anyone else. Do they even count as shorts?"

"Possessive much?" I tease as he buries kisses down the side of my throat, palming my ass in rhythm with each suck and pull of my skin into his mouth. God . . . he's going to mark me all over. And I want him to.

"The other day after our fight," he says, his lips pressing into my shoulder, "I was so scared of losing you and I played out all of these horrible scenarios, imagining someone else *having* you."

My back hits a tree trunk with a thud that I think I'll be replaying in my fantasies for years to come. "It's been driving me a little—"

"Wild," I answer for him, admiring the slightly crazed look in his eyes.

His forehead drops to my shoulder, his shoulders rising on heavy breaths. "Sorry . . ." he mumbles.

"No," I say adamantly, tugging at the back of his hair, driving my fingers into his curls. "I like it . . ." I whisper as our eyes meet. For one heady moment, there's nothing else in the universe but Caleb's hungry, cinnamon-colored eyes on mine. "Make me yours," I tell him.

With that, his mouth finds mine again. His kiss is forceful and heated yet concentrated and precise like a blowtorch operating against metal. His fingertips pry at the crease of my ass, spreading and kneading in rhythm with the jutting of his hips, soliciting involuntary moans from my throat as my back grazes the bark of the tree. My hands fist in his hair, paw at his neck, grasp at his shoulders and every other inch of him available to me and *god* I feel as if I'm getting drunk on it. Like every swipe of his tongue is a swig of wine, or a shot of something far better than liquor.

"I need more," I say between feverish kisses. "Put me down."

He groans, as if he'd rather die than do just that. As if any change will force us to leave the perfection of this moment behind. But I know what's best for us both. I want—no, I *need*—our clothes off. At least *some* of them. Enough of them to take what I want.

"I said put me down," I command, my hand gripping tightly on his jaw.

His beard skates across my palm as he slowly twists out of my hold and retreats a step, unpinning my hips from the tree. He backs away, putting his hands up as if he's dropped a weapon of some kind between us. Or, maybe, I'm the weapon.

I reach down to the hem of my tank top and tug it off, revealing the simple white bra I have on underneath. Caleb keeps backing away until his back hits the jagged cliff's edge. His hands explore the wall as his eyes remain raptly focused on me, and eventually he finds a ledge large enough to sit on. I walk over to him, undoing my bra as I go.

I expect a wave of nerves to follow, baring myself to him under the shaded daylight where *any* hikers could pass by if they find themselves off the trail—but my hands remain steady. And that fills me with even more confidence. Even in the privacy of our bedroom I'll often want the lights to be off before we get undressed. But there's something about being out here in the open that makes me feel recklessly alive. The vulnerability and the sweat and the grime and the earthiness of it all. *Something* about that indisputable desire in Caleb's expression that removes all possible insecurity.

I feel beautiful. I feel wanted. I feel loved. I feel so seen by him.

"Baby," Caleb says, dragging a hand down his chin as I place my shirt and bra on a nearby tree stump. I smile back at him, closing the distance between us. "Are we really doing this?"

"I think we are," I say, settling into his lap. I'm greeted by two large hands finding the center of my back, spread wide and reverent. He tilts me backward by lifting his hips and cradles me in his arms as my back arches. His lips make quick work of finding my tits, his tongue circling my nipples as he murmurs wordless praises against my skin. He licks from the hollow of my chest to the underside of my chin and it's not long before we're kissing again—just as animalistic and yet somehow still as tender.

We kiss and kiss and kiss. And it's as if I can *feel* our shared focus. Neither of us is imagining how to shed some more clothing. Neither of us is one step ahead. We're present, in this together enjoying *every* glorious second.

"Is it me or—"

"No, this is insanely good," Caleb says, in an almost-bitter laugh as he completes my exact thought.

I grind myself against him, twisting my hips to seek more friction. *More, more, more* my body chants.

"It's always been—" Caleb says, moving his hand to tighten around the base of my neck. "But this . . ." His hand is clasped there as he brings me back in for another heady kiss.

This, my thoughts agree, echoing my body. I pull my mouth away from his and the action is met with a ragged, agitated moan.

"Trust me," I say, rising off his lap to stand. I look down, admiring the hard lines of his cock outlined by his shorts. I bend over, each hand on one of his knees, and push them apart as I lower to kneel.

"Baby," Caleb whispers. The word somehow represents both halves of my husband that I've come to love. The doting partner who is audibly concerned about my comfort and the lust-filled man, praising me. "Your knees . . ." Again, it's as if both halves agree on the words but not the tone in which he speaks them. "Fuck," he whispers, in concern and celebration.

"I'm sure you'll bandage them up later," I say, reaching for the tie of his shorts. I tug on the loose end, undoing the knot with unwavering eye contact shared between us.

"Fuck yeah, I will . . ." he says, assisting me by lifting his lower half as I make quick work of pulling his shorts down past his thighs. I smirk in satisfaction as my husband's dick springs free, rock hard and flushed with need.

"I missed this," I say, licking my lips at the sight of him. My knees dig into the hard, unforgiving earth as I bring him into my mouth, taking every inch until he hits the back of my throat. I moan around him, and he shudders on a ragged whimper.

"Sarah," he pants, the muscles in his thighs tensing under my palms at the same time he moves to grip my hair. He fists my ponytail, straining and loosening his grip with every movement of my mouth. "Baby, slow down," he begs as I swirl my tongue around his tip before bringing my lips back down his shaft. "Oh my god," he says, voice tight. "Sar . . . I need you to stop."

I lick up the hard vein on the underside of him, bringing my hand in to fist the base of his cock. "Why?" I ask sweetly, smiling up at him.

"Up," he says, his jaw tenses as his chest rises and falls rapidly.

"I'm having fun."

"I know, gorgeous . . . But I haven't come in over a month and when I do again, it won't be in your mouth." *Over a month?*

"Cay . . ." I eye him skeptically. "You've not touched yourself?" I knew we weren't having sex since our fight at the fundraiser but surely he hasn't—

"I tried," he says. Caleb's throat flexes as he swallows, his eyes measuring the distance between his dick and my lips. "But every time I had to rely on my own imagination, I just thought about how upset you were and I . . . I lost it."

"That night in the shower? When I walked in on you?"

"I had been trying to, but I couldn't . . . I don't know. It didn't feel right."

I tilt my head to wrap my lips around the side of his hardness, pressing delicate, teasing kisses. "I love you," I say, lowering my mouth onto him once again. He cries out, his hand shaking against my cheek, as if he's fighting to gain control or, rather, to not lose every semblance of it.

And fuck if that doesn't turn me on even more. I love bringing him right to the edge and testing what that exact line is. I love any time I'm given the chance to steal my man's sanity while on my knees. Especially when it's *so* easy to take.

Caleb stands, robbing me of him. "No more, baby." He reaches down, tilting my face up to his. "Come here." He holds out his hand in offering to help me and I reluctantly take it. Once I'm standing, Caleb's heated gaze drops down my body and with one swift tug, my shorts land on the rocky ground.

I smile knowingly, watching my husband's expression shift. He licks his teeth behind closed lips, as his brow furrows to an almost comical point. "You cannot be serious," he chastises.

"We don't exactly have laundry out here." Though, my availability of clean underwear has *nothing* to do with my lack of panties. That's *all* for him.

"You wore those shorts all day with a bare pussy . . ." He circles around me, purposeful in each movement. I look over my shoulder to see him stop behind me, licking his smiling lips as his hands find the curve of my lower back, his thumbs pressing into my tailbone. "You are something else, woman."

"Impatient?" I offer. "Desperate?"

"Wild," he answers. "Put your hands on the rocks. . . ."

I turn forward and place one hand on the cliff's edge, and then the other, doing my best to avoid sharp stones. Naturally, I bend forward to do so, arching to the point where I can feel his upper thigh graze against my ass. *God,* I've never been this needy. "Like this?" I ask, twisting to press against him.

"Yes, perfect," Caleb says, pressing a kiss onto the wing of my shoulder blade. His arm wraps around my waist and his hand finds my left breast, then he does the same with his right hand too. For several bliss-filled moments he plays with my tits, grasping and pinching and plucking as he grinds his cock against my ass and lower back.

I'm preening for him, little gasps and moans pouring out of me as I fight to keep my grip on the wall in front of me. I can feel myself dripping with need for him, coating the insides of my thighs as he curls his body around mine from behind, kissing the back of my neck and shoulders. "Are you ready, baby?" he whispers against the sensitive skin behind my ear.

"Yes," I plead, gulping for air. "Please."

He drops his hand from my breast and caresses his way down my abdomen with the backs of his knuckles. Once he gives my pussy a quick stroke, he reaches between my legs to take a hold of himself and notches against my entrance.

"Fuck," I tremble, feeling the wide tip of him press into me.

"God, the feel of you," Caleb says in a heavy whisper. He slides himself into me and my eyes roll back into my head as his hands find my tits and begin molding me in his grip once again. We both gasp once he's fully seated inside of me. Nothing has *ever* felt this good. Every single one of my nerve endings, every pulse point, is awake and aware.

Caleb stills, planting kisses at the top of my spine as his nose presses into the base of my hairline. But I begin writhing against him, unable to help myself.

His arms cross over me in a tight hold, one hand wrapped over my chest and the other around my lower belly. "Stay still, baby."

"I need you," I whine, shutting my eyes tight as I tilt back into him.

"*And I* need to not lose it right away."

I bite my lower lip as it turns into a smile. "What happened to the grown man who knows how to take his time?"

Smack. Before I'd even fully finished my question Caleb's arm loosened around my belly and his palm found my left ass cheek.

"*He,*" Caleb practically growls, pistoning into me, "has been in withdrawal."

"You missed me," I say, pride flooding my veins as I sway my hips side to side within his hold.

"Baby, all I *do* is miss this pussy." He moves to cup it in his palm, gliding two slick fingers around my clit.

I laugh softly, rotating my hips against him as best I can in his rigid hold. "Then, take it already."

And take it he does.

With unrelenting thrusts, Caleb begins pounding into me from behind in rhythm with my quickened heartbeat. The relaxing sounds of nature that we'd previously been cocooned in transform into something far from it. Reverberating off the cliff's edge is the indelicate rhythm of skin slapping against skin. A chorus of grunts and moans and shuddered breaths in a cacophony of pleasure.

Baby and *fuck* and *yes* and *so good* spoken into the charged air between us. *Harder* and *shit* and *oh* and *oh* and *oh* and *Caleb* all chanted as I come undone over and over and over again.

Even at our best, on top of luxury bed linens in hotels with million-dollar views, tipsy on champagne, fresh from rose-petal baths, giddy with endorphins, and surrounded by helpful little vibrating toys, Caleb's never pulled so many orgasms out of me.

We've opened our hearts, let the ugly out, and welcomed each other's darkness with kind regard. And *this* is our reward.

Caleb's fingers work savagely at my clit as he slows his pace, his arm tensing around my waist as his breaths staccato. "I-I'm going to—" he stammers. "I'm close." His hand finds the vacant space next to mine on the wall's rocky surface and, hazy-eyed, I look up to watch the tendons in his arm flex as he supports his weight over top of me.

I lace my pinky finger over his thumb, shuddering out a long, anguished cry as I suspect what will be my final orgasm rolls through me. "Come with me," I beg. "Please," I whimper.

With that, my husband grunts and spills into me, a quaking "*Yes*" cascading out of him as he moves his hand from between my legs to my stomach, pulling me closer.

After he's finished, I let my head roll back, resting on the column of his throat. His hand moves from my stomach, then both of his hands take gentle hold of my wrists. He brings them in, crossing my arms in front of my chest in an *X*, like a self-soothing hug and comforting hold from him in one.

"Holy shit," I whisper, leaning into him.

Caleb whispers something indiscernible against my shoulder, pressing his cheek flush against my skin as he lowers to remove himself from me. Once he's back and wrapped around me fully once again, I turn within his arms to hug him, pressing my face to his chest.

With a kiss on my forehead, he palms my ass, massaging with both hands. I tilt back to smile up at him.

"Happy?" I ask.

"There aren't words," he answers simply, his face stuck in exhausted wonderment. "Having you in my arms like this. Feeling you . . . feeling you come around me. Being out in the open. I think I'm dead. I think heaven might be real. I think it's you."

"This may have beat our night in Paris," I suggest playfully, kissing him on the cheek before stepping out of his hold and turning in the direction of the tree stump where I left my shirt and bra. "Fuck!" I shout, putting my arms out in front of me as if I'm a blackbelt in karate and not the human embodiment of a couch cushion.

Sitting on top of my bra, really sort of *cradled* in my bra cup, is a rather perverted chipmunk.

Caleb can barely catch his breath as he laughs, struggling to pull his swimming shorts back on. "So we *were* being watched." He forces the words out through winded laughter.

I pick up my shorts off the ground and shake them free of loose dirt and debris. "Fucking creep!" I seethe as I lunge toward Chippy as he sniffs at my bra's strap.

"Don't be so hard on him. I'd live in there too, if I could," Caleb teases, picking up an acorn and tossing it at the ground near our new friend, who then scampers off. "There," he says.

"My hero," I reply dryly as I make my way toward my discarded clothes.

"Hurry up and put your tits away, Linwood," he says, crowding me from behind as he tugs his shirt back on. "Or we'll never get back to camp." He places his hands on my belly, his thumbs grazing the underside of my breasts.

I step away from him, glaring playfully as I pull on my bra and clasp it. "We both know you don't have another round in you, *wonder boy*." I pat his chest before throwing on my tank top and heading toward the trail. "Let's try to find that waterfall. I really need to clean up."

"It was worth the wait though, right?" he calls from behind me. "C'mon," he shouts as I begin to jog away from him. "Admit it!"

"Sorry, can't hear you!" I say, picking up my speed.

A LITTLE WHILE later, we're heading back to camp, having found the waterfall about ten minutes away from where we scarred that chipmunk for life. It wasn't so hard to find once we ditched the broken compass and my brain was less distracted by horniness.

"It's weird we fucked with *only* shoes on, right?"

"What?" I ask, stopping abruptly on the trail. Caleb keeps walking as if he's tunnel-visioned in thought—no idea that I'm no longer beside him as he rambles to his own shadow.

I jog to take my place next to him, catching him mid-sentence. "—and not that it wasn't fantastic, we've established that it was. But *only* shoes is weird, don't you think?"

I blink at him, struck by equal parts amusement and confusion as to why he's bringing this up *hours* after the fact. "I'm glad that's what's sticking with you . . ." I make no effort to hide my sarcastic tone, but it doesn't seem to register with him as he keeps his gaze forward and brow furrowed in thought.

I, for one, have been perfectly *without* thought since we washed our weary, sex-spent bodies under the stream of the waterfall together during what must have been the most perfect golden-hour of sunlight to ever exist.

"I mean, I've fucked you while *wearing* shoes, obviously, but just not *only* shoes."

"I understand."

"But I guess you've been fucked in only shoes before."

"Heels, yes."

"Then, there was the slight exhibitionism element, but I don't necessarily think—"

I reach out and grab his wrist, making him stand still long enough to search his eyes and quiet his words, if not his mind. "Are you okay?" I ask. "You seem to be . . . *really* thinking." I offer a timid, half-assured smile. "Not that I don't love that beautiful brain of yours but . . . what is it trying to do?"

"Sorry." He shakes himself. "I think I'm getting a little bit of pre-emptive performance anxiety."

"What do you mean?" I pick a piece of forest floor from his shirt's sleeve and brush my hand over his shoulder, removing any residual dirt. He ducks his chin, resting his jaw along my wrist until his lips press my pulse point.

"I want you to feel that good *every* time," he says, voice soft and low and shy.

"Me too," I tease, though I'm cautious with my laughter. "Why is that worrying you, love?"

"I'm trying to figure out what it is that made this time so different, so that I can recreate it."

Oh, my sweet man. I rise up to kiss him on the cheek, using a hand on the back of his neck for purchase as I lean on the tips of my toes to do so. "Cay." I sigh, shaking my head. "It's always good."

He places the backs of two of his fingers to the spot where I kissed him and his soft, amorous eyes find mine, glowing amber from the light of the setting sun. It strikes me, not for the first time but powerfully nevertheless, that I lucked out beyond measure in the husband department. I, earlier than most, found a man who can fuck me senseless, whispering all sorts of filthy litanies as he does so, gets lost in the mechanics of it all—his brain needing to rationalize and explain every phenomenon—and who then also turns bright red with a simple kiss on the cheek.

That duality is possibly his greatest strength that I have overlooked for far too long.

"Maybe it's just the air out here," he says, shrugging his shoulders. "That forest magic you mentioned."

My smile twitches. "I think that maybe sex is just better when you're on the same page emotionally and physically . . . at least for us. Plus, we had to wait for it," I admit begrudgingly.

He nods slowly, appearing deep in thought. Then, after a moment, a bashful, lopsided grin forms, slowly overtaking his features. "Well, thank you Yvonne and Helen then," he snickers. "They should put *that* on the pamphlet."

"You're such a dork," I say, pushing his shoulder. "I love you," I add, intertwining my fingers with his. He answers with a kiss to the back of my hand, held in his, and another to my forehead.

"I love you too," he replies as we begin walking. After a moment's quiet, Caleb opens up his thoughts once again. "You know what song I haven't been able to get out of my head since we got here? That one from the cartoon version of Robin Hood . . . 'Oo-De-Lally.'"

"Excellent choice . . . The real question is, am I Little John or are you?"

"Oh, I'm definitely John," he answers in a near scoff. "You're always the main character." I roll my eyes, my smile pointed at the ground as we trudge uphill. Once we reach the top, Caleb begins whistling the aforementioned, familiar tune.

I look up to the sky and wonder if it was too good to be true. If life could be this sweet and simple. If we'd be able to keep it this way once we returned home.

TWENTY-ONE

DAY FIVE OF REIGNITE

WE STARTED OUR HIKE BRIGHT AND EARLY THIS MORN-
ing because it will be our longest yet. Less than an hour from now
we will be at our final campsite of the week, which already feels
like far more than a week's worth of time. For the next two nights
we will be sleeping in a conservation area not far from where our
trip began. I, for one, am very excited for a shower. I am also
really excited to sit to pee. It's the little luxuries in life, ya know?

Things between Caleb and me have never been better. We
stayed up late last night talking and reminiscing and everything
felt so effortless, like it used to. We had a session with Yvonne and
Helen where we went over our ten-year plan and I'm genuinely
excited to get back home and begin the next phase of our life.

I feel stronger, both physically and mentally. I finally think
that Caleb and I are on the same page. And, though I'm not quite
ready to share this with anyone else just yet, I'm beginning to
think that my mom *would* be proud of me. That she'd be able to
see how hard I'm trying to make the most of the life she gave me,
the time I've been granted.

Our group is split in half once again. Just like last time. My walking partners are Nina, Maggie, Helen, and Kieran.

"I cannot stop looking at you," Nina says, smiling with her perfect teeth on show. "You're beaming."

I place my palm in front of my face, hiding my unshakable grin. It's true, I'm in an obnoxiously good mood. "I can't stop." I let out a fluttery laugh. "I'm imagining the shower I'm going to have before bed tonight," I say, half serious.

"Uh-huh, sure," Kieran says, bumping his shoulder against mine. "Not at all because of the *rule-breaking* that you and Caleb snuck off to do yesterday."

"Or this morning," I whisper, flaring my eyes wide in Nina's direction.

"Can we tell them now?" Maggie asks Kieran in a hushed tone over her shoulder. She's using a long branch she's found as a walking stick and is keeping pace next to Helen just ahead of us.

"I don't have a stick to protect *me*," Kieran says dramatically. "You tell them!"

"Every damn year . . ." Helen mutters, shaking her head as it bows forward.

"What am I missing here?" I ask as we step off a rocky ledge and back onto the dirt path.

"Confession? There's no abstinence rule," Kieran says. "It's sort of this hazing joke that Phil started with Henry and me two years back. Then we did it to Jai and—" He stops himself before mentioning Jai's ex. "And now you three . . ."

I gawk at him, a disbelieving laugh breaking free. "You little shit!"

"I didn't interfere because I do believe in allowing group dynamics, however, I will point out that no one *ever* asked Yvonne and me about it and we did *not* lie," Helen says, looking over her shoulder briefly.

"Yeah, yeah, as if you don't think it's funny," Maggie says teasingly.

"I never said it wasn't funny . . ."

"I also have a confession," Nina says to me, wincing playfully. "Jai sort of told me on day two."

"And you—"

"I was sworn to secrecy! And it's not like you guys *actually* waited!"

"A little forbidden fruit is always sweeter," Maggie says, waggling her eyebrows in my direction.

"I knew I never liked you people," I joke. "I cannot wait to tell Caleb, he's going to short-circuit. And . . ." I say slowly, "I call dibs on lying to the new couples next year."

"Permission granted. It's a rite of passage," Kieran says.

"Forgive me?" Nina whispers, her big eyes sucking me in like a cartoon deer's.

"I—" Helen's walkie-talkie siren goes off, interrupting me. It's a rhythmic, high-pitched noise like a car alarm. It *keeps* going until Helen manages to remove her backpack and find it deep inside her bag. "Geez!" I shout, reeling back. "Does it have to be so loud?"

"They're probably at camp by now, right?" Nina says, covering her ears. "Maybe they're calling about our food orders."

"Again, do we know for *sure* there is a camp store?" I ask. "Or is this wishful thinking?"

"There isn't, and there is no way they've already made it there," Kieran says, walking over to us as he checks his watch. "We're probably another fifty minutes out and they're less than thirty ahead."

"Maybe they walked fast . . ." Nina says, her voice trailing off as we collectively turn toward Maggie and Helen, who exchange a worried glance as they dip their heads nearer to the walkie-talkie.

Helen inserts a headphone jack and then there's nothing but the subdued sound of a breeze passing through trees and the dirt grinding under Nina's boots as she shifts her weight.

Something in my gut twists but I push it down, lift my bag up to bring my weight forward, and close the distance between me and the two women up ahead.

"What's wrong?" I mouth to Maggie. She swallows, then reaches out to squeeze my forearm. I take her hand in mine when she offers it. "Maggie, what happened?" I say, out loud this time.

Helen holds up a finger, signaling for me to wait as she continues to listen, her expression fiercely concentrated.

"What did you hear?" I whisper, beginning to feel anxiety build in my chest, growing harder to ignore with each passing second of fearful expressions and weighted silence. Nina and Kieran approach cautiously, completing our circle around Helen.

"I-I . . ." Maggie stammers then rubs her lips together. "I just heard the words 'accident' and 'ambulance' and—"

"Is he conscious?" Helen asks, silencing all of us once again.

My heart drops, and my eyes instantly search and find Nina's. I don't want it to be Caleb as much as she doesn't want it to be Jai, and our expressions say just that. I force myself to turn away from her and realize we're all wrestling with the same problem. Kieran doesn't want it to be Henry and it's the same for Maggie with Phil. But it's one of them. One of our men. One of our group.

At least it's not Libby.

"I'm sure it's all right," Maggie whispers, reaching out for Nina's hand, who reaches for Kieran's but he shakes his head and steps away.

"We shouldn't just be standing here," he says, skittish and jumpy as he drags a hand down his face. "At the very least we should be trying to catch up to—"

"I'll let her know. Right. Okay."

Kieran blows out a breath of relief that I both understand *and* resent.

My grip on Maggie's hand tightens. In all likelihood, it's probably Phil. He's older. It could just be a simple sprain or small fall or—

Helen lowers the walkie-talkie, clasps it on her belt, and turns to face me directly.

Fuck.

"*No,*" I whisper, shaking my head. "No," I repeat, dread creeping in and tunneling my vision.

"All right," she says softly, her expression pleading in a way that says *You cannot lose your shit right now.* "There's been an accident. Libby fell through a footbridge and Caleb jumped in to help get her out. After he helped Libby up, he slipped and hit his head. Jai and Henry were able to get him out, but he did lose consciousness for a minute or two. He's awake now, but groggy, and he has a head wound. Yvonne called rescue services and they dispatched before she called us, so we will need to move quickly if we want to get there in time for you to go with Caleb in the ambulance."

"A-ambulance," I repeat, nodding as nausea climbs up my throat, burning like bile. I drop Maggie's hand and bring my palm up to my neck, feeling the throbbing of my heartbeat under my fingertips. I feel myself drift slightly outside of my body, as if one strong gust of wind could take me into the clouds away from my skin and bones.

Helen zips up her pack, hoists it on, and turns back toward me as she fastens it across her chest. "He's awake now and he's talking . . ." She says it to reassure me, but *everything* about Helen looks uneasy.

"I'm sure he's okay," Nina says quietly.

I nod eagerly, revealing the desperate way in which I *need* that to be true. We all start off, walking faster than we have all day.

Nina stays close to my side as Maggie and Kieran fall behind us and Helen leads.

We move in stealthy silence with an unyielding urgency. I keep my mind focused on the next step, the horizon, the feeling of the blisters on my feet rubbing against my boots—opting to face a tangible, conquerable pain over the hypothetical. I wage war with my thoughts, recentering every time they drift to the worst-case scenario. With every step I push away all thinking and seal myself behind a steel-safe door.

I need to get to him, is the only thing I allow to reverberate against the walls of my emptied mind. *I need to get to him, I need to get to him, I need to get to him.*

Eventually I see Jai, standing at the bottom of an upcoming downward slope. He's pacing back and forth in circles until he spots our group approaching, and then he moves to meet us half-way up the path.

"We're just up ahead." He gestures for us to follow, and we do. "Yvonne sent me because it's a little bit off the trail."

"What were you all doing leaving the trail?" Helen asks, audible annoyance in her tone.

Jai swallows, looking toward Nina. "It was only supposed to be a short detour. Libby saw the bridge and wanted to—"

"Poohsticks," Helen softly interrupts. She sighs, stretching her neck. "Of course."

"What? What is that?" Nina asks.

"It's this silly game from the Winnie-the-Pooh books. Virginia, her mother, used to play it with her. You throw sticks off a bridge into the water below and then see whose comes out first on the other side."

"Caleb offered to go with her," Jai explains. "I joked that the bridge looked dodgy but . . ." He turns toward me, guilt heavy in his eyes. "I didn't think it would break. When Libby fell through

Caleb jumped in so fast. I swear, he's like Clark Kent or some shit."

Through a patch of dense trees and bush, I see some of the other group. By the root of a large oak tree, Yvonne sits with Libby in her lap, holding her closely. Not far from them, Caleb is laid down on the side of the riverbank and Henry is kneeling next to him.

"Here, let me take that." Jai reaches for my bag and slips it off my shoulders. As soon as the weight is off my back, I take off running the rest of the way.

"She's here," I hear Henry say as I approach, my chest heaving as I fall to my knees next to Caleb.

"Hi, baby." Caleb's voice is slow and barely above a whisper. His eyes are mostly shut but fluttering.

There is a lot of blood. Blood on Caleb's forehead. Seeped into his beard. Down the side of his neck. A little bit on the leaves beneath his head and the rolled-up sweater being used as a makeshift pillow. It's mostly dry but the cut above his ear is still bright red and wet.

I force myself to blink, take a deep breath, and fight against every impulse to throw up my breakfast. I scan the rest of his body slowly until I reach his boots. He doesn't seem to have any other injuries. But I notice his clothes are still wet and there's a pile of discarded wipes, gauze, and bloody tissues at his feet that have me fighting not to gag.

"Baby?"

"I'm here," I say, reaching out to touch his arm, squeezing his biceps with both of my hands. "Are you okay?"

"I think so," he says weakly. "Woozy . . . I've been told not to move."

"He fought me on that one," Henry says, moving to check on

Caleb's wound. "First thing I learned in first aid was to never move someone with a head injury. He's pretty banged up. . . . He'll definitely need stitches."

"What hurts, Cay?" I ask.

"My head," he answers, the corner of his lip quirking up a tiny bit, "and my pride."

"Hey. You should be proud," I say, trying to steady my breaths as queasiness washes over me in waves. "I heard Jai call you Clark Kent."

"Libby fell," he says, then sputters out a cough. I wince when he groans from the pain, his eyes shutting tight as he fights through it.

"I know, love. It's okay. You helped her. She's all right now," I say, briefly looking over my shoulder toward Libby and Yvonne as they wrap themselves around Helen.

"I'm sorry I ruined the end of the trip," Caleb says, voice slowing as his eyes lull.

"Stay awake buddy." Henry pats his chest twice. "C'mon, just a few more minutes."

"You didn't ruin anything," I say adamantly, squeezing his arm once again.

"Keep him talking," Henry directs me. "I'll be right back."

"How?" I ask, feeling desperate.

"Ask him questions."

I look down at Caleb, lost for words and too scared to think straight. "Have you seen any good movies lately?" I laugh softly as a tear falls down my cheek and then another, and another. When they begin to pour, I wipe my chin with my shoulder, refusing to take both of my hands off him. "Cay?" I sniff.

"Are you crying, baby?" Caleb opens his eyes weakly. "Don't cry."

"I'm okay." I shake myself. I have to keep his eyes open and on me. "Did you get the chance to talk to Henry? About your work stuff?"

"Yeah . . ."

"Good," I say, brushing his cheek with my thumb. "Do you feel good about it? Do you think you'll be able to do it?"

"Mm-hmm."

I move one hand to his chest, patting him as Henry had. "You have to stay awake, love. Please."

"It hurts," he whimpers. I feel my heart splinter, and my tears begin coming in faster.

"I know." I move my hand to cup his face. "I know it does. You want me to go beat up that bridge? I'll do it. Just say the word."

"The rock," he answers.

"Okay, I'll beat the shit out of that rock as soon as the medics arrive."

"Good," he whispers with the hint of a weary smile. "Fight for my honor."

"I will," I say, brushing my hand over his chin. "I'm so sorry you got hurt. It's not fair."

"Not your fault." His tone is steadier, but just as quiet.

"Well, I dragged you out here."

He grunts his disapproval. "We needed this."

"What is the old saying? You needed it like a hole in the head?"

"Yes, but that's not applicable."

"Only *you* would use the word *applicable* minutes after a head injury." I wipe my tears onto my shoulder once again. I don't know if it's just anxiety mixing in an explosive cocktail with adrenaline, relief that he seems to be okay, or fear of what *could* have been—but the tears won't seem to stop no matter how hard I try.

"Maybe I'll get another cool scar."

I sniff as a broken laugh comes out of me. "Maybe," I whisper.

"Hey, Caleb," Kieran says as he and Henry approach. "Mind if I take a look at your eyes?" he asks, kneeling beside Caleb's head. "I used to play rugby and got pretty good at spotting a concussion."

"Sure," Caleb mutters.

Worry twists in my gut as his eyes remain mostly closed.

"Can you open them wider for me?"

We all wait as Caleb struggles to open his eyes.

Kieran won't look at me. "No worries, man . . . We'll leave it to the professionals," he says. I try not to allow myself to panic when I see Kieran and Henry trade concerned expressions.

"Stay awake, Cay," I remind him again when I notice him drifting.

"Mhm."

I find myself watching the rise and fall of his chest, and feel my fear lessen with every strong breath in and out. "How long will they be?" I ask Henry.

"Any minute now," he answers.

Caleb lifts his hand off the ground and places it onto my bent knee. "Sar?"

"Yes?" I move closer, shifting my hip against the side of his abdomen.

"I love you," he says with a heavy breath.

"I love you too," I say. "I love you so much and you were so brave to jump in after Libby. I'm sorry you got hurt doing the right thing . . . But you're okay," I tell him. Or, perhaps, I tell myself. "You're going to be okay."

"You would have done it too," he says, before his eyes drift completely shut.

"No, love, stay awake . . . Cay? Cay, c'mon."

He grumbles in response.

"They're here," Kieran says, patting my shoulder. I look up to find Phil leading a group of four paramedics over. They're carrying a stretcher and medical supply bags.

"Hey," I say, tightening my grip on Caleb, "the medics are here now. I'm going to give them some space to look you over, okay?"

"No," he blindly reaches for me. "Don't go," he says, voice scratchy and low.

"I'm here," I say, moving to stand. "I'm not going anywhere."

I stay as close as I can to Caleb as the medics get to work assessing him. Henry answers their questions as Nina moves to my side, weaving her arm under mine and holding me steady.

After what is probably about ten minutes but *feels* like a lifetime, the medics carefully roll Caleb onto their stretcher. They work in unison with precision and speed. One of them begins tidying up their equipment while the two others strap Caleb in and secure his restraints. The last of the four men makes his way over to me. "We're ready to go, ma'am."

I nod, wiping more tears away. "Okay."

"We'll drive your car over," Henry offers, moving to my side. "You can leave your stuff with us."

"Thank you." I hug him. "The car keys are in Caleb's pack."

"Take this," Helen says, hustling over toward me as two members of the paramedic team check the straps across Caleb's body once again. She hands me a phone. "So Henry can find you later."

I nod, tightening my grip around the simple flip phone.

"Thank you," I whisper.

"Sarah," Yvonne says, walking toward me with Libby tucked tightly against her side. "We're—" She cuts herself off as her voice waivers, shaking with emotion. "Tell him thank you from us," she says softly.

"All set," the medic behind me says. They move in formation to lift Caleb.

"You okay?" I quietly ask Libby.

She nods.

I smile, tears still pouring down my cheeks. "Good."

"I'm sorry," she adds.

"One, two, three, lift . . ." The team of medics say in unison.

I feel emotion clog my throat but fight it back to smile at her. "Don't apologize, you did nothing wrong. I'm glad you're okay," I tell her before turning and following the medics out of the woods.

TWENTY-TWO

THE AMBULANCE RIDE WAS SHORT IN COMPARISON TO the amount of time it took for us to hike down the rest of the trail. The team had to stop a few times to lay the stretcher down and switch carriers. Every time I held my breath as they lowered Caleb to the ground and picked him back up again. But our slow descent gave Henry and Kieran the time to get ahead and find their way back to the motel where we'd left our cars for the week.

They arrived at the hospital shortly after we did, Henry in our car and Kieran driving behind him in theirs. I gave them Helen's phone, and in exchange they gave me my car keys, Caleb's bloodied glasses, and a hug. The first thing I did was get my phone out of the glove box to call Win. They left shortly after helping me find my way back to the waiting room and making sure the nurses knew where to find me.

I hate the sight of blood. Always have. But seeing *Caleb's* blood? There isn't a strong enough word. Detest, despise, loathe, abhor . . . What are some other words I know? *C'mon brain, think of words.* List them off. Synonyms. *Anything* is better than thinking of—

No. I won't go there.

The big clock on the wall ticks yet again. It's now one hour and fifty-four minutes since we arrived and they rushed Caleb away and told me they'd come find me when they could.

I don't know if I can stand to sit here another moment, soaking in my own anxiety. *What could be taking so long?* If he's waiting somewhere, for a room or a scan, why can't I wait with him?

I ask myself what I'm supposed to do over and over until I realize that Caleb would probably want me to call his mom. I take my phone out of my sweater's pouch pocket, but my hands are shaking so violently that I nearly drop it. Still, I manage to pull up Chellie's contact and hit *call*.

"Sarah?" she answers on the third ring with an immediate urgency to her tone. It makes sense that she'd perhaps presume it's an emergency. I don't think I've called her since . . . maybe *ever*.

"Hi, Chellie," I reply, my voice breaking as a bubble of fear threatens to burst. I clear my throat but it's no use.

"What's happened?" I hear a soft thud. It might be a door closing or the shutting of a book. Maybe a mug being set down. Or a knife being placed onto a cutting board? I don't know what Chellie would be doing at 4:11 P.M. on a . . . what day is it? Thursday? But she stopped whatever it was. "Hello? Sarah?"

"Sorry, here, um . . ." I sniff, still trembling. "Caleb . . . he-he's okay. But—" I blow out a long, shaking breath. "But there was an accident."

"What sort of accident? Where is he?"

Fuck. When Win had asked me which hospital we were at, I'd just read the sign outside. Now, I don't remember. *Shit-shit-shit,* why don't I remember? I should remember. God, my *only* job right now is to remember!

"We're in Huntsville." I look to the big, cruel, ticking clock that's turned forty-six minutes since we arrived and then to the walls surrounding it, finding an emblem on the wall. "Memorial," I say abruptly. "We're at Memorial Hospital," I repeat. "When we got here, they took him to do some tests, a brain scan, because of swelling or bleeding or—"

"Sarah, calm down," she commands coldly. "What happened?"

"Sorry," I say, trying to replay today's events. "We were hiking and Caleb got hurt. There was this old footbridge and a little girl fell when one of the boards snapped—"

"Not Win's little girl?" she asks urgently. I appreciate her concern; it feels like the closest thing to caring about me or those in my proximity that Chellie has ever demonstrated.

"No, Win and Bo aren't with us. Another friend of ours."

"All right."

"Libby, the little girl, is okay. Caleb saved her. After he got her out of the water he slipped and smacked his head, hard."

"So he's unconscious?"

"He was unconscious when we got here and they haven't let me see him," I say, emotion stealing my voice nearly entirely as tears begin to pour. "I just want to see him." My words are a warbled, wet mess.

"Well, there's not much you could do . . . You'd just be in their way."

I nod, forcing my upper lip to stiffen. "Right," I say, drying my face before placing a hand on my hip. "Yeah, yeah, I know."

"I'll call Cora and ask if she is able to take off work early and drive me up there. Caleb's father is still in Beijing on business so he—"

I turn to look down the hall and find a middle-aged white woman in scrubs walking toward me. "I have to go, someone is here," I interrupt.

"All right, well, let me know what they say, and I'll let you know what we decide."

"I will," I answer, then immediately hang up the phone. I

stand, looking to the scrub-wearing woman for answers. "Hi, can you help me? I'm Sarah. I'm—"

"Caleb's wife," she answers for me, nodding slowly. "I'm sure it was all a bit of a blur but I was one of the folks who met the ambulance when you arrived. I'm Doctor Wenarchuk." She gestures for me to sit, so I do. She lowers into the chair two down from mine and places a clipboard on the vacant seat between us. "The good news is that Caleb's condition is stable. However, there is a fair bit of swelling around his brain."

My throat tightens, forcing me to hiccup when I intend to breathe.

"We've sedated him, which will allow us to keep him comfortable while that little bit of swelling takes some time to go down. Sometimes these sorts of head injuries, especially when they go untreated for a few hours, can cause further complications. Keeping him unconscious will prevent any strenuous activity that could cause further damage and allow the body to put all of its energy into recovering. We currently see no signs of lasting or permanent damage but head injuries can be precarious and we want to be extra careful. He will most likely be kept asleep for at least the next twenty-four to forty-eight hours, and we will continue to run further tests and reassess. In the meantime, you are more than welcome to stay with him in the ICU. There's a fold-out bed in there, a few chairs. If there's someone who can come keep you company, we can help you both be comfortable. Have you eaten anything today? My colleague mentioned you were—"

"The ICU," I interrupt, then swallow as dread sends a cool shiver across every inch of skin. "Caleb, my Caleb, is in the ICU?"

The doctor nods, lowering her head to catch my gaze softly. "Yes, he is. And I know how scary that can sound but—"

"Caleb Linwood . . . Curly brown hair? Six foot? Looks like he could solve a Rubik's Cube?"

"Yes, dear."

"But it was *just* a fall . . . he was *just* talking. He was hurt but he was talking and joking and he—" Another chill passes over my entire body as a cold sweat begins to form on my palms and face.

The ICU is where people go to die. . . . That is what Aunt June said to me just days before Mom passed. She grabbed my shoulders, held me straight, and said, "You have to stop fighting and get ready to say goodbye." I was hell-bent on talking to every doctor, every nurse, every specialist.

I was demanding answers. Demanding fixes. Demanding *help*. I was a menace. I was breaking into the staff lounge to use their printer to leave new research studies for ALS patients on the attending's desk. I was calling Dr. Torres, begging him to do something. Deep down I knew that it was over. That Mom's body was tired and spent and ready to stop. But selfishly, I didn't want her to.

I felt as if my mother was the only person who could help me grieve her. How could she leave me to do that alone?

Now, I want Caleb. I *need* Caleb to talk me down. To tell me everything will be okay. To help me breathe right.

"He's in the best possible place he can be," the doctor assures me. "I swear to you, he's in very capable hands."

It's happening again. The shifting axis. The ending of worlds. And Caleb, my stable force, isn't here to help me through it. "I-I can't," I stammer, panicked breaths coming in quick.

"Sarah," Bo's voice booms from down the hall. I lean forward to see him. To see *them*. Bo's holding my niece, August, against his shoulder as Win takes off jogging toward me.

Relief settles into the space between us at the same time an unshakable heaviness falls over me. As if it's safe to fall apart, the moment she's here to pick up the pieces.

"Hi, babe," Win says, kneeling in front of me and wrapping me up in a tight embrace. "Hey, it's okay. We're here . . ."

"Gus," I choke out. "I don't want her to—"

"She's not going to remember a single thing, okay? She's fine. There was no way Bo was going to stay home once I told him what happened. We packed everything we could grab into the car and broke about seven traffic laws on the way, but we're here now. What's going on?" As Win speaks she leans back, looking between the doctor and me. "Hi, sorry, I'm Win, her sister."

"Hi," Dr. Wenarchuk says warmly. She then calmly repeats everything she'd just told me moments ago for Bo and Win. Bo sways side to side as he holds Gus, who's contentedly resting on his shoulder, thankfully turned away from us playing with the paws of a stuffed dog. I couldn't stand for her to see me like this. I couldn't look at her sweet little face right now without totally losing what's left of my mind.

Bo's eyebrows pinch together as he nods, taking in the information. He's far more serious than I've ever seen him before and, for whatever reason, that adds to my disbelief that this is truly happening. Happy-go-lucky Bo is not supposed to look so solemn. Gus is never supposed to see us afraid. I was never supposed to cling onto Win in a waiting room ever again. Caleb should certainly not be in the ICU.

Win rubs slow circles on my arm and shoulder as she rises to stand behind me, asking questions I'd not thought of and can hardly make out through the humming in my ears as the hallway begins to rotate around me.

"I can show you to his room, but we do have a strict visiting policy regarding children, unfortunately. No visitors under the age of sixteen in the ICU after five, which we're quickly approaching."

"I don't want Gus to—" Bo says, shaking his head silently as he looks at his wife.

No, I agree. None of us want her to see her Uncle Cay like this.

Win loosens her grip on my shoulder and moves to sit next to me. "Sar, I need you to listen to me carefully." She ducks lower, trying to get my face to turn to face her. I can't really see her past the tears flooding my vision, but I look at her anyway.

"Okay," I whisper, feeling my lips curl into a deepening frown as I hold back a sob fighting its way up my throat.

Win's glacier-blue eyes tear up, but she takes a long breath and straightens her shoulders, and the tears seem to retract somehow. "This is what we're going to do," she says with total authority. "On the drive here, I booked a room for four at the hotel down the street. There's two beds and we have Gus's travel cot. Gus will not go down for the night without me yet, so I am going to take her to the hotel now. Bo will stay with you until we can swap places, okay? Or, you can come back to the hotel for the night. Whatever you need . . ."

I nod, unable to do anything but inhale a shaking, wet breath.

"Have you eaten anything?" Bo asks, switching Gus to his other arm.

"We'll get her fed. You too," the doctor says, looking at Bo. "Any of you."

"Win?" I whisper, leaning in close to her as she wipes a tear off my chin. "I'm really scared."

"I know," she says firmly, eyes holding mine as she places a steady hand on my cheek. "But Caleb is going to be fine, I promise."

"What if—"

"Sarah, I mean it," she says, her voice cracking, as her bottom lip quivers half a second before she grips back into control. "This is not like last time." Then, she's hugging me again. "I'll be back soon," she whispers into my shoulder before she stands, takes Gus from her husband, says something to him, kisses his cheek, and then leaves the same way she entered with my niece in tow.

Bo walks toward me and extends a hand in my direction. I immediately place my palm against his, and he wraps his fingers tightly around my whole hand. "It's just you and me, kid." He smiles softly, despite the heavy anxiety behind his eyes. "Let's go see our guy," he says, tugging me upward.

I cling onto him for life as I stand on shaky legs. He moves to hold me steady with an arm outstretched over my shoulder, and eventually I find enough strength to follow the doctor toward the elevators down the hall.

When we stop in front of the elevators, my phone vibrates inside of my pocket. I pull it out to see a message from Chellie.

CHELLIE: Cora is unable to get away from work tonight, but we will be there first thing tomorrow.

I type out a quick reply as the elevator doors open and Bo guides me inside.

TWENTY-THREE

CALEB'S LYING IN A HOSPITAL BED IN THE CENTER OF a large, bright room with light blue walls, a square window overlooking the roof of the lower portion of the hospital, and gray-tiled flooring. The bed has crisply folded white sheets and there is a thin blue blanket draped across his lower half.

What I notice first is the IV in his arm and the tubes taped to his forearm and hand. His hand, with the Bunsen burner scar. Then, I notice the sleeve above the IV. He's been changed into a gray-and-white-patterned hospital gown. Which means someone, probably a nearby nurse or two, cut off my husband's clothes and changed him while he remained entirely unconscious. That thought alone makes me queasy, and the sensation only grows as I scan the monitors and screens surrounding him.

A machine in here distinctly sounds like Darth Vader's breathing, which I think Caleb would point out if he could. But he can't.

Try as I might, I cannot bring myself to look at his face.

"I know it is a lot to take in, but all of this is just keeping him comfortable." Dr. Wenarchuk comes into the room and slides the door closed behind her. "We'll get you both visitor passes, then you can come and go freely. The kitchen and family lounge is to the left of the elevators we passed through. We just ask that you don't bring any food back with you."

Bo clears his throat twice. "Can, uh, can he hear us?" The discomfort in his voice is obvious, and I shut my eyes tight as I feel more tears forcing their way out.

"Many patients who come off sedation say they could hear their loved ones or the staff, so, there's a chance. I like to think of it as a deep sleep. Like when you can hear a song in your dream that turns out to be your alarm."

"And he's comfortable?" Bo asks.

"Absolutely. He isn't in any pain or discomfort."

I turn toward Bo and open my eyes on a long deep breath. "Good," Bo says, a somber, crooked smile greeting me. "That's good."

"I'll give you both a moment and then I'll let Caleb's nursing team know you're here. They'll want to stop in and say hello. They might even have some updates for you," she says sweetly. "Things can change quickly around here."

I remember, I think. "Thank you," I say as she pumps the hand sanitizer device on the wall and swiftly exits.

"Do you want to sit?" Bo asks. I nod vigorously, then drop his hand.

"Sorry," I apologize when I notice the red marks left by my grip on his skin.

He pulls over a chair and places it beside the middle portion of the bed. "Don't be." He gestures for me to sit. "Win nearly broke my wrist when she was in labor. I'm tougher than I look."

Bo has angled the chair toward Caleb. Toward his face. My breaths start coming in short and shallow as I shake my head repeatedly.

"Hey . . ." he says, moving toward me. "Try to take a breath, if you can."

"I haven't looked yet." The words fall out of me. "I can't. I can't—"

"Okay, that's okay." With one grip he turns the chair to face him. "Sit." I do. Then, Bo moves across the room to get the other armchair, and moves it over, placing it directly across from me. Then he sits, our knees almost touching.

I work to slow my breaths with both of my hands placed on my chest.

"There you go," he says softly. "No rush."

"Sorry."

"Don't be," he repeats.

"I'm sorry you got stuck being here too."

"How about this . . . I accept a blanket apology for any and all things that you might say or do so long as you stop apologizing."

I laugh softly. "Okay."

"Caleb is my best friend," Bo says, his eyes drifting over my shoulder to the bed behind me. "I want to be here."

"Okay," I say alongside a sigh, lowering my hands to my lap.

"And you are one of my best friends too," Bo says, placing his hand on my knee. "I want to be here for you."

"I'm not good in hospitals." The words come out light, but I communicate the heaviness with my eyes.

"I know, me either," he says as his face falls, a sorrowful memory seeming to wrap around him for a split moment. "I never wanted to be back in a room like this." He twists his foot, looking down at his prosthesis that begins just below his knee.

"Same here," I say, placing my hand on his. "I'm sor—" He raises a brow as I lean back in my chair, putting distance between us. "Sooor glad you're here," I say, recovering in a near-Australian accent.

"Nice save." He swallows heavily. "How, um, how were things going? Before the accident? Win had told me that—"

"Really good," I cut him off. "If you tell Win I said this, I will break one of your action figures, but she was totally right . . . This week has been life-changing."

"I do not have action figures."

"Sorry, your dolls."

"Collectibles," he corrects, smiling softly.

"I think I'm ready now," I say. "But could you maybe wait outside?"

Bo's standing before he even answers. "Of course. Just text me when you want me to come back, okay? I'll go grab us some coffee."

"Thank you," I say after him as he walks toward the door.

My heart beats so hard and fast in my chest it feels as if it's swelling, but I gather my strength and turn around to face the bed, keeping my eyes low. I reach for his hand, rubbing my thumb against his. I close my eyes, take a deep breath, and turn my face to see his.

If my heart splintered while we were downstairs, it has now officially shattered.

The face that I had found more familiar than my own suddenly doesn't feel familiar at all. The face I've marveled at for seventeen years. The face I've memorized, now barely visible under an oxygen mask, tubing, and bandages.

And I swear, I'll never take that familiarity for granted ever again. Because, suddenly, I remember *not* easily recognizing someone you love is far, far worse.

I lean onto the side of the bed's railing and place both of my hands onto my husband's chest, feeling the warmth of his body seep into my palms, and the rise and fall of his breathing. The beating of his heart, still steady. And a little voice in my head tells me what to do next.

I close my eyes and attempt to pray. After all, desperate prayer is the only kind I've ever known and this, by far, is the most desperate I've ever felt.

Even still, the words don't come. I cannot seem to find the right phrases to beg, again, for the healing of someone I love. I try, and try, and try, and try. But I'm distracted by an undercurrent, an emotion growing fuller in my chest. Under my desperation, I locate a dense layer of anger. A bottomless well of helplessness and resentment and bitterness that grows with every moment I fail to do what my mother taught me.

Then, it dawns on me. The reason behind the anger. The realization that all of the hardships my mother experienced could have been prevented by the god that she prayed to, and that they chose to do nothing.

Not a single fucking thing . . .

So, I let them have my anger instead. I pour out hundreds of complaints that I've stowed away trying to protect the peace of a god I don't think I ever believed in.

I think of Libby, and her mother. I think of me, and mine. I think of every loved one separated too early. Too suddenly. Too brutally. I open my eyes to see Caleb, who has a machine breathing for him. A man who's never caused anyone harm. A man who's done his best to love people well. A man who is sweet, and kind, and loved by so many.

In the place of prayer, I offer my pain. I let it all go until I'm spent and emptied and nothing but a sopping mess of tears. Until my head and heart both ache with it. Until I feel like there is nothing left.

In the aftermath, it's silent.

I think I'll always instinctively call out to some form of deity or greater force, it's what I was taught to do, and I am proudly my mother's daughter.

But I know now that if there is *someone* or *something* out there . . . I can't rely on them as I once did. I have to believe, moving forward, that they are as human as me, as powerless. Because anyone who had more control than I do, more ability to intervene, to save, to help, wouldn't allow so much suffering.

I *have* to believe that.

So, before I finish, I apologize to them for their lack of control. I commiserate with them, knowing that we must feel the same. I thank them for their time. For the slight relief I feel, having laid the hurt out for them.

And, I say goodbye.

For now, and forever after, I will have to stand on my own two feet.

Amen.

TWENTY-FOUR

"YOU SHOULD BE SLEEPING," WIN SAYS FROM THE CHAIR next to Caleb's bedside. I have no clue how she knows that I'm awake, my back is to her on the pullout cot I'm laid out on. "I told you, I'm watching him."

I sigh, tucking a hand under the pillow the hospital provided. "I know . . ."

"Is it the monitors?" she asks. "Or the lights?" The nurses dimmed the lights to a soft, orange glow and turned the volume down on the machines just after Bo left to trade places with Win back at the hotel. But neither of those things are what is keeping me from sleeping.

"No, I keep drifting off but then jolt awake seconds later thinking something's wrong." I lift the blanket off me, sit up, and move to the second chair next to hers. Win is in her favorite navy sweatpants and a long-sleeve gray camp shirt. Her knees are bent up to her chest and she holds a large water bottle between her legs. "You should take the bed." I mirror her sitting position and place my chin onto my knees.

I'm grateful that she thought to bring me some of her comfy

clothes as well. And, that the hospital had a shower I could use just down the hall. At least I no longer smell as bad as I feel.

"No," Win says, turning toward Caleb. "I'm not tired." I watch the rising and falling of Caleb's chest once again and find myself syncing my own breathing to his rhythm. "What time did they say they'd run more tests again?"

"Six-ish, before shift change."

She glances up to the digital clock on the wall, and then back to Caleb. After a brief second, I see her wipe her cheek against her knee. Then she sniffs, confirming what I'd suspected—she's crying. Which, in turn, makes me cry too.

In an unspoken, mutual understanding, we decide to do nothing but hug our knees and let the moment pass as we sit and cry together.

"I texted my mom," Win says after a few minutes. "She's offered to come up, to watch Gus or stay with you. I said we'd let her know tomorrow."

I love Aunt June deeply but that woman hasn't made a situation easier on anyone in her entire life. "If you need her for Gus," I say softly. "But I think we'll be okay. They all keep saying they're taking extra precautions . . . That this is just protocol when someone loses consciousness. I don't want to waste her time."

"Right," Win agrees. "You're right." But I see her lip quiver just before she turns around.

"Babe," I say, reaching out for her. "It's okay."

Win turns toward me, her red-rimmed eyes in contrast to the sweet smile that she offers. "I'm sorry, I should be comforting you, not the other way around."

"If you want your mom here, then tell her to come."

"No, it's not that. Obviously, Mom shouldn't be here, she's like an emotional bull in a china shop. But she may annoy Caleb enough that he wakes up."

I laugh, though I probably shouldn't. "So, what is it?"

"I just hate this."

"I know, me too."

"And, I'm so frustrated that I'm not keeping my shit together in front of you."

"In your defense, I should be sleeping."

"Yeah, you're right. It's so rude of you to interrupt my scheduled meltdown time."

I huff, in an almost laugh. "My apologies."

"Seeing him like this . . . It feels so vulnerable," Win whispers. "It's bringing back all the memories of . . . Well, you know. And, sitting here, I've realized that we give Caleb such a hard time and—"

"Win, he knows how much you love him," I interrupt.

"Yeah?" She looks at me, a sad sort of hopefulness in her eyes.

I nod. "Yes, definitely. You're in his top five favorite people, *remember*?" Caleb had one too many gin and tonics at Bo and Win's wedding reception and made a *very* long-winded toast that concluded in him ranking his all-time favorite humans. Bo was fifth, Win was fourth, Gus was third, and Leonard Nimoy was a close second, apparently, to me.

"I'm sorry I cannot protect you from this," Win says, reaching out to cup my face. "I would if I could."

I pat her hand twice before she pulls away. "Right back at you, babe."

Win sits up straighter in her chair and I watch as she literally shakes herself, sniffs once, and blinks back tears. "Caleb's walking out of this hospital by the end of the week." She speaks with such authority that I find myself nodding in agreement as she gives direct eye contact. "I promise you."

Deep down I know that she doesn't have any right to promise anything, that she's just as helpless as the rest of us. But I decide to allow myself the kindness of believing her. At least for tonight. "Okay."

"Are you really not going to sleep?" she asks.

I shake my head. "Do you want the bed?"

"No, I want to hear about your trip. How was it?"

"It was great until it wasn't," I answer.

"Tell me about the great parts."

So, I do.

I tell her about Yvonne stopping the rain, the other couples, Libby, the fake abstinence rule, the first hike, being dragged back to the tent by Caleb, our public fight and the conversation that followed, the communication, the playfulness, the sex—of which I spare no detail. Win laughs with me, cries with me, sits patiently while I gather myself as we approach the timing of the accident and my thoughts scatter. For some levity, I pull out my phone and we make quick work of finding Nina's Instagram. We joke about how absurdly gorgeous she and Jai are. How unjust the world is to bestow such beauty upon one couple. I talk about my session with Yvonne and the revelations that have continued to follow in the days since. How much steadier I feel . . . Or, felt.

"So, university then? That's huge."

I nod. I feel a wave of fresh anxiety wash over me, looking toward Caleb over her shoulder. "It felt simpler yesterday, though. To plan and dream for the future."

"This is a *slight* hiccup," Win says, teasing as she grimaces at her obvious oversimplification. "But you'll get yourself there."

"I'm not really interested in *any* version of life without Caleb," I say. "And right now, any thoughts of the future are freaking me the fuck out."

"And you won't have to know what that looks like," Win says calmly. "And, I'm sorry."

"What? For what?"

"For not seeing it before. For not seeing how you were feeling all these years. You seemed so happy, and content, but I should have known better. I should have asked . . . I'm proud of you for figuring it out, but I'm sorry I didn't get the chance to help sooner."

"I'm okay," I reassure her. "And, I think it had to be this way. I had to decide to change for myself."

After a few more shared memories, tears, conversation, and one smuggled-in bag of chips the nurse *definitely* sees us eating and chooses to allow, we both fall asleep at Caleb's bedside.

When my eyes open again, it's morning. Caleb's nurses are checking on him, sunlight is pouring in from the window behind us, and Chellie is standing outside the glass sliding door, talking to a doctor I've yet to meet.

"Oh boy," Win says, spotting her too as she fixes the bun on top of her head.

"Here we go." I stretch my sore neck before I move to stand. "Chellie, hi," I say, sliding open the door. She immediately hugs me. It's brief, and rigid, but initiated by her, which is new.

"I'm glad you could get some sleep," she says, looking me over. "I don't think I'd be able to if it was Cyrus laid up in there."

I swallow my words, and put on a soft smile, turning to the doctor. "Is there any news?" I say, glancing between them both.

"I was just explaining to your mother-in-law that I'm not on Caleb's support team."

"And *I* was just inquiring as to why the lead attending in the ICU isn't *attending* to my son," Chellie responds.

I turn back toward the room, wondering if Win is witnessing this. And, of course, she is. Her mischievous face is peeking around the curtain with wide eyes as she whispers something to the amused nurse taking Caleb's blood pressure.

"Caleb has had great care so far," I assure her. "There's two nurses in there now who I'm sure would be happy to—" Chellie holds out her hand to me, so I stop, pulling my lips in tightly.

"Doctor—" She only gets one word out as she squares up with the doctor before he interrupts her.

"Rest assured, ma'am, you do *not* want me on your son's case. If I were his doctor, he'd be in a much worse condition."

"Why, because you're incompetent?"

His jaw ticks, but his smile remains cool and collected. "No, because I get the difficult cases. Now, if you'll excuse me . . . I have a patient next door who's already tried to die on me three times this morning." The doctor walks away and Chellie turns to me, visibly offended.

"I cannot *believe* he just said that," she says.

"Is Cora with you?" I change topics abruptly.

"No, uh, she's at a hotel a few blocks away. She's onboarding or deboarding or doing *something* with a new client and . . ." Her words die off as the nurses begin to wheel Caleb out of his room, his equipment in tow.

"They're doing another CT scan this morning," I explain. "To check if the swelling has gone down."

Chellie clasps her purse in front of her jacket, holding on to it as her eyes remain glued to Caleb as they wheel him down the hall. "He's . . . He looks . . ."

"I know," I say, reaching out instinctively to hold her elbow. "C'mon. Come sit with us."

"Winnifred," Chellie says in greeting, her voice distant, as I help her into what had previously been my chair.

"Hi, Chellie," Win answers back, then turns to me with a soft smile. "The nurse said his vitals were looking good. They'll bring him back in about an hour and they should have the results of the CT scan soon after. It would probably be a good time for us to go get breakfast."

"Do you want to go see Gus?" I ask her.

Win shakes her head. "I'm sticking with you. Bo's taking her to some indoor playground for the day. We'll switch off again after dinner for her bedtime routine."

"Are you sure?"

"Definitely."

I turn toward my mother-in-law, who's looking more and more out of her element by the second. I suppose it is strange how quickly I've adapted to my surroundings but it's not my first time in a place like this. "Chellie, are you hungry?"

"I couldn't possibly eat hospital food."

"It's actually pretty good," Win says. "They've got a bunch of fresh fruit and pastries and there's even one of those fancy cappuccino machines."

"Plus, I could use a change of scenery," I add.

"I'll stay here, in case he comes back early," Chellie says, opening her purse just to shut it again. I exchange a look with Win and she nods, hearing me without a word needing to be spoken.

"You know what, I'm not really hungry, so could you just bring me back a coffee when you're done?" I ask Win, who's already standing.

"For sure."

"Me too, please. A tea. Chamomile, if they have it."

"You got it."

I take Win's seat and angle it toward Chellie. I watch as she looks everywhere but in my direction. The floor, the red plugs and buttons on the wall, the light on the ceiling, the hallway as a nurse passes by. "Chellie?"

"Hmm?" she returns absently.

"It's okay to be upset."

"Well, it won't solve anything."

"It might," I offer. She turns to face me. "If it helps, almost every nurse that has come into this room in the past twelve hours has assured me that Caleb will probably not be here for very long."

"Good."

"He lost consciousness, so they had to sedate and intubate him, it's hospital protocol."

"Right."

"But once the swelling on his brain subsides, they can take him off of it and—"

"I'll speak with his doctor later, thank you," she interrupts curtly, then pulls her phone out of her purse. I fall back into my chair, resigned. But just as I'm about to try again, to tell her that I am on her side, Chellie makes a call, putting her phone on speaker. On the sixth ring, Cyrus answers, his brief greeting drowned out by the sound of clinking dishware and many other voices.

"Darling, it's me," Chellie says loudly into the phone, holding it up to her mouth.

"Yes, hello?" Caleb's father returns.

"I've just gotten to the hospital. I wanted to catch you before you go to bed." This is the first time I'm hearing that Cyrus knows that Caleb is in the hospital. I suppose that's not shocking, but it is disappointing considering he hasn't reached out a single time for updates. Though he could be getting those from Chellie. But a check-in would have been appreciated too. *Hello, daughter-in-law whom I've known for seventeen years . . . How are you holding up?*

"It's only seven P.M., Chellie. I'm at a client dinner."

Well, excuse the fuck out of your wife for not knowing what time it is in Beijing.

"I don't know your schedule, Cyrus."

Tell him, girl.

"Can this wait?" he asks.

Chellie's face falls, and I swear I can see the faintest hint of tears gathering at the corners of her eyes. Which is a *big* deal considering I've never once seen this woman cry in all my years of orbiting their family. Not even at Opa's funeral.

Chellie is built of steel. That mask I've never been able to wear well, the one of the good, calm, hospitable wife, has been her impenetrable armor she doesn't seem to ever take off.

My heart hurts for her. For the first time, I feel *pity* for Michelle Linwood. I hate that she doesn't feel able to ask for what she needs from her husband, which is clearly comfort. It's tragic that she has become so excellent at covering up her own emotions that she's no longer able to fall apart when the time calls for it.

That's her baby they just wheeled out of the ICU. Her unconscious, hurt, *only* son. And if she doesn't have the strength to ask for what she needs, then I'll do it for her.

She clears her throat. "I suppose it can wait . . . *But—*"

"Great. I'll call you back when—"

I rip the phone from Chellie and before I have a moment to regret it, I'm speaking. "Cyrus, it's Sarah. Your son is in the ICU and your wife is freaking the fuck out and needs you. Say goodbye to your little friends and talk to your damn wife. Better yet consider getting on your buddy's private jet and flying back here. Or at least *offer* to do so like a goddamn father should! Also, her name is Michelle and it's a beautiful fucking name, you cantankerous, self-indulgent dick!" With a slow breath out, I calmly hand the phone back to Chellie, who is the definition of stunned.

"It's for you," I say far too calmly. She gawks at me, rendered speechless as she glances between the phone and my smug grin.

God, that felt good.

I stand up to leave, deciding that I *am* in the mood for breakfast after all.

TWENTY-FIVE

"YOU CALLED HIM CANTANKEROUS?" WIN'S GIDDY SMILE
spreads as she smothers a bagel in cream cheese. "What does that
even mean?"

"Honestly, I'm not entirely sure. It's one of those words that
just feels cathartic to use. . . . Try it."

"Cantankerous," she says, then takes a hefty bite. "*Cwan-tan-
kros,*" she repeats, her mouth full.

"It feels good, right?"

She swallows. "It really does, I'm gonna add it to my reper-
toire." She licks her lips, then stares over my shoulder absently.
"So, what now? Are we fighting with Chellie? Do you need me
to—"

"I don't care," I say flippantly, then take a long sip of coffee. "I
don't care what Cyrus or Chellie have to say about me or say to
me . . . And that is *so* freeing and *long* overdue."

"Fuck yeah," Win whispers, mindful of the other families in
the lounge. "Okay, so, we're playing it cool, I guess."

"I mean, other than the fact that my husband is in the ICU, yeah. Cool as a cucumber."

"Right," Win whispers, wincing. "Other than that."

I check the time on my phone and realize we should be heading back soon, to be at least ten minutes early for Caleb's expected return. I'm not taking any chances. First, I fetch Chellie a chamomile tea and I even double-cup it to be sure to not melt her ice-cold exterior. I am sticking up for myself, sure, but I'm not a *total* bitch.

"Are you sure you had enough to eat?" Win asks as we scan our visitor passes and wait for the ICU doors to open.

I smile at her softly. "Yes, thank you, Mom."

"Hey, it comes with the territory now."

"Are you sure Gus is okay without you for the day?"

"Gus is totally oblivious and living her best life in a hotel robe as we speak." She shows me a picture while we continue walking down the hallway toward Caleb's room. In the photo, August is sitting in the middle of a huge bed, drowning in an adult-sized white robe, a cup of milk in her lap as she watches cartoons on the hotel's flatscreen.

It helps to know that at least one of us is totally okay. "She was *born* to live a lavish lifestyle," I tell my best friend.

"Yeah, well, she better not get used to it. Her parents might be broke soon. We've poured so much money into the camp and apparently—" Win cuts herself off. "Sorry, not important. Not now."

"Later?" I ask, as I reach out for the sliding glass door.

"Yeah," Win agrees.

AN HOUR LATER, Caleb's still not back from his CT scan. Chellie is glued to her phone, silently playing solitaire. When I returned with her tea, she took it with a quick nod of appreciation, but I haven't seen her eyes since.

Win and I snuggled up under the hospital blankets on the cot next to the window. Win suggested that I read to take my mind off things, but I've recently discovered—as in, today—that there are *some* things a good book cannot fix. At least not now, when everything feels as if it's hanging in the balance.

So, instead, we talk about Gus, as she seems to be the only entirely safe topic of conversation right now. I tease Win about giving me another niece or nephew, and she remains *adamant* that the camp has to be successful before she'll consider it, much to Bo's chagrin.

"Bo is persistent, I'll give him that."

Win leans in close to whisper, giggling. "I swear to god, I might have to hide my birth control pills from him or they'll go missing."

"It's not like you and the pill have an excellent track record regardless," I tease.

"That was before I knew how fertile I was!"

"You always underestimate yourself," I say, feigning sincerity. "But I'm team Bo on this one. More babies!"

"Yeah, because you get to snuggle, play, and ditch."

"Exactly. I—" I'm interrupted as the door slides open, and the same two nurses begin to wheel Caleb back inside. Behind them is a doctor I've yet to meet, but I suppose Dr. Wenarchuk has ended her shift by now.

"Hello, ladies," the new doctor says, her voice as peppy as her beaming smile. She shuts the door and then uses the wall dispenser of hand sanitizer to clean her hands. "I'm Doctor Ofori." She bypasses Chellie and extends her hand to me. I don't have time to stand before she reaches me, so I remain sitting. She shakes Win's hand, and then turns over her shoulder. "Why don't you come sit over here with us, my friend."

Win attempts to hide her grin. Chellie isn't exactly the *my friend* type. But she stands and begins sliding her chair over toward us as the nurses make quick work of getting Caleb situated. Dr. Ofori sits in the chair across from the cot and smiles sweetly as we wait for Chellie to settle into her seat. "Wonderful," she says brightly. "Well, today my job is nice and easy. I get to take over Doctor Wenarchuk's case and immediately deliver some good news."

Win grasps my knee over the blanket. I clutch her hand in response and squeeze.

"Caleb's CT scan shows signs of a concussion but no further trauma. The swelling that his team was worried about yesterday has greatly improved and I don't see any other reasons to keep him sedated any longer. His injury is mild enough that we believe he can heal just as well awake."

"Isn't it a bit soon?" Chellie clutches her *literal* pearls.

The doctor turns toward her, her genuine smile never fading. "Keeping patients with mild traumatic brain injuries sedated for longer periods of time has been shown to decrease cognitive function when they do wake up and prolong the side effects of a concussion. I know my colleagues were concerned yesterday as he had lost consciousness a few times, but between us," she leans in closer toward Win and me, "men tend to do that." She sits back in her chair, grinning.

"Could we get a second opinion?" Chellie asks.

"Oh, absolutely. I went ahead and called in a neuro consult while we still had Caleb downstairs and my colleague agreed that we should start working on getting him off of all this machinery." She waves her hand flippantly toward the medical equipment and folds one knee over the other, her full focus set on me. "We'd like to wean him off the sedative and remove his breathing tube, so he can start breathing on his own. Do you have any questions?"

"How long will it take for him to wake up?" I ask, blinking back tears.

"Times can vary from patient to patient. It's hard to know for sure. We like to say that waking up in the ICU is less like turning on a light switch and more like waiting for the sun to rise. Some patients can take just a few hours whereas others take a day, or even more. But given that he hasn't been sedated for very long and that he's in good health otherwise—I suspect he'll be on the shorter end of the spectrum."

"That's good!" Win says, shaking my leg with a talon-like grip on my knee. "This is *good*," she repeats, moving to hug me.

I'm in shock. At least, I *think* this is what being in shock feels like. I can't seem to speak, or think, or find anything to worry about—which must mean something is wrong. But I can sense it . . . the happiness and relief waiting to burst free like the contents of a piñata on its last strike. "A-and . . . he'll be okay? Like, he's going to wake up and—"

"We see *no* indications of any major, long-term side effects. Often our head-injury patients can wake up a little agitated, or groggy, or a little bit confused. That is totally normal and is almost always temporary."

"Okay," I say, nodding. "Okay," I say once more.

"Any other questions?" She turns to Win and Chellie, who both shake their heads. "Brilliant, I'll get the anesthesia team in here, then. I will have to ask you all to leave for a few minutes while we get started and remove his endotracheal tube. Have you already given the nursing station your cellphone number?" I nod. "Great, they'll give you a call when you can come back."

"Okay . . ." I look over her shoulder toward Caleb, holding my eyes on him. I hate having to leave. I don't *want* to leave him. I promised him that I wouldn't.

Dr. Ofori's eyes scan mine. "I'll give you some time to say a quick goodbye. I promise he's in good hands." She moves to stand. "If you have any questions or want to check in while you're waiting, feel free to call me." She hands me a business card with the hospital's number and her personal extension. "It shouldn't take too long. Promise."

"Thank you," Win says on my behalf as I take the card and stare blankly at it while the doctor makes a quick exit.

Chellie stands and moves over to Caleb's bedside as Dr. Ofori quietly chats with the nurses in the hall outside of the door.

"You okay?" Win asks me quietly.

"Yeah." A smile bursts from me, alongside an onslaught of tears. "He's going to be okay," I say, sputtering through sobs. She pulls me into a tight hug, and we both laugh in joyful disbelief.

"I'll see you both this afternoon," Chellie says sharply, picking her handbag off the floor. "I'm going to go back to the hotel and come back around supper time. Please call me if anything changes before then."

"Yeah, of course," I say, wiping tears away with both hands. Chellie moves to make a speedy exit but I'm faster, tossing the blankets off my lap and jumping off the cot. "Chellie, wait." She turns, and we nearly collide. I wrap my arms around her, hugging her gingerly—like an animal I don't want to spook. It takes her a moment, but she eventually relaxes into my hold and hugs me back. "He's going to be okay," I whisper to her, gratitude lighting up every syllable.

There is a weighted pause where neither of us moves or speaks. As I begin to wonder if we've been hugging for too long, Chellie sighs contentedly.

"He is," she says, her voice thick with emotion. She sniffs once, straightens her posture as we drop our hands, and wipes a single tear away before departing the room without another word.

Thirty minutes after leaving the hospital

THE HOTEL IS exactly 1.2 kilometers away. After hiking all week, the walk felt like nothing physically, but emotionally, it took its toll. I hate being away from Caleb. He seems so vulnerable, lying there unknowingly available to be poked and prodded and cared for. When we get to the hotel, Bo and Gus are still out having fun. We decide to order room service and watch a little bit of cable TV.

Ninety minutes after leaving the hospital

ONE PARTIAL EPISODE of Jerry Springer, a giant burger and fries, and two episodes of Judge Judy later—my phone rings. They're ready for us to come back. We don't even wait to hear if Lola is going to owe Michael the two hundred dollars for breaking down his door before we grab our shit and head back to the hospital.

One minute back inside the hospital

I TEXT THE group chat that Win made last night from the hospital's lobby. It's easier this way to update everyone at once. Quickly, it became thumbs-up responses from Cora and Cyrus, sharp and brief responses from Chellie, and long-drawn-out replies from my aunt June who cannot resist sharing the infinite wisdom from her current boyfriend who had a concussion nearly two decades ago and is therefore an expert on the matter at hand.

Win, Bo, and I are still texting in our regular group chat that also includes Caleb. Bo keeps giving him a hard time for not responding—which makes me feel a bit lighter. Soon, Caleb will be in on the joke too. Soon, he'll see how much we were all losing our minds without him.

Eleven minutes back inside the hospital

I NEVER THOUGHT I'd feel relieved to be back in the ICU, but I most certainly am.

"It all went very smoothly," a nurse says as she continues to wheel out equipment from Caleb's room. "He's breathing on his own as we'd expected, but we've put in the cannula just in case he needs a little bit of support later on." She stops, looking at the heart rate and blood pressure monitor. "But so far, he's doing great."

After I kissed Caleb's cheek, marveled at his now-more-visible, gorgeous face, and readjusted his blankets, we got settled back into the room. Win went to grab us ice chips from the machine down the hall and diet Cokes from the family lounge. When she got back, we turned the television in his room on, hoping to catch some more daytime television as we wait.

Two hours back inside the hospital

CALEB IS STILL sleeping, but he's been stirring every so often for the past thirty minutes. I've moved my chair as close as I can get to his bed, and I'm mindlessly stroking his arm while we watch *Family Feud*.

Four hours back inside the hospital

CHELLIE CAME BACK earlier than she'd told us she would. I think that was partially because I began informing the group chat, perhaps a *touch* overeagerly, every time Caleb moaned, groaned, or moved his fingers.

Still, the nurses are very optimistic it will be *any* minute. Until then, Chellie has gotten acquainted with *The Jerry Springer Show*. Which, I have to say, feels like a win.

"Of course he's not the father," she says calmly, sipping on her second chamomile tea. "That baby looks nothing like him."

"She totally cheated," Win says, shaking her head.

"I don't know," I say. "They do have the same chin . . ."

Five hours back inside the hospital

WIN KEPT JOKING that Caleb was going to wake up the *moment* I went to pee. Therefore, I have *never* peed so fast in my life. Honestly, I didn't wipe. I did a little jiggle of my business and then ran to *quickly* wash my hands. I grabbed sanitizer at every doorway, it is a hospital after all, plus the doors take so long to open I had to do *something* other than just stand there.

Even though it would have sucked to miss the moment Caleb woke up—I was a little disappointed that Win's superstitions failed. He was still asleep when I returned.

I forced Win to leave and use the washroom, just in case she was half right. But still, nothing.

I'm starting to worry again. I can feel it rolling in like an oncoming storm—not quite panicking just yet but hyperaware that it's approaching. Maybe they missed something. Maybe my husband's beautiful, genius brain needed more time before they attempted to wake him up. Maybe we were all too eager. Too quick to hope.

"Nothing?" Win asks me when she returns from the bathroom.

"Nope."

"I'll try," Chellie says, surprising us both as she stands to leave.

Win studies me, tilting her head as her brows knit together. "You okay?"

I shake my head as tears spring loose and I shut off the television. She holds me as I fall apart again.

Eight hours back inside the hospital

"NO, DARLING, HE'S still asleep. Yes, I'll tell Sarah you send your best. I'm glad you made your flight in time. I'll see you tomorrow night. I love you too." Chellie lays down the phone.

Win and I nearly break our necks with the speed in which we turn toward each other.

I did that. I made Cyrus Linwood do the *right* thing.

Nine hours, eight minutes, and eleven seconds back inside the hospital

"BABY?" A HOARSE voice whispers.

"Caleb," I say, all the breath leaving my lungs at once as I rise out of my chair. Unadulterated relief fills my body like helium in a balloon, lifting me toward my husband. "Hi, love. Hi." I kiss his shoulder and rest my head there. "How are you feeling?" I move away when he coughs, scanning him over with concern.

"Hey." His eyes open softly as he frowns in discomfort. "My throat . . ."

"Here," Chellie says, appearing at his side. She lifts a cup of water off the side table and helps him find the straw. He takes a long sip, then another.

Win moves to stand beside me, her hand next to mine on the railing of the bed.

"Mom?" Caleb blinks at her, visibly confused.

"Hello, darling."

He turns back toward me, slowly but as fast as I think he can manage right now. Even after waking up from his induced fugue state his facial expression is clear. *Things must have been bad for you to have called my mother.*

"You had us really worried." I brush my hand along his chin.

That is when Caleb spots Win and his eyes widen even more as he turns toward her.

"Wow," he says, then coughs again. Win takes the cup from Chellie and offers Caleb the straw for him to take another sip. "I feel pretty special right now."

I notice a nurse standing in the hall, watching the monitors closely through the window. She gives me a smile and waves. "You are special," I tell him, tears collecting along my lash line. "So, so special."

"Baby, don't cry," he says, moving his arm without the IV to place his hand on top of mine. All his movements are sluggish and seem to take a lot of effort. But he's moving. He's talking. He's come back to me.

"I'm happy," I tell him as a few hospital staff enter the room and stand against the wall, making their presence known but allowing us a few more moments. "I missed you so damn much."

"I'm right here."

"I know but you scared us. I love you. I love you a truly stupid amount."

"I love you too, baby," he whispers back to me, a sleepy smile pulling at his lips.

"We should let these fine people look you over," Chellie says, smiling warmly at me. "Then we're going to discuss what on earth possessed you to walk out onto a dilapidated bridge." She raises a brow toward her son.

"Don't go far," he says, tightening his weakened hold on my hand.

"We'll just be outside." I kiss him briefly on the lips and then move out of the nurses' way into the hall. Win wraps her arms around me from behind, nearly knocking me over with her enthusiasm.

"He's okay," she says. "Well, he's still Caleb. . . ."

I giggle, joy flooding my system as my shoulders relax. I watch as Chellie turns back toward us from down the hall and smiles *again*—which has to be some sort of record. "C'mon . . . I need a stiff drink."

"It's a hospital," Win argues, following me.

"A coffee, then." I smile to myself, simply because I cannot seem to stop.

TWENTY-SIX

TWO HOURS LATER, WE ARRIVE IN CALEB'S NEW ROOM downstairs in the general ward. He's got nothing attached to him anymore, and he's even stood up to walk to the bathroom with my help. The nurses and I keep reminding him not to push himself, but he's always been an overachiever.

Chellie left shortly after we were allowed back into the ICU. She gave Caleb a gentler lecture than I think any of us had been expecting and told him she'd be back tomorrow with Cyrus in tow. Win left shortly after Chellie did, to have some time with Gus before her bedtime.

Standing at Caleb's bedside, I wheel over the tall side table so it stretches over his lap. Then, I place his water cup and glasses down. He eagerly reaches for his glasses and puts them on. "Much better," he says, blinking to focus.

"Welcome back," I say, crawling onto the narrow bed next to him. I snuggle into his side. He lifts his arm over my back and draws small circles on my ribs with his fingertips. "Are you hungry? You must be hungry."

"A little bit . . ."

"Okay, I'll—" As soon as I try to move off the bed, ready to scrounge up some hopefully not-disgusting cafeteria food, he holds me tighter to him.

"Not yet," he says softly. "This first."

I relax back into him, breathing him in. "You scared the shit out of me, Linwood," I tell him.

"I'm sorry." He kisses my forehead. "Didn't mean to."

"I know," I say sarcastically. "You just *had* to go and be a hero."

"How is Libby doing?" he asks.

I lift off the bed slightly to pull my phone out of my pocket. "Yvonne texted me a few hours ago just to check in. They decided to end the trip a night early. Libby is totally fine, though she's obviously a little shook up. She was worried that we were mad at her."

"I hope you—"

"I told Yvonne to tell her that we were definitely not mad and still wanted to go to her recital next month."

"Good," Caleb says followed by a sigh. "Everything's a little fuzzy memory-wise."

"I bet."

"I remember hitting my head, lying down, talking to Henry, and then you."

"Right," I say, nodding.

"But . . . Did Jai call me Superman?"

I cannot help but giggle. Of *course* that is one of the few things he remembers. "Clark Kent, I think it was, but yes." He smiles proudly in response, soliciting more of my laughter. "You'll be pleased to hear that Jai has checked in a few times," I tease. "I found Nina on Instagram, and we swapped numbers. I think we both made new friends."

"Well, who wouldn't want to be friends with you?"

I tilt up to look at his face and then brush my palm over his beard. For a moment, we just stare at each other, holding softened eye contact. In our little happy bubble, everything feels just as it should be. Monitors beep, announcements sound, and nurses chat outside the door, but in here—it's perfect.

Caleb smiles a *new* smile I've yet to see. Something like regret in his eyes in contrast to the serenity in his crooked, subtle grin. "I don't want to wait ten years," he says softly, in almost a whisper, "to have the life we want. You are the *only* thing that matters to me, and I'm tired of pretending otherwise. If you're okay with it, I'd like to start scaling back the company as soon as possible."

I know it's probably the exhaustion and the *literal* head wound talking, but I smile just the same. "We can talk about it tomorrow. You should be resting. It's—"

"I've *never* felt clearer," he says, cupping my face in a tight hold. He brings our foreheads together as he sighs. "I'm not wasting another moment. . . ." He pulls back, his eyes held firmly on me as emotions rise and tears begin to sting my eyes. "I'm finally asking myself, 'What would Marcie Green do?'" He reaches out to wipe a tear that's rolling down my cheek with a bent knuckle, then laughs gently. "I don't really like white wine, but I *do* want to give when I'm able, help when I can, and not waste my one shot at life."

"You remember?" I ask, pouting up at him. "You remember my speech?"

"Of course I do."

"Okay," I answer him. "Whatever you want . . . But—"

"Fuck the ten-year plan. All that I could ever want is in this bed right now." He leans down to kiss me. Our lips meet tenderly. Warmth radiates between us as tears roll between our mouths, making our kiss taste like an ocean breeze. It's soft and sweet, and not very long before a quick knock at the door separates us.

Just as I think we're about to get told off by a nurse for sharing Caleb's bed, I spot Bo through the square pane of glass in the door.

"Come in!" I call out, shuffling higher in the bed to sit up as Caleb takes a sip of water.

"Hey," Bo singsongs, leaning through the door, his broad smile locked on Caleb. "We thought maybe you'd be hungry?" He reveals a huge box of pizza, bringing the other half of his body inside of the room. Behind him walks Win, holding August.

"Well, this is a nice surprise," I say, hopping out of the bed and practically skipping toward my niece. "Hi, Gussy girl."

"Who cares about a bedtime on such a special day?" Win says, angling so I can take Gus from her.

"I missed you." I kiss the side of her head, turning back toward the bed. "Did you have fun with Dada?"

"According to my husband the park was great until the geese came. . . ." Win answers for her, flashing me a grin.

Bo places the pizza box down onto the table and rests his hand on Caleb's shoulder, smiling down at him with a warmth that makes my chest ache. "You look good, man," he says, his voice rough, as he pats my husband's arm. "Real good."

"Oh, yeah?" Caleb smirks. "Do you like my new outfit?" He gestures to his hospital gown.

"Beautiful," Bo returns, stepping back to mime taking a photo. "But don't make a habit of wearing it."

"They're disgustingly cute," Win says snidely for only my ears, stepping around me to grab a chair from the far corner of the room.

The five of us sit together, surrounding Caleb's bed as we eat pizza and catch Caleb up on what he's missed in the last forty-eight hours. We specifically focus on the way I bitched-out Cyrus on the phone and Chellie's new affinity for Jerry Springer. Then Gus tells us all in great, toddler-pronounced detail about the playground she'd visited today with her dad and the "bird bullies." Geese, as they're otherwise known.

We talk, and eat, and tease, and bicker, and repeat it all in tandem until there's nothing but pizza crusts left. Gus falls asleep in my arms as time ticks by until it's probably long past visiting hours—but no one comes to tell us off, so we stay. I listen to the contented rumblings of Gus's heavy breathing against my chest, and find myself drifting off too—the exhaustion of the last few days settling in.

When I wake and fade slowly back into awareness, Caleb is telling Bo all about his ideas for Focal with unbridled enthusiasm not suited to a man in a hospital bed. Try as I might, neither of them listens to my pleas for Caleb to rest when there's an opportunity to nerd-out and calculate something. They keep going, and I can't help but listen—admiring Caleb's newfound passion for scaling back our lifestyle and uplifting his employees. It's exactly what I didn't know we needed. I've never felt prouder to be my husband's wife than hearing him decide to step out of his father's shadow and try something new to do right by his employees.

When Caleb mentions my plan for university, Bo's ears perk up and he and Win both smile at me proudly, then each other. It's a small, subtle type of smile that says *She's going to be all right.* It's the same one Caleb and I exchanged after we spent time with Win and Bo for the first time post-Gus conception. I tell them that my plan is to apply for an undergraduate degree in English— hopefully start in the fall—and then to simply try my best.

It's not long after that the two men slip back into talking numbers. Bo mentions a house for sale down the street from theirs and Caleb's face lights up. *God,* I don't know which pairing out of the four of us would be more codependent if we lived even closer. Still, I agree to go look at it when Caleb's given the all clear to leave the hospital.

"Hey, you," Win whispers, leaning in as she brushes the hair out of her sleeping daughter's face. The maternal warmth in her eyes as she looks at Gus always stirs up a nostalgic comfort inside my chest.

"Hi," I whisper back, admiring the side profile of my beautiful friend while she slowly glances around the room, grinning at the two men nattering away across from us, her daughter, and then back toward me.

"You know, I keep thinking about what you said to me when I was pregnant with this one. . . ." She strokes her daughter's cheek.

"I say a lot of things," I reply. "Remind me?"

"*You deserve good things.*" Win lifts her chin on an exhale. "And I think you were right. I think we do. I think we have them. I think Marcie would be very, very proud of us."

I nod softly in reply. "You know what? I agree."

I rest my cheek on top of my niece's head and close my eyes to capture the exact feeling of the moment. The comfort of having my family in one place. How glad I am to know and be known by them all. The relief of sensing that it will all be okay. The knowledge that we'll all be here for one another if it ever isn't.

Filled with gratitude, I send up a prayer of thanks for the first time, directed at no one in particular, but anyone who'd hear it.

Thank you for Gus. Thank you for Win and for Bo. Thank you for interfering, for intervening, and making them a family. Thank you for Caleb. Thank you for bringing him into my life exactly when I needed him. For allowing me to find my soulmate earlier than most so I would never have to be alone. Thank you for making him kind. Thank you for my mother, for the time I had her. Thank you for this one, beautiful, messy shot at life. I promise to not waste another moment of it. Amen.

EPILOGUE

TEN YEARS LATER

"A LIMO? SERIOUSLY?" WIN LAUGHS, STANDING NEXT TO me in a tight-fitting purple dress that shows off her *huge* baby bump. She has sworn that this, their fourth baby, will be their last. Gus, my eldest niece, is in an equally beautiful dress next to her, grinning ear to ear as the limousine approaches from down the street. Win's other two girls are at home with a sitter, though I'm fairly sure they're begging Bo to stay as he's yet to join the rest of us outside.

"Dad's going to make us late," Gus says, looking down the street *just* as their front door, only a few doors down from ours, opens. Bo comes running out, fixing his bow tie as he sees the limo and whistles a catcall.

"Run, Forrest!" Aunt June calls out toward Bo, laughing obnoxiously loud. She timed her yearly visit around this evening, and while I'm grateful, I'm *also* praying that she doesn't embarrass me tonight. "Where is Caleb?" she asks me, pulling out her red lipstick from her sparkly clutch bag.

I sigh, shaking my head as I feel a lopsided smile grow. Then, I point to the limousine door seconds before it opens, and Caleb pops his head out.

"Need a ride?" he asks me, with a wink.

"You are *ridiculous*. . . ."

"Oh, come on! We had to travel in style! How many times in my life will I get to go to the premiere of my wife's play?"

"Is there champagne?" Aunt June asks, peering in the window.

"Hopefully we will get to do this many times so some of us get to drink next time," Win says, leaning on the side of the car, rubbing her belly. "Now move, I need to sit down." She shoos Caleb away from the door.

Caleb moves, opening the car door wider, and continues to hold it open for everyone as they pile inside.

"Such a gentleman." I step toward him, pressing the front of my body into his side and tilt up to kiss his cheek. "Thank you, love."

"Don't thank me, *you* paid for it," he says mischievously, smiling down at me.

"Ah, well, what's mine is yours. . . ." I say, biting my lip playfully.

Six years ago, I finished writing *A So-called Little Life*. A novel heavily inspired by my mother and a story that she had loved, wherein one woman, on her deathbed, is able to visit the hundreds of different lives happening concurrently in alternative universes. Since then, I've written three other novels and published two. But none have been quite as successful as the first, which, as of today, is a stage play, beginning its tour in Toronto.

For the leading role, we've been blessed to have none other than the Tony Award–winning actress Gianina Rossi, whom I know better as my dear friend, Nina. Nina and Jai got married last year in a *lavish* wedding off the coast of Italy, two months after she won her third Tony; and though she certainly could do much, much bigger things with her time, she's agreed to a one-year run with us.

"Still, thank you . . . for, being so supportive and excited for tonight and for leaving me those minisized Kit Kats in my desk drawer to find over the last few weeks. They're the only reason I finished edits this time around."

"Of course, baby." Caleb smiles, dipping down to kiss me. "I'm so proud of you," he says, bringing his hand to my neck.

"Are we ready to go?" I ask.

He nods, slowly. "Did you feed Helen?" Helen, our now eleven-year-old rescue pup, is not as spry as she once was. The name Helen, however, is still as funny as it was ten years ago when we found her at the shelter. Human Helen, as she's now referred to, gets a kick out of it too. So does her granddaughter, Libby, who has dog-sat for us between college semesters when we've gone away. We see them all often, though we never did go back to Reignite. We decided, following Caleb's accident, that we are officially *not* outdoorsy people.

"Yeah, I did. Gus let her out to pee while I was slipping this on," I say, shimmying in my tight black-velvet number. "Which took *forever.*"

"I bet it'll be easier to take off," Caleb whispers, licking his lips as he tugs on one tendril of my hair. I return a bashful smile, leaning in to kiss him long and slow.

"Move it, you two!" Aunt June shouts, followed by the giggling of her twelve-year-old biggest fan. "The theater waits for no one!"

With one last peck, Caleb moves to help me into the limo and shuts the door behind us.

"You look amazing," Win says, leaning back in her seat to try and take a photo of me.

"Here," Bo says, pulling out his phone.

"Both of us," I say, tucking myself closer to Win as we smile toward the camera.

"This is giving me prom flashbacks," Win says.

"We didn't take a limo to prom," I tease. "We took Caleb's LeSabre."

"I had hoped it would be ready in time . . ." he says, grimacing. "But it wouldn't have fit everyone, anyways."

Caleb has been fixing up his Opa's LeSabre in his spare time with his dad, who retired last year. They still don't have the perfect relationship, and Cyrus still will never comprehend Caleb's choice to make Focal a "socialist-propaganda posterchild," but they're both trying their best to get along, for the sake of Caleb's mother who has turned over a refreshingly independent, appropriately demanding new leaf. She even goes by Michelle again. With all of that progress, the car is still no closer to being fixed than it was a year ago. In fact, it may actually be worse off. Still, I let Caleb pretend to be a successful blue-collar man.

"Sure, wonder boy . . ." I say, leaning across the aisle to pat his knee. He rolls his eyes, smiling even still.

"You'll see . . . we'll be driving around in that car again someday."

"Driving? No. What I'm really looking forward to is—" Win interrupts me by clearing her throat, correctly guessing what I was about to say as she flares her eyes at me in the direction of her daughter. "*Seeing* . . . the backseat again."

"Are Cyrus and Michelle coming tonight?" Bo asks, changing the subject.

"Yeah, they are," I answer proudly. "I think they actually might beat us there too. . . ." I pull out my phone to see a long string of messages from Michelle. "Yes, they're already there . . . and wondering if there is a VIP section." I chuckle.

"Tell them that the VIP section is on their way," Aunt June says, beaming with smugness.

"Will do," I say teasingly, typing out my reply.

Three and a half hours later, the play finishes without a hitch.

Shortly after, I'm pulled onto center stage by Nina as the audience stands in applause. The stage lights are blinding at first, and I have to squint to see the front row, but the applause only grows louder as I bow and clutch my chest as it fills with gratitude. Roses are thrown onto the stage by my aunt, Michelle, Cyrus, Win, and Gus, while Caleb throws something different that lands at my feet. He's folded the playbill into a paper airplane. I pick it up, deciding I'll want to keep that forever.

I smile toward him, feeling proud to be standing here, but even prouder to be his wife. For all the work he's done to make Focal a better place, to scale back, to be more present in our lives. For everything I've done to get myself here too. We've grown so well-planted side by side.

"Here. Take this," Nina says, removing her small taped-on mic from her forehead and holding it out to me. "Speech!" she shouts above the applause, and the audience falls quiet, ready to listen.

"Oh, uh, oh no! I didn't expect to have to say anything—" I laugh nervously, holding the tiny microphone, still somewhat attached to Nina, between my thumb and forefinger. "Well, firstly, thank you all so much for being here tonight. None of this would have been possible without the amazing stage crew, performers, the theater staff, ticket holders, and of course, my beautiful friend, Gianina. . . ." I hold out for applause for them all, then continue. "But of course, I also have to thank the *three* great loves of my life. My best friend, Win, who's never once doubted me. My husband, Caleb, who has dutifully loved every version of me, the good, the bad, and the even worse. And my mother,

Marcie, who is not only the inspiration for this story but also the inspiration for *everything* I do."

Caleb puts his fingers to his mouth and whistles loudly, gaining a laugh from the audience and another round of applause.

"Oh!" I say, twisting to avoid Nina's grasp as she reaches to take the microphone back. "One last thing! Fuck you, Cecelia Floodgate!"

The reviews hit the morning paper the next day. I didn't dare look, I don't read them anymore unless I want to schedule an additional session with my therapist, but Win did. She cut out a few of her favorites and left them for me to find in my mailbox this morning alongside a note that said, *Marcie would be so proud.*

My personal favorite clipping read:

Toronto's newest play based on the beloved novel, *A So-called Little Life,* starring three-time Tony Award-winning actress, Gianina Rossi, is off to a rip-roaring start. The evening, by all accounts, was a huge success. Both fans of theater and the novel itself are flocking to attend, with tickets sold out well into the spring. But the novel's author, Sarah Linwood, did leave all of us in attendance with one question following her curtain call speech: Who is Cecelia Floodgate?

Caleb went out to buy a frame immediately. We decided to hang it in our office next to our degrees, a photo of Helen graduating her puppy training, a picture from our twenty-year anniversary, when we renewed our vows on a most perfect Sunday afternoon at a nearby library, and a shit ton of artwork hand-delivered by our nieces.

"We did it," Caleb says, wrapping me up in his arms from behind as I set our hammer down on my desk. "The ten-year plan is complete and then some."

I laugh, admiring the wall. "We're getting old, Linwood," I tease.

"No, baby," he says, tucking his chin against my neck, those aged but familiar features that I love so much burrowed into the side of my face. "We're just getting started."

ACKNOWLEDGMENTS

WE DID IT, FOLKS! MY TRADITIONALLY-PUBLISHED-from-conception debut! There are so many wonderful, kind people to thank that helped get this book out into the world, so please bear with me.

Thank you, first, to everyone who has supported my career in any capacity over the last few years. Namely, all the Instagram content creators, BookTok folks, readers, and booksellers who push the HBY agenda—I owe you more than I can ever say. Your creativity, generosity, and enthusiasm is truly what got me here. I cannot properly thank you for that, but I will continue to, regardless. Thank you.

I want to thank the women who surround me, build me up, keep me grounded, and hold me steady that inspire friendships like Sarah and Win's. I am so incredibly fortunate to have a community of beautiful, soul-filling friends who show up for me time and time again.

To Abi, Mel, and Nicole—my first ever book club readers and

dearest friends—thank you for your unwavering support and friendship throughout this wild journey. I love you.

Alyssa, Sarah, Maddison, and Vanessa, you have been my friends through many phases and stages and, by some miracle, have stuck around—so, thank you. I love you.

Thank you to my dearests, Millie and Taylor, for your support, patience, humor, and wisdom, and above all else, your never-ending chisme. I love you.

My Catfish ladies—AKA Taylor, Chas, and Sam—my life would be so boring without you perfect weirdos, and this book would have never been finished without you three. I'm so grateful to whatever force brought us together from across this great big continent (it was social media but let's pretend otherwise). I love you. Elena, thank you for your lovely words on the cover, our unhinged chats, and your kindness.

Sophie, my true sister, thank you for holding my sanity together, loving Sarah and Caleb like I do, and being the easiest person to talk to in the world. I love you.

Thank you to my author pals who share my highs, lows, and woes. Becka, Meg, Jillian, Lyla, Chloe, Julie, Clare, Zarin, Hannah, Becs, and Tori. I treasure each of you.

Thank you to all of those I met on Taylor Swift's internet, who I'm now honored to call friends. Amani, Candace, Esther, Laura, Tabitha, Erin, Brandi, and Logan . . . thank you for not being fifty-year-old men irl and for all the joy you bring into my life.

Thank you to Natasha, my champion and most big-hearted friend. I'm devastated that this will be the last book we will work on together. I miss and love you dearly.

I also want to thank all my beta readers who offered their time, skills, and effort so graciously. You're so very appreciated and I'm so sorry I still don't really understand how commas work. I'll be better next time.

To all the wonderful people working at Bookends Literary Agency, but most especially my agent, Jessica Alvarez, thank you for literally everything. Without your wisdom, guidance, and emotional handholding I would be totally lost. Jessica, you deserve a six-month vacation without email access but please don't do that.

To every person at Dell and Penguin Random House—whether you've been hands-on in publishing my books or not—if it wasn't weird, I would kiss you on the mouth. You're simply the best and I unabashedly beg you to keep letting me write books for you fine people. Shauna, my editor extraordinaire, I thank you endlessly for the opportunities you've given me to grow and learn and create. Thank you to Taylor, Meg, Mae, and Brianna—the dream team—who work tirelessly to promote these silly books of mine. To all of the copyeditors, formatters, designers, and Leni Kauffman for the beautiful cover art, I extend another massive thank you.

Thank you to Carolyn and all the lovely people at Bedford Square, my UK publisher, for their hard work and dedication.

Last, thank you to my husband, Ben, for your support, understanding, enthusiasm, and love during this and every project I've taken on since I was fourteen. Not bad for two dumb kids, huh? We're just getting started.

© MEGAN PREECE

Hannah Bonam-Young is the author of *Next of Kin, Next to You, Out on a Limb,* and *Set the Record Straight.* Hannah writes romances featuring a cast of diverse, disabled, marginalized, and LGBTQIA+ folks wherein swoonworthy storylines blend with the beautiful, messy, and challenging realities of life. When not reading or writing romance you can find her having living room dance parties with her kids or planning any occasion that warrants a cheese board. Originally from Ontario, Canada, she lives with her childhood-friend-turned-husband Ben, two kids, orange cat, and bulldog near Niagara Falls on the traditional territory of the Haudeno-saunee and Anishinaabe peoples.

hannahbywrites.com/
Instagram: @authorhannahby
TikTok: @hannahby_writes